KV-373-638

ABOUT THE AUTHOR

Charles L. Grant is a prolific novelist, editor and short story writer, with 100 books and around 200 stories to his credit. He is a three-time winner of the World Fantasy award, as well as the recipient of two Nebula Awards, and the British Fantasy Society's Life Achievement Award. After publishing several science fiction novels, he began to develop his unique brand of 'quiet' horror in such books as *The Hour of the Oxrun Dead*, *The Nestling*, *The Pet*, *For Fear of the Night*, *In a Dark Dream*, *Something Stirs* and *Raven*. His short fiction has been collected in *Tales from the Nightside*, *A Glow of Candles* and *Nightmare Seasons*, and he was the editor of the acclaimed *Shadows* and *Greystone Bay* series of anthologies. He has also written humorous fantasy and teenage fiction under a number of pseudonyms. Grant lives with his wife, novelist and editor Kathryn Ptacek, in a century-old haunted house in Sussex County, New Jersey, and his most recent projects include three novels based on the cult TV series, *The X Files*, and Raven Books' forthcoming Young Adult volume, *Horror at Halloween*.

THE TEA PARTY

CHARLES L. GRANT

RAVEN BOOKS
London

Robinson Publishing Ltd
7 Kensington Church Court
London W8 4SP

This edition first published in the UK by Raven
Books, an imprint of Robinson Publishing Ltd, 1995

A copy of the British Library Cataloguing in Publication
data is available from the British Library.

ISBN 1-85487-347-4

Printed and bound in the UK

10 9 8 7 6 5 4 3 2 1

To Doug, who knows a good suit when he sees one;
And Lynne, whose fetish of the month is Doug;
For knowing, and caring, and for coming to the party.

PART ONE

THE HOST

The fog had been there from the beginning.

When the Appalachians rose in dark volcanic flame and the sea slid back boiling, when the centuries-old glaciers gouged and ground and crushed their way through to pulverize the land and create the narrow valleys, when the lakes filled with rain and the beasts returned to prowl the forests, the fog was there, barely shifting, seldom rising; when the trees finally grew and the land became fertile, when the birds returned to roost and Man was born, the fog was there, breath of the night and mirror of the moon, scuttling to shadow ahead of the sun, returning at dusk to reclaim its place.

It settled in a rolling meadow much longer than it was deep, a meadow boxed on three sides by a low wooded hill, bordered on the south by the dry shallow grave of a long-dead creek.

With the sun high the fog dissipated, strands and arms of it lifting toward the sky, pierced by the wind, faded and scattered by the light; strands and arms of it fleeing to the forest, finding burrows and caves and hollows in trunks, settling and waiting like air before a storm. With the sun lowering it grew again, seemingly out of the ground, out of the branches, out of the rock—white blades of grass that stretched into white vines that wove themselves swiftly back into a slow tumbling cloud.

Unbroken by trees, untouched by passing creatures, unnoticed except for the Indians who avoided the

3

meadow by taking their hunting elsewhere, and by the colonists who decided that the valleys beyond were somehow better places to establish their farms and their mines.

There were no stories of ghosts or demons or giants; there were no spells cast or curses leveled or monsters reputed to keep their lairs there.

There was only the fog that had been there from the beginning—grey-white, always moving, always shifting, never still . . . until a man and his family came with their lives strapped and bound in their road-battered wagons. They stopped there in spring, on the last day before summer, stopped on the creek bed now turned to a rutted road, and watched the fog writhing under the sun's morning light.

No trees, no creatures, but every so often the shifting moving white was broken by the backs of large grey boulders, like stolid, patient sea-things lurking beneath a constantly changing surface. The man was a stonemason, his family numbered ten, and when the fog cleared and the meadow was revealed, this, he decided, was where he would stay.

There was no argument from the family; they were weary of travel and anxious for a place they could finally call their own. The fog vanished by noon. The land was claimed shortly after.

The mother of the family's eight children was fortunate enough to be clever, and within a month of their arrival she had learned the language of the Lene-Lenape, who taught the family much about survival, since the area's white residents wanted little to do with them. No reason for this is known, yet the family remained, undaunted and proud and determined not to be bested by either Man or Nature.

By the end of 1690 they had established a crude working farm and were, if not thriving, at least holding their own.

By the end of 1691 six of the eight children were dead.

A smallpox epidemic swept that section of the colony during early May, and the four middle offspring were the only ones touched of the stonemason's brood. They burned with high fever, thrashing and screaming in their sleep, and lost so much weight that their arms became sticks, their faces hollow skulls; their hair turned brittle and fell out in dried clumps, and though as much was done for them as could be, they died one by one, coughing and vomiting, gurgling as if they were drowning in a well.

In October, while hunting for wild turkey, the eldest son slipped crossing a stream and struck his head on a rock. He drowned while struggling back to consciousness.

In 1692 a sixth child, a girl seven years old, was brutally mauled by a female bobcat surprised in her lair shortly after giving birth to the season's first litter. The dying child stumbled and crawled ahead of the wake of her own blood, two miles back to the temporary log cabin before collapsing at the gate. She had no strength to scream or call out, and so her mother, working in the garden not fifty yards away, never knew what happened until she came to the wall to look for her baby.

Despite these tragedies, the stonemason persisted in using his skills to build a more permanent home. He ignored his neighbors when he wasn't working for them, in spite of the fact that they warned he was staying on long-cursed land.

The house was completed in 1699.

It was christened Winterrest, to celebrate the protection it would offer from that harshest of seasons, and because the last stone was laid the day of the year's first heavy snowfall.

The family—which now included, aside from husband and wife, the eldest surviving son and his wife and two children, and the youngest son with his spouse and three children—moved in their possessions shortly before Christmas.

Their neighbors, after swallowing their objections both to the place and to the people, tried visiting them before the turn of the year and received no response for their knocking. They left, relieved of their responsibility by the hostile silence they faced.

A year later a tinker passed the estate. He later claimed that just as he reached for the gate-latch, he heard agonized screams from within the house. A group of farmers, fearing the family had been slaughtered by brigands and that they might be next, went to Winterrest armed and angry.

But the house was empty.

There was no sign of struggle, no blood, no corpses. There were no foot- or hoofprints in the grass, no way of telling how many had entered and how many had left the large grey mansion.

In 1702, one mile farther east, Deerford village was founded.

The fog never returned.

But Winterrest was its color.

PART TWO

THE GUESTS

ONE

1

The season was summer, not known for dying.

The weather was stifling, with no sign of storms.

The densely wooded hills were low and unimposing, the thick heavy foliage a slow-fading green. The hazed, white-hot sun had bleached the blue from the sky for well over a week, yet the streams were still deep enough for trout to hide in the shallows. Crows with talons, hooks and beaks open circled low, hunting carrion on the roads; hawks with eyes hooded, talons tucked, coasted high, hunting anything that moved. A blue jay stared at an acorn on the ground. An aged copperhead dozed on a bed of exposed slate. Pasture-land cleared the slopes in uneven arcs where dairy cattle grazed and alfalfa grew for hay and an occasional yellow tractor belched black exhaust into the grey dust clouding the horizon. The contour-hugging, two-lane roads that once were cowpaths were dull ebony and deserted. No breeze touched the ponds. The dogs that watched the farms lay in deceptive shifting shade, panting, dreaming, ignoring the swarming flies.

But under the trees that had lost their spring's shine it was cooler, though not cool, and the buckskin mare that picked her cautious way along the dirt trail seemed less weary than ambling, once in a while reaching for a tempting moist leaf, her heavy black tail switching flies from her rump. She skirted the few deadfalls without having to be guided, tossed her head and snorted whenever she caught the sharp scent of the greenland in the valley.

The trail followed the hill's contour halfway up its southern slope, dipping only when it had to around huge boulders or sudden hollows. Her rider knew it well; the buckskin knew it better.

Douglas Muir slumped comfortably in the tooled western saddle, left hand holding the reins, right hand flat along his thigh. He wore brown boots a season too old, jeans patched and faded, and a loose blue plaid shirt that let his skin breathe. His hat was a rumpled Stetson, once a startling white until the day he'd brought it home, dropped it on the living room floor and kicked it around with his bare feet until the stiffness was gone and the color less sterile.

He shifted, and the saddle creaked—the blue jay squawked and vanished, the copperhead tested the air with its tongue, uncoiled and slipped beneath a dark copse of briar.

He massaged his knee, the back of his neck, checked his watch and smiled. It was nearly four, almost suppertime, something his stomach had already told him. He began to whistle randomly, not quite on key, until he settled on a spirited rendition of "The Flight of the Bumblebee," which he preferred to remember as the theme from *The Green Hornet*. The buckskin tossed her head and whickered a protest. Doug laughed and urged her forward—faster now, until the trail aimed straight down the eastern slope, flattened, and the trees stopped.

A tug at the reins, and the horse paused blowing at the clearing's shaded edge.

They were on the left side of a two-acre expanse of grass, a nonprofessional but functional paddock enclosed by a greyed split-rail fence whose two upper corners were hidden by stands of thick-boled oak. Not twenty feet from the fence, at the back and on the far side, the hill rose again, almost vertically nearly two hundred feet; most of the trees there were white birch and spruce, and the underbrush gave way to stacks and stairs of boulders.

Doug slipped out of the saddle and opened a plank gate to lead the animal through. Once the gate was relatched, he and the horse walked side by side, paying no attention to the grey squirrels that bounced away, scolding.

A second gate, the grass here worn in patches to the ground, and they were behind the garage, house, and stable.

The house was clean and weathered, a two-story log cabin with a steeply pitched slate roof, small windows top and bottom, and a single screen door off a narrow concrete stoop. The dark red garage was to the left, the matching low stable to the right, the backyard itself less than ten yards wide. There were no rusting tools here, or lawn chairs and redwood tables beneath a suburban sun umbrella; only a raised and covered stack of drying firewood to one side of the stoop.

The horse needed no prodding. She headed directly for the tackroom and waited patiently, eyeing Doug, who took his time crossing over and smiled when she finally pawed at the ground.

"You're worse than a wife, you know that, Maggie," he said, stripping off her saddle, blanket, and bridle. And as he turned to put the gear in its place, the buckskin reared, whinnied, and raced back through the gate. She sped across the grass, bucked, called again and rolled on the ground to scratch her back and sides.

He shook his head slowly, stepped back outside and pulled the tackroom door closed. *You really have a way with animals, almost like you can talk to them,* he'd been told more than once. But talking to Maggie had nothing to do with it. It was training, patience, and a damned healthy respect for a big dumb creature that could squash you flat or bite through your arm if it decided it was angry. Not to mention the hooves that could take a piece of your skull without half trying.

Still, he thought as he headed for the house, there were times when he almost believed the twelve-year-old mare could actually read his mind.

He had one hand on the doorknob, ready to turn it, when something made him turn around.

Maggie was standing abnormally still, her ears pricked high and stiff, her tail snapping hard from side to side.

He stepped down to the grass and pushed his hat back.

Then Maggie's ears flattened and she reared, her forelegs kicking out as if aiming for an invisible, dangerous target. Her teeth were bared, and her angry snorting punched the air like the sound of muffled gunshots.

"Maggie," he called, "what's up?"

His head cocked in bewilderment as he watched her lash out, then settle back to paw fiercely at the ground and shake her head violently.

"Hey, Maggie?"

She bolted suddenly, racing toward the back fence, circling once before ducking under the oaks to stand trembling behind the largest trunk.

Worried now and perplexed, he was halfway to the gate, ready to break into a run himself, when he felt it—a stirring of the ground, a sensation of *rumbling* without the earth moving. He looked down, frowning, until the *rumbling* passed like a train beneath his feet.

Maggie snorted, backed away, and pawed divots from the grass.

Son of a gun, he thought, and felt something else that made his head snap up.

The air was moving not quite in a breeze, and carrying with it a definite slice of winter. He looked around, the fingers of his left hand snapping nervously. Glancing between the stable and the house, he could not shake the feeling that whatever was coming had started on the other side of a tree-hidden wall, the northern boundary of the Winterrest estate.

The light seemed to shimmer, blurring the foliage, making him blink to clear his vision.

Maggie called out, defiant from behind the trees.

He scanned the hilltops—what the *hell* was going on?—and saw the trees begin to quiver, sway, give rasping voice to the breeze that quickly became a wind.

A strong wind.

A gale.

A hurricane's high keening that charged without warning around the front of the house and lifted a swirling crest of hard-edged dust and sharp dead leaves from the yard, surrounding him with it, pelting him with small stinging pebbles as he rushed back toward the door.

He heard Maggie again.

He hesitated, and something cracked viciously across the backs of his knees, shoving him forward with his spine arched and his head up. He whirled with a half-spoken curse and was hit again, harder, and fell face down with hands out to catch himself, turning away from the wind that howled now, grew to a shrieking, and made him gasp with the cold that sliced through his clothes, while his hat was yanked off and spun toward the garage.

Maggie challenged—high-pitched, almost screaming.

A knobbed section of dead wood thudded against his side and made him grunt with pain, and he quickly covered his head with his hands and curled himself into a tight ball, still kneeling, leaning to the right to keep from falling over.

The tackroom door was thrust open, cracking over and over against the stable wall.

Grit stung his cheeks and slipped beneath his eyelids; twigs knifed across the exposed backs of his hands; another branch slammed into the center of his spine, and he yelled in anger and surprise.

His nostrils clogged and he opened his mouth to

breathe, and it instantly filled with dust he could not spit out.

The cold intensified, and he felt his skin tighten and split across his knuckles.

A rock bounced off his ribs, another off his elbow, and he could feel his shirt beginning to tear along the seam on the left side. He was hard put to keep from dashing for the house, knowing that the moment he raised his head he would be pummeled unconscious.

Sound was muffled as the air pressure altered and his ears were stoppered.

Deafened, partially blinded, he was prepared to wait it out until he realized that in a very short time the banshee gale was going to pump the air from his lungs, that the cold was going to freeze him—that in the middle of July he was going to be battered to death or die of the cold.

And as he opened his mouth to shout . . . it ended.

As abruptly as it had begun, it was over, and he toppled onto his side, no longer braced against the wind.

"God . . . damn!"

He lay for several long seconds gulping for a breath before he moved his arms down, slowly, to avoid cramping. His chest ached, and his legs stung and throbbed in a hundred different places. The taste of blood mingled with dirt made him spit several times. Then he lifted his head and pushed himself up until he could sit with his forearms draped over his knees. The backs of his hands were an angry red, and a thin line of blood trickled down over one knuckle. A palm ran gently over his sides to test for broken ribs. He blinked once and hard, and shook his head vigorously before realizing that the heat had returned and sweat was already breaking out under his arms. The yard had been scoured clear, and dead branches were piled in a huddle on the garage's far side.

Maggie was beneath her oak, grazing.

The trees were still.

"Jesus," he whispered, and struggled awkwardly to

his feet, dusted himself off, and stared at the sky. There were no storm clouds that he could see, no thunder he could hear; only the sun heading west and the humidity's clinging haze.

"Jesus, what the hell was that?"

Maggie raised her head, shook her mane, snapped her tail at a fly.

When he felt he could take a step without falling, he walked clumsily to the fence and leaned heavily against it, watching the calm buckskin shift from spot to spot in search of the perfect meal. There was no indication she was still disturbed, and when he called to her, she only lifted her head, shook it, and snapped at a green leaf spiraling out a tree.

He grunted, more than willing to believe it had all been a hallucination brought about by the week-long heat wave; more than willing, and virtually praying, until he saw the divots Maggie had tossed aside in her inexplicable rage, and felt the dull pain in his thighs and side where the rocks and branches had struck him.

The only plausible explanation was the arrival of a new frontal system; here in the eastern foothills of the Appalachians it wasn't unusual for abrupt, powerful winds to sweep through minutes ahead of a changing weather pattern. And though they were often preceded by impressive cloud formations, neither was it odd for a front to barrel through out of a perfectly clear sky.

He checked the mare again and decided that that answer was just as good as any. Just as good, and it would have to do.

A brisk shake of his shoulders as he recalled the knifing cold, and he exhaled as loudly as he could in forced relief. The aching subsided. The stinging on his hands faded until he could ignore it. He strode to the back door, opened it, and stepped inside without turning.

Just as good, but he didn't like it.

* * *

The kitchen was the smallest room in the house, with just enough space for a table by the back window, and the appliances, counters, and cupboards, none of which were more than six years old. To the immediate right a doorway opened onto a cluttered study/office lined with bookshelves, and he glanced in without entering, wincing guiltily at the drafting table by the window.

He supposed he ought to get to work. The ostensible purpose of the ride had been to sweep his head clear of conflicting ideas, to settle on the design so he could take care of it the instant he walked back through the door. The trip, however, had taken longer than he'd planned, and the incident with the wind made him a little jumpy. No sense trying anything now. He'd have to calm himself a bit more, no question about it; and no, he answered a small nagging at the back of his head, I'm not procrastinating.

A quick grin; he was a liar.

The water ran disturbingly cold when he turned on the faucet, and he waited a second before he rinsed out his mouth, spitting, grimacing at the blood that swirled down the drain. A tentative prod found a loose tooth on the right side; another rinse, and the bleeding stopped. Then he washed his hands without soap, and dried them on a succession of plain paper towels. After taking a can of beer from the refrigerator, he walked stiffly down an unlighted hallway to the large front room that swung away to his right, twenty feet square, a cathedral ceiling, and a gallery off of which opened four doors.

The walls were paneled in white pine, the fireplace on the west wall was made of fitted stone; the floor was pegged and bare, except for a worn throw in front of each of two armchairs and a long, three-cushioned sofa that faced the raised slate hearth. A walnut stereo cabinet stood in the far corner, its four speakers wall-mounted below the gallery's level. Old newspapers and magazines lay in a tilting pile beside the fireplace, and here too a number of shelves nearly filled with books.

Shades of brown, shadows of gold, a spot here and there of deep red and dark green. Even the draperies over the wide front window were splotched with the hues of the woodland outside.

It seemed spare, not for frequent company, and apparent even to him that he was the only one in the house.

A long drink, a longer sigh, and he walked over to the stereo. It was time, he thought, for a little culture, an uplifting of the spirit.

A jumble of cassettes lay beside a dusty tape deck, and he plucked one up without looking at the label, fitted it, and stepped back to the center of the room. The speakers hissed. He set the beer can on the floor and raised his hands just in time to begin conducting the opening theme of *Lux Radio Theater,* then glowered theatrically as the medley deepened into the pounding of *The FBI in Peace and War,* grinned at *Fibber McGee and Molly.* By the time he had guided the Lone Ranger through the *William Tell* Overture, he was laughing.

"Ah, Douglas," he said as he turned off the tape and retrieved his beer, "you were born too late. You could've been a star, the greatest maestro of the airwaves."

If he didn't feel entirely at ease then, he felt considerably better than when he'd walked in. The cassettes were hastily shoved into a stack that tipped over the moment he turned away, and he stood there a second before deciding that his passion for old radio shows was not to be sated this afternoon. This wasn't the time to listen to a gravel-throated Rochester try to mollify Jack Benny.

He pulled the drawstring to open the draperies, turned a leather chair around, and sat down to watch the world.

There was no sign of the windstorm.

He wondered if he ought to call Judy or Liz and tell them about it, changed his mind because no doubt it had done the same to the town. Besides, Judy would be opening the tavern about now, and Liz would be at her county seat office, juggling court cases and muttering about the way some judges still looked at women lawyers. She didn't need to waste a minute while he told her he was frightened.

"You're a coward," he told himself then, knowing full well she'd be glad to hear his voice. "And you're not frightened, you're just plain dumb."

Or unsettled. Anyone would be, even Captain Marvel.

Ten minutes later, the beer forgotten and warming in his hand, he started when he thought he saw someone staring in at him through the window.

i didn't murder him
he's still dead
i did not murder him
but he's still dead, you killed him

He almost bolted, then sagged back again when the face receded into the sunlight that had him squinting.

he's dead

His reflection, nothing more—a man's round face tanned and pleasantly lined, thick auburn hair beginning to show traces of grey at the temples; a small mouth, small nose, eyes in contrast just a shadow too large.

He touched a steady finger to his chin; the reflection did the same. Simon says do this, he thought, and put the beer can on the floor.

you killed him

"Shit," he muttered, and without warning he was once again a wide-eyed twenty-four, living in Seattle. He had just completed a major project, not his first by any means, and had come racing home from the office, the *wunderkind* architect, hired right out of college. He'd rushed to the eighth-floor apartment he shared

18

with his fiancée Ellen, two hours before he was due.

He called out cheerfully when he entered, stopped and dropped his briefcase when he heard muffled noises in the bedroom. Another call, no response, and he hurried, heart abruptly leaden. She was there, but she was not waiting; she was in their king-sized bed with a man he didn't know. He was immobile, she was hysterical, and the man leapt from the bed, not bothering to fetch his clothes, evidently deciding that taking the offensive would drive Doug away. But Doug felt a rush of heat that blinded him, deafened him, and a single step forward had him in a fight.

It was a graceless battle, more wrestling than punching, staggering around the room, bouncing off the walls, crashing into an end table, finally ending at the low-silled window.

He heard Ellen shriek an obscenity, and the rage crumbled to disgust. He threw the man aside as hard as he could. All he wanted now was to leave; all he wanted to do was get away from the woman who knelt naked on the bed and shrieked at him to leave her poor lover alone.

He grabbed the man's arms and threw him away.

The man's legs struck the sill, his momentum slammed him back. There was a shout, and a scream. The window cracked, shattered, and the man fell through, eight stories to the ground where he landed on his back.

When Doug looked out, the man was staring up, blood fanning from beneath his head, the rain filling his dead eyes.

Arrest and prosecution; charged with manslaughter in the first degree because the prosecutor couldn't prove actual malice. Four years in prison before he was paroled, four years more in Washington before they let him leave the state.

The *wunderkind* was dead, a convicted killer, and

the only one in Deerford who knew it was Judith Lockhart.

In the beginning he had said nothing because he feared reaction to his past; then he had fallen in love with the place, and feared that after years of drifting they would force him to leave.

"Shit," he said again, and stared at his reflection.

For months at a time he managed to avoid thinking about it at all, and the nightmares were at last only something to remember. Now it was coming back, and he knew the reason why: Judith and Liz—he was terrified of loving either because of Ellen and her dead lover.

"You," he said to the face in the window, "are a mess, pal, you know that, don't you. God, what a mess."

The reflection grinned at him; no argument there.

His nostrils flared then, and he looked at his lap and at his hands. Definitely a shower, he decided—to wash off the ride and the dust from the windstorm, and not incidentally wake him up for a decent night's work. And it had better be now, or he'd sit here for hours, until it was too dark to do anything but stare at the stars.

With a grunt at his aching legs he rose, stretched, and stripped off his shirt as he headed upstairs. The right-hand door led to his bedroom, a twenty-by-twenty haven over the dining room below. The furniture here was cherrywood and heavy, the king-sized bed under a wooden canopy bolted to the wall. After flicking on the overhead light, he dropped with a sigh onto the quilt and yanked off his boots.

The mattress was soft, the pillows inviting.

Shower! he ordered when he felt himself leaning back.

He laughed and left the room, avoiding after a check the darkening bruises spreading over his thighs and the side of his chest; and he laughed again when, as he dressed in fresh clothes much like those he'd taken off, he found himself deliberately avoiding a look at the bed.

Muir, he thought as he hurried down to the kitchen, you've no time for naps if you want to pay the bills.

As he headed for the stairs, a cold gust of wind rattled the panes.

2

It was reputed to be the best car on the road—this great, marvelous, unsurpassed BMW. It was supposed to zip through rush hour traffic like a shadow, tear along the interstate like the wind, and not cost her more than an arm and a leg because if you want to be crass about it, the dollar-for-dollar resale value was higher than any other machine on the road. It says here. It says here in the impressive, leather-bound, plastic-preserved letter the salesman showed her, just one glowing testimonial among many from other, eminently satisfied customers who would sooner trade in their children than trade in their sedans.

Bullshit, Elizabeth Egan thought.

The car was the color of chocolate, inside and out, and it showed every spot of dust, every nick from a thrown stone, every tiny dent and scratch from every parking lot she'd been in since picking the thing up. It also had the personality of one of Piper Cleary's hounds—it ran when it felt like it, and if she was in a hurry, it took a vacation without leaving word at the office.

Like now, as she stood helplessly at the front fender, hood up, staring in at the warren of wires and hoses, trying desperately not to scream her frustration. Today! Today of all days it had to conk out. And it knew, it damned well *knew* she had to be home by five to feed herself and the kids, then shower and dress in time for Clark Davermain to pick her up. Today, when she was sure he'd propose, and was just as sure she didn't know what she'd say—because she didn't want to say yes and didn't have the courage to say no.

Goddamnit, it *knew*, and it was mocking her.

Liz, she thought sternly, get hold of yourself.

She immediately grabbed an elbow in a palm, looked down and started giggling.

Get hold, Lizzy, get hold.

She grabbed the other elbow, wrapped one foot around an ankle and stood there on the shoulder of a two-lane country road less than two miles from home, and giggled until she'd calmed down. She was sure more than one passing motorist thought she was drunk; she was just as sure she didn't give a damn.

She laughed.

This was insane, and it would get worse if she didn't get home soon and find solace with her children. At least their problems weren't defined by the Constitution or a medieval judge who believed in an eye for an eye and thirty days, no bail; at least with Keith and Heather there was hope for the world.

A glance down dampened her mood again.

Her cream satin blouse was stained with perspiration; her rust skirt was wrinkled, her matching shoes dusty. She could feel the dust settling in her blond hair curled under below the nape, coating her narrow tanned face and accentuating her pugged nose. Making her ugly. Gathering under wide hazel eyes in pouches to deepen her cheeks' hollows and make her chin like a dagger. At thirty-four, others still called her pert, but with a layer of Jersey roaddust she could easily pass as Gretel's stepmother.

Oh hell, Liz, stop feeling sorry for yourself.

Yet even the view didn't brighten her mood.

The woodland was beautiful, rich with tall maples and caged birch, with a smattering of evergreen darker than the rest. No houses for miles, not even a gas station until Deerford, and as far as she knew, if she died right now she wouldn't be found until August.

22

And it was quiet.

The engine had stopped its cooling ticking; there was no breeze. When she kicked at a pebble, it bounced across the road without making a sound.

She decided then she was being punished for her treatment of Clark, taking him too much for granted when she knew, if she were honest with herself, that she wouldn't be taking anything else if she could help it. Punished for being blind to how truly serious he was—about her, and the future. They had crossed briefs almost a year ago, at the county courthouse in Newton, bitterly, loudly, and she had come out the winner. That same afternoon he had called her office and suggested a drink, perhaps a meal, that same evening.

Much to her own astonishment, she had accepted.

They saw each other frequently after that, and the attention pleased her so much she had not noticed his gaze, or felt the way he held her when they danced, or caught any of the hints he had cast timidly in her direction. But today, hearing his voice on the phone, she knew, and for a long time she sat alone, staring out the window, seeing nothing, afraid that if she took the chance and gave her kids a father, Doug Muir would suddenly come around and give her what she wanted.

Damn him, she thought; damn them both.

Doug could solve everything if he'd only stop stalling.

Yet, though she sensed in him the attraction and the need, he refused for some unknown reason to let himself go. The several dates they had had together had been fun—they dined, held hands, kissed lightly, and laughed—and the moment they seemed ready to make some sort of commitment, he had quickly but politely backed off into the role of a nice, dependable, stalwart good friend.

She didn't need a friend; she needed a lover, and a sharer, and a father for her children. With Clark, that was two out of three, but sharing was something she didn't think he understood.

So she sought calm on the drive home, a moment to reflect and gauge and hunt for a decision; unfortunately, once she had reached the sweeping highway curve, the BMW had choked and died, and after frantic attempts to restart it she had flooded the engine. The only thing she could do now was have a smoke and wait.

She returned to the door and raided her purse for a cigarette, a lighter, then leaned back against the fender to watch the woods across the way. After initially complaining about the wilderness that surrounded her daily, she liked now the way the trees were packed close together, putting shadows in the air as well as on the ground. She was drawn to them. Whenever she had the chance, she walked among them for hours, once found herself talking to them, telling them about the office where she was treated like a niece instead of a junior partner, and how the competition with her colleagues was worse now that the firm was cutting back.

Never kidding herself, she knew she had landed the job because of her sex; the remnants of the New Frontier had made her superiors nervous about feminist lawsuits. And she never bothered to explain that she wasn't the type to take legal action just because she wasn't hired.

What made the current situation more frustrating was the admission of the firm's founder that she was, without a doubt, one of the best attorneys he had.

Of course, she could always hang out her shingle in Deerford. Everybody asked her advice anyway so she certainly wouldn't lack for clients.

It would be hard, no question about it. Litigation between farmers and shopkeepers wasn't exactly the road to great or lasting fortune. On the other hand, she would be rid of the unrelenting pressure to perform, and the kids would have her home more often. They were old enough now to understand why she had to work so hard, and so late; but they were also starving for the sight of her, the touch of her, even the way she scolded them.

A scolding much like the one she'd given only that afternoon.

Keith had called (hastily claiming his sister had forced him into it) to ask if they could take their bikes over to Winterrest to explore after their household chores were done. She had said no. He had pouted. She told him that the estate was private property and no one, not even God, was allowed to walk there without permission.

When he passed the obviously expected response on, she could hear Heather demanding justice for young adults and gee whiz all the other kids do it.

"Well," she said with impeccable parental logic, "you're not all the other kids. Stay away. I don't want you near it."

It was curious, actually. She had no idea why she felt that way. No one had lived there for years, and the older kids frequently crept over the low wall and did whatever kids did in the dark these days.

But while Winterrest was for some a comforting declaration of Deerford's existence, it unnerved her, and she could not say why.

She glanced at her watch; it was a few minutes past four. Time to see if this heap would start moving.

She flicked the cigarette across the road and had half turned to open the door when she felt rather than heard a subterranean *rumbling*. A light cloud of dust lifted from the tarmac, hovered and settled only to rise again, flecked through with black motes like gnats swarming at dusk.

An anxious look up the highway, searching for the truck that had to be careening wildly toward her, thinking for a moment she ought to move into the trees in case the driver didn't see her and slammed into the car.

The *rumbling* increased, and she felt a thrumming

vibration penetrate her soles, tingle her calves, tighten her thighs.

Then, before she could decide what was happening, the ground trembled.

She started, and stared at the narrow verge, at the blacktop still cracked from the previous winter's freeze.

The ground *rippled*.

A flock of crows bolted into the sky, calling hysterically, wheeling, swinging sharply overhead before disappearing south.

The car creaked and began rocking, and she jumped away, holding up her hands as if afraid it would scorch her.

"Hey!"

Beneath her feet the rumbling became thunder, and the trembling became a quaking, rolling and violent. Before she could grab the door the hood slammed down, and before she could call out again she was thrown off her feet.

The trees became palsied, saplings swaying like frantic whips until they blurred grey and green. A large gnarled branch crashed onto the road, bounced, and shattered into splinters as if it were glass; an oak lifted groaning out of the ground, roots dripping black dirt and dark wriggling things, screaming as it fell against a smaller, younger tree that bent under the weight and snapped like a gunshot, the landing raising a cloud that spun away as though the quake had given birth to a wind.

The grumbling swelled to a roaring, a deafening bellow that made her ears ache.

Liz was rolled into the middle of the road, jagged pieces of blacktop scraping her arms and legs while she screamed and tried to cover her head.

A moss-stained boulder moved ponderously out of the forest and onto the verge.

The car bounced on its tires, and the hood flapped and clanked like a toneless cymbal.

She was tumbled toward the woods and tried to stop

herself by spreading her legs, digging in toes and heels wherever she could. It didn't work. The ground hunched and threw her, and she landed face up in a shallow ditch, the breath punched from her lungs; and she looked skyward to see a forty-foot tree leaning down toward her.

She screamed for the children and crossed her arms over her face, drew up her legs and tried to stand, was thrown back again, her head slamming on a rock.

The bellowing climbed, a dragon prowling the woods.

She cried as the tree lowered, its shadows creeping along her chest, its rough-bark bole groaning in the effort to keep itself whole. A leaf raked her brow as if trying to skin her.

She swore as she tried to squirm out of the way, and found herself pinned by a branch against the ditch's wall, prayed when she could smell the bark, the leaves, the heaving roots lifting blackly.

And she blinked when the dragon abruptly fell silent, the throes of the earthquake suddenly ended.

The ground settled.

The leaves stopped husking.

In a nearby tree a cardinal was singing.

"Good . . . lord," she groaned as she sat up and pushed a twig away from her legs. "Good—"

The kids! God, the kids are home!

Her legs wobbling, her breath hard to come by, she staggered to the car, swallowing and gasping, her hands outflung to regain her balance.

Midway there she stopped.

The windshield was spiderweb-cracked on the passenger side from a rock striking it head on, a horizontal dent creased the driver's side door, and the paint was badly faded by the dust raised by the quake.

The only thing that surprised her was that the engine was running.

No doubt there was some highly technical and for her totally incomprehensible reason why the engine

27

had restarted during the earthquake, but as she left a smoking plume in her haste to get home, she didn't really care. It had started, was still running, and that's all that mattered until she reached the kids to see if they were all right.

The back of her left hand swiped a tear from each cheek, then regripped the wheel while her right hand plunged into her purse to find a cigarette. By the time it was between her lips and burning, she had slowed down, and was frowning, leaning forward and staring through the windshield at the view ahead.

It was impossible, but nothing seemed damaged beyond the spot where she'd stopped. The blacktop was unmarred, the trees were still standing, and when the blinking amber light came into view at the T-intersection turn into town it wasn't even swinging. As it should have been—perhaps even dashed to the ground—if in fact the earthquake had actually happened.

Don't be ridiculous, Liz; you were there, for god's sake!

There, and terrified, and she could have been killed by that slow falling tree had the quake continued. Right now she could be broken and dead at the side of the road.

Her arms went suddenly and frighteningly cold, her legs went numb, and her eyes began to blur. She pulled over and turned off the ignition. She could walk now if she had to. Though there were trees on her right, on the left side of the road was the backyard fence of the first Meadow View home. She couldn't recall who it belonged to, but there was wash hanging from a line strung from the back door to a weeping willow. A pudgy woman in a pink floral robe was pinning a sheet to the cord.

Up ahead, beyond the warning signal, a county maintenance truck came toward her. When it was abreast of the BMW she stared at it, at the men sitting in back amid rakes and shovels and pots of steaming tar. They grinned, one whistled, and she half turned to watch until they disappeared around the bend.

Ordinarily, she would have ignored them.

Ordinarily, she wasn't caught in a New Jersey earthquake.

"It happened." She reached out to touch the windshield's crack. "Damnit, it happened!"

She restarted the engine, pulled off the shoulder, and drove to the brick pillars that marked Meadow View's entrance. She took the rest of the way at walking speed, to the last house in back. A split-level mock Tudor. Green fields behind it, green lawn in front shaded by the two red maples Ron had planted the afternoon he died. He had been standing by the last one, hosing water over the roots when suddenly his face paled, his mouth opened—he looked at her on the steps, and he keeled over.

The doctor said he was dead before he hit the ground.

Six years ago, at thirty-five, his heart had given out.

She pulled into the driveway, sat for five minutes trying to see if she would scream, then opened the door just as her children ran out of the garage.

Keith was eleven, husky, and blond, wearing coverall jeans and a Conan T-shirt; Heather would be fourteen in December, and was in one of her father's denim workshirts, and a pair of red shorts. Both were barefoot, both demanding her immediate attention, and both were stunned when she threw her arms around them and hugged so tightly Keith began to gasp.

"Mom, are you all right?" Heather asked when she finally extricated herself. "What happened to the car? Did you have an accident? Are you okay?"

"Did you hit a tree or something?" Keith said, staring in astonishment at the crack in the windshield. "Jeez, you musta been going ninety. Jeez."

"Fine, I'm fine," she said shakily. "I . . . didn't you feel anything here, about twenty minutes ago?"

"What," Keith said, wrenching his attention from the wrecked car to the wreck his mother was. "An earthquake?"

She almost nodded, then changed her mind. Instead, she hugged them again and her son protested loudly.

"Hey, can't a mother hug her kids when she wants to?"

"Child abuse," he muttered, and danced out of the way of her stinging palm.

She watched them rush inside, and followed slowly, looking around until she was dizzy, finally convinced that whatever that nightmare was, it hadn't struck here.

And once in the kitchen—sunny yellows and copper, a round white table in the center, a cloth calendar by the fridge—she had to force herself to believe it had really happened while she spun a swift tale of being forced off the road by a speeding truck.

Heather swore piously she'd never drive that way, and Keith was all for forming a lynch party instantly. The concern made her feel good, made her smile, albeit somewhat weakly.

"Mother," Heather said then as she opened the refrigerator and pulled out a can of Dr. Pepper, "would you please tell Keith that my room is off limits to little boys? He keeps going *in* there without my permission. And I wouldn't give it to him anyway, even if you said to."

"Mom," Keith said, sitting at the table and folding his arms over his chest, "would you please tell Heather than I don't take orders from anyone named after a weed?"

"Mother!"

She sat, took the soda, and drained half the can. A glance around the room to be sure the walls weren't cracked, the windows were still intact, and she drank the rest without taking a breath, held out her hand until Heather gave her another. A belch rose, and instead of stifling it she let it out, loudly, crudely, and both her children gaped before starting to laugh.

Normal, she thought; thank god, it's all normal.

Then, with her hands cupped around the can, she listened as they told her about their day, about the way

Keith's truly dumb friends—who called themselves the Mohawk Gang—had been absolute *pests* from the moment she'd left for work, how Heather was getting too snotty just because she was almost fourteen and thought she was a big deal, and how they were going to have to learn to ski next winter because otherwise they were completely and *totally* going to be the invisible man if they didn't.

"That's nice," she said, grinning. "And when did you find time to straighten up the house, like you were supposed to?"

Keith looked at her as if she were crazy, and Heather only rolled her eyes toward the ceiling.

"Sorry," she said, "I must have lost my mind. It looks all right, anyway, I guess."

"Mother," Heather said, "are you going out to-night?"

When she nodded she couldn't help noticing their reaction—Keith's gaze went blank for the briefest of moments, and Heather's eyes narrowed just as long.

But she knew it wasn't the date that bothered them, it was the man taking her on it. Clark Davermain was not exactly the hit with the kids he thought he was.

On the other hand, if it had been Doug, they would have personally carried her up the bathroom, scrubbed her back, washed her hair, and made sure she had washed thoroughly behind her ears.

Well, maybe not quite that bad, and they really didn't *hate* Clark at all. They were polite, and they conversed, and they laughed quietly at his jokes. And she blinked with the realization that what they were doing was tolerating him. For her sake. Because they thought she cared for him.

Oh, Christ, she thought, this is a hell of a thing.

And when a light push of wind rattled the screen door, it was all she could do not to scream in their faces.

31

3

The two-story colonial three doors down from the Depot Tavern was, on that Friday afternoon, darkly immersed in shade that seemed too much like winter shadow clinging to the maples towering over the building. It looked like a normal Deerford residence—white, a house-long porch complete with rocking chairs and a padded bench-swing, the windows flanked by dark green shutters, with cream shades with braided pulls, and white filmy curtains permanently tied back; it looked normal except for the narrow pine-plank sign on the gaslight post at the end of the slate walk, a sign with "The Antique Bazaar" burned into it in lettering the owners supposed looked like Old English. The entire first floor had been transformed into a shop, various polished bits and sets of furniture, bric-a-brac, and display cases of gold- and silverware painstakingly arranged to resemble a maiden aunt's attic in which treasures were to be found.

There was track lighting on the molding, and a few of the lamps were fitted with low-watted bulbs, the effect designed for a pleasant browsing atmosphere and for preventing the casual but ready shopper from seeing too much too soon, before the sale was made.

Now, all the lights were on though it was only just past four—the maples' persistent but noncooling shade made it feel as if it were considerably past sunset.

The front door was open in a vain attempt to vent the heat, and on the threshold stood a young man slight and tall, whose light brown hair had already retreated around a monk's cap at the back of his skull. He wore pressed brown slacks, a pin-striped shirt folded open at the throat, and at the moment he was crushing a cigarette beneath his loafered heel. Then he turned from his survey of the empty street and put his hands in his pockets.

"Ollie, I have made a decision," Bud Yardley announced to the woman he was going to marry in less than three weeks.

"Really," she uttered, not bothering to look up. Bud was always making decisions; it was part of his charm.

"Yes, I have. After a great deal of careful consideration, I have decided that this weekend, and for this weekend only, we will do nothing but sell the original stuff from the Retirement Room, and none of this crap we have out here."

Olivia West looked up from the cash register set on a four-foot long counter just inside the door, and she frowned. "What the hell are you talking about, Charles?"

Bud winced at the scolding and what he thought was an upper-class pronunciation of his given name, and decided that the marriage contract would somehow have to include a prohibition of its use.

"I mean it, Ollie," he said earnestly. "Let's do some real selling for a change."

Ollie shrugged. "Whatever you say."

"Well, it isn't only what I say," he told her, wondering at her attitude. She had been distracted all day, but wouldn't tell him why. "You are the other half of this partnership, you know."

A shallow crease appeared in her smooth high forehead as she counted the bills in their slots, lifted the tray, and counted the bills and checks beneath it. "Okay. Then I say you're wrong."

Bud bit down on the inside of his cheek. For a moment, just for a moment, he was tempted to take hold of the thick brown braid dangling down her back to her waist; just for a moment he wanted to give it a vicious yank to pull some sense into her skull. But he knew he wouldn't, just as he knew she would never permit him to sell the only true antiques in the shop.

They had known each other for five years, since both were twenty-one and freshly scrubbed out of

33

college. Both trained to be teachers, and while they had not found jobs, they found each other instead and a vast companionable interest in colonial American history—the social history that emphasized the way people lived. They were also equally fascinated by furniture—Bud made it in a small workshop in the basement, Ollie restored it, and it seemed only natural that they should open a place together.

They also discovered it didn't hurt that they had fallen in love.

They pooled their money, cadged loans from each set of not-quite-approving parents, and set out to create a name to be reckoned with in the field of domestic antiquities.

The first attempt had been a disaster, down in South Jersey where the people were too interested in making a living in the present, and where the credible buyers seldom traveled in the numbers they needed to survive. The following year they traveled north, closer to New York City, where they hoped to attract a more well-heeled clientele. That project failed too when a blossoming of urban renewal literally brought their building down around their heads.

A fluke of driving that summer—Bud got lost, Ollie couldn't read the map—landed them in Deerford, found them the empty house, and found them Eban Parrish, who took them under his wing. Their loan now long since repaid, they had become one of the regular stops for those looking for honest deals. And for those tireless wives who dragged their husbands out on weekends, and those pompous, all-knowing husbands who believed everything they read in books, there was the assorted furniture in the front—just enough real goods to keep suspicion at bay, the rest of it simply old and well kept and seldom worth half the asking price.

In the back, however, was a room filled with genuine stock insured for more than half a million dollars, and it was Bud's constant dream to clear it out in a single afternoon, salt the resulting fortune away, and go off on a real buying trip, to Pennsylvania or New England.

The Retirement Room, their whole lives bound in carved wood and tufted velvets.

Ollie, however, kept reminding him that it had taken them almost five years and a lot of debts to build that much of a showroom. What would they do in the meantime, live on love and orange peels?

She looked up again and saw his disappointment, the way his lips were not quite twisted into a pout. She smiled but did not relent, instead skirted the counter and slipped her hand around his waist, two fingers insinuating themselves between the buttons of his shirt. She was only an inch shorter than his own six feet.

"You're feeling guilty, that's all."

He took a deep breath and looked out the door. "I am not."

"You hate it when some wicked city woman sashays in here and picks out a table she calls mid-Victorian that you knew damned well was made in Albany in 1931, and you don't tell her she's wrong."

"Well, it's cheating."

"It's giving the public what it wants."

Their routine was simple: his earnest boyishness took care of the women, her somewhat earthy and frank sultriness usually lined up the men. They were also experts at picking out fellow experts, and never once had they tried to pass a bad deal on someone who could do them irreparable harm by dropping the wrong word.

If people wanted to be fools, on the other hand, they were more than willing to accommodate them—if the opportunity arose and the sucker asked for it with a smile.

"You wanna go upstairs?"

He was being consoled and he knew it, and he also sighed at the way her fingers scratched at his stomach.

"No. Someone might come."

"It's after four. No one's coming now. C'mon, let's

35

go." She tugged at him gently and leaned over to kiss his cheek, gently pressing her chest into his arm. "Huh? You wanna?"

He did. He always did. He could barely stand it when he hadn't touched her for over five minutes, and was worse when he saw her with a male customer, playing her role, just out of reach. He felt his blood pressure rising when he saw a male friend give her a hug or kiss her or flirt openly with her. She loved the attention, and she loved him as well, and as far as he knew she had never been unfaithful.

But the other men drove him crazy.

She kissed his ear, and her tongue circled it once.

"Hey!" he said, jerking his head away. "Jesus, Ollie, someone could see you out there."

She checked the road—no traffic, no pedestrians, Parrish's office across the way was closed for the day.

"Besides," he said glumly, "you told me you weren't feeling well."

"I never said anything of the sort. And my not feeling well," she said, nuzzling his neck after a brief hesitation, "has nothing to do with what I have in mind. I may not be up to par, but I ain't dying either. C'mon. Smoke a little, do a little. What about it, sailor?"

His arm found her shoulders, and he pulled her closer. "I love you, you know, even when you're wanton."

She grinned and relaxed; his pouting was over. "I love you, too. You wanna get married?"

"Never. I don't want to spoil it."

"Let's go."

She released him and threaded her way along the deliberately complicated system of aisles and passageways created for the shop's layout. The stairs to their rooms above were off a short hallway in back, opposite the Retirement Room's locked door. There was nothing in the hall but an overhead light, and seven fire extinguishers on the floor, and on the walls.

Ollie wriggled her hips once in a gentle parody of

36

seduction, stopped at a polished milk can, and opened the first button of her shirt. A raised eyebrow, a silent whistle, and she laughed as she turned around.

"All right, all right," he said, stepped inside and shut the door, turned the *Closed* sign outward and hurried in her wake. It was crazy the way she maneuvered him, and there were times when he wondered if it was unmanly. But at least she didn't nag him. There was no pressure to make a million dollars before they were thirty, no pressure to fill their house with children, no pressure to do anything but pay the bills on time and continue learning their craft.

He reached the stairs and looked up to the landing. She was waiting, the shirt open and off her shoulders, her breasts not large but filling the transparent bra to give her what he thought was marvelously ample cleavage. She stuck out her tongue, slowly, reached into one cup and pulled out a breast, and he took the stairs two at a time, had his hands out to grab her when she whirled to the left and raced up the last three steps.

"You're a pain, Olivia," he said in disgust at her playing. "You're a regular pain in—"

He stopped, frowned, sniffed.

"What?" she said.

He sniffed again. She saw him this time and did the same. And her eyes opened in fear.

"Bud? Oh god, Bud?"

He looked down fearfully, and gasped when he saw dark ribbons of smoke curling rapidly from under the Retirement Room door.

"Oh my *god!* Ollie, the extinguishers!"

"But the smoke alarm didn't go off!"

He ignored her as he dashed back down and snatched an extinguisher from the wall. Then he took hold of the doorknob. It was warm, not yet hot, and he wondered what in god's name was going on. No one had been in there since this morning, and the back window pane was over two inches thick—anyone breaking in would be heard all over town.

With his free hand he fumbled with the key chain

clipped to his belt. "Come on, come *on, come on!*"
The smoke wrapped around his loafers, snaked up his
legs. He shook his head violently, then closed his eyes
prayerfully when the bolt turned over. A deep breath
to steady himself, but when he threw open the door he
nearly dropped to his knees.

Smoke. Filling the room like a caged, pacing thun-
derhead, acrid and swirling, thick and blinding, shot
through with flashes of flickering red and gold.

He choked, put one hand over his face and moved
in, squinting to locate the source of the flames, hearing
Ollie enter behind him and give voice to her shock.

"Help me!" he shouted. "Get this shit outta here!"

Ollie dropped the extinguisher she was holding and
began pulling and yanking and dragging and kicking at
everything within reach, piling it haphazardly in the
hall and returning for more.

Tears blurred his vision, smoke drew bile into his
mouth as he aimed the nozzle and played it over a
Sheridan chair, an Empire headboard propped beside
it against the wall. He could feel but not see Ollie
scuttling around somewhere else in the room; he could
see nothing but his arms and the pointing black cylinder in the smoke that filled his lungs, the flames that
curled the hairs on his arms and scorched the hairs on
the back of his neck. Sparks wafted out of the grey-
black and landed on his wrist, landed on his cheek, and
made him wince at the stabbing. He shook his head
because he didn't dare stop to brush them off.

Then he heard glass breaking, and the smoke began
to move. Slowly, ponderously drifting toward the
smashed window. The flames roared now, and he
realized he had spent the extinguisher. He stumbled
back back into the hall and grabbed another from the
floor.

He swallowed and coughed, spat black phlegm onto
the wall, and ducked his head to one side as he plunged
in again.

"Ollie!"

The flames had moved to the far wall, and he attacked them at their base, adding cold smoke of his own to the already stifling room. His arms were stinging, and he was sure he could feel flames crawling up his back.

"Olivia!"

"Here!"

The smoke was thinning, and he could see her in the corner drenching a Revere cobbler's bench and sobbing. When she was done, the extinguisher thunked to the floor and she staggered past him, shaking her head angrily when he reached out to grab her. A look around, and he realized they had beaten it. More noise and smoke than actual fire, and after ten minutes of poking numbly through the charred rubble, he threw his extinguisher through the broken window with a despairing yell, lashed out with his foot at whatever stood in his way, and fell into the hallway, gasping, coughing, ready to weep.

Ollie was on the stairs, her face in her hands. She parted her fingers, looked at him, and laughed.

Oh hell, she's hysterical, he thought as he pushed himself to his feet; now she's gone and gotten hysterical. He limped to sit beside her and hold her in his arms, comfort her, tell her everything was going to be all right, they could start over, don't worry, no problem.

She giggled, and he was ready to slap her when she pointed to the open door.

"I know," he said soothingly, stroking her hair, kissing her cheek. "It's all right. I know."

She shook her head and laughed again, pointed again, then grabbed his cheeks and forced his head around.

"Ollie, I can't—holy shit!"

The room was clean.

The window facing him was unbroken.

When he examined the length of his arms he couldn't find a single burn, or see a single ash.

TWO

1

There was no organization, official or otherwise, known as the Deerford Historical Society, nor was there a handful of old-timers who indulged in colorful oral history around a cracker barrel in the general store. As far as anyone knew, Deerford had been here before Sussex became a county, before New Jersey became a state, though after Winterrest had been built in its meadow. What people did know was that at one time it had been a coach stop, that it served as a place for buying staples for the area's farmers, and when vacationers wanted to get away from it all, they passed through Deerford on their way to wherever "away" is.

There were very few corners, and its only traffic light blinked monotonously at the county road. All the houses—clapboard or brick, colonial or Victorian—were on or just off Deerford Road, set back behind elms and maples whose trunks were almost as wide as the porches. The children attended a regional school, the adults either had their own shops or they commuted to the county seat in Newton to work as clerks, secretaries and, once in a while, lawyers.

There was the Depot Tavern, a Mogas station, a general store with a post office, five houses whose first floors had been converted into antique shops and a handmade toy shop, the Shade Tree restaurant, and Eban Parrish's real estate office.

No one really cared that Deerford never grew. The reason the two thousand year-round residents stayed was because they could count on stability, count on their friends, count on the fact that aside from those who stopped at the restaurant or an antique store no one was going to bother them with progress. The county maintained the roads and the sewers, the cable company gave them television, and whenever there was a problem they held a town meeting.

Permitting construction of the Meadow View development had been a mistake, and everyone knew it. It had opened with six basic models duplicated four times, and stayed that way. It took the developer four years to sell the nineteenth house, and he never bothered to build any more. To live in the country was one thing; to live close to nothing at all but rolling fields, treed hills, and a traffic light that never turned red was something else again.

Those who did remain did so because they either couldn't afford to move again, or because they realized that Deerford was what they had been looking for all along. It wasn't unusual, then, that the "new folks" were the most militant about restrictions in town, the most enthusiastic about local affairs, and the most eager to be accepted.

And for the most part they were, and by the time the sapling maples planted along the curving streets had grown large enough to have foliage worth the name, it seemed as if they had been there forever.

And the last time a farm went up for sale the whole town chipped in and hired Eban Parrish to buy the land for them and lease it to a farmer who would work the fields hard and leave none of it to fallow.

If it seemed boring, it was only because some people had lost the knack of imagination.

And if it seemed tranquil, it was only because Winterrest was still sleeping.

2

The darkened house just to the left of the Depot was a squat, bulging Victorian that had been, at some time in it's recent past, shorn of the ornate gingerbread that had coiled around the rim of its house-long porch, the tiny-paned gables at each corner, and just above the sagging eaves on the black slate roof. It was freshly painted white, its shutters black, and its windows low enough almost to be square. Just inside the solid oak front door was a tiny vestibule barely wide enough for guests to utilize the coat closet on the left; and the inner, glass-paned door couldn't be opened if the closet was in use. Few visitors lingered there; it was too much like being in a glass-fronted casket.

The large, high-ceiling parlor which held most of its original, overstuffed, or back-breaking furnishings was on the left, the dining room with a refectory table and eight-foot china closet was on the right, and a narrow, red-carpeted staircase loomed directly ahead, climbing to a broad landing above which was a rose window perpetually dark.

The walls were papered in floral patterns now faded, the trim was dark and polished, and the fireplace in the parlor was made of grey stone.

At night the house, because it was not air conditioned and the untended attic did not have a circulation fan in either its front or back windows, tenaciously held the summer's worst heat to an unpleasant degree; it was, however, cool during the day.

Judith Lockhart sat on the heavy, embroidered couch facing the long front window and watched the day's light traffic pass by on Deerford Road. Her short-sleeved blouse was pale green, her jeans were faded, and her feet were bare with the toenails lacquered dark red.

She was alone.

All the other shades in the house were down, and she shivered in the faintly golden light, rubbing her thin arms and thinking she ought to go upstairs and find herself a sweater. It was ludicrous; hot outside, and here she was raising a bumper crop of gooseflesh on skin that had very little meat beneath it. What she ought to be doing was getting some sun—lying in the standing hammock in the backyard and listening to the trees tell her stories and the squirrels telling her to mind her own business; or trimming the dense privet hedge that surrounded her property; or going to the Depot to get ready for Friday night.

She ought to be behaving like ordinary people.

Instead, she sat in the midday gloom and watched the traffic, and listened patiently for signs of her brother returning.

And as she did she thought about Douglas Muir, and the trouble he was causing her because he was so damned stubborn, and so infuriatingly polite, and so maddeningly determined not to relinquish any control over his life.

He was getting to be a pain in the ass.

But it was almost time to force him into a decision. Not that he wasn't aware of her plans for him, and not that he had ever given her any solid encouragement. On more than one occasion over the past five years she had thought with certainty he would ask her to marry him, yet she had not pushed him because she knew she had plenty of time. She had not pushed, and Doug had not asked, and more than one tavern regular had told her with a sly wink that if she didn't get moving she'd surely lose him to that blond lawyer who lived over in Meadow View with her two children.

She had not pushed, and time, without her realizing it, had run out on her. Only a few days remained, if that, and then it would be too late.

She knew it would help her courage a lot if she loved him, but she wasn't sure she knew exactly what love was, or would even know it if it came up and bit her on the rump. God knew she had had her share of failures, spectacular and otherwise, the latest though not the most painful one with a man from New York City who thought it marvelously quaint that she lived in what he laughingly called bucolic isolation, a throwback to the pioneer days when men were men and women were women and the only thing they had to do in winter was fuck their little brains out while the snow piled up to the roof.

That he was a lousy lay didn't help, and that he refused to leave the city for Deerford sounded the death knell.

She shook herself to shed the disgust, ran a steady hand though her curly black hair and stood, walking stiffly back into the kitchen where she busied herself with the kettle and the instant coffee. She checked her watch and sighed. Two o'clock. One more hour and she would have to head next door, open the tavern, and get ready for the influx of the Friday crowd. There were a few, generally the newcomers like those in Meadow View, who wondered aloud and not very politely why she didn't open the place as early as the law allowed. On Saturdays she did; the rest of the week there was no call for it. The Shade Tree had its own liquor license and the lunch crowd, such as it was in a place like this, and she didn't think she really had to work herself frazzled to the nub just to provide a shot of rye for the drunks and Bloody Marys for those desperate for the hair of the dog.

And she certainly didn't need the money. The Depot provided for her well enough. Her needs were quite simple. Certainly more simple than most of them knew. Deerford proper never complained, and the others . . . they only waited for her to open the damned bar.

Now if she could only get Doug to move his butt out of the Hollow and into her bed, she could show him that just because she didn't have big tits or long legs didn't mean she didn't know a thing or two about screwing around, or making love.

44

Her abrupt laugh was short, bell-clear, mirthful, and she shrugged. In good time, Judy dear, all in good time. Don't panic. Keep calm. If you lose him too it won't be the first time.

The coffee made, she took her cup to the back door and looked out, hoping that maybe Casey would be there. He wasn't. Her eyes closed and she muttered a short prayer, warning him to be careful, warning him to stay away from Winterrest today.

Damnit, Sis, I saw that light, he had protested vehemently on Tuesday morning. *It was upstairs, in back, one of the bedrooms, I guess. It was there, and I wasn't drunk.*

But he was drunk when he told her, or well on his way—the first time he had slipped in over a year. She had been so furious at him for his weakness, and for what he might say to the wrong people at the wrong time, that she had hauled off and slapped him, so hard her palm stung and she had to blow on it to keep it from bursting into flame. Casey had staggered back a step, his eyes gone wide, his lower lip trembling, and before she could turn away he had burst into pathetic tears. He stumbled around the house weeping, raising his fists to heaven and demanding justice for himself, and retribution for the sister who wouldn't believe him if he gave her the time standing in front of Big Ben.

Then he had left. And stayed away, returning only that night to snore in his bed. He was gone by dawn Wednesday, was sober by the afternoon, and that night in the Depot she was begged by several of the regulars to chain him, or lock him up, but for god's sake do something because he was driving them all crazy with his talk of folks moving back into the estate.

She understood their nervousness.

Winterrest wasn't a place you visited willingly, even at noon.

At three o'clock there was still no sign of him, and though she was worried, she was furious as well. She should have known that her brother wasn't strong enough to face the dying again.

She wasn't really sure she was either, but considering the alternative, she didn't give herself much of a choice.

Ten minutes passed while she rinsed out her cup, dried it, set it back in the cupboard, emptied the copper kettle, put away the jar of coffee, rinsed off the teaspoon and placed it in its drawer.

Casey was still gone.

She wondered what people would say if he tried to tell them what was happening. Crazy, is what; drunk, stoned, and Christ, Judy, don't you think he ought to be looked at or something?

Her red lips parted; it might have been a smile.

The hell with you, pal; you're on your own now.

Shortly before four she switched on the neon Miller sign in the Depot's window, unlocked the door, and checked the bills and change in the register drawer. She hummed. She assayed a buck-and-wing across the floor to turn on the lights. A glance at her watch proved it broken again, and she dumped it in the trash; watches and she did not get along—a sign, perhaps, that Time and Judith Lockhart did not mean much to each other.

She hummed louder. Once in a while she pulled out a compact and examined her makeup, pursed her lips, fluffed her dark curly hair, smoothed her ruffled red blouse down over her chest. *I made you love me,* she sang silently to an image of Doug striding through the door; *you didn't wanna do it, you didn't wanna do it.* She opened the blouse's top button and told herself it was all in a good cause and the hell with what her employees thought.

Then she looked down at the cleavage and groaned loudly; if she wanted anything to show she'd have to gain about thirty pounds; then, for good measure, shove a box of tissues into her bra.

Not quite that bad, actually, but loosening a provocative button would only make someone ask her to redo it.

"Judith," she told herself as she pulled out the week's work roster, "you are insufferable. And very, very sick."

And Casey still hadn't shown up, though he knew damned well he had to work behind the bar tonight.

The sonofabitch had probably forgotten.

Or was too frightened to show his face.

It really didn't matter now; she had her work to do.

Being Friday, there'd be waitresses in to help her after six, local girls under orders not to wear tight skirts or blouses or sweaters, to wear honest-to-god Wranglers or somewhat baggy slacks and definitely not something out of a designer's wet dream; she wanted her customers to concentrate on their drinks or each other, not a single hip, breast, or rolling buttock that worked for her. She checked the big-screen TV to be sure it was tuned, checked the jukebox to be sure it wasn't going to balk again. There was no need to go in back; Gil Clay had been in earlier to count the weekend stock and take the deliveries, and she noted with satisfaction that he was, as usual, right up to snuff. He was a good man, if a bit on the thin side in meat and hair for her taste, and though in the early days of their relationship he had come on to her, she had made it clear that what she wouldn't tolerate from her girls she wouldn't tolerate from herself. Amazingly, he had understood, and they'd been friends ever since.

The stool behind the register was high and padded, made especially for her by Bud Yardley, who lived in the next house down from hers. She could sit and rest her feet, yet still see everything that went on in the tavern. As she settled down and waited for the first drinker, she noted that her feet barely reached the first rung. Short. Very short. But not too short, she comforted herself; she didn't even mind hiring girls taller than she.

A sudden grin sent many of her freckles sliding into her dimples.

Girls. God almighty, here she was only a handful of years over thirty—and lord, if they only knew how over thirty she was—and here she was calling women under twenty-five girls. Jesus, that had to be symptomatic of something or other.

At fifteen past four she heard the wind—soughing, then screaming, though none of it reached the Depot; at the same time she thought she smelled smoke, and could definitely feel a subtle, subterranean *rumbling* that set the tiered glasses in front of the bar's mirror to trembling.

Singing to each other softly.

Settling after several minutes into a crystal-bright, brittle silence.

She touched a hand to the register drawer and slid off the stool, walked unhurriedly to the pay phone by the side door, and dropped a dime into the slot. Dialed. Waited as she looked blindly at the walls, the floor.

The handset was picked up at the other end.

She said nothing but her name; then she only listened.

A moment later she rang off, hummed some more, and turned with a big smile as Piper Cleary walked through the door.

THREE

1

Dumpling was barely two years old, the youngest of the last litter Piper Cleary's old bitch coon hound had whelped before Piper had decided he'd had enough. She was also the most stubborn, and Piper had had a hell of a time teaching her that staying in the yard on Hollow Lane was a much better deal than a round of heavy-handed slaps on the nose or rump for straying out of sight.

But Dumpling was pregnant, and hungry, and Piper was inside listening to music, having forgotten to fill the bowls that lined the steps on the sagging back porch. The other three hounds lay in whatever shade they could find, patiently waiting for dinner while they panted through the heat and weakly tailed off the flies.

Dumpling couldn't wait. When she failed to gain his attention by scratching and whining at the back door, and when none of the other dogs would help her, she hunted anxiously around the yard for something to gnaw on, something to ease the ache in her belly and the pressure her own pups were causing below. There was nothing. All she could find, and all she knew she would find, was dry grass, brittle weeds, and drooping brown shrubs that separated the back of the yard from the trees. She barked once, and moved in a switchback trail away from the house. When she looked over her brown-and-white shoulder, she saw that the others weren't looking, and Piper hadn't come to the door to scream at her hoarsely.

The hunger grew, and she snapped at her side, chased her tail and yelped when she caught it.

A dash into the trees, then, to begin the fervent search for a morsel—an egg dropped from a nest, a wounded bird on the ground, a hare's burrow, an acorn.

Then she raised her head, her dark eyes steady, her nose twitching, the skinny white tail lifted. A scent; there was a scent, and it was raccoon, nearby.

All her training, all the long hours in the woods at the end of Piper's leash, battled with her to turn around, to run back, to sound the alarm. But she was hungry, and there was something inside her demanding to be fed. She whimpered, lowered her nose and followed the erratic spoor until she came to the stone wall. After circling frantically, she lifted herself awkwardly onto her hind legs, resting her forepaws on the top to look over. She sniffed the air, found the scent, and saw all that fresh and moist green grass just waiting for her.

Dropping to the ground she circled again, yelping, wagging her tail, once flopping onto her side to lick at her swollen belly. Then she roused herself with a single sharp bark and took the wall at a single leap.

The grass was cool, the raccoon scent overpowering, and she raced with her tail whipping like an antenna in the wind.

She had run just thirty feet when she saw the dark brown rock half buried in the ground. A puzzled snort as she approached it cautiously; it looked like no 'coon she had ever seen, yet there was no question that here is where the scent originated. Another bark, this one high and querulous, and she considered the possibility that her prey was underneath.

She approached it, jumped back yelping to warn it she was there and knew its hiding game, approached it again, and made a tentative start at digging.

The rock moved.

Her ears pricked high, her soft brown eyes went wide; she was so startled that she backpedaled and ended up on her haunches. With her head cocked to one side she studied the rock, her tail slapping softly at the grass.

A *rippling*

A series of barks then to prove she hadn't been fooled at all, that she knew where the quarry was, and she lunged forward with both forepaws digging furiously.

rippling

Salivating now at the prospect of at last feeding herself and her unborn young, Dumpling ignored the way the rock elongated and grew taller, ignored the way her claws seemed to dig through the earth without touching it. She was too busy now, sending hasty gouts of dirt and grass between her legs, snarling, growling happily, determined to finish before Piper found her and she was punished.

The hole widened; the scent grew stronger.

She eased back and circled, sniffed the ground as her tail pointed skyward. Then she attacked the rock again, knowing there was food, determined to find it and feed herself and her pups.

Barking angrily when she discovered that her left leg was caught somewhere down in the hole.

Barking fearfully when she tried to dig it out and had her right leg snared as well.

rippled

Whimpering at the pain that climbed into her chest. Howling her distress when she felt her bowels go. Tugging, snarling, realizing she wasn't going to escape, finally gnawing and biting frenziedly at her own flesh, tasting her own blood, digging in her back claws as she was dragged slowly forward.

Her head slipped into the hole and the barking was muffled, was stopped; her chest followed, and her tail slapped feebly at the grass; the swollen veined pouch for her pups split darkly, redly, yet her hind legs kept clawing, kept scrabbling, until there was nothing left on the lawn but a large brown rock, and a spattering of blood that shimmered in the heat.

51

2

Dinner was over by seven, the kitchen cleaned, and Maggie fed and watered and brought to her stall. Doug stood restlessly in the living room, trying to decide how to relax before beginning the new design. It hadn't been easy returning to work, but over the past three years he had been picking up a house here, an addition there, and it was almost to the point where he could, with luck, stop living off his savings.

The telephone on the sofa's near end table rang. He blinked at the intrusion, and told himself immediately it was that wind which had made his nerves so sensitive.

"Doug," a woman's voice said before he had a chance to give a greeting, "I've got a problem."

Slumping onto the couch, legs stretched toward the hearth, he tried not to sound too effusive. "Ah, the elusive Miss Lockhart! So good to hear from you, my dear. I was given to understand from your week's silence that you had gone on a trip around the world."

"Knock it off, Doug, okay? This is serious. Casey's at it again."

He allowed himself a half smile and burrowed deeper into the corner. "I thought your brother was on the wagon."

"There isn't a wagon built in the universe he can't fall off of, and you know it. Please? Do you think you could cover for him tonight?"

A guilty look to his right, into the dark study. "Judy, I'd like to, really, but I've got a commission on the board that's due Tuesday. And then there's that new house for the guy over in Branchville. If I don't finish that one pretty soon, his wife is going to have him out on his ear."

"So? You've got the weekend, right?"

52

"Judy, I haven't even started Tuesday's project yet. In fact, I'm seriously beginning to wish I'd never taken it on in the first place. It's probably going to be a waste of time."

He could hear sounds behind her voice: tinny laughter, tinny country music from the jukebox overlaid with conversation turned babble by the number of the Depot's early customers.

He could sense her disappointment, yet he knew that if he put off working tonight he wouldn't get to it until Sunday. He wasn't in danger of starving by any means, but neither was his portfolio so fat or his reputation so secure that he could afford to antagonize new contacts or customers.

"Douglas?"

A little girl's voice, pleading and grinning. A shameless tactic she used whenever she felt him wavering, and a tactic he didn't mind because two years ago he had decided it was possible for him to fall in love again, and Judy was one of the women he felt strongly about. One of two. After so many years, suddenly there were two. Judy had been polite and aloof, accepting his clumsy advances with good humor, and no solid rejection; then, abruptly, two weeks ago, she began making sly jokes about harnesses and yokes and rings through men's noses.

He hadn't questioned her turnabout, but it had started him thinking twice about what he was doing.

Because the other woman was Liz Egan, and his emotional confusion only doubled when he found himself thinking about her, a state that was increasingly hard to ignore.

He cleared his throat. "It's important, this job, Judy."

"Please?"

Another glance over his shoulder—the empty house, the wind. Maggie slicing the air.

"Damn your ass, Douglas Muir, if you—"

"Of course," he said quickly, "it is only an addition.

53

One of those solar greenhouse things for some judge over in Newton."

"Right."

He crossed his legs at the ankles, stretched an arm along the couch's back and tapped a finger on the wood trim. "I mean, I guess I could let it go until tomorrow."

A pause. "Right."

He held out his arm and stared at the mouthpiece, then pulled it back and frowned. "Judy, is something wrong?"

"I told you," she said with a quiet, nervous laugh.

"Well, I guess I'm a little on edge, too."

"Oh, yeah," he said, remembering, and feeling a sympathetic twinge along his left leg. "That wind was enough to jar anyone's teeth. I thought for a minute there Maggie was going to light out for Canada."

"Wind? What wind? Doug, what are you talking about?"

"What . . . ?" He pointed to the window as if she could see him, dropped his hand and shook his head. "Never mind."

"Hey, are you all right?"

"Yeah, sure. I think the pressure must be getting to me. Presidents can't hold a candle to architects with customers who have angry wives."

She laughed, cut herself off and asked him once again if he wouldn't please, *please* fill in for Casey tonight before she went crazy and burned the place down.

"I guess," he said. "Sure."

"I know I'm asking a lot, but he's acting up, real weird lately, and I've only got two hands, y'know? My god, you'd think he'd know better, today of all days."

"Judy, I said I'd come, okay?"

"I tell you, Doug, that man oughta be shot, he makes me so mad. If he wasn't so big, I'd chop him to pieces."

Then he knew: another boyfriend had been lost in

making sure Doug was the one she actually wanted. Her trouble was, he thought, she didn't know what she really wanted, and didn't know how to stop looking.

And his own indecision wasn't helping matters any. "I mean, really, Doug. He knows this is payday, and he knows there are a zillion stupid tourists out looking for their dose of rural reality, and damnit I get so *mad* sometimes just thinking about what I've done for him, putting him through—"

"Judy, Judy, for god's sake!"

"—college, nursing him when he got sick, all that—"

"Judy!"

"What!"

"I'll be there in half an hour."

Silence.

"Doug?"

"Yeah."

"Casey said he saw a light in Winterrest the other night."

The telephone rang and immediately he replaced the handset. He thought it was Judy again, and had a quip ready to fire when he heard, faintly, hoarse breathing on the other end. Bubbling, as if the caller's lungs were filled with water.

Then: "Mr. Muir?"

A smooth voice, cultured to the point of having an accent almost British. Ageless, as was the man it belonged to.

"Good evening, Mr. Parrish," he said, leaning his head back until he was staring at the ceiling. "How are you?"

"I am fine, Mr. Muir. I trust I'm not interrupting anything, but I am calling to see if you have found the time to think over my client's proposal."

Doug shook his head. Two days ago, Parrish had called to make an offer for his house. A client whose name he would not and could not reveal had an

55

interest. And a great deal of money. He would pay cash, full price on signing, and more money than Doug hoped to see at one time in his life.

Eban Parrish was in real estate, and by all appearances he was doing very well.

"Mr. Parrish, to be truthful, I haven't thought about it a great deal at all."

"Ah. Well, I'm sorry to hear that."

"No, you don't understand. I haven't thought about it because I don't want to sell."

He heard the bubbling again and wondered if the curious old man were under treatment for something.

"I see."

"I'm flattered, of course, that someone likes this old place so much but . . . well, let's face it, Mr. Parrish, I've a lot more than money invested in it now."

"I understand perfectly."

"I just hope your client will understand."

"Oh, I am sure of that, Mr. Muir. Absolutely. And by the way, I think you should know I have been in close contact with a gentleman from Florida who is interested in purchasing the Winterrest estate."

Doug waited, saying nothing.

"He has, if I may say so, some extraordinary plans for establishing a condominium resort there."

"What?" He sat up abruptly. "You're kidding."

"I do not kid, Mr. Muir, in matters of business."

Before he could respond, the man had rung off, and he was left staring at the mouthpiece.

God, he thought, and hung up. He was about to leave when he remembered something that had caught his momentary interest in the study. Something about Parrish. He frowned, looked into the darkened room, and saw himself leafing though some old magazines. Pictures of homes, pictures of designs . . . a picture of a man who vaguely resembled Parrish.

He scoffed. It couldn't have been, and now his nerves were telling him lies, making him recall things that weren't so.

Christ. Lights in Winterrest, winds out of nowhere,

and Eban Parrish on the phone shilling for invisible men. M'boy, he thought, you need a drink. Fast.

The bronze-painted, canvas-top Jeep was a god-send, he thought, if not a miracle. It managed to get him up the road and around the skirt of the steep rocky hill to the unpaved flat a half-mile from the county highway without once losing control and skidding into the trees—something he had done too often after he'd first purchased the vehicle. The road was canted downward to the right, and he was constantly fighting to keep from sliding off the seat while, at the same time, maneuvering the Jeep straight ahead. In winter it was hell with the road sheeted in ice, and he seldom left the house; the rest of the year it was only a pain in the ass.

On the other hand, the road's deplorable condition prevented unexpected visitors, salesmen or otherwise. And few of the local people he knew wanted or dared to trust their axles to a genuine deathtrap.

Once on the flat, however, he relaxed and sped up, noting absently the half-dozen ramshackle dwellings he passed on the way. He knew by name all the families living there, but only one—Piper Cleary and his incessantly fighting brood—had any specific dealings with him, which was fine with him and evidently perfect for them. Most of the houses, no matter how large, seemed to have been cobbled together with spit, hasty prayers, and ten rolls of tarpaper; if there wasn't a rusting truck or car in the front yard, there were plenty of scratching chickens, angry geese, and the occasional grazing goat or two.

If the people saw him, they waved politely enough, but no one made a special trip to the front door when they heard him coming; not even Cleary, unless he was looking for work.

A hound bayed; a hawk coasted.

The temperature began to slide as the sun began to drop.

Fifteen minutes later he reached the unmarked T-intersection with the county road and was about to swing left and head for Deerford when he recalled Judy's whispered comment abount Casey seeing lights in Winterrest. It was probably nothing. Casey was not known for his sober observations. Still, now that he knew from Parrish what was in the estate's future, there might be something to it after all. He looked right, shifted gears, and pulled out onto the tarmac, drove for another mile between a high wall of evergreens before slowing, pulling onto the verge, and stopping.

There was nothing special about Winterrest except that it was there—in the middle of nowhere, an out-of-place mansion on a meadow unmarked by a single tree.

Driving toward Pennsylvania, the passing tourist saw only a three-foot greystone wall three hundred yards long which, by assumption, enclosed the estate. In its center was a simple wood-slat gate that opened onto a narrow graveled drive leading directly to the house one hundred yards back. There were no trees lining it, no shrubs or ornamental fountains. Only grass. Acres of it, seemingly miles of it, reaching out to the flanking hill.

The house was two stories high, of large greystone blocks, its windows placed one above the other, narrow and arched, evenly spaced on both sides of a tall wooden door. There was no porch, just three steps to the threshold. Above the highest windows were gables that broke up the steep pitch of the black slate roof. He could count eight chimney stacks, none of which he had ever seen smoking.

Casey said there was a light.

Parrish had said someone wanted to build condominiums there.

He left the Jeep and ambled over to the gate, leaned on it, and stared, but could see nothing through the distorted reflection of the lawn in the windows. There was no other building on the grounds, no garage or servants' cottage, and he could see no cars parked anywhere near the front. An angled glance to his right and he could see the heavy stand of oak that marked the division between this land and his own.

Back to the house, then, and he smiled. He loved the place, had spent hours walking around it in covetous wonderment. The stones had been blocked, set in place and trimmed, and as far as he could tell not a single speck of mortar had been used to hold it together. The construction was flawless, a superb job that left no seams, no cracks; a job that few, if any, could do anymore, and he would kill for the chance to build just such a house.

His envy for the unknown master craftsman was enough to make him want to turn in his pencils, burn the drafting board, and raise horses instead of blueprints.

He moved along the waist-high wall a few paces, put his hands on the top, and had another look around, thinking that the local high school kids must be making a fortune mowing all that grass.

Suddenly, he snapped his hands back and gaped at the stone.

The wall had moved.

He could have sworn it had moved.

It was cold on first contact, rough and gritty. Then, without warning, it had *rippled* as if it had turned to water, *shifted* as if ready to make room for his hand.

It had moved.

The stone had moved.

He stepped back, reached out, and poked a finger at one of the blocks. Cold again; hard. He looked around, expecting a prankster to be watching him and laughing. He pushed; it didn't give. He frowned and moved closer, lay his palms on the top and leaned on them, hard. The wall didn't move, didn't give, and he returned to the Jeep with a shake of his head, slid in behind the wheel, and looked at the house again.

Though the estate was carefully maintained, it was obviously deserted. Despite the odd feeling he'd just had at the wall, there was no sense of habitation, of menace, of decay. It just *was,* nothing more.

Casey, he thought, you must have been drunk.

But the wall had moved.

God *damn,* it had moved.

Quickly, he swung the Jeep into a U-turn without bothering to check for traffic and sped down the road, passed Hollow Lane and raced south toward the overhanging traffic light he could see in the distance.

"You're nuts," he muttered as he wiped a hand across his chest. "Nuts, like old Sitter."

3

Sitter McMahon had no first name as far as anyone knew. He lived in a small, neat, white clapboard home just north of the traffic light, at the T-intersection where the county highway swept past the narrow road into Deerford, and he spent every dry day except in winter sitting in a green lawn chair in front of the ten-foot-tall hedge that barricaded his home. His hair and lumberjack beard were dark red, his face continually flushed, his eyes squinting at the sun even when it was blocked by the wooded hill that dropped its steep slope to the shoulder directly opposite him. Each day without fail he wore a worn, red plaid shirt, brown corduroy trousers, and hiking boots whose laces were wrapped five or six times around the tops.

And he waved.

At every car, van, truck, that passed him he shot out his arm and hand in a stiff-elbow wave.

And he smiled.

At every driver, every passenger, no matter how startled.

Most of the tourists and those just passing through were too astounded to respond, or they ignored him as a nut; the locals, however, and a handful of others, waved back enthusiastically, especially the children, and odd as it may seem he made them all feel good.

On Friday then, in July, he sat in his customary place and waited, but he wasn't smiling, he wasn't still. He squirmed, and he kept looking north, up the road toward Winterrest, noticing but paying little attention to the Jeep heading his way. There was something odd about the day, and he wondered if anyone else felt it—the change in the weather, the change in the town.

Sitter wasn't surprised, though. He was nearing sixty come November, and it was something like fifty years ago when he last felt the change. He didn't know what it was then, and his folks dead and buried twenty years had never said a word. But it was there, and when he woke up last Monday morning he remembered it as if it had happened only the day before.

The only trouble was, he couldn't remember what the change meant. If it was a change. If it meant anything at all.

On the other hand, Mr. Parrish didn't pay him to think about things like that. He was paid to sit, and to watch, and to count the people leaving, count the people coming in; the waving was his own innovation—because he liked to make people happy.

He shifted again, and scratched hard at his beard. It would be a while before the next car came by—people from the Meadow View development just east of the light coming home from work. Some of them even waved before he did because their entrance was a good fifty yards away. Some didn't like him, though, and that hurt. He wasn't bad, not as bad as some and maybe even better than others. His house was clean, he washed and combed his hair and beard every morning, and he never bothered anyone at all. Never. Ever. In fact, as far as he could remember, he hadn't spoken more than a couple of sentences at a time to anyone since Pop and Mom died.

Except for Piper Cleary.

And except, of course, for Mr. Parrish.

And he didn't mind not talking, either. Mr. Parrish paid him well just to stay where he was, and since he couldn't do anything else, he wouldn't want to lose his job.

A job where all he had to do was count, and make people happy.

4

As soon as Doug made the turn onto Deerford Road he relaxed, slowed down, slumped back in his seat, and shook his head. His laugh was explosive and short, and he startled himself so much he nearly drove off the road. But leave it to old Sitter to make him feel better, chase away the willies, keep the clouds from his sun; and not for the first time he promised himself that someday he was going to stop and ask the man why he did it. But that, he knew, would undoubtedly spoil the effect. If the guy was drunk all the time, or stoned, or just plain off his rocker, waving to him would never be the same again.

Just like a lot of things weren't the same anymore—his fear of loving *(you killed him)*, his slow-moving work *(it was an accident)*, even the dreams that continued to haunt him while he was awake *(but you killed him you killed him)*.

"Yes," he whispered.

murderer

"No. Damnit, no!"

His grip on the steering wheel became a stranglehold, and he closed his eyes briefly, holding his breath until he was able to see in his mind's eye not the shattered window and the ugly hate on Ellen's face, but Sitter, in his lawn chair, waving and grinning and no strings attached.

Thanks again, pal, he thought with a glance to the rear view mirror. Thanks. I owe you.

Five minutes later he swung into the Depot Tavern's narrow, graveled parking lot and braked alongside the single-story building. It looked very much like three freight cars placed one behind the other—and it was. When the DL&W was selling off a portion of its rolling stock to all comers back in the late twenties, an enterprising young innkeeper from just outside town thought they would make an unusual and profitable attraction. Damning the expense and the jeers of his neighbors, he had them hauled all the way from Newark, settled their massive iron wheels on a specially made reinforced foundation, then knocked out the interior walls to make room for the bar, booths and tables, and a kitchen that served only slightly less greasy food than the grill it was cooked on.

The man went broke a year later, and Judith Lockhart bought it at a sheriff's auction. Now it was painted a garish, fire engine red, the windows were outlined in white, and the chimney pots were a dingy grey. It had been redone only that spring, with the help of half the town and the Mohawk Gang, a group of kids determined to raise hell and be saints, both at the same time. Despite the dust born of the heat wave that wouldn't quit, the paint still gleamed, reflecting street-light and starlight like the memory of an old ballroom.

Tonight, however, it looked too much like blood.

Doug paused as the door hissed shut behind him. Seattle was long gone, along with the moving wall, the wind, and Eban Parrish's call. Now there was noise. People noise, drinking noise, and he was glad for a change that Casey had gotten drunk.

The slightly curved bar was thirty feet long and cut from white pine logged from the nearby hills; the nine round tables between it and the twelve booths at the front were filling slowly, mostly with men and women in for a quick easy meal before heading off to a movie, the drive-in in Newton, or the shopping malls at Port Jervis. A few of them raised hands and voices in boisterous greeting when he walked in, and he smiled and nodded back, heading directly for the bar, where he pulled a starched apron down from a peg and slipped right into the ordering rhythm without turning a hair.

Judith was tending the register, and when she looked around and saw him, she allowed him a harried grin and a wink. She was his age, perhaps a year or two older, with curly black hair and a plump pale face touched with dark freckles. She moved quickly without seeming to, small hands darting, red lips moving. Her red shirt with sleeves rolled to the elbows, and black slacks covered by a red checkered apron, were neither too snug for her slight figure nor so loose that she fooled the males into thinking she was a boy.

She was attractive without being intimidating, and more than one man, after seeing her, was reminded with a bittersweet pang of a high school sweetheart he had never seen again after sharing that last, graduation night kiss.

When she had a moment, she hurried over to him, got up on her toes and kissed his cheek.

"You're a lifesaver."

He nodded and saluted. "Yep. Sergeant Muir of the Yukon, with his trusty Jeep, King. Where's Casey?"

She slapped angrily at the bartop with a towel, scooped up a tip and dropped it into a empty coffee can next to the rinsing sink. "I don't know. I don't care. I hope he falls in a goddamned well."

"Not very familial."

"If my father were alive today, he'd shit a brick if he saw what his son was doing."

"Your father, by all you've told me, hated his guts."

"He's over there in the corner, by the TV."

"Who? Your father?"

Exasperation made her scowl. "No, idiot. Casey. He came in about five minutes ago. And if you want to keep your scalp, don't you dare sell him a drink."

He laughed softly and squeezed her hand, then deftly filled several orders and passed quips with Piper Cleary about the state of his beloved coon hound, Dumpling.

The wind still bothered him, and his knuckles still stung.

"What about the light your brother saw?" he said to Judy as he nodded to one of the waitresses picking up her tray. "Was he drunk or what?"

"I don't know. Maybe somebody's moved in."

"I don't think so."

"Then he was drunk."

He leaned closer, barely moving his lips. "Parrish called me just before I came over. He said there was someone ready to buy the place, land and all, and turn it into some kind of leisure resort. You know, condominiums and like that."

Judy tilted her head, and looked at him sideways. "You're kidding, right?"

"That's exactly what I said to Parrish. He said, very indignantly, that he wasn't."

"Jesus. Well . . . Jesus!" She plucked at her hair and glared at the register. "Well, we can't let it happen, you know that, right? I mean, we just can't. God, you mean Casey was actually . . . we'll just have . . ." Someone called her name and she nodded. "We'll talk about it later."

"Sure," he said, wondering how he could bring up the afternoon wind and not sound like a fool. "Okay."

She put a hand on one hip and set her back to the bar. "Doug, what's bothering you?"

He gave her a painfully false smile. "It's nothing," he insisted. "I'm still . . . I guess I'm still back there at the old drawing board."

It was obvious she didn't believe him, and didn't know the right question to ask; the trouble was, he didn't know the right question either.

"Later," she said.

"Right."

People came, people left, and it was close to nine o'clock before lank and mustached Gil Clay, the night bartender, arrived with apologies for being late, and Doug was able to lean back and watch the crowd.

It never changed, and he didn't care.

There were towners in their cliques, a few travelers trying and failing to fit in, and in the high-backed, red leather booth by the door two men he knew instinctively were not here just to pass the time. They were dressed casually, but not in jeans; they were watching the steady flow of patrons without seeing a thing. A couple of times he thought one of them was watching him as well, but he had dismissed it as a lingering of his dark mood not yet quite banished.

Now he wasn't so sure.

The man was dark-skinned, dark-haired, his dark blue shirt opened halfway down his chest to free a thatch of black hair that climbed almost to his neck. He wasn't wearing dark glasses, but he gave that impression, and Doug looked away just as he reached across the table to touch his companion's arm.

"Friends of yours?" Judith asked, sweeping past him carrying a tray stacked with empty glasses.

Someone turned on the projection TV at the far end and a crowd gathered to watch the Mets play baseball.

he's dead you killed him

"No," he said when she swept past again. She stopped, and looked at him curiously.

"Are you all right?"

"Yeah, sure."

She looked over her shoulder. "They look like Mafia types."

"Hey, there's no such thing as the Mafia, don't you know that?"

"Boy, you have lived in the Hollow too long," she said, poking a thumb in his waist. "You ought to read a paper now and then, get in touch with the world." She looked again. "Maybe it's the guys buying Winterrest. Yeah, how about that? Jesus, I'd like to spike a drink or three of theirs."

He smiled, but didn't look at her. The second man had finally leaned forward, and looked around the booth's scalloped edge.

"Oh . . . Christ," he whispered, half under his breath.

Suddenly, someone shouted angrily, and his attention was diverted to the television corner, where he saw lumbering Bernie Hallman from the Mogas station squaring off against Judy's brother. Casey was not much taller than his sister but weighed well over two hundred pounds, most of it, it seemed, solidly planted in his chest and shoulders. His black hair was straggly, his puffed cheeks flaring red, and as he circled the garage owner, he spat disgustedly on the floor.

Judith screamed at him, even as the baseball crowd made way and started betting.

Doug looked to Gil, who only shrugged and filled an order. Hell, he thought, took off his apron, and started around the bar. He had no intention of getting into the fight, but he wanted to be close by in case someone needed help.

But the fight moved too fast for him to get near or follow clearly. Casey was swinging and Bernie was ducking, a few punches landed, and they grappled their way across the floor toward the entrance. The door opened. He saw a flash of metal and realized Casey had drawn a knife.

Everyone froze.

Judith, who was fuming behind the bar, shouted, "Goddamn you, Casey Lockhart, put that thing away!"

Then the two men in the end booth sidled out and slipped past the combatants through the open door, but not before Doug saw their faces clearly and sagged in relief. They weren't anyone he knew, no one from Seattle. Strangers only, given false places in his nightmare.

Then Bernie raced outside, Casey followed with a bellow, and Doug didn't move again until he heard a woman scream.

5

By six dinner was finished, all plates and glasses in the dishwasher, and Heather admitted that she had neglected to give her mother a telephone message.

"Honestly, girl," Liz said. "There are times when I wonder what's in that brain of yours."

"Mush," said Keith. "Girl mush."

Heather glared at him, changed expressions to contrition, and pointed to the wall phone by the hallway. "It was Mr. Parrish. He wants you to call him back."

"Ugh," Keith said, grimacing and shaking his hands. "That guy's a creep."

"Keith," Liz scolded absently, and looked at the clock.

"He said to call anytime."

"He wants to take you out, Mom," Keith told her as she crossed the room to the phone and dialed. "He wants to marry you and give you all his money."

"That isn't funny," Heather said quietly, and Keith shrugged as he left for the front room.

Parrish answered on the first ring.

Liz toed off her shoes and sighed silently as the amenities were cleared away, then straightened just as she was about to slip the belt from her waist.

"Say that again, Mr. Parrish?"

"Mrs. Egan, the reason I wish to speak to you is that I have a client, a rather good client, who wishes to purchase your home if you are willing to sell."

"Mr. Parrish, I . . . there's never been any intention of selling this house. Never."

Heather looked startled, almost panicked, and Liz shook her head sharply to calm her.

"I see."

"Uh, would you mind telling me who this person is?"

"I'm afraid that would be impossible, Mrs. Egan. At

68

least, for the moment. But I can assure you the offer is quite legitimate. And very generous."

"I can't argue with that at all, Mr. Parrish. It's three times what Ron and I paid for it, and frankly, three times what it's worth."

"Well, in my position I have learned there is no accounting for some people's interests."

She made a noise that might have been agreement, or a cough from the meal that was trying to make her belch.

"In any case, Mrs. Egan, thank you for returning my call. And do think about it, if you will. As a favor to me. And should you change your mind . . ."

"Thank you," she said, "but I don't think I will."

She rang off and stared at the grey-tiled hall that ran toward the screened front door until Heather reminded her that Clark Davermain would be here soon and was he really going to be their new father? She smiled and patted the girl's shoulder. "I really don't know, love. I do think he'll ask me to marry him, though."

Heather's eyes widened. "What are you gonna say?"

"I don't know that, either."

"He's fat."

Liz's expression turned diplomatically blank. "He is not."

"He pulls my pigtails."

"I'm sure you'll survive," she muttered as she opened the refrigerator. "Tomorrow's Saturday. What do you think about a salad for dinner? I don't think I'm going to feel much like cooking."

"It's all right with me, Mom, but Keith's gonna croak."

Ten minutes later the weekend sally began.

"Mom c'*mon!*"

"Keith," she said wearily from the top of the stairs, "I hate to keep reminding you of this, but you are only eleven years old. And it gets rather dark out here in the country, in case you've forgotten."

Keith dropped gloomily onto the bottom step, faced the front door, and slammed his elbow onto his knees, his cheeks heavily into his palms. "Aw, Mom, the Gang's gonna fall apart if I'm not there. I promised them."

"The Gang," she said, not without sympathy, "will just have to muddle through alone this one time, okay? If they can't come here, you can't go there. You are not to leave the neighborhood, and that's final."

"But Heather—"

"—is only going to Mary Grum's, two very short blocks away. She'll be back when it's dark, and you two can watch TV until your eyes fall out."

"But there's nothing on, they're all reruns!"

"Then read a book."

"Jeez, what a pain."

"If you want to leave the house alive, young man," she said sternly, her arms folded across her chest, "you will explain that remark."

He looked up quickly and pointed to his right knee. "A pain," he said, wincing proof of his agony. "I hit it with my elbow."

"Nice," she said. "Good work, you get to live."

She stood anxiously at the bathroom mirror, hunting for the lines beneath the makeup, hoping the sun wasn't drying her out. Her nerves forced a faint tic by her right eye, and she pressed the heel of one hand against it, to kill it.

"Mom, do I have to?"

Heather stood in the doorway, downcast, already defeated and making the most of her martyrdom.

"Dark is dark, my dear. You know the rules when I'm gone."

"But I'm thirteen years old! I'll be fourteen soon!"

"And I'm already past thirty and I'll be home by midnight. It isn't my fault I can't get a sitter on such short notice."

"A *sitter?* Mother, you've got to be kidding. I would

70

just *die* if Mary ever found out. God, Mother, please promise you won't tell her you were thinking about a sitter."

"If you don't want a sitter, you'll be home before dark, and you'll look out for your brother."

"Great. That's just great."

She turned and saw with a start the girl she used to be, and not for the first time felt a little ill at ease. Despite her slender, not quite sexless figure, Heather could have been her at every age since birth.

The girl smiled suddenly, all teeth and dimples, and ran into the room to hug her mother snugly. "I know, Mom. It's just that it's summer, y'know?"

"I do know," she said gently. "Believe it or not, the mother really does know."

Then she kissed her daughter's forehead and shooed her out while she finished dressing—short-sleeve print blouse, cotton slacks, and sandals on her bare feet. And as she examined and criticized her mimicking reflection, she tried to reach some conclusions about her relationship with Clark.

He was certainly handsome enough, and through all his occupational bombast he occasionally let slip more than a thin slice of wit. He had money, position, and was thinking of making a run for the State Senate next year, a run he would very likely complete successfully. But what else was there? He was generous, and tried very hard to make friends with the kids; yet there was a reserve in his manner, a puzzling distance she'd not been able to bridge. She had never discovered what really made him tick. When it came right down to it, she really didn't know Clark Davermain well at all.

He certainly, most definitely, wasn't Douglas Muir.

"Lizzy," she told her reflection as a brush passed fast and hard through her hair, "it's about time you either fish or cut bait." She leaned closer to the mirror. "If you don't love the man, don't do it. The kids are doing fine, and Doug won't be a monk forever."

She jumped then when someone slammed the front

door on the way out and grimaced at the mess she'd made of her lipstick. A tissue for correction, and she stood back and sighed.

For slightly more than a year after Ron's death she had locked herself away in this split-level, thin-walled mausoleum and watched her world fall apart by splinters and chips until she could no longer stand the sight of herself in the morning. Then Keith wet his bed once too often, and when she had raised an hysterical hand to administer a spanking she saw Heather in the doorway, thumb in her mouth. Seven years old, in second grade, with her thumb in her mouth.

Ron was dead. He wasn't coming back. She was trained to be a lawyer, and there was no looking back.

But it wasn't until a year later that she had whipped up her courage and had gone out on her first date. She felt like a fool. All she had talked about was her late husband, and all he talked about was his job. It was another six months, on her birthday, before she went out again. She had a quiet party with the kids, got a sitter, and went down to the Depot for a drink with Judith Lockhart and her brother.

It was the first time she met Doug, and the first time she realized that while she wasn't actively hunting for a man, she wouldn't have minded a bit if he had taken her back to the Hollow, stripped off her clothes, and ravaged her in the yard. The feeling had been so strong, she'd excused herself and ran all the way home and found herself in a cold shower, laughing hysterically, and crying.

Since then she hadn't exactly been a nun; on the other hand, she had never had more than a handful of dinners at the Shade Tree with him, and not once had he ever asked her to join him for a nightcap. The only consolation was the fact—carefully gleaned by roundabout interrogation—that Judith was similarly left out in the cold.

Heather rapped a knuckle on the door frame, and stood there, her hands primly at her waist. "Mother,

Mr. Davermain is waiting for you downstairs. Shall I tell him you'll be down in a moment?"

Liz inhaled loudly.

"Is that a yes or a no?"

"Good lord, girl, what have you been watching?" she asked as she pushed past her daughter and hurried into the bedroom. Heather followed, giggling while she told her it was from something she had seen on PBS. Liz turned as she reached for her jewelry box on the dresser. "PBS? *You* watch PBS behind my back?"

"It's very educational, Mother," the girl said righteously, then giggled and jerked her thumb over her shoulder. "He's still fat, Mom. You can see his stomach through his shirt."

"Heather Egan, aren't you supposed to be watching your brother?"

"Not until dark. He's out on his bike with those stupid Mohawks somewhere. I'm supposed to be at Mary's."

"Child, go away before I sentence you to a dust mop."

She was gone with a laugh, and Liz felt a slight burning in her eyes, her love for them both sometimes uncontrollably overwhelming.

"And he is not fat!" she yelled, looked into the hallway, and realized Heather was gone. *Christ,* she thought, *I hope Clark didn't hear me.*

Heather was right, she noted with a sinking feeling; Clark's stomach did poke through his shirt. It must be his suits, artfully tailored to cover the defects and accentuate what he obviously believed were his strong points: the mass of brown hair so carefully brushed back from a widow's peak to give him a vaguely satanic look, the large brown eyes, the patrician nose, the square-block jaw that seemed always outthrust. He was deeply tanned, and his white shirt and slacks ably and deliberately served to heighten the effect.

The trouble was, his stomach forced the lower buttons of his shirt to separate, and made visible a swatch of skin that had her wondering how many sunlamps he owned.

As they turned right into Deerford, he grinned and jerked his head toward Sitter McMahon. "What is he, local color?"

"He likes the fresh air, I guess," she said, almost defensively. She would have turned to wave, but she was afraid to move. White inside and out, the Mercedes made her feel as if she were covered with mud, that a single move might splatter the dashboard, or Clark's shirt.

"So this is Deerford. I've heard of it, you know."

"I'm surprised you've never been here, living all this time in the county."

"No need," he said. "I'm too busy elsewhere."

"Oh." And when he reached for and found her hand, she tensed and held her breath; then she told herself to relax. He had not given her any indication he was going to pop it; if the night was miserable it was only because she'd done it to herself.

"Hey, that restaurant, the Pear Tree?"

"Shade Tree."

"Yes, right. Some of the guys have taken their wives there on weekends. Sounds like a nice place."

"It is, very."

He looked at her, his left hand draped lazily at the wrist over the steering wheel. "Liz, forgive me, but you don't sound right. Is something wrong?"

The concern in his voice made her give him her best smile and make some excuse about worrying about the children.

"Don't worry, it's okay. I promise to have you back before you turn into a pumpkin." He smiled. "And I'm really glad to see you, Liz. It's been two weeks. I've missed you."

She didn't trust herself to speak.

"You know," he said admiringly as they reached the first homes and he saw the care with which the buildings were kept, "it sure does look nice."

"It's perfect."

"Well, I don't know about that. A little too isolated for my taste, I think."

She would have said something then, but had to direct him into the Depot's parking lot, to an open place near the front door. He turned off the engine and stretched his right arm along the back of the seat, his fingers kneading the back of her neck.

"Liz, look," he said solemnly, "there's something I have to tell you before we go in there tonight."

Oh great, she thought, here it comes.

"I'm here under semi-false circumstances."

She looked at him sideways, puzzled but still wary. "Oh?"

"Yes. You know . . . well, you know how I feel about you, I think." He paused. "Right?"

She had no choice; she nodded, and gave him a tiny smile.

"And you know that I have never once since we've been seeing each other mixed business with pleasure. I didn't want to give you the wrong impression."

She covered his hand with hers and said, "You haven't, Clark, believe me. I—"

He shook his head and grabbed the steering wheel with both hands. "This is dumb."

"What?"

"I said, this is dumb."

"Well, it is if you don't tell me."

"Yes, true." He considered a moment, then cleared his throat. "I had a call today, a man who said he worked for a client who wanted my services. Something to do with an estate somewhere out here."

"Oh, sure, Winterrest," she said immediately. "It's the only place like that within twenty miles. And the man was Eban Parrish?"

"Right! How did you know?"

"What did you tell him?" she asked.

"I told him he had a perfectly good lawyer right out here."

She watched him carefully, touched by the mild

distress on his face. "Thank you," she said finally, quietly.

"Yeah, but he didn't want a woman lawyer. He said he didn't trust them."

Her eyes narrowed, and her hands balled into fists. "Why that two-bit country sonofabitch."

"My sentiments exactly," he said. "I wanted to tell you, in case this guy walked in and said something."

"I appreciate that," she said gratefully, though her anger still simmered.

"My pleasure." He grinned and leaned toward her awkwardly, and she accepted the kiss with half-closed eyes, thinking that perhaps he wouldn't propose at all, that tonight they would have fun and maybe screw around a little.

When they separated, he kept a hand lightly on her shoulder, searching her face, examining her, breathing as though inhaling her very essence. Then, with a rueful sigh, he shook his head.

"Liz, there's more."

"What more?" she said, touching his cheek.

"The man, this Parrish guy, he wanted to know if I would be interested in assisting him in selling this estate."

She froze, blinked once, and frowned. "You're mistaken."

"Nope. That's exactly what he said."

A burning started in her cheeks. "The bastard," she said flatly. "The little bastard."

Clark held a tenuous smile. "Is that bad, selling this Winterrest?"

"Clark, I could take or leave that ugly heap of stone, believe me, but it's practically an historical landmark, not only for the area but for the county, maybe even the state. Jesus, Parrish better head for the hills when this gets out."

"He didn't seem to care."

"He didn't huh? And he doesn't want a woman lawyer, huh? Well, that overaged land shark is in for a surprise or two. C'mon, Clark," she said, opening her

76

door. "Let's have a drink. I believe that's a custom before you start a war."

As she straightened and waited for him to hurry around to help her, two men rushed from the tavern and walked quickly toward the far side of the lot. She paid them little attention, only took Clark's arm and started for the entrance.

A woman's voice shouted then, and they stopped.

"Oops," Clark said. "A little excitement, I fear."

They were at the steps when the door slammed open and two men barreled out, one of them backwards, the other lunging forward with a knife in his hand. Clark grabbed Liz's waist and started to pull her away, but the man with the knife was too intent on his charge.

He lunged with a grunted curse, but he missed the top step and stumble sideways, off balance.

In a moment slowed by shock, Liz could do little but watch as the blade swung out, flaring gold in the light from the Depot window. She saw the lines of it clearly, and threw up a desperate hand, heard Clark cry a warning, heard her own breath pass her lips in a scream more a hissing.

She and the man collided, and she fell, vision blurred, her side burning where her hand gripped it against the pain.

And the last thing she saw was the deep red of fresh blood flowing over her fingers.

6

"It must have been the dope," said Bud, sitting on the edge of the bed to pull on his socks and slacks. He pointed at the ashtray on the nightstand and nodded once. "It must have been laced with something, y'know? I've heard about people doing things like that. They get their kicks out of watching people go bananas."

77

Olivia lay behind him, lightly scratching his back, a drowsy smile on her lips while she stared at his shoulders.

"It's really sick, y'know, doing stuff like that. I mean, it's really damned sick." He grunted when she slipped a finger below his waistband, into the split of his buttocks, and he slapped her hand away, lightly. "Sick. We must've had a flash, or flashback, whatever it's called."

"That's with LSD," she said dreamily.

"Yeah, well . . ." He stood, sucked in his stomach and hitched up his pants. Then he looked down at her. The sheet was drawn to her neck, but her unbraided hair lay in a fog over her chest. "I love you," he said.

"Good. Then tell me what happened."

He sat again and held her hand. It was cold, just as cold as his in spite of the day's heat and the heat of their lovemaking. "I don't know. But it must've been the grass, Ollie. It had to be. Maybe we're doing too much, do you think? Maybe we oughta cut down a little."

Her cheek floated to his arm. "No, that's not it. It sounds good, but that's not it."

The telephone rang.

"Don't answer it," she pleaded when he reached for the receiver. "Let's pretend we're in Monte Carlo, we've broken the bank, and now we're gonna ball the rest of the night. C'mon, Bud, leave it. Leave it, okay?"

"Jesus, Ollie," he said, wondering what the hell had gotten into her. First her lousy mood, then her lousy lovemaking, and now this. He shrugged off her hand, picked up the phone and listened, slammed it down thirty seconds later and lunged for the shirt he'd thrown on the floor. "That was Gil Clay."

She punched the mattress. "Damn! There are times, Charles—and this is definitely one of them—when I wish to hell you'd never joined that little club of yours."

"It isn't a little club!" he shouted as he raced from the room and flung himself down the stairwell.

And it wasn't. It was the local Emergency Squad, and he felt he owed it to the community to do something besides providing a tourist or two for the restaurant and bar. Anyway, it made him feel good that he was helping people—he had willingly taken all the courses, from lifesaving to first aid, studied every book on practical medicine he could find, and spent hours at the hospital emergency room watching doctors and paramedics treat patients for shock, for bleeding, for cardiac arrest.

And the first and only time he delivered a baby while the ambulance ran for the hospital, he had cried in awe most of the night.

At the bottom step he paused to tuck in his shirt, and looked at the Retirement Room, completely bewildered. Obviously, it had been a hallucination, and just as obviously it had been triggered by what they had been smoking, no matter what Ollie said. It just had to be. There was no smoke, no damage, and by the time he had stumbled back into the room to see for himself, his clothes were clean, there was no soot on his hands or face, and his lungs didn't feel as if he'd been dragged down a clogged chimney.

Astonishing, he thought as he ran for the front door, what the human mind can do when it's doped up, or horny.

He took the steps to the walk at a leap, veered left, and sprinted over the intervening lawns toward the Depot. There were already people spilling out of the doorway, a few more gathered around someone lying on the ground. As he vaulted the low hedge that bordered the blacktop, the red-and-white ambulance van screamed from its place behind the tavern and stopped just beside him as he pushed through the crowd and looked down.

"Oh god," he whispered, and dropped to his knees.

It was Liz Egan, and blood was rapidly staining her

filmy blouse. He could hear a scuffling somewhere ahead of him, between two cars, some shouting, some curses, but he tuned it all out as Clay dropped the black bag beside him and rustled up two men to help him fetch the stretcher.

The blood froze him for a moment, bile rose burning into his throat, but a hard swallow and an oath rid his system of the shock. He worked as gently as he could, cutting away the shards of fabric clinging to the wound, staunching the bleeding with packs of gauze and white tape. Liz was still unconscious, and her skin was clammy and sweating. Pleased that his hands moved without conscious direction, he was smoothing out the last bit of tape when a hand reached suddenly down over his shoulder, brushed over the wound, lingered, and vanished. Perplexed and annoyed, he glanced up and saw Eban Parrish shouldering his way back through the crowd.

Jeez, he thought; I didn't know he cared.

Gil, still in his bartender's apron, came up with the wheeled stretcher and, the four of them working perfectly and without a sound, soon had Liz up and in the back. Clay instantly raced around to the driver's seat; Bud had one foot up and in when an overweight man tapped his shoulder.

"Please," he said, and pointed to the unconscious woman. "Please. I was with her."

Bud shrugged. It didn't make any difference to him if the guy wanted to tag along, as long as he kept out of the way and didn't ask stupid questions. When he nodded, the man him gave a tremulous smile and climbed in. Bud slammed the doors shut and the van backed out of the lot, hitting the road with lights flashing and the siren wailing high and low.

"How is she?" the man asked.

Bud said nothing. This was the first time he had seen anything this bad, and he wished to hell the town's doctor wasn't on his damned vacation. But he knew what to do. First the blanket, then the temperature, then the safeguard IV to be sure she had fluids.

From behind the wheel, Gil looked around and caught his gaze.

"A bitch, ain't it."

Bud nodded, and did not sit back until he was sure he had covered everything he could. The rest was up to Gil's driving and the depth of the wound.

"How'd it happen?" he asked.

"Some asshole stabbed her," the overweight man said. "He came out of that . . . that *bar* after some other guy, and he just stabbed her."

"Casey," Gil explained when Bud looked to him, puzzled.

"You're kidding."

"He's been nuts all week. He's been under the wagon this time, telling everyone he's seen lights in Winterrest."

"No shit."

"He was drunk, like I said."

The van swerved onto the highway and headed south toward the hospital, ten miles distant. There was no sound in the back but Liz's labored breathing, and the overweight man cracking his knuckles.

"Funny," Bud said at last, trying to keep his eyes away from the blood-stained arm that had slipped from under the sheet. He reached out, tucked it back in, and wiped his hands on his knees.

"What is?" the man asked, then introduced himself and asked the question again.

"Nothing. Nothing really. It's just been a funny week."

"I know," Davermain said eagerly. "As a matter of fact, there was this weird little guy, called himself Parrish, he—"

"Parrish?" Bud said. "You know Eban Parrish?"

"In a way," said Clark, almost shrugging.

Liz groaned, her head beginning to drift from side to side.

"He is funny, a little," Bud ventured in a whisper.

"I could tell that."

"Came up to me and my lady on Monday, said he

had a client who wanted to buy out my store." He shook his head at the wonder of it all. "Weird, y'know? Wouldn't say anything but made me an offer that almost blew my mind. Christ, I couldn't make that much bread in fifteen years."

Clark asked if he were taking the offer.

"Are you kidding? Leave Deerford? No way, Mr. Davermain. No way in hell. This is where I want to spend the rest of my life."

FOUR

1

Keith had changed from his coveralls to his jeans, had taken his ten-speed from the garage, and was gone before Davermain drove up in his Mercedes. He didn't want to see this guy, didn't want to stick around so that his dumb sister could boss him when Mom was gone. There were important things to do, things Heather would never understand as long as she lived. All she cared about was talking about boys and standing in front of the mirror and combing her stupid hair. She was okay, he supposed, but boy was she dumb.

He rode to the end of the block, bounced up over the curb and onto a narrow bike trail that led across the pasture stretching behind Meadow View. In the distance, almost at the near horizon, he could see the darkening farmhouse, barn, and silo that belonged to the man who had sold Meadow View's land. A barbed wire fence marked the boundary, and when he reached it he swerved right toward a narrow stand of trees.

The Gang was already there, waving as he skidded up and leapt from the saddle, letting the bike tip slowly over.

"Mohawks," he said as he dropped cross-legged to the ground.

"Mohawks," said Dirk Snow, the skinniest kid in the world with the most hair Keith had ever seen.

"Mohawks," muttered Artie Mancuso, plucking at grass and dropping it on his fat belly. This was a guy Keith knew he had to watch.

"Yeah, Mohawks," said Ian Backster eagerly. At nine, he was the youngest member of the Gang, the only one with glasses, and the only one who sunburned like a lobster instead of tanning like a human being.

"Gotta plan," Dirk said, stretching out on the ground, his chin on the backs of his hands.

"Who cares," Artie grumbled, and plucked more grass.

"Oh shut up," Keith said. "What's the plan?"

"Well, there's two, really, and man, are they both excellent. The first, see, is that we leave the bikes here and go on back, get into Sitter's house and—"

"No," Artie said, thick lips pursed in derision. "That's dumb. I mean, that's really dumb. Really dumb. I mean, who the hell cares about that crazy old fart, right?"

Dirk shrugged the bones that passed for his shoulders. "Okay, then why don't we go to Winterrest and break a few windows?"

"All *right*," Artie exclaimed. "Now you're talkin."

"No!" Ian said. "No, we can't do that."

"Why not?"

" 'Cause it isn't right, that's why. Tell him, Keith. Tell him it isn't right."

Keith rubbed the back of his head patiently while Artie laughed and Dirk whistled shrilly. When they were quiet again, he looked to Ian and wondered how many times he was going to have to explain this before the runt understood—that the Mohawk Gang had been formed to do a lot of good things around town so people would smile at them when they rode by, pat their heads, and say good things to their mothers. Like the time they wasted a whole Saturday helping to paint the Depot, or the time they mowed the church lawn for nothing, or the time they went around taking branches off the streets after a windstorm last fall. Good stuff, that made people like them.

Then, when they really wanted to have fun, no one would believe that the Mohawk Gang had done it.

He had seen it on TV; it worked there, and it was working here. No one, but no one believed they had painted the Shade Tree windows red last Halloween, or let the air out of the ambulance tires in back of the Depot, or threw enough cherry bombs on top of creepy Parrish's office roof last month to start a small fire that had the whole town running around like it was at war or something.

No one believed it because they were the Mohawks.

Ian was a new member, and when Keith had finished he shook his head sadly. "I don't know, Keith. It isn't right. My father would kill me."

"He won't find out, stupid," Artie sneered.

"I'm not stupid."

"The only way your old man will find out is if you tell him, stupid."

"I'm not stupid!"

Artie pushed his bulk up until he was kneeling; Ian was standing with his fists at his sides.

"Take it back," the boy said, the sun reflecting red in the lenses of his glasses. "Take it back."

Artie sniffed and grinned. "Make me."

"Oh, knock it off, huh?" Dirk said in disgust. "You guys are sick, you know that? Really stupid."

"I . . . am . . . not . . . stupid."

"Aw shit."

"Shut up!" Keith shouted. "Damnit, you guys, shut up!" They stared at him, shrugged, sat again and waited. It was the heat, he knew. The heat did really weird things to people, made them fight all the time, and this time the heat had lasted nearly all week, making you feel like you lived in an oven. Maybe he should've stayed home like Mom told him to. "It's a great idea, Dirk," he said with quiet enthusiasm. "Really great. But I can't do it."

"See?" Ian said.

"Why not?" Artie challenged. "Why not, huh?" Then he pointed. "I get it! Your momma's not home, right? You gotta be in by dark. You gotta be babysat by your fairy sister!"

Ian couldn't understand why that was such a big deal, but when Keith, looking sour and angry, didn't deny it, Artie and Dirk started hooting, rolling on the ground, pulling at the grass, and laughing until their faces turned red.

Keith took it as long as he could, staring at the ground and at the fists on his knees. Then he jumped up with a shout, a shout so loud the others fell immediately silent and saw him standing angrily over them.

Dirk instantly looked shame-faced, but Artie only said, "Uh oh, the chief's ticked, men," and stood up, his attitude a dare that Keith desparately wanted to take. He didn't. He only met the fat boy's gaze as long as he could before he was chilled by disgust, shook his head, and walked slowly to his bike. This wasn't fun; the heat was making them all crazy.

"Hey, where ya goin?" Ian called.

"He's goin home to momma," Artie explained loudly, shaking off Dirk's restraining hand. "He's goin home 'cause he's a little pissant, 'cause he's chicken."

Keith froze, his hands already out to grab the handlebars.

"Cluck," Dirk said softly.

This, Ian understood. "Cluck," he said gleefully.

Keith turned around. "I am not chicken."

"Pissant," Artie said. "Pissant chickenshit."

"I said I wasn't," he insisted, and was ashamed to feel a stinging behind his eyes.

"Okay, then," Artie said, "I call for a torture."

Ian's eyes widened; he remembered the torture he had to go through to become part of the Gang, and he knew that calling for one now meant that Artie wanted to be chief instead of Keith. He hoped they wouldn't make him try to take something from the Mogas station like he had to—god, Mr. Hallman was a giant, hated kids, and had almost caught him. God, he hoped they wouldn't make him do that.

Dirk stood beside Artie. "You heard. A torture, Keith. You gonna do it?"

It wasn't fair. He had started the Gang; it was his idea and they were having a great time. Now that fat slimeball was trying to take it all away. "Sure," he said as calmly as he could. "Sure, why not?"

"What's it gonna be?" Ian asked, and Artie said without a moment's hesitation, "Winterrest."

Keith didn't blink.

Artie studiously examined the field, the horizon, then turned his head slowly and grinned mirthlessly at Keith. "You gotta go to Winterrest and bring back something that proves you were there. And you gotta go alone. And you gotta go now."

Dirk clapped his hands, Ian followed though doubtfully, and Keith knew he was trapped. When he didn't respond right away, Dirk said, "Cluck," and Ian yelped, "Cluck-cluck," and he glared at Artie, sending him a clear warning that as soon as this was over he was going to pay, and pay good.

Artie only smiled. "Cluck," he said. "We'll be waiting."

Keith squared his shoulders and mounted his ten-speed. He rode off with the guys cheering behind him, but he didn't look back. Winterrest was off limits, and Winterrest was spooky, and if he ever got out of this alive he was going to kick somebody's ass all the way to the ocean.

He didn't stop until he had reached Meadow View's pillars on the highway.

There was no traffic.

The sun was nearing the horizon.

His foot tapped nervously against the pedal, and he held onto the pillar to keep his balance on the bike. On his left shoulder a miniature version of himself paced up and down, demanding that he either get on with it, or go back and admit that he was really pissant chickenshit, just like Artie said. In any case, he had better not be caught here on his own or his mother would kill him.

"It's scary," he whispered as a painted van shot past.

87

Little keith strutted up and down his shoulder, snapping his fingers impatiently.

"Scary."

'course it is, stupid, that's half the fun

A glance over his shoulder. That dumb German shepherd in the ranch house was barking at a crow picking at garbage on the curb, and someone hit a softball a good half a mile from the sound of the crack and the shouts of the players.

"It's empty," he said, stroking the shoulder.

that's right

"Nobody can chase me off."

right

He could be there in ten minutes, take a look around, come back before they knew it. He would bring the guys what they wanted and they'd never challenge him again.

right again

He smiled, looked around and saw nobody watching.

cluck, cluck, keith, you're gonna lay an egg

"Shut up," he muttered, pushed off the pillar, and rode north, his legs pumping as fast as they could, his body leaning over the handlebars as his eyes squinted in the wind. The little keith on his shoulder vanished the moment he began to move, but he didn't need his buddy now because now he was flying—past the traffic light with a guilty look to his right down Deerford Road to be sure there was no one there who could recognize him and tell his mother, seeing Piper Cleary on the side of the road and praying the old hound dog man hadn't seen who it was; past Sitter McMahon who snapped out his arm and smiled, while Keith flashed him a grin and hoped he was as crazy as all the kids said he was. If he was, Keith was safe, because his mother would never believe a crazy man who said he'd seen her son, just flying and flying down the road to Winterrest.

Past Hollow Lane, where Mr. Muir lived, a very weird man who hardly ever showed himself in town, and according to Heather built houses made of glass for rich people and crooks who paid him in diamonds.

One of these days he'd go down to the Hollow and see what his place was like. Mr. Muir had a horse that Heather went to see every time she got the chance, but the only other thing that he really knew about him beside the fact that he was an okay guy was that whenever he was walking with his mother in town, and Mr. Muir came by, his mother would grab his hand and nearly squeeze the bones out.

His mother, he thought as he checked the road and crossed it in a blur, was going to marry again. He knew that and wasn't sure what he thought about it. But his mother better ask him first, or there was gonna be trouble.

The trees ended then and the stone wall began, and he slowed down and stared at the low grass on the other side, and at the house that was set down, plunk in the middle, its windows red from the red setting sun, the greystone almost purple. There were no trees except around the wall's outer edges. There were no cars, no lights, nothing at all but the house.

He stopped at the gate, leaned the bike against the wall, and gnawed at his lower lip.

cluck, cluck

He glared at his shoulder; little keith was smirking.

cluck, cluck; cluck, cluck

He put his hands on the wall, took a deep breath, and grunted as he clambered over.

2

Sitter watched the boy pedal furiously past him, and fifteen minutes later saw the boy's mother ride into town in a big white car driven by a stranger. He tugged at his beard, pulled at the hair that barely reached his ear. That's three not good things that happened in the past two hours, and he didn't know what to do about any of them.

First there was Piper Cleary walking by on the other side of the road, heading for the Depot, and he didn't even call a hello, and that meant trouble though he couldn't figure out why.

Then the little boy whose mother was a lawyer who had helped him keep his chair when some of the development people wanted him to go away. The little boy was going to Winterrest. He didn't know how he knew that; he just did. And that was bad. Later, maybe, it would be all right. But now it was bad.

Then the mother herself, riding toward town with a stranger in a white car.

A stranger, Piper, the little boy. Sitter was confused. He guessed he should tell Mr. Parrish what was going on, but Mr. Parrish had told him that he was never ever if he wanted to keep his job to call him or go to him or do anything to get in touch until Mr. Parrish himself came around. Once a week. After nightfall.

But nightfall was still a good hour away, and there was no telling if Mr. Parrish would be here at all.

A stranger. The little boy.

Sitter was so upset he stood, folded his chair, and went through the gap in the hedge and into his house.

He didn't come out until he heard the siren wailing.

3

Piper Cleary was a man much too small for the skin he carried; it hung from his arms, from his neck, seemed to slip down his face in imitation of a bloodhound. His large teeth were nicotine yellow, and he always seemed five days away from his last decent shave. His hair was a thick and unruly brown unsure when it was supposed to turn white, and forever squashed beneath a tweed deerstalker cap. A sheathed hunting knife was clipped to his belt, and his hiking boots were open at the top and folded down. At last count there were thirteen patches on his jeans.

He saw the boy speed by on the bike going north on the county road, but he didn't care. It wasn't his kid, it was Sitter's job to keep track of people moving about, and besides he had more important things to worry about. Like the demons. Like going back to the Depot and sitting there in the corner with his drink not really a drink but actually ginger ale and thinking about how he was going to take care of all those damned demons getting ready to take over the whole world from the cellar at Winterrest.

He knew they were there.

He knew they were after him.

And he knew that unless he did something about it, they were going to break out pretty soon.

He kicked angrily at a stone and switched from demons to Dumpling, hoping the poor little bitch hadn't gone wandering too far. She was due any minute now and he would be damned if he was going to lose a litter just because she got it into her stupid little head to take a damned walk.

Besides, the demons might get her.

As he came abreast of the Shade Tree, he considered visiting his daughter-in-law and his son. Maybe they had some ideas where he could look for the dog. He snorted, and crossed the street. Nell-the-Bitch for sure would have an idea—get rid of all the hounds so the house wouldn't smell like dogshit all the time—that's what she'd say. Or—get rid of all those horrid scratchy records so we can have some peace, for god's sake.

But what the hell did she know about Carmel Quinn anyway? Could she remember Arthur Godfrey? Could she remember Frank Parker and that gorgeous little Hawaiian girl singing their hearts out for the whole goddamned country? Hell no. She couldn't remember how the glorious Miss Quinn would lift that sweet angel's voice of hers, putting every other singer to shame and tears in a strong man's eyes. Hell, she wouldn't remember that at all.

But Piper did.

Piper Cleary was in love with Miss Carmel Quinn, had been for twenty years or more, and if Mr. Parrish didn't have anything for him to do this weekend, he was going to stack up the records, turn up the volume, and hope that Nell would run screaming out of the house.

If he was lucky, she'd never come back.

He climbed the Depot steps, opened the door, and paused to look back at Parrish's office. There were no lights, no sign the man was watching. But he was. He always was. He always knew when to come by the house and tell him to load up the rocks and take them . . . away.

Away to get rid of them, though he never remembered where, and he never remembered why.

Like only yesterday. For most of the day he had been behind Winterrest, picking up the rocks and loading the wheelbarrow and carting them across the grass to the wall behind his own house. Eighteen trips at least, dumping the rocks over and loading them into the pickup.

He had a feeling he would be taking them someplace soon, maybe even this weekend.

But he didn't know.

He never knew until Mr. Parrish told him.

He shivered as a cool breeze touched his shoulders, then lifted his nose to test the air and tugged the deerstalker low over his eyes.

Bad, he thought suddenly; it's gonna be bad.

The only thing was, he wasn't sure it was the demons.

4

Keith sat with his back to the wall, hugging his knees, staring at the house. Now that he was here, he didn't know what to do. He couldn't just tell the Gang he'd come because they wouldn't believe him. Artie sure wouldn't; he would hardly believe it if he were sitting right next to him.

He didn't know what to bring back as proof. A blade of grass was silly, and there were no signs around that he could steal.

The only thing he could think of was somehow getting inside the house and taking something out. But it looked locked from here. Even though it was a football field away, it certainly looked locked, and he sure wasn't going to break a window and really get himself in trouble. Maybe, though, there was something around back. A piece of wood, or something left behind by whoever was in there last. It wasn't the greatest idea in the world, but it was the only one he had; besides, he'd done all right so far, hadn't he? He'd gotten over the wall without anyone yelling or chasing him away, and he hadn't seen a single ghost or monster in the windows, not a single one of Sitter's dumb witches or Piper's silly demons.

He winked at himself, shifted into a crouch—a runner at the starting blocks—whispered "onetwothreego!" and sprinted over the lawn.

The house bobbed erratically ahead of him, the panes flaring red, flaring gold, dying a nonreflective black. It seemed awfully far away, and there were an awful lot of rocks in the grass he hadn't noticed before. One of them almost tripped him; he swerved and gave the rock the finger. As he reached the near corner he gave the house wide berth, swinging out in a half circle until he was in back and hidden from anyone looking in from the road.

There was nothing here.

The windows were the same, the door in the center was probably locked, but other than that there was only the grass that reached back toward the hill, flat at first before lifting in low rises.

And the shed.

He couldn't believe his luck. The Gang would crap in their pants if they knew.

Not twenty feet from the right-hand back door there was a little shed whose sides were canted slightly inward . . . and its door was open.

All right! he thought triumphantly as he sprinted forward again; alright, Keith! What he'd do then is, he'd run in, grab the first thing he found, and run out again. He'd take the bike, get back, and shove whatever it was right up Artie's fat hairy nose. All right, Keith, all *right!* Go Mohawks, charge!

The shed was barely taller than he, and the door was open just wide enough for him to pass through without having to turn. He checked the house for prying eyes, checked the grass back to the hill and the trees, and was inside before he could talk himself out of it.

It was empty.

After his blinking eyes adjusted, he could see that there were no windows; it was dark, but enough dusty light slipped in through the doorway to show him that all his excitement had been for exactly nothing.

"Oh . . . nuts," he said with a mournful shake of his head. "This ain't fair, it ain't fair."

He made another quick examination in case he had missed something small hiding in a corner, then sighed and turned to leave.

And the door slammed shut, screaming on its hinges.

"Hey, cut that out!" he yelled as he reached for the knob. "Hey?" he said when he discovered there was none.

He kicked at the door and yelped when he learned it wasn't wood at all, but stone. A glance around, a deep breath, and he punched at it, pushed at it, shrieked Artie's name because it had to be him, who else but the Gang knew he was here.

Artie didn't ansawer; neither did Dirk or Ian.

It was cold now, it was dark, and when he thought about digging a tunnel under the door like they did in the movies, he discovered that the shed's floor was made of solid rock.

"Ian! Dirk! Hey, let me out! C'mon, you guys, this isn't funny."

The shed groaned.

He froze, and listened.

The shed groaned. Like something tall and unstable shifting in a high wind, something tall and heavy balanced to fall.

He swallowed and backed to the door, palms spread behind him and his legs braced to lash out at whatever was there, back there in the dark. The door pressed against his back. His left foot slipped in the dust beneath his shoes and he jerked a bit until he was balanced again, then reached out blindly for the door and leaned against it while he caught his breath.

And felt the stone moving.

It *rippled*.

It *shifted*.

It grew awfully warm.

And he knew it wasn't true because stone didn't move because stone wasn't alive. Maybe, he thought in a fierce whimpering effort to curb his imagination, there's a back way out. Sure there is. Sure.

He stepped cautiously forward, his hands out to meet the rear wall after shuffling only two paces. He shook his head. That wasn't right. The shed was bigger than that; he knew it. He'd seen it. It was at least eight feet deep and six feet high. He turned to find the door again, and suddenly it was right *there*.

The shed groaned.

The stone *shifted* like the back of a large animal leaving sleep and stretching.

And when he spun around again, his head bumped against the ceiling.

He screamed.

The shed was shrinking.

He screamed.

And heard something new: a thumping—deep, slow, vibrating through the stone, vibrating through his bones, filling his head with pictures of hearts beating, drums beating, hammers beating against skulls.

Thumping, echoing, until it all blended together somewhere deep in his head.

He screamed for his mother to get him away from this terrible place, screamed for his sister, screamed for his dead father as he dropped heavily to the floor, his pants drenched and stinking as his bowels loosened, his hands clutched against his chest while the shed groaned, *shifted*, the thumping growing louder, louder, the awakened animal angry now and stomping through the ground to come up and get him.

And he couldn't stand it anymore because he was all alone in the dark, and no one knew where he was, and this wasn't right; it wasn't a joke, and he knew it wasn't right.

The shed grew warmer.

The thumping grew louder.

His hand, trembling so hard his wrist began to ache, reached out to see how close the ceiling was now.

He felt it less than four inches away, yanked back his hand and reached out again; and there was no screaming left, only a tiny, soft whimpering.

The hand reached out, and passed into the stone.

As his legs passed in when the shed collapsed upon itself, and his arms passed in, his side, his hips, and finally his head while his eyes streamed with tears, his eyes widened and stared, his eyes searching the dark for the terror out there.

shifting
groaning
thumping

Until there was silence, and a crow flew over the house, circled once and landed on a large grey boulder twenty feet from the back door.

On the boulder's west side was a thin line of blood.

5

Sitter stood in his doorway and watched the ambulance fly south down the highway. He hoped it wasn't anyone he knew. That would be terrible. If it was someone he knew then he would want to go to the hospital to visit them and make them happy, help them get well. But he couldn't do that, because Mr. Parrish wouldn't let him.

So he hoped it was a stranger who wasn't hurt all that bad, and returned inside where he walked through the tiny kitchen into the tiny living room and sat in the recliner in front of the TV he had bought two years ago because it had a big screen and a lot of pretty colors and he wouldn't miss anything he was looking for.

He pressed the remote control unit he had taped to the chair's arm, turning on the news channel he got with the cable. He didn't watch anything else. Only the news. He couldn't watch anything else because something might happen that he had to know about, something about the witches that lived in Winterrest.

He watched for an hour, and the sun went down.

He watched the sports news, and the Wall Street news, and the news about the president leaving on his vacation. He took note of the weather in Alaska and New Mexico, in California and Maine, took note of the special segment on water safety for boaters in the East.

But there was nothing about the witches.

He was glad.

Another day gone, and still he'd heard nothing about

the witches he knew lived on the estate, who did terrible things every time there was a full moon, who kidnapped little children and who murdered adults and who, his mother had told him one night before he slept, cast evil spells over anyone who tried to climb over the walls.

Sitter had never been over the walls of Winterrest.

And he had never told Mr. Parrish about the witches, because Mr. Parrish wouldn't understand.

But they were there, and they were restless, and maybe they were the cause of the change he was feeling.

6

The scanner on the nightstand crackled, and Ollie sprang out of bed. It was Gil's voice, alerting the hospital they were coming in with a stabbing victim. Her heart pounded against her chest, her eyes watered, and she didn't calm down until she heard at the end of the broadcast the single word, "flower," a signal to her that Bud was all right, that it was someone else they were taking to the emergency room.

She sighed and slumped into a chair, and wondered if she were going nuts. Here she was, at twenty-six living in a no-horse town, sitting in a bedroom full of furniture every stick of which had been made by Bud in his cellar workshop—from the wall-canopy nineteenth-century bed to the Edwardian vanity, to the Spanish oak chair she was sitting in now. A decorator would have had a heart attack just glancing inside, but she loved it. All she had to do was exclaim over a piece she saw in a magazine, and Bud would vanish downstairs whenever he had spare time, reappear weeks later with a duplication just for her.

It almost compensated for the bouts of jealousy, and

for the fact that he'd made her promise they would never have children.

Hell, what was she talking about? It did compensate for all that, and did a lot more. It showed her how much he loved her, and taught her how to handle him whenever his moods grew too much to bear. For all his posturing, he was still a teenager; for all his bluster and rage, he was still more like her teddy bear than he would ever admit.

But she had promised they would never have children, and so how was she going to tell him she was pregnant?

And not your ordinary pregnant either. The doctor, whom she visited while telling Bud she was going out to shop for some new clothes, said she was at least four months on the rails.

She looked down at the tiny bulge beneath her loose shirt. Bud thought it was cute, that little pot belly there. Bud didn't know that little pot belly was filling up.

Her eyes closed. One scare over, another still in progress. How in hell could she be four months pregnant and not even know it? The doctor said it happens. She said, not to me, pal, not to me.

It scared her. It scared her so much she hadn't said a word to anyone. Not even to Bud. But today, after they'd made love and he'd rushed out to save the world, she felt something down there, something pushing at her belly as if trying to get out. She hadn't said anything even then, but she was going to have to now.

Later, she thought. Bud is on the move, and you're all alone. She decided there was no sense waiting for him to return. She wandered to the stairwell, paused when she reached the bottom, and had walked past the Retirement Room when she changed her mind, turned, and opened it.

The stench was gone, the panes in the window untouched, yet there was the empty extinguisher lying on the floor. She had it cradled in her arms when she saw a large stain on the center cushion of an eighteenth-century Indian lounge. Oh my god, she thought as she leaned closer; Bud's gonna die. There was no way in hell a stain like that was going to come out. The lounge was ruined.

But a touch of her finger made her freeze. The brocade was stiff, brittle, and a piece of it flaked off when she rubbed it. Suddenly it was cold in the room. She knelt before the lounge and sniffed at the dark spot. Burned. It had been burned.

A look to the window, and down to the extinguisher in her arms.

It was real, then. Somehow, in some way, that fire had been real enough to damage this lounge.

The cylinder dropped unnoticed to the floor as she lay an unconsciously protective hand over her stomach, rose, and backed out into the hall. She made sure all the night lights were on and went over to the Depot, to see what had happened, to seek some reassurance that she wasn't losing her mind.

The tavern was full, the noise from the jukebox swamped by excited conversations at the bar, the tables, the overflowing booths. It's like a dumb convention, she thought as she made her way to the bar, found a space at the end, and took a stool from a kid who couldn't have been more than eighteen. He eyed her, and she smiled at him and turned away just as he was marshalling his nerve to make a move. Doug Muir, she saw then, was washing glasses in Gil's place.

When he spotted her, he came over and answered her questions with curious detachment. Oh wow, it must've been a doozy, she thought as she ordered a draft beer and tried to catch Judy's eye down at the register. It took several minutes before she saw her, and by then she'd eavesdropped enough to know that it was Casey who had done the stabbing, that the attack was a mistake, and Casey had taken to the hills after fighting off three men and breaking one's glasses.

"I am moving to Florida," Judy said when she joined her, folding her arms and resting her forehead on top. "I am disowning my brother, selling this dump, and moving to Florida. To the Everglades, where I'll find a rich alligator to take care of me."

"What the hell made him do it?"

Judy turned her head; her eyes were red and puffed. "I don't know, Ollie. Jesus Christ, I don't know. He's been babbling all week about someone moving into Winterrest, but he won't—"

"No kidding?"

"Oh, it's bullshit," Judy said. "He gets all his inside dope from the bottle."

Wonderful, she thought; that jackass oughta find a cliff and fall off it.

Judy groaned and sat up, fussed with her hair, and gave Ollie a silent apology before appropriating the beer and taking a long, gulping drink. "How's Bud?" she asked when she was finished and had pushed the glass forward for a refill.

Ollie almost told it all; it was on the edge of her tongue and ready to be spat. "Same," she said instead.

"You guys still getting married?"

"Why?" She laughed nervously. "Is there a pool?" When Judy grinned, she leaned closer and nodded toward Doug. "What's with him? You two have a fight? Or did Liz pop the question?"

Judy stared at her so hard, she began to feel warm.

"Hey, did I say something wrong?"

"It was Liz who got stabbed, Ollie. Casey knifed Liz."

"Oh shit. Oh no, shit."

She saw then the expression behind Judy's eyes, the hurt and a trace of anger, and she grabbed for the fresh beer, took a drink, and said something about Casey, how funny he'd been acting.

"Yeah," she said when Judy didn't respond. "Funny. That's the word around here this week, and not just your brother. Funny peculiar, I mean. Like,

101

did you know Bud and I had an offer for the shop on Monday? Jesus, can you believe it? Who the hell would want to bury himself in this town?"

"You did," Judy said lightly.

"Yeah, but I'm nuts. It's either here or they lock me up."

"Me too."

"You? Bananas?"

Judy swept an encompassing arm toward the room. "You see what I have to put up with. Damn, I'm lucky they haven't come for me already." A dramatic sigh, a silent glance. "You feeling all right, Ollie? You looked a little pale. You also, excuse me, look like you're gaining a bit."

"My cooking," she answered hastily. "I'm into pasta this month."

They looked at each other for several long seconds and would have said more but one of the waitresses called out. With a quick smile Judy was gone, and Ollie changed her mind about going back home. She wanted the noise, and the people, and she didn't mark the time, didn't notice when the crowd started thinning out, when she was finally alone, only Doug and Judy with her.

When she looked up at the clock, it was only eleven.

When she looked at the door, Bud walked in, walked straight to the bar without saying a word, reached over and grabbed an open bottle of Southern Comfort. Judy gaped, Doug stared, and Ollie hurried to his side as he drank what amounted to a full glass before taking a breath.

"What?" she said, taking his arm to force the bottle down.

"Is it Liz?" Judy asked, moving closer to Doug.

Bud shook his head, wiped his mouth, and brushed alcohol tears from the rims of his eyes. "Gil's parking the ambulance in back."

"All right," Ollie said calmly, without feeling calm at all.

"Liz," he said then, and looked as if he were going to cry.

Judy saw his expression. "Oh my god," she said.

Ollie suddenly felt sick to her stomach.

"No," he told her. "No, she's not dead. She'll be fine."

"Then what's wrong?" Ollie asked.

Bud spread his hands. "Nothing is wrong, and that's what's the matter."

Doug took the bottle, poured a shotglass and handed it to him despite Judy's disapproval. "The doctors took care of her," he said, his voice tight.

"Nobody did," Bud said loudly. "Damnit, nobody had to. By the time we got there, she was all better." When they looked at him blankly, he slapped a hand on the bar. "Goddamnit, Doug, when they took off the blanket and looked under the bandage, there was hardly anything there. Don't you see? There was hardly anything! I swear to god she was stabbed, but there was only a fucking scratch!"

FIVE

1

Doug excused himself shortly before two, leaving the others to close up the tavern. No one tried to stop him, though Judy gave him a look that almost turned him around. But he couldn't stay. He kept looking at the windows, at the doors, expecting any minute to see someone else, another reminder of what had happened. It was foolish. It was ridiculous. He knew it. Yet the day had loaded his imagination with too many demons and he decided it was about time to rid himself of this plague once and for all.

If he didn't, he'd be an emotional cripple for the rest of his life.

As he had been during his flight from Seattle after his parole ended. It was evident he couldn't practice his profession there because of his past, so he took the money he'd invested and headed cross-country, hitching when he could, working in forgotten diners in places he had never heard of and never wanted to hear of again. He had no credit cards, so he had to use cash; he had virtually no identification, so he used whatever name came to mind whenever he was asked. When he arrived on the East Coast he stayed away from the larger towns because the fraternity of colleagues had big ears and old gossip, and landed in Deerford when his last ride did.

He had slept behind the tavern without anyone knowing.

He discovered the Hollow the next day, discovered

104

Parrish's office and learned the land was for sale. Parrish, to his credit, didn't blink when Doug pulled out his bankroll; he just gave him Piper's name as someone reliable enough to help build his house.

It was six years later, and time he stopped whipping himself.

He drove as fast as the dark would allow, skidding into Hollow Lane, slowing only when the streetlamps stopped, seeing nothing but the twin trails of his headlamps as he jounced along the road. His back and shoulders ached with tension, his hands cramped around the steering wheel.

The noise of the engine thundered, the tires ground like an angry mill, the creak of metal was like gunshots that struck him in a hundred numbing places.

Liz. Oh my god, Liz.

And he heard himself telling Bud that if Liz really hadn't been hurt, then the blood on her blouse belonged to someone else. Bud resisted. Doug, calm and aided by Ollie, suggested that perhaps Casey had really stabbed Bernie, and Liz had only been splattered. The excitement, the panic; with Liz there and Bernie gone and still not found, it was an understandable mistake.

"No," Bud had insisted. "I cut away the blouse. I *saw* the damned wound."

"You *thought* you saw the wound, Bud. You could have been wrong."

Bud had said nothing more, and to keep their minds occupied with something else besides the fighting they spoke of Parrish's attempts to buy up their homes. It didn't make sense, but then what did? Doug didn't mention the wind, and when the last gossiping customer had paid his tab and left, he had wiped the bar down and left without explaining.

Liz, he thought after he garaged the Jeep and went inside. Liz, for god's sake, be all right.

There was, again, a temptation to go and see her; there was, again, a reminder that Clark Davermain was staying with her.

He drank a can of beer, stared at the phone, and steeled himself to call the hospital. No big deal, Muir. You're just asking about a friend.

But Bud had said there was no cut, not a scratch.

Liz . . .

He looked into the fireplace and forgot about the time.

He looked, and he waited, and he listened to the night.

2

Casey Lockhart was afraid, his throat dry, his lungs screaming at him to slow down. But he couldn't. He had to keep running. Bad enough Hallman had told him he was nuts to his face, bad enough his anger had found the knife in his pocket. Then he had to go and pull the sucker out, flash it around. When Judy yelled, he panicked for the first time and plunged out the door behind Bernie with no intention of sticking him at all.

Then that goddamned lawyer woman popped up in front of him and he tripped trying to backpedal away; his right foot had twisted out, his left foot had kicked back, and before he could do anything he felt the knife go in and heard her screaming and what the hell could he do but get the hell away? He was drunk, and he knew it, and who would believe he hadn't been aiming for that prick, Bernie Hallman?

Three guys cornered him between two cars. By then he had dropped the knife, had only his fists, and they had forgotten how good he was with his terrible fists. It took less than ten seconds, time enough for five or six solid punches made invisible by the night air and he was away like a shot, around the back of the tavern, cutting through his own backyard, and darting across the darkest part of the street on the far side of the

Bazaar. He heard the ambulance, the shouting, and he bulled his way through a hedge into the trees beyond.

The ground rose, and he scrambled up with it, using branches to pull him, boulders to propel him, telling himself it was wrong to run, he should stay and tell the truth, but who the hell would believe him? Who would believe a drunk? He had fallen off the wagon, and no one cared about the lights. Bernie had stood right there and told him he was nuts, there hadn't been electricity in that place for over fifty years, who the hell would believe him?

He ran.

Over the hill and down, slowing as he approached the houses on Hollow Lane. He was tempted to make his way to Doug's place, hide in the stable until daylight, then show himself and plead his case. Doug was all right. He knew things, and knew how Casey was when he was drunk. He knew, and he would understand, and he would help with the police.

Casey vetoed the idea almost as soon as it was formed.

That wouldn't work. Doug would believe the part about the knife easily enough, but he wouldn't believe the part about Winterrest. Casey wasn't precisely sure why it was so important—there was only a whispering in his head that warned him it was—but if he could only find out who was there, then he would be believed about everything. So Doug would have to wait. Casey would make it back to the Hollow before dawn and tell Doug everything, and Doug would tell Judy and then she wouldn't come down so hard on him anymore.

He slithered, then, and slid, became as softly silent as the breeze tailing him overhead. A few chickens muttered at him, Piper's hound dogs barked a few times, but he managed to get across the road and down the rest of the hill without being spotted.

Once into the trees again, the open ground beyond a soft and beckoning white, he fell against a tree trunk and closed his eyes. He was sweating. His oversized chest was drenched, and his shirt clung to it coldly; his legs were cramping, inside his head something was thumping, and he could hear the blood tumbling through his veins by his ears.

Heart attack, he thought then; twenty-two and I'm having a stupid heart attack. God, I hope Liz is all right.

He swayed, dropped to his knees, and vomited into the weeds.

He could *feel* the knife as it slid into her side, *feel* the give of flesh, *feel* that brief spurt of blood on the back of his hand before he had leapt away. He gagged again, trying to turn his head away from the stench, finally wiping his mouth with his sleeve and pulling himself to his feet.

Another hundred yards and he reached the estate wall.

3

Judy was alone, and glad she didn't have to talk, to pretend, to play the worried friend of a friend who had been injured.

She had been so furious at Casey that she'd been tempted to join the others and chase after him, her only reason to catch him first and beat the living shit out of him. The murderous impulse passed, however, as soon as she heard the scream and Gil charged back inside to grab the ambulance keys from its hook beside the cash drawer. She heard a shout, Liz Egan stabbed, and the first group of men stampeded out the door like a pack of Piper's hounds on a fresh scent. Instead of following, she stationed Doug at the register in case someone thought to take advantage of the confusion, and bustled around the room, getting as many people as she could back into their seats. She made it as far as the door. The ambulance was pulling out by the time she had elbowed her way through, and four or five men were pelting across the street, yelling, pointing, proving to her at once that they hadn't the slightest idea where Casey had gone.

Christ, she thought; Casey, watch where you're going.

She was called back inside, and taking care of the remaining customers took all her patience while Doug stood behind the bar and went through the motions of mixing and serving, as if he were a robot. She tried a dozen times to get him to talk, but he answered only with sickly grins and noncommittal grunts, and she gave up in disgust, wondering why the hell a little fight should affect him this way.

That self-deception lasted only a few moments.

She knew damned well what was bothering him, and hadn't hesitated at all to press on him the necessity of his staying behind with her. Gil was gone, the waitresses nervous, the crowd rowdy, and he was the only other man in town she could trust to keep the place from being torn apart. He'd agreed, but he might as well have gone for all the company he was.

Then worry over Casey soon turned to anger—if he was dumb enough to go to the estate, then nothing she could do would stop him from paying. Unlike her brother, she remembered early; and unlike her brother, she didn't mind a bit.

When Bud returned and told them that story about the knife wound, she almost screamed.

Then Doug left with only a quick word and a nod, and by two-thirty she was alone, rinsing out the last of the glasses, taking the cash from its drawer and stuffing it into a canvas sack whose mouth she tied closed with a broad leather strap.

The lights winked out, the neon sign lingering even after the switch was thrown.

She walked to the house through a gap in the hedge, and went through to the kitchen without turning on any lights. The sack was dropped into the freezer, the safest place in the house since she never bothered with

109

a safe. Then she walked to the telephone and dialed Doug's number.

Four times she dialed, and four times she hung up before his end started ringing.

Then she sat alone in the parlor, in the dark, hands clasped in her lap, and she thought about Casey running through the hills, thought about Liz Egan lying bleeding on the ground.

Her left foot began to jump, and she grabbed her knee, forced it still.

She didn't know whether to laugh or to cry.

She thought about dying.

4

Bud sat on the edge of the bed, hands clasped on his knees. He was naked. Ollie was asleep beside him, murmuring now and then, her hand once brushing his hip. Below him the shop was quiet. Outside, he saw the round white cages the streetlamps dropped onto the street. A dove sounded, an owl answered.

I *saw* it.

He watched himself jump the Lockharts' hedge, saw Liz on the gravel, saw his hands working, the smooth slice in the roll of fat at her side and the blood slipping out as if from a razor's cut. He saw the gauze pads, the white tape, the stretcher, the man named Davermain, the ambulance lights muted against glare. He watched the hospital approach, swinging dizzyingly away as Gil took the entrance curve, dizzyingly back as he pulled up to the emergency ward door and saw the interns racing out, followed by a nurse.

The back doors swung open.

There was talk, nervous laughter, and Liz was gone, Davermain beside her, Bud climbing out and grabbing hold of the van's corner to steady himself. He had been nervous, frightened, worried to death he had done the wrong thing and Liz would die because he had missed something in his training. He was scared, and Gil hadn't helped by standing beside him and cursing Casey's shitty aim. As if Bud would feel better if it were Bernie on the stretcher.

I saw it, he said a dozen times to the intern who could barely suppress his rage at what he thought had been a joke. Liz had a wicked bump on the back of her head where she had fallen, and that was what had knocked her out. There was no blood; there was a cut, but less than one you would get rubbing against a sharp twig. The intern hadn't believed his story about Casey; Gil had hustled him into the van and they had left for Deerford, leaving Liz to be checked and re-leased later that night.

When Gil showed him a fist if he didn't shut up, he'd slumped into the corner and watched the road, and couldn't understand what he'd done wrong. Even though Doug's perfectly reasonable explanation had triggered the memory of the bogus fire, he was positive. Less positive because of that fire, but so damned *sure!*

Now he couldn't sleep.

Ollie had done her best, even agreeing to help him call around to see if they could locate Hallman and find out if Doug had been right, that it was Bernie's blood they had seen. But no one knew where Bernie was, and a few were already making jokes about Bud's needing glasses, preferably the kind with soda bottle lenses.

When he began making noises about going out again, to inspect the parking lot, maybe drive back to the hospital and see Liz, she had rebelled. She told him bluntly that he was forgetting what had happened to them that afternoon, and it was obvious even to a blind man that's he'd had another flashback. It was a horrible thing, most likely brought about by his concern for Liz, but it was just another hallucination.

She went to bed.

He sat in the living room at the back of the house and tried to make himself believe it.

He undressed and sat on the edge of the bed and tried to make himself believe it.

He walked back down to the Retirement Room, unlocked it, and switched on the light. The furniture waited for him, dark, patient, telling him there was no fire, that he couldn't still smell the smoke or see the flames or watch the grey and black smoke billowing through the open window. There was nothing wrong here. It hadn't changed at all. Until he saw the Indian lounge, and the scorch mark on the cushion.

He walked back upstairs and into the bathroom, lifted the lid from the toilet tank, and pulled out a large plastic bag. Water dropped onto his bare feet. He raised the bowl lid and opened the bag, dropped the marijuana into the water shred by shred and flushed it away. Then he returned to the bedroom and slipped under the covers. The night was still warm, but the room was cold and his teeth began to chatter, his legs began to jump, and when Ollie awoke to see that was the matter, all he could do was stare, and whisper, "I *saw* it."

5

Liz huddled next to Clark in the Mercedes, a thin hospital blanket around her, the stench of disinfectant filling her nostrils. Every few seconds she reached up and gingerly touched the lump of bandage on the back of her head, and that would trigger the sight of Casey leaping out at her from the bar.

She grunted when she felt the knife passing into her side, and Clark tightened his arm around her shoulders.

"A miracle," he said. "It's a miracle you weren't hurt."

But I was, she thought; goddamnit, I was.

Clark had prevailed upon a nurse to drive him back to the tavern so he could pick up his car. It wasn't difficult. He simply smiled through his tan and the woman practically fell into his arms. Then, quite on his own, he had driven over to the house where he found Heather waiting. In his best (she assumed) lawyer/fatherly manner, he'd explained what had happened, apparently giving it a rather romantic twist—it was Liz who had seen the fight, Liz who had recognized the danger and, without thinking, interceded to halt it. By the time he had finished, Heather was eating out of his hand and it was nothing for him to suggest she remain where she was until he'd brought her mother home.

"You ought to have that idiot arrested," the intern had said to them as he walked them to the car. "God."

"It wasn't his fault," Liz had insisted. "He thought . . . it was because there was all that blood. . . ."

"Asshole," the intern had muttered. "You people ought to get a real doctor over there, then things like this wouldn't happen."

Liz shivered.

the blade had cut her

Clark drove unerringly to the house and parked at the curb. All the lights were on in the living room, and before she was out of her seat, Heather exploded from the doorway and raced into her arms. Clark stood to one side, making himself busy locking the doors and fussing with his key case. Then he followed them up the short walk to the brick steps, and to the landing just inside. Stairs led down into a darkened family room, led up to a hall and the living room on the left. The rooms were white, with a few wildlife prints scattered along the walls. Liz dropped onto the three-cushion sofa and held Heather close. Clark found himself a chair that faced them and settled in, crossing his legs at the knee, folding his hands in his lap.

Over in the corner a grandfather clock chimed twelve.

The chattering slowed, and Heather finally pulled out of her mother's embrace and stared at her as if she were a woman she'd never seen before. "Mom, you're a hero!"

"No, not really, dear. And where is your—"

"But Mr. Davermain said you tried to stop that fight!"

Liz managed a scolding look that Clark shrugged off, and let the blanket fall from her shoulders. Heather looked immediately at her side and reached out a finger to touch the unbroken fabric.

"Mom, I thought he stabbed you."

"No, dear. We *thought* he did. All that happened was that I fell down and cracked my skull a little."

"There's no concussion," Clark reminded her. "Just a bump."

"A bitch of a one, too," she said, wincing and slapping at Heather's hand when she unhesitatingly prodded at the lumpy bandage. "Look, I thought Clark explained all this to you."

"Oh, he did," Heather agreed. Then, quite without warning, her eyes reddened and she started to cry. Liz felt her own tears on their way down her cheeks, and over her daughter's shoulder she asked if Clark wouldn't mind putting the kettle on in the kitchen. When he was gone, all too eager to be away, she stroked the girl's back and looked down the hall toward the rooms at the far end.

"Where's Keith?" she asked gently.

"Oh Mom," Heather sobbed, "I thought you were dead. When Mr. Davermain came in looking like that, I remembered—"

Remembered the way the guests had come to the house after Ron's funeral. Solemn at first, condolences, remembrances, then standing around and avoiding looking at Liz and the children until the food and drink were served.

"I know, dear, I know," she said as she willed her

114

son to get his butt out of bed and come comfort his mother.

"God, I thought—"

"Keith," she said suddenly, sharply, pushing the girl away. "Heather, where is Keith?" She rose just as Clark came out of the kitchen with two cups of tea. When she asked him about her son, he looked bewildered, stammered, and finally just shrugged.

"Heather," she said, ignoring the thumping in her head, "are you covering for him again? Damnit, has he come home yet?"

Without waiting for an answer, she strode furiously down the hallway, listening to Heather indignantly protesting her innocence behind her. The first door on the right was Heather's, the first on the left the bathroom. At hall's end were two more set into the corners—her own on the left. She opened the right-hand one without pausing, and stepped in.

"Oh my god," she said, "oh god, no," and fell heavily against the jamb.

"What is it, Liz?" Clark asked, his voice once again tinged with professional concern.

"Mom? Mom, what's wrong?" Heather ran up behind her, looked in, and gasped.

The bed was empty.

"Where is he?" Liz demanded, turning on her daughter and grabbing her shoulders. "Where *is* he?"

Heather paled as her mother's fingers dug into her skin and dragged her closer. "Mom, I—"

"Damnit, girl, where is your brother?"

"Listen, Liz," Clark began.

"You keep out of this, Clark," she snapped without looking at him. "Just . . . oh, go make some tea."

"Mom, please, you're hurting me."

She glared into the girl's wide, frightened eyes. "I'll do more than hurt you, Heather Egan, if you don't tell me right now where Keith is! You were supposed to be watching him! You were supposed to be *watching* him!"

She could hear herself yelling, could see the medication she'd been given fuzzing her vision until it seemed as if she were peering through gauze. But she couldn't help herself. She lost one man in the family already, and now her only son, eleven years old, was out there god only knew where, in the dark, in the middle of nowhere, and all this child could do was complain about a little pain. What the hell did she know about pain?

Her bedroom door opened.

Keith stumbled out, rubbing his eyes. "Mom? Mom, what's all the noise for?"

6

Casey could see the mansion squatting in the middle of his sixty acres, a dark formless lump untouched by the moonlight. The windows reflected nothing; the rolling lawn was bleached white as if buried by frost. A bird flew low and fast across the ground, leaving no shadow. Behind him one of Cleary's hounds started barking again.

Shit, he thought; if Piper's home, I'll never get a chance.

He lay his hands on the wall's top and climbed over smoothly, dropping on the other side, instantly running.

In the open like this he was vulnerable, a cinch target, and he tried to hunch over, but his weight was concentrated above his waist and he felt himself tipping. It didn't matter. Upright or not, he was clearly visible from all sides. So he gulped deeply and began to sprint, staring at the house as if by his will he could bring it closer than it was.

Halfway there, he heard a noise.

It was a rumbling, like a subway train deep in its tunnel approaching its station; a grinding, as if the grass had turned to glass; a whistling, as if it were a late autumn wind coming down from the hill.

He glanced over his shoulder, puzzled, thinking maybe it was a hundred men vaulting the wall to give him chase, the sound of their feet striking the ground the sound that he heard.

It wasn't a posse, and it wasn't the wind.

It was a boulder. A jagged globe of grey stone that rumbled along the ground as though it were plunging down a steep slope.

And it was heading straight toward him.

He faltered in surprise, tripped, and sprawled to his knees. It wasn't the boulder so much that kept him scrambling until he was up again and running; it was the sound. It was the fact that as it came closer it began to grow larger. A trick of the moonlight, but as the sound increased, so did the stone.

The ground rose, and he veered right to climb with it, broke over the top, and raced down again, into a deep trough swirling with shadows. His footsteps were muffled, his panting harsh and edged with fear. After twenty feet he struggled up a second rise and stopped, hands limp, jaw sagging while he tried to find air. The boulder, or whatever the hell it was, was hidden by the first knoll he'd come over.

But he could still hear it.

He could still feel the ground trembling beneath his feet.

Then he saw it.

A wedge of it slowly lifting above the grass, a grey-black moon moving up in its orbit. Stalking. Higher. Shadows flitting across its rugged surface. Higher. Slower. Winks of mica like trapped stars. Higher, until it finally reached the top.

And stopped.

"I'll be damned," Casey said, shaking the sweat from his eyebrows. "I'll be damned and gone to hell."

The boulder rocked on its base, forward and back.

Casey leaned toward it, narrowing his eyes, cocking his head.

The boulder rocked again, toward him and away.

His eyes widened. He looked behind him to the house to see which way to run next, and saw a wavering light in an upper story window. A candle. Someone was walking through the rooms, carrying a candle. Hot damn, he thought; I was right! I was right!

With a soft grinding, a crunching, the boulder rolled back down the slope and out of sight.

Casey checked to be sure it was gone, wondering how the hell the guys had done something like that, but he wasn't going over there to find out and get his ass caught, and started down to the level grass, Winterrest's back lawn. He walked at first, then broke into a slow trot, and didn't hear the rumbling until he was at the bottom and ten yards along.

Jesus, he thought, they don't give up, do they?

He turned as he ran, and froze, and opened his mouth to scream.

The boulder shot over the second knoll as if it had been punched from a cannon, spinning and climbing, and kept on going, into the air.

As big as the moon, bigger, and grey-black. It rose and it spun and the shadows turned to black bands that wound about its circumference and sharpened its edges and whistled its own wind, while Casey gaped and shook his head, and finally realized what was happening and started running again.

whistling

High-pitched and atonal.

whistling

And climbed.

whistling

And fell.

Casey stopped.

He had remembered at last why Judy didn't want him talking about the house.

He remembered, and he screamed.

whistling

Louder.

He was facing the house when it landed squarely on

his back, cutting off the scream, slamming him into the grass, into the earth, only one leg showing, one convulsing hand, droplets of blood showering over the lawn.

The boulder squatted in the moonlight, rocking back and forth, turning side to side, silently grinding Casey into the ground.

PART THREE

THE INVITATIONS

ONE

1

On Saturday morning the sun rose over the eastern hills, the sky was blindingly clear, and the temperature promised considerably more moderation than the previous day.

Such a morning in Deerford was usually marked by preparation. The proprietors of the various shops knew this was the time when the casual driver stopped by to inspect offered goods and perhaps spend a little unintended money. So they had to be especially clean, especially well stocked. The owners of the Shade Tree, Wilbur and Nell Cleary, whipped their small kitchen into shape in anticipation of their most profitable day. Friday nights were fine but mostly local; Saturdays brought the strangers, first-timers, and those who had been pleased the last time around. There was sweeping to be done, salads and dressings to make, vegetables to start steaming, and late breakfasts to be served to the likes of Gil Clay, who, according to Nell, wouldn't know how to start an electric stove. Bernie Hallman would grumpily get ready to pump several hundred gallons of watered-down, expensive gasoline, Deerford being farther off the beaten trail than most drivers anticipate. Judy Lockhart would sleep as late as she could, then check on the Depot to see what damage had been done the night before. If Gil and Casey had done their jobs well, if the waitresses hadn't botched theirs, she would walk back to the house and fall into bed again until the middle of the afternoon. Elderly ladies in pink dresses and sensible shoes headed for the church to clean, to sing, to gossip while they polish. The children swam until noon, then split into their factions and headed for the fields and ballgames, the streams for some fishing, the woods for some hunting in and out of season.

Driveways sprouted cars that needed washing and polishing, clotheslines sprouted limbless creatures that flapped and resisted the wind, and once a week from June through August a silver and red chartered bus pulled up in front of the Shade Tree and took a handful of generally middle-aged people off to Atlantic City for a day's gambling, or into New York or Pennsylvania for a day's shopping. The county sheriff stopped by or sent one of his men to see what crimes had been committed during the week, unless such crimes had already been reported, and already solved. Piper Cleary would don his deerstalker and call Doug Muir to see if there was work, then take his favorite blue tick coon hound and her pups and disappear into the woods for a little off-season hunting, and a little training for those animals he intended to sell one day. Sitter McMahon cleaned his lawn chair with a chamois, made sure he had enough beer hidden behind the hedge, and staked out his spot on the highway for a good day's waving.

In the distance, if you stopped long enough to listen and most people did, you could hear tractors and tillers and shredders working on the farms; you could hear hawks and crows overhead, jays and sparrows and starlings in the trees, dogs barking lazily in the shade, engines being tested, an argument or two if someone's windows were open; you could hear the foliage shifting, traffic on the highway like the faint buzzing of mosquitoes, lawn sprinklers hissing, a call to children for lunch and children answering and not going.

This Saturday in Deerford wasn't anything like that.

The bus drew up to the Shade Tree already more than half filled, and a few people stood on the pavement and complained about the company's lack of adequate preparation; Gil was the only one around who worked a hose on a vehicle; there were no birds, no dogs, no traffic on the highway; the sheriff had other business, and the deputy at the substation wasn't about to ride all the way in just to find out nothing had happened; Judy was worried about what her brother might say to someone who found him; Bernie Hallman was wondering what all the fuss was about just because Casey had gone on another bender, and was insulted that folks thought the idiot had either the skill or the luck to cut him with that toy; and Piper Cleary couldn't find that goddamned stupid Dumpling, who was due any day now and he didn't want the pups dropped in the almighty woods.

On the grass behind Winterrest a large boulder rocked.

2

The old, single-story brick building on the west side of Deerford Road was small, nestled between the Shade Tree restaurant and a high picket fence that separated it from a blue and white salt box devoted to antique glass and lamps. Two plate glass windows flanked an indented doorway, and in an arc across each of the panes were the words *Parrish Realty*. Passersby had to slouch a little to see the name through the low branches of an elm that had buckled the edge of a slate walk, but except for the name the windows were blank, backed by Venetian blinds which were open during the day and closed after five. The door itself had a shade that was raised during business hours, but reflections from the street prevented the curious from seeing anything but ghost images of themselves.

Directly inside the door was a single room, fifteen by fifteen. Two small, walnut desks facing each other on either side of the threshold had atop them neatly centered, leather-trimmed blotters, a marble-based pen and pencil set, a vase with a single flower to fit the season, a black telephone, and a series of large black notebooks in which photographs and details of properties were given.

No one in Deerford remembered ever seeing anyone in either of the black swivel chairs behind either of these desks; and no one ever commented on the tawny film of dust they saw undisturbed there.

Past the desks was a low wooden barrier carved to resemble a ship's railing. Past the railing was a third desk, similarly outfitted, though behind it were two tall filing cabinets and a water cooler. Between the cabinets was a door, and it was assumed that this led to a tiny apartment where Eban Parrish spent his time after hours. It had to be, since he did not own a house, did not rent rooms, did not as far as anyone was aware own an automobile for commuting from a neighboring town. That the door was never seen open, or that he never invited anyone in, didn't surprise anyone.

Eban Parrish sold real estate. Other than that, he was left alone.

On this Saturday, in the office, the air was still, a pocket of autumn twilight trapped by the shade and blinds. It was cool, and it was quiet. Not a sound from the outside penetrated the windows.

And Eban Parrish sat in his chair, behind his desk.

Of medium height, he favored three-piece blue suits with faint black pinstripes, a carefully done dark tie, and a flat white shirt. French cuffs with silver cufflinks, each embedded with a chip of grey stone. In the breast pocket a dark red handkerchief perfectly folded, seldom touched, never used. Black, patent leather shoes that tie. Dark blue socks.

His hair was a gleaming black and sufficiently thin to allow glimpses of his scalp, sufficiently stiff to keep breezes from unsettling its sideways combing; no sideburns; no strands tickling his collar. His face may have been round in his youth, but was thinning now, his cheeks slightly puffed at the ridges, his nose just this side of being fleshy. Thin, barely visible lines slanted down and away from pale and disturbing grey eyes. His lower lip was pressed forever upward, giving the impression that the corners of his mouth were drawn forever down. His hands were thickly veined, his nails straight and clean, and an occasional liver spot appeared just below his knuckles.

He could have been a trim fifty, or a well-preserved seventy, but only the fog knew exactly how old he was.

The sun rose higher, just to the right of the Antique Bazaar, caught the gold cross on the steeple of the First Methodist Church, and flared into the street. The chrome on the ambulance brightened. The cornfields and pastures beyond the town lost their shadow-blankets, and what livestock there was began the day's grazing.

The air in the office stirred warmly. Dust floated from the ceiling, danced, and settled.

A faint but perceptible shudder began at Parrish's shoulders, drifted down his arms, his chest, to his legs and feet. His hooded eyes blinked once, slowly, and he pushed back his chair, rose effortlessly, smoothed his lapels, and touched a straightening finger to the knot of his tie.

Walking soundlessly to the door, he raised the shade with one hand, reached around to either side, and opened the Venetian blinds. Then he stood with his hands clasped behind his back and watched the street.

Though the Depot was closed, he could see to his right a shirtless Gil Clay in the empty parking lot, hosing down the ambulance, polishing the lights and siren cone, standing back every so often to admire his work, stroke his thin mustache thoughtfully, and scowl when he located an elusive, stubborn smudge. Judith Lockhart, her shirttails tied in a knot just below her breasts, called to him from her porch; he turned,

127

motioned lazily toward the back of the tavern and shrugged. Her sigh was almost audible, so expressive was the disappointment on her face before she returned inside.

Directly opposite him, the door to the Antique Bazaar opened and Ollie West poked out her head, took a deep breath, and started choking. She looked inside, then leaned down to shove an iron doorstop into place. She rubbed her stomach and was gone, replaced a few minutes later by Bud Yardley, who carried two plastic garbage bags down to the curb. He called to Gil, laughed, dumped the bags, and hurried back into the shop.

Farther up the street Bernie Hallman came out of the Mogas garage office, unlocked the pumps, and pushed up the two repair-bay doors. He turned when Gil shouted to him, waited as the bartender ran up the sidewalk and grabbed his arm, trying to pull him to the antique store. Bernie shook his head. Gil argued. Bernie lifted his shirt and pointed to his side, rolled up his sleeves and pointed again. Then he tapped a temple with one finger and broke Gil's hold, said something shortly and went into his office and slammed the door. Gil stood there, shaking his head, started back and paused at the Bazaar's walk, shook his head again, and kept on walking.

Parrish nodded.

He waited to see if there would be any more tiny dramas, then returned to his desk and opened the center drawer. He did not sit. He looked in, cocked his head as if listening intently to someone whispering over his shoulder, and pulled out a ribbon-tied packet of small, square, ivory-tinted envelopes. He tapped the packet several times against one palm, then shuffled through it, reading the names so painstakingly hand-printed on each face, nodding to himself, once allowing himself a vague smile. Then he very carefully divided the packet in half, put each half in each inner jacket pocket, and sat in his chair.

The air continued to warm; the dust continued its dancing.

For the next hour he did not move, did not blink, did not once tap his black shoes against the bare oak flooring.

At precisely eleven he shuddered, from shoulders to feet, and flipped his desk calendar over to the present day. He touched briefly the dimpled space between his upper lip and his nose, and took a deep breath. His lips pursed, and he sigh-whistled tunelessly while he rose and turned to the door behind him. He took hold of the knob and pulled, pulled several times more before he was satisfied it was locked. Then he patted each side of his jacket to make sure the envelopes were still there. A glance at the telephone, and he pushed open the railing gate, walked to the door, and closed the Venetian blinds, pulled down the shade.

He stepped outside and blinked in the sunlight fragmented by the elm.

Parrish began delivering the envelopes at the last home on Deerford Road and worked his way forward.

He walked up to whatever served the house as mailbox and placed one envelope in each. The proper name, of course, the envelope's flap folded in, not sealed, in case the recipient was in a hurry.

He spoke to no one; it wasn't the time.

He did have occasion to nod politely to those he knew, to manage a paternal smile for an inquisitive child, to wait at the curb and lift a hand to a passing car or pickup, but he neither initiated nor encouraged anything remotely resembling conversation or prolonged greetings. The dogs didn't bother him, and the cats kept their distance.

And when he was finished with Deerford Road and its sidestreets, he headed for the highway. He walked slowly, on the shoulder, and not a speck of dust lightening his suit; he walked without feeling the slightest bit tired. When he checked the sun and saw it was after noon, he quickened his pace, though the difference wasn't noticeable to anyone's eyes.

By two o'clock he was finished.

All the envelopes were delivered, and he was back in his office, the blinds and shade up, sitting at his desk and not moving a muscle.

Eban Parrish was patient. He would wait there all day.

Saturday had begun, and Winterrest was waking.

TWO

1

Olivia avoided Bud as best she could. She made breakfast in a hurry, and told him she had to take another shower before joining him downstairs to open the shop. He grumbled but said nothing beyond a grudging declaration that it seemed to him her brain was turning into some kind of mush.

When he stomped down the stairs, she ignored him.

As soon as she was sure he was gone, she went into the bathroom, closed and locked the door, leaned over the toilet, and threw up until there was nothing left in her stomach.

Then she stripped shakily, turned on the shower, and stepped into the stall, thinking as she did that she had to talk to someone. Maybe Liz wouldn't be out with Clark today, not after last night. Maybe she'd be home, and maybe she could advise her.

It wasn't until she'd wet her hair and reached for the soap that she looked down and saw her abdomen.

Her hand clamped over her mouth as the soap bar thudded to the stall's tiled floor, and her scream was muffled by the water, by her palm, as she fell back against the wall.

She had grown.

Overnight, her stomach had grown twice as large.

2

Doug awoke in jarring stages, like an elevator too old and trying to find its level—smoothly at first, sliding out of a deep exhausted sleep that abruptly altered and thumped him into partial wakefulness. Minor aches penetrated the night's fading haze—a stiffness deep in his legs, ringing his neck, yoking his shoulders until he stirred to ease it all. He groaned softly once and shifted in the chair; his head lolled, the elevator lurched again, and his eyelids began to flutter, admitting flashes of light he attempted to drive off with one hand; a series of small settlings, and by inches he became aware he was climbing out of sleep, by inches felt the discomfort in his limbs, by inches reluctantly grasped the chair's armrests and hauled himself upright.

It was dawn.

He was looking into the charred mouth of the fireplace, frowning until he recognized it while sensation returned and he swallowed, coughed, and staggered to his feet. He didn't want to think, refused to allow himself to remember anything at all. Instead, gripping the chair's back with one hand, he passed a knuckle from eye to eye while his tongue tried to clear the fuzz from his teeth. He had to use the bathroom but when he looked up at the gallery, he wasn't sure he could make it. A deep breath made him dizzy, and he lurched to the stairs. The bannister felt slippery and he pulled himself up with both hands, palmed open the bathroom door and fell in. He caught himself on the edge of the basin counter, opened his eyes as wide as he could and was amazed that the man there in the mirror had any resemblance to anything human.

The miracles of nature, he thought as he stripped, turned on the shower, and let it run hot.

The sound of water drumming on the porcelain made him think of spring rains that lasted all night.

The steam made him sleepy again.

And through the steam from the pebbled window over the tub he saw the first light of day, and paused with one foot on the tiled floor. The light was soft, almost bronze; and if he could slant the panes of that damned greenhouse, frame them in . . .

Maybe. Just maybe.

The owner's original demand had been nearly impossible—give me a passive solar greenhouse on the south side of a weatherbeaten colonial, and make it look as if it belonged. Doug had had the commission for just over three weeks, and had done little on it save a preliminary sketch or two after checking out the cost range within which he was working, and taking a dozen photographs of the house itself, from as many angles as possible. He had been stalling because he didn't think it would work; but now . . .

He showered quickly, and while he was drying off an image came of the Branchville house, the design almost fullblown, and he snapped eagerly at it, held it until he was sure he wouldn't lose it, then threw on a tartan bathrobe and, still in his bare feet, hurried down to the living room. There he put on several cassettes at random, mostly episodes of *Lorenzo Jones* and *Our Gal Sunday*, background noise to keep his mind on track. Then out to the stable to feed Maggie and open the paddock, back into the study where he pulled out the stool, his materials, and stared at several sheets of blank paper until, just before eight, his right hand moved.

He smiled until his cheeks ached. It was the first time in a long time that he'd done anything remotely resembling difficult work. Designing houses these days wasn't all that hard since most people could see only the uninspired styles prevalent in developments; anything else was out of their league. On the other hand, grafting solar technology onto the early nineteenth century was a challenge, and he loved it.

He felt today as he had years ago, when the *wunderkind* was in full swing and the ideas were flowing.

It was a small thing, of course, this slanted wood and glass structure, but a step ahead just the same. A major step because it had sparked the necessary impetus for the Branchville place, yet another commission to prove he was still able to put dreams on paper and translate them into something solid, something he could point to and mark as his own no matter who lived there.

He was frustrated that he couldn't use one hand for each project; and was exhilarated that when he was finished he would not be ashamed of what he saw on paper.

When the rush ended four hours later, the radio tapes long since over, he sagged on the stool, dropped the sketching pencil and applauded himself loudly. Magnificent it wasn't; stunning, far from it; but it was good. It was pretty damned good. No ego involved; just appreciation for recognizably decent work, and it felt so damned fine he applauded himself again and shook his head at the giddiness that made him start to giggle.

Then he looked up over the top of the slanted board and saw Maggie kicking up her heels, denying her age, actually chasing a squirrel foolhardy enough to invade her paddock when she was feeling queenly.

"Go to it, Mag," he whispered with a wink, then stretched and went upstairs to dress. He was just drawing on his boots when he heard the ring of the telephone and nearly fell the last three steps in his haste to catch it before it stopped.

"Doug, have you got a minute?"

He smiled at the empty room. It was Liz, and the thought struck him that he was awfully lucky to have two women interested in him at the same time. He wasn't unaware of Liz's confused feelings for him—or of his own reluctance to help her—just as he was aware of Judy's increasing desire to get him into her bed. It felt good, actually, and at the same time he knew their interest was making him overcautious.

"Douglas, are you into heavy breathing these days, or are you just listening."

He sat on the arm of the couch and turned so he could see through the front window. "I'm here, Liz. Just thinking, that's all. How are you?"

"I think I'm crazy is how I am. Last night—"

"Yeah, I know."

"Doug, look, I can't talk on the phone. I need to see an honest-to-god real human being. The kids," she lowered her voice, "they don't know anything except that I stopped World War Three last night, thanks to Clark's imagination. I can't . . ." Her voice threatened to break. "Look, would you like a free lunch?"

"Sure," he said, an automatic glance at his watch surprising him by showing it was just past noon. "I have a couple of things to do first, then I'll stop by, okay?"

"You sure it's all right?"

"Sure, no problem."

She exhaled loudly and laughed. "Thank God! You know, I'm really not with it today. After all that earthquake business busting up the car and—"

He sat up, frowning. "What? What earthquake?"

"Never mind," she said, entirely too quickly. "I—"

"Liz, there are no earthquakes in New Jersey."

"I know that," she snapped. "Don't you think I know that?"

He rubbed a finger across his cheek, into his hair behind his ear. "Hey, Liz, take it easy." *Wind? What wind?* "Liz, this is going to sound dumb, but do you remember what time this . . . this earthquake happened?"

"Doug, if you're in a bad mood, I can call someone else. Today of all days, I do not need to be laughed at, or humored."

"I'm not humoring you," he assured her gently.

"You know me better than that. Look, was it sometime around four, maybe a little after?"

When she didn't answer immediately, he felt a cloud pass over the sun, felt shadows stirring in the fireplace.

"I'll be there as soon as I can," he said, standing.

"Doug, wait! What do you know about that earthquake?"

"I don't know anything about an earthquake," he said calmly, realizing he had sounded too anxious, too intense. "But I sure do know something about a hurricane out of season. Put the kettle on. I'll look for . . . I'll do my stuff later. Fifteen minutes, Liz. Maybe sooner, okay?"

"All right," she said. "And Doug?"

God, he thought, c'mon, Liz, c'mon.

Gently then: "Yeah?"

"I've got news about Parrish, too. The sonofabitch is trying to sell Winterrest out from under us."

The phone call; he snapped his fingers. "Right! I nearly forgot. Some guy wants to turn it into condos and stuff."

"He told you, too?"

He nodded, rose, and stood impatiently by the endtable. "Yep. Yesterday. Now I don't know if he's trying to spook us or rally us, but that's something we'd better not let go too long, either."

"I know. But first the lunch. Please, Doug, don't be long."

"Then hang up, counselor, or I'm gonna sprout roots."

He rang off before she could respond, walked to the kitchen door, and looked out at Maggie. She was grazing, switching her tail at flies, every so often raising her head to check for marauding squirrels. He had no idea why she went after them the way she did; it was a battle she'd been waging since he'd gotten her, at four.

He smiled, cocked his head, then hurried back to the

phone and dialed the Lockharts' number. Liz's call had reminded him about the fight Casey had with Hallman, and he wanted to know if the idiot had been caught, turned himself in, or had been found, as usual, sleeping it off in the woods.

There was no answer. And none at the Depot. He debated calling Bud, and decided against it. If there was news, someone would have been in touch by now. Casey, the jerk, was probably still out and running. As soon as he was done with Liz, he would have to go over to the tavern and see how Judy was faring.

A replay of his recent conversation, and he scolded himself for scaring Liz with that nonsense about a hurricane. It wasn't important anyway, only odd. What was important was the Winterrest deal, and Liz's need to talk.

With a slow shake of his head he took a step toward the front of the house, and heard Maggie calling. When he asked himself how much of a real hurry he was in, he made an about-face and walked out to the fence. A clicking sound with his tongue on the roof of his mouth made the mare look up, snort, and walk slowly over.

"Girl," he said, "how would you like to visit Heather today?"

Maggie tossed her head and he laughed, opened the gate and followed her to the tackroom. Ten minutes later she was saddled, and he was riding her around the side of the house. Midway across the lawn to the drive, he saw something stuck into the gap between the front door and the frame. Maggie waited patiently while he leapt down and hurried over, plucked out an ivory-colored envelope and stared at his name on the front.

There was no stamp, no cancellation marks, and when he saw it wasn't sealed he opened it carefully and pulled out a square sheet of paper that crackled like parchment. The writing, he saw with mild surprise, had been done in fountain pen, and in a script that bordered on the Gothic style.

He read the invitation twice more, not knowing whether to smile or frown as he climbed back into the saddle, replaced the paper in the envelope, and slipped it into his shirt pocket.

"A tea party," he said to Maggie's nodding head. "Can you beat that, Mag? I've been invited to a damned tea party!" He laughed, and cut himself short. "Jesus, the fourteenth is tomorrow!"

3

When Doug reached the Clearys' house, Piper was standing in his front yard, a broom in his hand, and Doug eased Maggie over to the hedge. Piper looked up, grinned, and dropped the broom as he ambled over. His cap was jammed on, his face unshaven, and from the open front door Doug could hear singing.

"Well, if it isn't himself," Piper said genially, "and the old nag."

Maggie snorted and tried to reach her teeth over the hedge for his arm. He danced back and took a pugilistic stance, laughed, and flicked a thumb against his red-veined nose.

The music grew louder—the white-sweatered Clancy Brothers being boisterous about a cheating, loving tinker.

"How's it going, Pipe?" he asked.

"Could be worse, could be better, I could be right but I ain't. That fool hound of mine, Dumpling, has chased herself into the woods, she has. Her pups, I

138

guess. The idiot doesn't know how valuable she is." An emphatic headshake to show his disgust. "We got work today?" He asked so eagerly Doug knew the man's daughter-in-law had ordered him to clean house or else—a monthly command Cleary dreaded and sought escape from whenever he could.

"Not today, sorry."

The man shrugged. If he couldn't get out of it this way, there was always looking for the hound. He pointed at Maggie. "You riding posse or something?"

"Huh?"

"Lord, Mr. Muir, ain't you heard about Casey and the fuss at the Depot?" Piper pointed as though Doug didn't know the direction.

He nodded. "Sure. I was there."

"Oh, right." Piper touched at his cap; a slip of the mind. "Well, so was I. Outside in the parking lot when he comes barreling out like a madman." He lifted his shirt with a dramatic wince to display an ugly spreading bruise high on his side. "Damned fool gave me a clout into Ohio. Thought for damned sure all my ribs was busted."

Doug shifted, and the saddle creaked. "You heard anything?"

Piper spat in disgust. "Nothin, not a blessed word. But I tell you, Mr. Muir, that crumb ever comes around here, I'm gonna teach him a lesson he'll never forget." He laughed then, a hoarse wheezing. "Jerk stabbed himself, you know that? Stabbed himself with his own damned knife."

"No, no I didn't."

"Sure. Poor Bud Yardley thought it was the lawyer lady that got stuck, had her halfway to New York the way I hear it before he found out he had the wrong one." He laughed again, and a dribble of tobacco juice slipped from the corner of his mouth. He choked, wiped it away with a sleeve, and spat again. "Nice kid, that Yardley, but boy is he dumb."

"An honest mistake, Pipe. I thought Bernie got it."

Cleary's eyes widened. "Bernie? Are you kiddin?"

139

He scowled as if vital gossip had been snatched from his grasp. "Well, I'll be damned. "

Oh lord, he thought. "No, Pipe. I said I thought it was, but it wasn't. I take it, though, that Casey isn't back yet."

"Not until he sobers." Cleary folded his arms across his chest and looked up from under the cap's bent and stained beak. "The way I have it figured, see, is he's gotten himself over to Sparta or someplace, rousted a doc to fix him up, and he'll be back by tonight. Hung over, feelin stupid, and on the wagon again—until next week. 'Course he ain't never gonna live this one down, you can bet on it. Christ, what an idiot."

Doug squinted in the bright sunlight, wishing he'd worn his hat, and spied the Clearys' less than road-worthy pickup at the side of the house. In the bed was a jumble of grey stones.

"Building a fence?" he said, nodding to the truck.

Piper looked over, looked back. "Yeah, I think so." He grinned sheepishly. "Got a little under the weather, you might say. Don't really remember what the hell I was doin." Then he pointed at the envelope poking out of Doug's breast pocket. "Hey, you got an invite, huh?"

Doug looked down at his shirt, taking a moment before he focused on the envelope. "Yeah. You, too?"

"Of course," Cleary said indignantly. "I live around here too, y'know."

Doug managed a neutral smile. "Then maybe you know what this is all about. I thought the place was empty."

Piper spat, picked up his broom, and shrugged as he headed back for the house. "Beats me. But I sure don't ever turn down a shot at free food. Somebody probably bought it and wants to get in good with the new neighbors. Casey, the idiot, he's been talkin about lights over there since Monday. Now I ain't sayin he's got it right, but on the other hand, he must've been almost right or we wouldn't have got the invites, right?"

"Yes, Pipe, but nobody else—"

Cleary waved impatiently at the house, and held up the scrawny broom. "Look, Mr. Muir, I gotta get goin. Nell'll skin me if I don't do what I gotta. And than I gotta get after that damned dog before she does somethin stupid."

"But who delivered the invitations?" he called out as the little man reached the front door.

"Who knows?" Cleary yelled back. "Who cares? What the hell, a party's a party. See you later."

The door closed, not quite slammed, and Doug nudged Maggie back onto the road. He didn't know what high tea meant, but it sounded somehow formal, an affair that fit neither the town nor Piper Cleary. Right now, however, it was the least of his worries. He had seldom gone to any of the parties he'd been invited to. At first he had been afraid someone would recognize his name; and when he realized that the hot news from Seattle would hardly reach this far, much less linger for a decade, he had already established a lifestyle that accommodated his fears, one he eventually learned to believe was comfortable.

Left at the highway had him heading for the traffic light, Saturday drivers passing him, staring, especially kids in the back seats, a few of them waving. He waved back, but twice had to talk to Maggie softly when a driver thought it great fun to lean on his horn in an attempt to spook horse and rider.

Just before reaching the intersection he frowned. Sitter's chair was there by the hedge, but the man himself was missing. A perfect summer day, and the town's unofficial greeter was absent from his post. He hoped the old guy wasn't ill. There had been other occasions when he had skipped a day or two, and Doug found it amusing that he should feel unsettled. That says something about something, he thought with a quick laugh, and checked his watch.

"Nuts," he said. He had spent more time with Piper than he'd imagined. "Maggie, there are too many cars for us to rush, but I think we're going to be in a hell of a lot of trouble."

4

The living room was dark, all the shades drawn against the afternoon sun. Sitter was in his favorite chair. He was nervous, and very uncomfortable. He had offered his unannounced guest the best seat in the house, but it was refused, and five minutes had passed before he remembered to turn off the television.

Now it was silent.

Except for the intermittent passing of a car outside, the room was quieter than midnight, and Sitter couldn't help tapping a finger against his leg.

Finally, he could stand it no longer. He mumbled something about his throat being awfully dry and escaped into the kitchen where he opened the refrigerator and grabbed a beer, pulled back the tab, and drained the can before lowering his arm. He reached for another, and changed his mind. His head was already buzzing, his stomach was telling him he should have eaten first, and a tic began pulsing on the side of his neck. He slapped a hand against it, willing it to stop.

An eighteen-wheeler thundered by and his left hand lifted automatically in an unseen wave.

Go back, he told himself. It isn't polite to stand out here while we have company inside.

He looked fearfully to the doorway, to the dim twilight beyond, and puffed his cheeks. But this wasn't right. This wasn't the way things were supposed to be. *He* wasn't supposed to be here, not here in the house.

Not in broad daylight where anyone could see. It wasn't right, and he thought about saying so until he searched and realized he couldn't find the courage.

He reached for a beer a second time, changed his mind again, and dried his face briskly on the clean towel drawn through the refrigerator's handle. When he was positive he wasn't going to be betrayed by shining skin, when his lower lip stopped its quivering, he drew himself up and returned to the living room, took his seat, and watched as his finger started tapping again.

He heard a horse's hooves and looked alarmed until the animal had passed.

"A splendid day for riding," Eban Parrish said smoothly, from his seat on the couch. His features shadowed, hands placed just so in the middle of his thighs. "You should take up riding, Mr. McMahon. The exercise would do you good. Sitting is no way to keep yourself fit."

"I . . . I don't like horses, sir," he said apologetically. "They're too big. They might fall on me."

"I see."

"They're very nice, though," he added. "Pretty. I like to look at them."

"Yes. I'm sure you do."

Sitter wished the man would hurry up and leave. This wasn't right, him being in the house like this in the middle of the day; he had to watch the news. If Mr. Parrish stayed too long, he might miss important word about the witches. And that would be terrible, so terrible he began to squirm.

"Tomorrow," said Parrish.

At last. Now he was going to learn something. And once that was all over, Mr. Parrish would leave him alone and he could watch the news. The news about the witches.

"Did you hear what I said?"

"Yessir, I did," Sitter said. "Tomorrow."

"Excellent, Mr. McMahon. Excellent. Now suppose I tell you a few things about tomorrow. You will have to listen carefully because I do not have the time to repeat them. Please listen, and if you have any questions about what you hear, you will wait until I am finished before you ask them. And when you ask them, be positive you are sure you want to know the answers."

Sitter was perplexed, but he said nothing. He knew better than to ask for explanations when he was told that the question period would come later. When Mr. Parrish said later, he meant later, and there was no getting around it no matter how silly it seemed. He would have to wait. He would have to be sure he was listening so he wouldn't have any questions to ask.

"There is going to be a party tomorrow, Mr. McMahon. What you might call a tea party. A large number of people from town have been invited." The voice softened. "You, I'm afraid, are not invited. I wanted to tell you that myself, so you would not be offended if you saw people going and wondered why you yourself were not asked."

"That's all right, sir," Sitter assured him. "I don't like parties. And I don't like tea. It's all right."

"Marvelous," Parrish said, by his tone informing Sitter he had transgressed by interrupting. "Marvelous."

Sitter nodded, told himself to shut up, and waited.

"This—and we shall continue to call it a tea party, if you don't mind—this tea party, Mr. McMahon, will be held at Winterrest."

Sitter closed his eyes; he didn't want to hear any more.

"I am going to ask you to do me a great favor."

No, please, Sitter thought; please don't please don't.

"I want you over there right away. As soon as I leave."

No, please; no, please.

"It won't take long. I know you have many things to do on a beautiful day like today. All I ask is a quick look around, to be sure none of the older children have been using it for their private playground. Bring a bag with you. Pick up any cans or bottles you may find. Bring the bag back here and dispose of it with your own garbage."

Sitter felt the ache in his eyelids, snapping them open when he realized Mr. Parrish had stopped talking and was waiting for his questions. That was all, then. He didn't have to go *into* the house where the witches lived. All he had to do was look *around* and pick up the litter. Today he was going to be a litter collector. That would be easy. That would be all right. It wouldn't take awfully long, and he wouldn't miss much of the news. That's okay, then.

He nodded.

Parrish rose, climbing through the shadows, and Sitter knew better than to rise with him. He sat obediently in his chair and stared intently at the blank television screen until, at last, he heard Mr. Parrish reach the front door.

"Oh. One thing, Mr. McMahon."

Oh no, he thought, panicked and sweating; oh no please no please no please don't make me go in there.

He turned his head slowly, blinking against the sudden flare of light that erupted behind Parrish when he opened the door. He was dark now, darker than he was before. When he spoke, Sitter wasn't even sure his lips were moving.

"Are you listening, Mr. McMahon?"

"Yessir, I'm listening. I'm listening."

"You are to say nothing to anyone—anyone!—about the tea party tomorrow. If they ask, you may say you know about it, but you are not going. That's not a lie, Mr. McMahon. You can say that without angering me."

"Yessir, I will. I mean, I will say that so you don't get angry."

"And Sitter."

"Yessir?"

"Watch out for the witches."

5

For the fifth time in as many minutes Liz looked up at the kitchen clock and brushed an impatient hand back through her hair, gathered it in a fist, and pulled it over her shoulder. She stroked it absently, then looked at what she was doing in faint disgust. A snap of her wrist sent the hair back to her spine.

Damn, she thought.

"Damn," she said aloud.

Fifteen minutes; he absolutely promised me he would be here in fifteen minutes. She checked the clock again. Over an hour since they had spoken. She had tried calling his number three or four times, but no one had answered. He was gone, then, on his way, and after the third try she decided that someone had probably waylaid him and he hadn't been able to extricate himself. The odds were it was Piper Cleary, angling for work and going on, and on, and insufferably on about the magnificent new strain of hounds his bitch was producing this year.

As if Doug really cared; as far as she knew he hated dogs, tolerated cats, was comfortable only with Maggie.

That, she believed, was a fair portion of his trouble—he was too damned polite, too considerate of other people's feelings. A smile parted her lips, an eyebrow raised in affectionate tolerance. He was indeed an odd sort of man. She had seen him talk to a pair of dowdy, militant Jehovah's Witnesses for over an hour because he didn't have the heart to order them from his house, finally easing them out by purchasing a handful of their publications and promising he would think seriously about what they had said; she had watched him in the bar listening to Casey Lockhart spill out his woes both drunk and sober, without telling the young man to stop feeling so damned sorry for himself, get off his butt, and get himself to work.

She, on the other hand, had no patience with those who wasted what they had because what they wanted wasn't handed to them on a silver platter. Which, she supposed, accounted for no small part of his attraction—she couldn't understand why he was so kind when others returned that kindness with what she believed was imposition.

Sudden loud voices in the backyard startled her into half rising from the chair. Keith and his sister were arguing, and she was too upset to go to the door and tell them to either shut up and play nice, or take their silly battles elsewhere.

Easy, counselor, she admonished when she sat down again; easy, take it easy.

Her right hand drifted to her side, and she winced in anticipation. But there was nothing left there now but a faint scratch, one so miniscule she could barely see it even when she leaned in as close as she could. Yet she *knew* she had felt the blade sliding in.

Her fist truck the table.

She rose and walked to the counter, looked at the slices of white and rye bread, Swiss and American cheese, baked Virginia ham all artfully arranged on a wooden tray. The ham made her mouth water. Her stomach gurgled, reminding her that she hadn't fixed herself breakfast. Yet another look at the time and she decided that Douglas Muir could go straight to hell; she wasn't going to wait a second longer. And to think she believed him so considerate of others, when he hadn't even bothered to call to tell her he'd be late.

A moment later, a thick sandwich in hand, she hovered at the back door, watching the children perched on the back fence. They were almost comically intent in whatever they were discussing, and she wondered if they were talking about what had happened last night.

She wouldn't have been surprised.

After all, she had nearly taken Keith's head off when

147

he had appeared out of her bedroom, scaring them all half to death. His absence had so frightened her, she hadn't bothered to find out until much later that he'd come home while Heather was still at Mary's, and had gone into her bathroom to the shower since it had the massage attachment he loved so much. When he was done and Heather still wasn't home, he'd fallen asleep on the floor, listening to her radio while he waited for his hair to dry.

It was perfectly reasonable; he had done it a hundred times before and it had evolved into a standing family joke.

Last night, however, the joke had lost it edge. Last night she had caught herself just in time to keep from slapping his head off his shoulders.

Then Clark had left with a "Have a drink to help you sleep, I'll call you tomorrow," and the kids were jabbering at her, about her, around her until she'd chased them off to bed.

For another hour she had sat on the sofa, hands clasped in her lap. Once in a while an icy tremor would make her whimper. Once in a while she would pull at her blouse to see if the blood was still there, dried, caking, drifting in tiny flakes to the carpet. She got up only once, to make herself a Scotch, no water, and had left it on the coffee table, untouched.

Fright does curious things to people, Clark had said at the front door. Lord knows you've seen it yourself a hundred times, when you've questioned witnesses, right? When she'd nodded reluctantly, he had patted her shoulder. Well, he explained, the same applies here. She had seen the fight at the tavern door, had been frightened when she spotted the knife in the guy's hand, and when the jerk leapt off the steps in her direction she feared the worst, and it had happened. In her mind, it *had* happened. Then he had touched her bandaged head tenderly, kissed her forehead, and left her alone.

But she had sat there, on the sofa, and could not believe a single word he'd said.

She reached up now and probed the edges of the dressing, tense as she waited for pain to spark another headache, realizing only when the examination was done that her head was still resting quite safely on her shoulders.

Keith and Heather were still talking.

The air sifting through the screen door was April-cool and lulling.

She finished the sandwich without recalling its taste, poured a glass of soda, and stood at the table, facing the front of the house. Her fingers snapped at a revelation: Judy! Judy had called Doug about her brother, and he had detoured there to see what he could do. Of course he would. All Judy had to do was crook her little pinky and Doug would salivate like a dog faced with a kennel packed with prime, ripe bitches. Sure; he was comforting the barmaid sister of an addle-brained barfly while she was still here, slowly going insane.

"God, you're a bitch," she murmured at herself then.

She couldn't help it. She learned how much she really cared for Doug when she'd called him for help instead of Clark, Clark who had not once contacted her today.

So much for the proposal.

So much for her patience with Douglas Muir.

He was at Judy's and *she* needed him *here,* and what are you going to do about it, stand here like a jackass and talk to yourself?

The handset was up and poised by her ear, her finger touching the first button, when the doorbell rang. It wasn't Doug; he would have come around the back, climbed loudly up the steps to the redwood deck and called in through the screen door. When it sounded a second time, long and insistent, she stared down the hall and saw Olivia West waiting on the stoop.

"Hey, Ollie, hi," she called. "Come on in." She hung up the telephone and went to the counter. Doug could wait now, the sonofabitch. "I was just having lunch. Nothing gourmet, just a sandwich or two. You want something?" She turned around the tray in her hands to show what she was offering, and almost dropped it. Ollie was already at the table, a tie-dyed shirt hanging out of her jeans, and tears streaming down her face.

"Jesus, Ollie," she said, hurrying to the woman's side, "what happened? Are you all right? Is it Bud? You want me to call—"

Ollie shook her head vigorously and mumbled something she only partially heard.

"You're what?" she said, kneeling on the floor beside her chair.

"I said I'm pregnant!" Ollie blurted, hiccoughed, and cried even harder.

Liz was on her feet instantly, dropping into the opposite chair and staring.

"Oh *hell*," Ollie said. "Oh *hell,* hell, *hell!*"

She scrabbled in her pockets with both hands, and came up empty. A pleading look, and Liz gratefully left for the hall bathroom. She grabbed a tissue from the container on the toilet tank, grabbed another, then threw them both down and grabbed up the box. On the way back she took her time, to give Ollie a chance to get composed, and to give herself a chance to figure out what to say.

Judging from the woman's distress, congratulations were obviously out of the question; both she and Bud had made it clear from the first day they had moved here that kids were not part of their immediate, if ever, future. Kids were things other people had, were nice for an afternoon as long as they didn't tag along home at the end.

This then had all the ingredients for a major catastrophe, and the first thing she said while Ollie was blowing her nose was, "Does Bud know?"

Ollie shook her head. "Not yet. I haven't . . . aw, shit, Liz, what the hell am I going to do?"

"Then this isn't . . . it isn't common knowledge?"

When Ollie told her no, that Liz was the first one she

had said anything to, she checked the back yard and noted with relief that the kids were gone; no unauthorized ears picking up gossip. A short delay to get her thoughts together, and she returned to the counter, put on the kettle, and began fixing them both lunch. Ollie protested, and Liz told her she probably hadn't eaten all day and as of right now there was a moratorium on talk about anything having to do with babies and men until they were finished. Don't argue. Just sit there.

Ollie pouted but acquiesced, and they ate in silence. Liz was ashamed of the appetite that assailed her while Ollie just nibbled at the bread and sipped at the instant coffee. But only when the table was clear and the kettle simmering again did she take her seat, fold her hands in front of her, and nod. Once.

"From the beginning," she said. "And whatever you don't want to tell me, don't. Okay? Sort of . . . sort of lawyer and client stuff." And she smiled.

The smile she received in return was heartening, however tremulous it was, and she leaned back, brusqueness gone.

Ollie snatched up a tissue, just in case, and the muscles at the sides of her neck stood out in the effort to prevent the tears from interrupting. "I don't know what to say." Her face contorted in confusion and fear; she looked to the ceiling, and to the remains of her lunch. "I . . . I'm pregnant. At least I think I am."

"You think? What do you mean? Haven't you been to see a doctor?"

A quaking nod as the tissue crumbled in Ollie's fist. "Well, okay, right? I am. I am. And I've been sick every morning since last Monday. You know, throwing up and everything. And I can't look food in the face anymore. I just want to be sick and die."

"Believe me," Liz told her lightly, "I remember that all too well. It's one of those things those guys who write the books can't really prepare you for." She kept smiling gamely, though she couldn't help thinking of what Bud would say when he found out, how his famed ill temper would surely trigger an explosion. To keep Ollie from thinking the same, at least for now, she asked about her breasts (were they sensitive?), about cravings (fruit? juice? things loaded with sugar?), about anything else she could remember.

Ollie's answers, given through half-swallowed dry sobs, were all affirmative.

"Then I guess you are, all right," she declared, thinking that perhaps the younger woman for some odd reason needed further confirmation, this time from someone who had already been through it all.

"But," she added when the woman's eyes filled again, "you still haven't told me what the dotor said. I mean—"

Ollie forced a harsh laugh, daubed at her puffed eyes, and took a deep, trembling breath. She was calmer, and the tension in the kitchen eased considerably, though Liz could not yet understand the reluctance to talk about her visit to the doctor. Then she snapped a finger.

"You're frightened, aren't you," she said, and smiled at a sudden memory. "Scared the hell out of me, too, when I found out I was carrying Heather. Not of her being born deformed or anything, but scared for *me*. The deed was done, and suddenly I wasn't so sure I believed in that instinctive motherhood stuff. I mean, I was going to be a mother, for god's sake, and there wasn't anyone in the world who could tell me what to do every step of the way. I tell you, I was ready to either throw Ron off a cliff for doing this to me, or slit my throat." Then she grinned. "But that lasted only about ten minutes. After that, I was impossible to live with, I was so damned happy."

A look, and she saw that she'd missed the point. There was still something about all this that Ollie would not, or could not yet, tell her.

And suddenly, she knew she had it.

"Who's the father?" she asked quietly.

Ollie sniffed. "Liz, you have to believe me when I tell you that ever since I met Bud I have not slept with another man. Not one. Damnit, not a single damned one!"

She backed away from the vehemence of the denial, and was on the brink of believing her when she stopped in midthought. "Wait. What are you saying?"

"I told you you didn't get it."

Exasperation was beginning to wear her temper thin, but she would not lose it, nor would she lose her patience. Instead, she poured herself another cup of coffee, and sipped at it until she could speak without shouting.

"Ollie, listen to me. If you haven't slept with anyone else, and I'm sure you haven't if you say so, then the father has to be Bud, right? That's the way it works. Logic—"

"Logic?" Ollie stood so quickly her chair tipped over and clattered against the wall. She strode to the back door, whirled, and stood in front of her, leaning over, red eyes glaring. "Don't tell me about logic, Liz Egan. Don't you dare give me all that lawyer shit about logic and evidence."

"Now wait, Ollie—"

Her shoulders were grasped so hard she gasped. "Liz, I swear I have not slept with another man since I started living with Bud. I have been so damned old-fashioned and faithful it's sickening. And this is not Bud's child! It can't be!"

"Why the hell not?"

"Because," Ollie shouted into her face, "nobody gets this pregant this freaking fast!"

Liz grabbed her hand for fear the woman was going to hit her, held it, and told her mutely she still didn't understand.

"The doctor—"

"That frigging doctor out there doesn't know a goddamned thing," Ollie said wearily, all violence gone, only confusion remaining. She wiped a hand slowly over her face, and down across her breasts where it settled on her stomach before jerking abruptly

153

away. "Look," she said, stopped, and shook her head. "Look, okay? Every six months Bud and I have complete checkups because, he says, we have to keep an eye out for cancer, right? Every six months we go to the hospital clinic and get the whole works. We get poked, needled, X-rayed, all of it. The last time we went, Liz, was three weeks ago."

Liz waited, head tilted in question.

"Liz," Ollie whispered, "three weeks ago I wasn't pregnant."

She wanted to laugh until Ollie pulled her other hand free, dug into her hip pocket and tossed a crumbled mass of papers on the table. "Forms. All the goddamn so-called scientific results of the last visit straight from the freaking computer's mouth. Take a look. Go ahead. According to these I was not pregnant on July second."

Liz refused the dare. Instead, she leaned back and waited.

"You don't believe me?" Ollie said, and stood back. "No?" She pulled up her shirt. "Take a look. Take a good look."

She did. The top button of the jeans was undone, the better to accommodate the slight swelling of her stomach. A small bulge but unmistakable—it was the gentle protrusion of a woman somewhere around five months pregnant.

My god, that's impossible, she thought with a chill. She remembered seeing Ollie in shorts and a halter only last week and wishing her own stomach were as proudly and as solidly flat. And when Ollie jerked away, she realized she had spoken the thought aloud.

"See? See, I told you."

"Well, there's got to be an explanation," she said lamely. "I mean, surely you must have had symptoms before this week."

"Nope," she said, and smoothed the shirt down over her waist. "Not a single damned one." Then she began to tremble and grabbed for the nearest chair, sat heavily, and put her hands to her face. "Liz, this isn't happening, you know. This just isn't happening."

"The doctor," Liz said, trying to sort it all out and give it some sense. "Look, the guy at the clinic wasn't looking for pregnancy, so he didn't find it. That's simple enough, and not unusual. You had—"

"The tests, right," Ollie said tonelessly. "Hey look, I'm not stupid. I know what the symptoms are, I know what to expect. So when I got them again Tuesday morning, I kind of got paranoid, y'know? I don't always remember to take the pill, but nothing's happened before. So when I tossed breakfast again, I figured . . . I got scared is what happened. So I went back to the clinic and told them to get a rabbit. And do you know what the guy said to me when he called me at the shop on Thursday? He said I should go out and celebrate, that I was healthy as a horse, and may the kid live to be a hundred." She inhaled loudly. Closed her eyes. "He told me, Liz, I was at least four months gone."

"It's a mistake," she said automatically.

"Oh, of course it is," Ollie answered sarcastically. "And do you want to know something else?" she said, her voice tight with hysteria. "Do you want to know something else?" She laughed, a cold and unearthly sound that raised gooseflesh on Liz's arms. "Are you ready for this?" She pointed to her stomach, her knife too much like a dagger. "That . . . that *thing* wasn't that big when I went to bed last night."

6

"You're nothing but a big fat chicken," Keith sneered in disgust.

"Oh yeah?" Heather said, flipping her ponytail as though giving him the finger. "Well, who won't even try to feed a horse, huh, smarty? Who's so afraid of horses he practically wets his pants every time he sees one?"

"I am not," he insisted loudly. "I just don't like them, that's all. Besides, I could get hurt bad. Even Mr. Muir says so. He says if you don't hold your hand just right they could take off a finger."

"Yeah, well, who won't even try, huh? Who won't even try to feed Maggie?"

They stood at the Meadow View pillars, each leaning against one, facing each other across the narrow road in undisguised disgust. They had already talked out the bewildering events of the night before and had reluctantly concluded that their mother was right, that she had only tripped over someone's feet in her rush to get away and had hit her head on the ground—she hadn't stopped Casey Lockhart from killing anybody at all.

And, as usual, Mr. Davermain was wrong.

That was too bad. It had been fun for a while, thinking Mom was a hero, and if it had been anyone else telling them—like Mr. Muir, or Ollie West—they would have probably believed it for practically ever. Mr. Davermain, on the other hand, wasn't the best source for legends. He wasn't, as far as they were concerned, the best source for much of anything, not even a few loose dollars when he wanted to be alone with their mother and they were giggling and perverse enough to hang around until someone got testy.

He was, Keith had once told her, a big fat shithead.

She had scolded him for his language, but she had also been forced to agree. Mr. Davermain was fat, and he patted her on the head, and he acted as if her brother was still in diapers. It was humiliating when he was around, mortifying when he came by and one of their friends was at the house. Like that time in June when he came over and Mother talked him into mowing the lawn and he took off his shirt and looked like a blubbery whale puffing around the grass. The only good thing about that day was the great sunburn he got so bad that he couldn't even put his shirt back on. Mary Grum had been there, and wouldn't stop teasing her about how would she like to have that for a new father.

Heather had almost cried.

Though they had long since given up saying their prayers at night, they both managed a plea or two before falling asleep that their mother should not be so stupid as to marry fat Mr. Davermain just because she thought they might need a father.

"Cluck," Keith said. "Cluck. You're an ugly hen that can't even lay an egg."

"I'm not a chicken either, Keith Michael Egan, so you can just stop that right now. I'm as brave as you are, that's for sure. It's just that Mother said—"

"Mother said, Mother said," he mimicked, high-pitched and derisively. "That's all you ever say." He jammed his hands into his pockets, took them out again, and pointed. "You're no fun anymore. Just because you're thirteen going on fourteen you think you're so big. Well, you're not. You're just a big chicken."

When she didn't respond, he glowered as fiercely as he could at her, pushed off the pillar, and started for the highway.

Heather frowned uncertainly. "Where are you going?"

He paused without looking back, started walking again.

"Keith, where are you *going?*"

"Where do you think?"

In dismay, she ran after him and grabbed his arm. "Keith, you can't go there alone! Mother'll kill you!"

He smiled, and slowly removed her hand. "I went there last night. While you were over at stupid Mary Grum's, I went there all by myself."

Fury turned her hands to fists and made her blush. "I *knew* it. I just *knew* it! All that crap about falling asleep on the floor. I knew you were lying, I knew it, I knew it."

157

"Then why didn't you tell, smarty pants?" he said, turning his back on her to continue on up the road.

She hurried to keep pace, arms swinging wildly at her sides. "Because she'd kill you, that's why. She'd just kill you."

"Well, thanks for saving my life. The next time you say you're at Mary's and you're out in the field with Barry Mancuso smoking cigarettes, I won't tell either."

"Keith, that's a lie."

"Okay."

"Well, it is."

"I said okay, didn't I? You never, never go out into the field with Barry Mancuso, smoke cigarettes, and then chew gum so Mom doesn't smell it on your breath. You never do, and Artie never told me."

Heather slapped his shoulder, but not very hard. "Oh, Keith, you're impossible. You're really and absolutely impossible."

"See?" he said. "I told you you sound just like Mom."

They walked silently to the intersection and stopped. The road was empty in all directions. Sitter McMahon's chair was there, but he wasn't in it, and Heather was glad. She didn't like the way he looked at her when she passed him; she had heard about men like him at school, and whenever she decided to walk into Deerford she always crossed the road long before she got to the intersection.

The light blinked amber; a single dark cloud drifted over the sun, drifted away, and it was summer again.

Heather looked behind her, and wrinkled her nose. "They taste horrible, anyway," she said, the admission an attempt to get Keith to talk. "Really terrible."

"Then why do you do it?"

"I don't know. Barry says it's cool."

"It's stupid. It'll stunt your growth. You'll be a midget when you're thirty."

"Who told you that?"

"Mom."

158

"Mom isn't always right, you know."

Keith lifted a hand; he didn't care.

She checked the empty road again, the empty chair, the rocky hillside across the way. "You're really going?"

"Sure. Just to the wall, that's all."

When he started off again, she stayed with him, her attitude clearly informing him that she was going along just for a little way, and don't you dare get any smart ideas of getting me into trouble.

Then: "What was it like?"

He grinned. "You really want to know?"

"No," she said casually. "But just in case somebody asks."

They passed McMahon's house before he stopped and looked her straight in the eye. "You're not gonna say anything?"

"Cross my heart," she promised, matching gesture to words.

"Really?"

"Keith, I crossed my heart, didn't I? C'mon, what's it like over there?"

"Well, first of all," he said, "there's this really neat little house, kind of like a shed, out back."

7

Bernie Hallman was pissed. All that extra gas he had ordered for the weekend rush, and now there wasn't one. Hell, he hadn't had a single customer since noon. It was a bitch. And wouldn't you know the damned phone was ringing and the office door was stuck again and shit on it, he should've listened to Wanda and stood in bed. As a wife she wasn't much good for anything but keeping the sheets warm in winter, but she always knew when there would be days like this.

Yep, no question, he should've declared himself a goddamned holiday and stood himself in bed.

Damn, it was a bitch.

The warped door finally gave with a rusty scream, and he slammed it open with a broad, callused palm, paying no attention to its crash against the cinder block wall. He grabbed up the pay phone with a strangle hold that turned all his knuckles white.

"Yeah?"

"Mr. Hallman?"

Bernie stared through the large plate glass window, trying to see through the shade to the real estate office down the street a ways. He turned his head and cleared his throat, his free hand unconsciously brushing through his hair and smoothing down the front of his shirt.

"Yes, Mr. Parrish?"

"Mr. Hallman, I do hate to disturb you since I'm sure that Saturdays are terribly busy for you, especially during the summer months, but I am somewhat pressed for time, and would like to ask a favor of you."

"Hey, sure thing," he said expansively, sitting on the corner of his metal desk, shoving aside the credit card press with his rump. "What can I do for you?"

"I have a very dear friend who is just recently arrived in town, Mr. Hallman, and he seems to be having some trouble with his new automobile. I am not a vehicle owner myself, as you well know, so I am unable to give him the advice he requires."

Bernie stretched, but didn't see anything that looked like a new car parked at the curb.

"Well, what's the problem? I'll see what I can do."

Parrish gave him a short, self-deprecating laugh that made him stare at the receiver. "That I couldn't tell you either, I'm forced to admit. Which brings me to why I'm calling. The favor I'm asking is this—would you be so kind as to have a look at the car personally?"

"Well, jeez, Mr. Parrish, it's Saturday, y'know, and

I ain't got anyone working with me today. Tell you the truth, I don't think I could leave—"

"Mr. Hallman," Parrish interrupted smoothly, "my friend is, to put it bluntly, rich. He is also generous to a fault, something I have often chided him about, alas to no avail. But I don't believe I'd be very far off the mark if I said that one hundred dollars for fifteen minutes of your time would not be entirely unthinkable."

"A hundred bucks? Are you shittin—are you pulling my leg, Mr. Parrish?"

There was silence, and Bernie gave up trying to see Parrish in his lair.

"All right, I guess I could make it. But I, uh, don't see a car anywhere, Mr. Parrish. You'll have to give me directions to where your friend is stuck."

"No directions needed, Mr. Hallman. You'll find my friend and his vehicle waiting for you at Winterrest."

8

"See?" Keith said as though she should have trusted him all along. "There's nobody here. We can go right over and I can show you that place."

Heather was doubtful. Standing at the wooden gate, she could see the bulk of the mansion, the beautiful lawn flat in front and rolling behind, and the tops of large greystones poking up here and there through the grass. It looked okay, but her mother's frequent admonitions were as strong as the temptation Keith dangled in front of her. She shook her head, not refusing, not agreeing.

"C'mon, Heather, what can happen?"

What could happen was that someone could drive by and see them sneaking around, know they weren't supposed to be there because no one was ever supposed to be there except maybe for Mr. Parrish, and it wouldn't be long after that before their mother found out. And if she did, Heather would be grounded for so long she'd practically graduate high school before she would be allowed to go out again.

"I . . . I don't know."

Keith sneered at her nervousness and climbed up onto the wall. His balance was precarious and she felt her heart leap, skip, stutter as his arms flailed wildly.

"Keith!"

"It's okay," he said absently, intent on finding the proper distribution of his weight. And when he had, he strutted up and down, stopping at the gate, daring her to dare him to try to jump to the other side. When she didn't rise to the bait, he rolled his eyes skyward, and marched a hundred feet westward, returning with knees high and arms swinging as if he were a drum major and the band was right behind him.

"See?" he said, standing over her with hands on his hips. "See? It's easy."

She looked up, and the sky was glaring behind him, shading his features, a cardboard cutout wavering in the breeze.

"God, it's not gonna fall down, y'know."

"Well, I know that," she snapped, and to prove she wasn't entirely frightened to death, she took a bold step closer and put a hand on the stone. It was cold. Much colder than it should have been under the July sun, and she snatched her hand away.

"Cluck," said Keith, and he jumped to the ground on the other side. "Cluck, cluck, cluck."

Nervously, she glanced up and down the highway. "Keith, you better get out of there. Now."

"I thought you were goin with me?"

She looked away haughtily. "I've changed my mind. This whole thing is silly. It's for kids." A groping, then, for the ultimate insult: "It's something that stupid gang of yours would do."

"But what about the little house?" he said, paying no attention to the jibe.

She leaned her elbows on the wall and stared at him. "I thought you said it was a shed."

"Well, a shed's sorta like a little house."

A raspberry made him jump back. "I know what a shed looks like, Keith, and it's not a little house. It's like a shed, and that's all."

Finally exasperated at her intransigence, Keith flung up his hands and started to walk away, stopping ten paces beyond the wall and turning. "God, the Gang isn't chicken like you, y'know. The Mohawks come here all the time and they aren't afraid."

Her expression told him what she thought of his gang. "And I'm not afraid, either. I'm just being careful."

"Yeah, yeah."

"Keith, this isn't right and you know it."

He took a long step back. "Well?"

"No," she said, retreating nervously to the shoulder. The house was dark in spite of the sun, the panes reflecting nothing but the grass—a dozen green eyes, cats' eyes looking right down at her, right through her own eyes and into her mind. Her left arm was chilled, and she rubbed warmth back into it, her gaze flicking from the house to her brother and back again.

And when a sudden stiff breeze raced across the lawn, the green rippled and danced.

Keith picked up a stone and tossed it up, caught it, tossed it up, caught it. He was smiling, but she saw nothing funny about the green eyes he had suddenly, where the light caught them just wrong and the green rippled, like all the windows.

"Keith, please."

"Cluck," her brother said.

This wasn't her brother. This was a stranger.

"Cluck."

This was silly. He was only a kid, and she didn't have to do it just because he called her a chicken. But if she didn't, he'd be clucking at her forever and she would be totally and absolutely miserable, and she wouldn't be able to say anything to Mother about it because then she would have to tell why, and then she'd be in just as much trouble as if she'd actually gone over the wall.

A sigh for her predicament, and another check of the road.

"Cluck." Softly, on the breeze. "Cluck."

So, she thought, as long as I'm gonna get in trouble anyway, it might as well be for a reason.

Not wanting to give him the satisfaction of knowing that he'd maneuvered her, she picked up a pebble and tossed it at him without much strength behind the throw. He laughed when it fell far short of the mark. She threw another one, stepping closer. A third, and she was at the wall. Keith danced away and lobbed his own missile; it struck the wall and bounced back.

"You . . . !"

The wall was low. She had no trouble vaulting it sideways and landing on her hands and knees. Keith yelled with delight and ran a few yards toward the house, picked up another rock and waited, tossing it up, catching it, tossing it, smiling.

The house seemed large over here, cats' eyes, rippling green and black.

"Heather, come *on*."

Well, as long as she was this far.

She broke into a trot and Keith cheered, ran up and took her hand.

"Neat," he said. "Boy, is it neat. Wait'll you see it. Come on, let's go."

They were halfway to the house when she stopped, yanking him off his feet. He sprawled on the grass, rolled over, and scowled as he got up again.

"Jeez, Heather, you almost killed me!"

The house was huge now, the lines between the stones filled with shadows that crept down to the ground and over the grass toward him. She shook her head, suddenly disgusted with herself. This was dumb. This was really dumb. He and the Mohawk Gang could go to hell for all she cared; it was Saturday, and tonight

Barry was going to come over and they were going to listen to records, and if she were caught now she wouldn't see Barry again until he had a beard.

"Look!" she said, pointing sharply over his shoulder. "Wow, look at that!"

Keith followed her finger, saw nothing, and when he looked back she was already racing for the wall.

"Bye!" she shouted. "And if you don't come with me, I'm gonna tell Mother!"

Keith watched her take the wall in a clumsy leap he had sure skinned off half her right knee. He shook his head. His eyes were no longer green; they were black, and they were angry.

He was even angrier ten minutes later when Bernie Hallman drove up to the gate in his tow truck, saw him standing there and started yelling. He wasn't supposed to be seen. He was supposed to be gone by now, everything done and over. Now that creep Hallman was standing there, yelling, looking around, and oh shit climbing back into the cab.

The anger drained; his eyes slowly regained their normal, placid color.

The *buzzing, whispering* he had felt in his head since morning was gone. Now he was alone, at Winterrest, and he didn't know why Heather was gonna snitch.

Now he was gonna get it. Boy, now he was gonna get it good when Heather told Mom. He walked slowly to the wall and leaned on it, felt it moving so quietly beneath his arms that he smiled at the feelings that *rippled* and *caressed* over his skin. Gonna get it good, he thought; and he swallowed a whimper without knowing why when he saw Mr. Parrish walking toward him up the road.

9

They moved into the living room, Ollie sobbing quietly while Liz fussed with throw pillows, sat, stood, and walked back into the kitchen. Through the screen door she could see the trees, the grass, the aging rail fence; it was normal, all perfectly normal. She thought about calling Bud, about taking Ollie to the clinic at the hospital, about pouring two very stiff drinks and searching for the reason why Olivia had denied her own pregnancy all these months.

"Liz?"

She brushed her hair back and returned to the sofa.

"Liz, listen," Ollie said eagerly, grabbing her hands and smiling tightly. "This could all be my imagination, right? I mean, this whole thing is all in our minds, okay? We . . ." She faltered, dropped her hands and sagged back into the corner. "I'm scared."

It was Liz who held hands now, shaking them, tugging at them to force her to meet her gaze. "I know you're scared," she said calmly. "I know that. But there's no denying it, Ollie. I mean, it's there, right there, and—"

"What about false pregnancy? It could be that, or hysterical pregnancy, y'know? That's why I came over. I mean, I snuck out, left a note for Bud that I was out walking, and I came here because I thought, well, you're a mother and all, and I thought—"

Suddenly, she tore open her shirt and lay a hand on her abdomen. A moment later she uttered a short, horrified cry and covered her eyes. Liz hesitated, reached out, and lay her palm over the swelling. The flesh was warm, taut, and it wasn't long before she felt the distinct pressure of a child kicking.

My god, she thought; my god my god.

"You felt it," Ollie said numbly.

She nodded.

"Yeah. Yeah." Ollie closed her eyes slowly, seemed almost to doze before they snapped open again. "I thought it was the dope. I thought maybe Bud was right and it was the dope."

Liz was puzzled and showed it.

"Well, he got some for us in the city a while ago," Ollie said, speaking as if Bud had only dropped over to the general store. "It was pretty good stuff, not bad, but . . . " She squirmed uncomfortably, pushed herself upright and scowled at her stomach. "Well, he said it might be laced with something, because of the fire yesterday, so when I woke up this morning and got in the shower and saw this . . . "

She pushed deeper into the corner, trying to get away from the swelling that terrified her so much she could hardly bring herself to say the word, or even look down.

Liz, while she sympathized, had latched onto something else. "What fire?"

Ollie seemed reluctant, but Liz prodded her, trying to get her to talk about anything but the baby until they were both thinking clearly enough to make sense of what was happening.

"Well, yesterday, after we closed the shop around four or so, we found a fire in the Retirement Room. God, it was horrible! All that smoke, I thought I was going to choke to death. But when we got it out, it wasn't there." The expression on Liz's face stopped her. "Did you hear me? I said it wasn't there. There was no fire, no smoke, even the window I broke wasn't broken. So it was the dope, though I didn't think so at the time. That's why I thought the baby was the dope too. I mean, that I was hallucinating. But when I came over to tell you about it, and you looked at it . . . "

Liz felt rather than heard a faint buzzing in her left ear. She rose to her feet slowly, pulled her shirt out of her jeans to expose the faint scratch on her side. Ollie stared, and shrugged her lack of understanding.

"Oh! Yeah!" she said when Liz thrust out a hip to be

167

sure she was watching. "Right. I was in the Depot when Bud came back. God, that must've been terrible, Liz, all that fuss for nothing."

Liz leaned down until their noses were almost touching. "It was *not* for nothing. I swear that as sure as I stand here that I felt that knife go right into my side. No! Don't say it, don't say anything, not yet. Let me tell you something else—yesterday, around four, around the time you had that fire that wasn't a fire, I was on my way home from the office and I was in an earthquake."

Ollie started to laugh, cut herself off, and shook her head. "There are no earthquakes in New Jersey."

"Exactly." She smoothed the shirt back into place. "Exactly. Yet something out there beat the hell out of my car. " She licked her lips, sucked noisily once between her teeth. "I called the police that morning. They said there had been an accident at the curve where it happened. There was nothing there, but they figure a large truck must have run off the road and knocked down a couple of trees." Licked her lips. Sucked her teeth. "There wasn't any truck. I was there. I know."

"Oh." Ollie put a hand to her mouth. "Oh."

"And do you want to know something else? "

Ollie shook her head; she had had more than enough.

Liz ignored her. "Doug. I talked to him around noon today, about last night, about what happened at the Depot. Somewhere in there I mentioned the earthquake, and he said that at the same time, over at his place, there was a hurricane."

Ollie giggled. "Now that's really crazy. I mean, that's wild, Liz." She closed her eyes, making a decision. "Last night," she whispered, "before I went to the Depot, I looked in the Retirement Room because I couldn't believe it was the dope. There was a burn mark on a lounge Bud had found in Maryland. A big mark. It hadn't been there that afternoon. But the fire was . . . no. No, Liz, it's crazy."

"Sure it is. But something happened to you, and something happened to me, and something seems to have happened to Doug. I think we'd better find him and do some more talking."

She reached out a hand to help Ollie to her feet, but as soon as she was up Ollie dropped the hand and stood back, looking down at the arm resting over her stomach.

"Liz, this isn't an hallucination."

"I know."

"Liz, something's going on. I've got to get to a doctor. I've got to know what's inside me!"

Liz pulled her toward the door. "Doug first, doctor second. One more hour to find out if we're all going nuts, and I promise I'll take you to the clinic myself."

She rushed into the kitchen and grabbed a notepad and pencil from the top of the refrigerator. She scribbled something quickly and attached the page to the refrigerator door with a magnetic ladybug. "Ugly isn't it," she said. "I put it here because it's the first place they go when they come in." Babbling; she was babbling. "No home should be without one." Babbling, because there was a grinding in her stomach, a sudden need to scream.

Ollie gave a quick laugh. "It's really ugly Liz. It's absolutely godawful."

She allowed herself to relax slightly. For that one sane and precious moment Ollie had forgotten her troubles. But it passed once they were in the car and Ollie saw the dents and cracked windshield; she began sniffling as they headed for the highway.

"It'll be all right," Liz told her, reaching over to pat her arm. "Listen to me, Ollie, it'll be all right."

Ollie nodded, then pointed suddenly. "Hey, that's Doug!"

169

10

Doug yelled and waved a hand wildly when he saw the
BMW glide between the pillars. Liz nodded quickly
and made a rapid U-turn, and he followed, reaching
the house shortly after the two women had left the car.
He gaped as he slipped from the saddle. Jesus Christ,
he thought, Ollie looks pregnant.

Maggie was tethered in the backyard, and when he
stepped into the kitchen, Liz fell into his awkward,
surprised arms.

It took an hour to sort out all the stories, Doug
refusing belief until Liz dragged him outside, pointed
at the damage, and drove him to the spot where she
had felt the quake. A road crew was working there, hot
tar steaming, steam roller waiting, while a dump truck
was filled with lengths of fallen boughs. He said nothing more until they returned to the house.

"Well, the way I see it," he offered with a lopsided
grin as they entered the kitchen to join Ollie at the
table, "we are the victims of a Communist conspiracy
to dominate the world through the introduction of
hallucinogens into the drinking water. We are affected
because we have particularly susceptible nervous sys-
tems, thereby enhancing the softening process of our
brains."

"You're full of shit," Ollie said, though her eyes
gave him a smile her lips could not manage.

He shrugged with his eyebrows, then inhaled slowly
while Liz poured them coffee. "You haven't told
Bud?"

"Are you kidding? After last night, he'd freak out,
Doug! He'd go so far around the bend he'd never find
his way back."

"Look," said Liz, "if we talked to someone who
knew about such things, I'm sure we'd find perfectly
good reasons for the wind and the earthquake. I mean,

there has to be." She toyed with her cup; it rattled on the saucer. "It's the fire, and Ollie, I don't know. I just don't know."

He rubbed a hand over his forehead. "It isn't coincidence," he said lamely.

"You're nuts," Liz said. "Coincidence—"

"I don't believe in it," he told her. "I don't believe we could be living here all this time and suddenly, in the space of a single day, have all this come down on us. It makes no sense."

"Well, it can't be anything else," she insisted. "If it were, you'd be implying some direction behind it all. Some connection."

"Well, maybe I am," he said without emphasis.

Ollie shook her head, swallowed, and headed for the bathroom. When she was gone, Liz took his hand and squeezed it.

"What is it, Doug?" she asked. "What's going on?"

"I wish I knew," he said, and felt the hand covering his, saw the eyes, the fall of hair, the lines of her face.

"You've been avoiding me," she accused lightly in an abrupt change of subject, and when he started to deny it she held his hand more tightly. "I don't mean that, I mean . . . you run away from me. Right? You run away, and I think I want to know why."

"You think?"

A brief smile. "Yeah. Maybe I don't want to know."

He waited, listening for Ollie's return, and before he could stop himself he told her about Seattle, all of it, and what he had dragged with him across the country. He never once met her gaze, but his hand stayed in hers. When he was finished, he waited forever before looking up. There were no tears, no smile, but she leaned over and kissed him solidly on the cheek.

He wondered if he should tell her that he felt much better for the telling, but he was interrupted by the slam of the front door. Liz was on her feet immediately, and he followed her up the hall to the living room where, at the window, they saw Ollie hurrying up the street.

171

"Damn," Liz muttered, and started for the door.

"No," he said, and took her arm. "I think Bud has to know first. With all this other stuff, she needs him more than she needs us. Besides," he added, "you and I have to talk."

11

Piper stood at the back door, an album cover in his hand. His housework was finally done, and Dumpling still hadn't come back, and despite the fact that it wasn't nearly as hot as the day before had been, he hadn't the energy to go tramping through the woods after her. He lifted the cover and looked at the face of a young Carmel Quinn. Behind him, Irish eyes were smiling from the throat of Dennis Day.

"Damn fool animal," he muttered, returning the album to its place. He shut off the turntable and straightened his cap. A visit to the kitchen filled his pockets with bits of roast beef, and he was soon walking down to the highway. At the intersection he flagged down Hallman's tow truck coming toward him from the west.

"What's up, Pipe?" Bernie said, leaning an elbow out of the window. His nose wrinkled, and he waved a loose-wristed hand. "Kee*rist*, man, you smell like last night's dinner."

"Have you seen Dumpling?" Cleary asked, ignoring the jibe, his Adam's apple bobbing against the stench of gasoline.

"Dumpling?" Hallman laughed shortly. "What the hell's a Dumpling?"

"A hound, you ape," he snapped, plucking at the loose skin on his wrist. "Gonna whelp any minute and the bitch's run away."

Hallman groaned. "Listen, I ain't got time for your

172

damned dogs, for god's sake. I just lost a bundle out at Winterrest."

Piper frowned and looked west. "What were you doin there?"

"Got a call from Parrish. Some rich joker with car trouble. All I saw was that Egan kid playing with hisself on the lawn."

"Must've been a joke. You didn't see my dog, did you?"

Hallman shook his head without an ounce of concern, shifted gears loudly and was gone, turning Piper away from the dust, pushing him toward Winterrest before he knew where he was heading. When he realized it, he stopped and turned around, and pulled off his cap. His left forefinger dug into one ear, wiped the wax on his jeans, then scratched through the thin white hair that laced across his scalp.

"Dumb dog."

Worry doubly creased his face. He needed those pups to sell come September; he needed Dumpling for another litter; and he missed her because she was the only dog who didn't try to bite off his ankle whenever he trained her. She was the best in a long line of coon hounds. She reminded him of his dead wife.

Well, hell. He didn't even know where to start, so he might as well head home, get himself something to eat, and go on over to the Depot for a Saturday night's watching.

He supposed he was picked because he was Irish, and the Irish were supposed to be fantastic drinkers. But drink made him throw up. Most of the time he nursed a ginger ale and an oath from Judy and Gil that they'd never tell a soul. He wasn't even really very Irish, not all the way through. He hated Tommy Machen, couldn't stand the raucous yelling of the Clancy Brothers either, but they were part of the damned act. He preferred Carmel Quinn and Dennis Day, solid professional Irishmen who could bring a tear to your eye and a lump to your throat just by winking them County Cork orbs.

173

But hell and damn the English, you can't have everything. After all, the money was good and the company was okay, and shit they'd all be on welfare if he wasn't for him since that damned feedbag of his son's hardly ever turned a profit.

A finger poked him in the middle of his back.

He whirled with a gasp, slapping his cap back on as if caught with his hand in the till, and had a curse at his lips until he saw who it was.

"Mr. Cleary, top o' the morning to you."

Piper forgot Dumpling, and the roast beef in his pockets. He nodded deferentially and touched his shirt pocket. "Got the invite, sir. Thank you. I appreciate it truly."

"Very good, Mr. Cleary. I trust you'll be there."

He sniffed and whipped a handkerchief from his hip pocket to wipe across his nose. "Got a lost pup, sir, need to find her."

"Mr. Cleary, your priorities are wrong," said Eban Parrish.

Piper allowed as how that might be god's truth, it being such a long time since the last time if Mr. Parrish knew what he meant. Mr. Parrish did indeed and without annoyance, then asked about the truck he had seen heading into town. Piper told him, word for word, inflection for inflection, what Hallman had said, and he almost ran when he came to the part about the Egan boy playing.

Parrish's eyes turned black.

It was just for a moment, but Piper knew they had turned black, and something in the back of his mind told him he had seen that look before. He said a quick prayer for the lad, then backed away, explaining again that Dumpling was missing, Mr. Parrish must know what a prize she was, and if Mr. Parrish didn't mind he'd be on his way, hunting for the fool creature before it got itself hurt.

Mr. Parrish didn't mind.

Piper smiled weakly. "I guess, then, sir, I'll be seein you tomorrow."

"You will, Mr. Cleary. You will."

Piper headed back up the lane, stopping only when he heard the soft whisper of his name.

Parrish was still at the intersection.

"Yessir?"

"Don't worry about a thing, Mr. Cleary," Parrish said. "It will be worth it, I assure you. You always did enjoy your little trips, as I recall."

Piper said nothing, making only an affirmative gesture with his hand. It was true he didn't mind driving off once in a while, getting away from Nell's nagging, but he never would quite remember where he had been, or why he had gone there.

Parrish touched the dark red handkerchief in his breast pocket and nodded a farewell.

Piper nodded back, and had half turned to leave when Parrish called him again.

"Sir?"

"I should be careful, though, Mr. Cleary."

Piper frowned. "Sir?"

"Well, you never can tell where you'll find demons."

12

Ollie stumbled through the back door into the tiny service porch and leaned against the wall to catch her breath. Her hand strayed to her stomach, and when she realized where it was she snatched it away and lay it against her cheek. The skin there was warm, and slightly slick with perspiration, and she tried as best she could to dry her face with her sleeves.

She was crazy, of course. But her insanity paled against the delusions Doug and Liz had thrown at her. It didn't matter that the fire seemed to fit right into whatever pattern Doug was hinting at; she had the dope to fall back on, but those two . . . she shuddered deliberately, smoothed her shirt down over her chest, and opened the inner door.

Bud would help her. He had to. She had been wrong when she claimed he would flip when she told him. On the contrary, he would get a little excited, then explain to her the nightmare, calm her, soothe her fears, and protect her as always. He was Bud, after all, and they had been through too much together for him not to stand by her now.

She moved down the hallway, past the stairs, past the Retirement Room, and saw him at the front of the shop. He was standing by the counter, randomly punching keys on the register without engaging them. She waited until he sensed her and looked up, and she struggled into a smile.

"Where the hell have you been?" he demanded sullenly as she came nearer.

"I told you," she said neutrally, "I went for a walk."

"To get flowers, yeah," he said, and stared pointedly at her empty hands.

"I couldn't find any I liked."

He turned his head toward the window. "Ollie, I've been thinking. A lot." His face was gaunt, his hair tangled. "I think we ought to sell this place and get out. Go west or something. Parrish made an offer, you know. He said—"

"I know," she answered quietly.

"What? You know?"

She nodded. She had been out walking one afternoon less than a month ago, going nowhere in particular, when Parrish called to her from his doorway. At first she had ignored him, sure that he meant someone else. But he called again and she veered, smiled, and thought nothing of it when he ushered her into the office and closed the door behind them. He had stood awfully close, too close for her comfort, and suggested that perhaps she and her companion might consider an offer he had just received for the building they owned.

176

His hand lighted on her arm, and she inched away, not wanting to seem rude, not wanting him to touch her. Before she could say a word, then, he had given her a figure she thought insanely high, and told him so, as well as telling him they had been through too much to give up on the shop now.

He understood, he said. And would they in the course of time be having children?

His hand again, this time darting out to brush over her stomach before pulling back and smoothing one of his lapels.

Not likely, she had told him. She and Bud were not into children or parenting or spooning mush into kids' mouths.

Parrish smiled as he suggested she would in all likelihood make an excellent mother.

She had smiled back, apprehensively now, thinking that if she didn't get out of this place right away this old fart was going to rape her where she stood.

Then he had placed his hand on the small of her back and guided her outside. Not another word passed between them, and she had nearly run back to the shop, her skin tight, her throat dry. She'd showered for nearly half an hour before she could rid herself of the feeling that she had been touched by the grave.

"You know?" Bud said again. "Jesus."

"I told him no," she said. "And I'll tell him again if he asks."

"Well, I think we ought to leave."

"Bud, look," she said, and stopped. When she tried to take his arm he backed away, nervously massaging the back of his neck, his gaze seldom lighting on anything for very long.

Oh god, she thought; oh god, he's still spooked.

"In fact," he said firmly, "I think I'm going to insist on it."

"Bud, we can't leave."

"Why not?" he asked, petulantly now.

She held her breath. "Because of the Bazaar, and you and me, and because I'm pregnant."

He opened his mouth, closed it, and stared at her waist. "I don't believe it."

Tears filled her eyes. "Bud, please, I am, and I'm scared." But when she looked for a hug, or a touch, or even a smile, she found nothing. He only stared, shaking his head in denial. Finally, he covered his eyes with one hand and drew it slowly down to his chin.

"You can't be."

Her tears could not be stopped.

"How long?"

She licked at her lips and tasted salt. "Five . . . five months."

"Five . . .?" He frowned. "But we went for our checkup. You weren't . . . what the hell are you trying to pull here, Ollie?"

"Nothing," she insisted, almost begging. "Bud, there's—"

"I don't believe it." He strode around the counter to face her. "I just . . . I don't believe it."

Her hand gripped his arm. "Bud, listen to me, please. I know I wasn't pregnant three weeks ago. But I am now. I am!"

He shook off her hand and opened the door. "You're crazy, right? You're really crazy."

"Bud!"

"How could you do it, Ollie? How could you do it? We agreed, goddamnit, and now you've—" He raised a hand, bunched it into a fist and punched at the air between them. "And I suppose you want to keep it."

She almost slapped him, and he backed away from the horrified expression on her face. "Bud, it's ours. I need help. I don't know how, I don't know why, but it's ours, Bud. And I'm scared."

"Ours," he muttered. "A month ago you weren't pregnant, now you look like a cow." He sniffed. "Christ, you're a lousy liar, Ollie. How dumb do you think I am?"

And he was gone before she could stop him, racing down the step and around the side of the house. A moment later the VW bellowed into the street, and all she could do was stand on the threshold and watch him leave. Crying without a sound.

And whimpering when she felt something move in her womb.

13

"I've been talking to Mr. McMahon and Mr. Cleary." said Eban Parrish.

Keith stood at the gate, hands clasped behind him so they wouldn't shake so hard. He thought he had done the right thing bringing Heather here—that's what he thought all the whispering had said—but Mr. Parrish looked mad, so he decided to keep quiet. It wasn't fair that he should have to find out stuff on his own, anyway. But maybe that's the way it must work.

He just wished he could be sure, just wished he could remember.

First . . . he was in the shed.

Then the shed took him. There was no other way to put it—the shed *took* him. And hurt him. Hurt him so bad he thought he'd never stop screaming.

Then the shed that was really a rock that was really, he guessed, just another part of Winterrest, then the shed light let go and sent him home. He wasn't sure that part was right, but it was close enough because the next thing he knew he felt little whispers in his ear. Like shadows talking low behind a door. It wasn't little keith, who told him this and told him that and told him how to start the Mohawk Gang; these were littler, cold but nice, darksoft, humming, and he figured that what he had to do was get someone else there for the stone to sort of . . . *take*.

And as he told that part of it to Mr. Parrish, it occurred to him that what he was saying was that

179

Sitter was wrong, and Piper was too—there were no demons or witches out there in the house.

What he was saying was that Winterrest was alive.

He said all this aloud, and winced when Mr. Parrish lifted a hand, took his arm and pulled it gently, until Keith brought his own hands around front. Then they started down the road. A man and a boy taking a stroll. The boy was terrified; the man was smiling.

"I am very pleased, Keith, that you thought that way."

Keith's legs nearly buckled with relief.

"It shows that you are very, very intelligent."

"Yes, sir," he said softly, realizing with a cold start that it was the first time he had ever called anyone "sir" in his life.

"I am not saying you are correct, mind you, but it shows me you will be a great help when I require it."

"For what, sir?"

"Soon," he was told. "Soon, Mr. Egan. Do not be impatient. It will all come to you, in time."

"Yes, sir, okay." He didn't understand, but he didn't want Mr. Parrish angry at him anymore.

"But I do not want you back here again, do you understand? Not until tomorrow."

He didn't ask why. And he didn't ask about the part about the stone being alive because he knew he had to think about it some more. His mother had always told him that all things were living in one way or another. But she never said anything about stones being alive.

He just nodded when they passed Sitter McMahon on the road. Sitter was heading for Winterrest, but Keith didn't ask why. He didn't ask why about anything at all. He just walked to the amber light, said goodbye to Mr. Parrish as politely as he was taught, then ran all the way home and used all the swear words he knew when he found no one there.

He was scared—really, really scared.

He didn't care what Mr. Parrish said.

There were darksoft whispers climbing around in his head, and he was scared, and he wanted his father.

THREE

1

Nerves, Liz concluded, or a form of mild hysteria. That's what it was. Any other explanation did not hold true, not when all the facts were examined beyond the taint of emotion.

She stood in the bathroom, the shower curtain blocking out most of the sun. It was nearly dark, she could barely see her reflection in the mirror over the basin, but she desperately needed the quiet, the time, without distractions or temptations.

Now that she knew about Doug, she could readily see how he was susceptible to periodic baths of guilt over something which had not been his fault. An accident was all it was. Tragic and beyond recalling, but an accident just the same; and his tirade against coincidence merely a search for a rational reason where none apparently existed.

And Ollie denied the pregnancy because of the pact she and Bud had made against having children—and her own fears about being capable of raising a child. That was the least surprising since she had seen more than one case of it herself among the many female clients she'd had as a public defender.

Bud, too, was anxious—he was almost frantic. This was their third try at making a go of their business, and he worked furiously hard because the specter of another failure was too potent to live with; and having a child now was precisely what he had convinced himself he didn't need.

Her dim reflection grinned sourly, wry amusement at the diagnoses she had managed for all of them but her.

Standing away from the bašin, she leaned against the towel rack and squinted. Mirror, mirror, on the wall, who's the biggest jerk of all?

Clark was coming over, and he was going to ask her to marry him. But after all the miserable, grueling, oftentimes satisfying work she had done since Ron had died, she was afraid now that another marriage would take it all away. Clark was an attorney. No matter how much he might protest (and he would oh yes he would), they were tempting the birth of an intracouple competition, and she could not help doubting that his vanity could accept the role.

So hey, there was a mild earthquake that was extremely rare but not unknown in the state where she lived; a hell of a strong wind blown stronger out of proportion; a fire not nearly as bad as claimed; an unwanted pregnancy.

So what?

She didn't know; god help her, she didn't know.

Doug was still in the living room, sitting on the couch with a highball glass in his hand when she returned. She sat beside him, close enough for their legs to touch. He stirred but did not shift away, set the glass on the coffee table and turned to her slowly.

"You think we ought to go after her now? She's had time to talk with Bud."

"No," she said. "I have a bad feeling he's not going to believe her."

"Yeah, me too. Maybe, though, we ought to be there anyway, to give her some moral support."

Her hand went to his hair and brushed a strand away from his forehead. His back stiffened but again he did not pull away, and she told herself this was neither the time nor the place to explore what she'd suspected she had felt all along. But before she could stop, he took hold of her wrist, pulled it to his lap and held her hand.

His finger moved gently over her knuckles, following the faint traces of her veins. Her hearing grew more sensitive, and she listened to the erratic pace of her heart and the almost hissing sound of his breathing; her vision grew more acute, and she saw the lines about his eyes, the ghosts of grey hiding in his hair; and she could identify the smell of him—the hints of stable, of cigarette smoke, of the house he lived in.

It was a moment startlingly intimate, and she could no more resist when he leaned forward to kiss her than she could lift the couch onto her back.

A brief kiss; tender, promising, and not at all touched with threat.

"Doug," she said when they parted, "I . . ." She laughed shortly. "I think I have a problem."

"Yep," he said. "Me, too."

"Mine's Clark."

"Mine's . . ." he pointed at his chest.

They kissed again without an embrace, and at the second parting they leaned back and watched the afternoon shadows grow longer on the ceiling. The silence between them was neither strained nor forced, and when she turned her head she saw the smile working his lips.

"We have to talk," she said at last.

"I know."

"But not now."

"I know that too. The outside intrudes, or something like that."

"Something like that," she agreed. "But later?"

"Definitely. Absolutely definitely."

They talked then of other things—the wind, and the quake, and none of it making sense—until she lighted on the Winterrest sale and felt herself growing excited. She complained about what it would do to their town, quite possibly their lives, and after nearly twenty minutes of pacing the room and waving her arms, she stopped and looked at him.

"Not bad, madam lawyer," he said with a grin. "You do that well in court?"

"I feel silly."

"Don't. In fact, hold on to that enthusiasm. It's good, and we'll need it. In another fact," he added as he got to his feet, "why don't we have a pre-tea party party? We'll organize, we'll form a solid front against the callous opposition, and tomorrow after we eat their food we'll spit in their collective eyes."

Liz applauded and hugged him, an embrace that held until the doorbell rang and Clark was on the stoop. He thought her smile was for him and hugged her, then heard Doug laughing. He tried not to frown when she dragged him up into the room and explained their war plan. He was clearly unhappy, clearly wanted her alone, but she would have none of it. She knew now what her answer would be, and that as much as anything buoyed her to giddiness.

Then she groaned when Heather walked in, demanding to know what Maggie was doing in their backyard, followed immediately by Keith declaring that he was starving to death and if he wasn't fed soon he and the Gang would have to raid the town, and pillage and plunder all the old ladies until their stomachs were full.

"It's okay," Doug said with Heather hanging onto his arm and pulling him toward the back door. "If you can't get a sitter, bring them along."

Heather gaped. "A sitter? Mother!"

Keith stood at his sister's side, scowling his support. "I don't want a sitter, Mom. Jeez, that's for babies."

"Now listen here, you two," Clark said sternly from Liz's side, "you will do as your mother says, and that's final. No more backtalk, period." He turned to her with a flourish, presenting her with a silent family as if he had been mediating squabbles all his life. "You make whatever calls you have to, Liz. Don't let them railroad you."

At any other time she would have lost her temper at his presumption of authority, but at a wink from Doug she only giggled and told the kids they could come.

Doug said yes, they could feed Maggie and listen to his tapes, and no, they could not climb the rocks in back. Clark, swiftly and expertly retreating to an I-was-in-favor-all-along stance, opened his wallet for the drinks they would need to buy, and agreed to pick up Ollie and Bud on his way back. Breathless orders were given—for god's sake, don't forget the food—and before she could blink, Liz was in the kitchen, alone, watching through the screen door as Doug and the kids pampered the horse.

The silence nearly overwhelmed her.

So maybe she was kidding herself; so maybe they were only postponing all the decisions they had to make. So what? For the time being, they also needed the knowledge that none of them was alone, and if some ridiculous development scheme was the temporary bind she would be an idiot not to take advantage while she could.

She called Judy without thinking twice, found her at the Depot and told her Clark would be in for some bottles in a few minutes, and told her why.

"You guys are nuts," said Judy, laughing.

"Yeah, but so what. Hey, can you get away? It wouldn't be right without you." She almost added, "And Casey, too," but no mention had been made, and she decided not to be the first.

"Sure," Judy agreed. "Gil's a big boy, and he's dying to prove he can run this show on his own. Well, as of now he's on his own. It'll take a while, though. I may be a little late."

"No problem," she said, watching Heather on Maggie, with Keith dancing for his turn. "And listen, maybe I can get the old fart to come in person. Maybe we all misunderstood."

"Don't bet on it," Judy told her. "He's got more tricks up his sleeve than Houdini. He's no dummy, Liz. He makes a buck like I open a bottle—the easiest way possible. He'll fold if he sees he's going to have to fight for that sale."

"Not a great recommendation."

185

"Fight and opposition aren't the same thing, Liz. Hey, gotta run. I'll see you later."

She dialed again and listened to the Bazaar's phone ringing, a worried frown creasing her brow when it wasn't answered right away. She was almost ready to hang up and try again when she heard the handset lifted on the other end. There was no immediate greeting, and she hesitated before giving her own.

"Oh," Ollie said, her voice strained, and distant.

"Ollie, are you all right?"

"Yes, I guess so."

Liz looked at the door, but Doug was still outside. "Well, look, do you think you guys could come over to Doug's later?" She forced herself to sound more jovial. "We're going to have a meeting of all the hotheads in this burg, to see what can be done about the Winterrest sale. You wanna burn down a few castles or something?" She softened her voice. "It's okay if you don't feel up to it."

"Bud doesn't believe me!" Ollie blurted in anguish. "He thinks it's someone else's kid."

"Oh, Ollie."

"Liz, he's left me. He took the car, and he's gone!"

"Don't worry," she said automatically, cursing herself for such an inanity. "He needs time, dear, that's all. Look, why not let Clark bring you over. The company will do you good."

Ollie wavered, then agreed in a soft, almost inaudible voice, and Liz wished she could wring Bud's thick little neck.

As the handset clicked onto its cradle she heard a shout outside, and turned just as Doug and the kids charged into the room. They were drenched, their hair gleaming against their scalps, their clothes spattered darkly. A glance to the window, and she saw the rain.

Hard rain, streaking out of the sky and cracking like hail against the panes. The kids were whooping as they raced for towels, but Doug remained at the door, looking down when she joined him.

"Shower," he said unnecessarily.

She could barely see Maggie huddled miserably under a tiny apple tree. The brisk wind was damp, unpleasantly cool, and she rubbed her arms hard to smooth the skin and bring it warmth. The sky was light; when she looked again she could see no clouds at all—the color above was a darkening blue.

There was thunder, no lightning; she was reminded of the sound the earthquake had made.

Thunder again as Heather returned, jeans replacing her shorts, her hair in a terry cloth turban. This time lightning flared and made them all squint, and the third clap of thunder rattled the windows, rattled on the cups on the table, and Heather moved closer, shivering.

"Wow," she said. "Wow."

The wind punched a chilling spray through the screen, yet no one moved to close the door. Gouts and spears of water rose from the lawn, slammed away from the sundeck, sheeting and wavering when lightning crackled over the fields; thunder rolled and crested and exploded like boulders dropped onto the roof. Heather yelped and grabbed her mother; Liz fumbled for Doug's hand, while Doug stepped closer to the door, shaking his head as he looked up, shaking it again as thunder and lightning followed in swift artillery fire, so loud Liz at last covered her ears and turned her head.

Keith was standing in the kitchen doorway, head cocked to the storm, eyes narrowed, and he was smiling.

2

Bud drove the rust-pocked VW recklessly, not caring that he had almost veered off the road twice. He took the jump into the driveway at speed, and braked hard only when the garage door filled the windshield. The bumper touched wood. He listened as the engine whined before he turned it off.

Blinking rapidly, he slid out and leaned on the roof, putting his head on his forearms until, with an effort, he jerked upright and swallowed. He headed for the front where, at the walk, he paused to look at the signpost, remembering how Ollie had bitched for an hour for him to be careful as he worked the scorching tool over the words.

The sun in its setting slowly turned red, and the air took the appearance of unnerving heatless fire. The trees were shifting to gold, the street to black blood, and the lawns were shimmering as a breeze touched the grass.

How could she do it? How could she sit there and tell him she had been pregnant and not know it? What did she think he was? Why didn't she tell him? God, they could have found a clinic and everything would have been fine, just the two of them again, for the rest of their lives. Fine. Great. Until she lied. He glanced to the bedroom window over his head. All that time up there, all those times at all times of the day—and she was pregnant.

The street darkened, and he hurried inside. A tear broke, and he didn't care because she had broken their sacred trust. What an idiot she must think him; five, six months gone and not even suspecting? What an idiot. What an ass.

He listened for several seconds before he knew he was alone. She was gone. He walked slowly through the aisles until he paused at the Retirement Room, went in and locked the door behind him. He sat heavily on the lounge and brushed a finger over the scorch mark. This was what was left of the rest of his life; this was all there was left to living.

He wanted to believe she hadn't known, but . . .

The dim light sifted out of the room.

He wanted to believe, but god, he wasn't a magician.

188

An hour later he heard her calling and jumped eagerly to his feet. And froze. He heard footsteps on the staircase, and she called his name again. No remorse, no tears—she was goddammed excited! No plea for forgiveness, no begging him to come back so she could make it right between them again. None of it. No goddamned nothing.

He sat and clasped his hands, knuckle-cracking hard. Needle-point pain erupted in his wrist, and he welcomed it while he told himself he was a fool, that trust was all there was, that Liz was right when she said this wouldn't be the first time that something like this had happened. There were all sorts of reasons, and he ought to give Olllie a chance to explain, for crying out loud. After all these years, she ought to have a chance.

Her footsteps were muffled, hurried. There was no calling him name this time, no begging, no entreaties.

Footsteps, running, and she was gone.

A few minutes later all hell broke loose.

The storm startled him to his feet, whirled him around to the window where he watched the lightning drive away the black, felt the thunder ring in his ears until they started aching. The building shook. The chairs and desks in blue-white strobic flashing jumped from the walls, crawled toward him, scuttled away. The panes rattled as if the glass were made of sheet metal. The floor vibrated, and he made his way to the sill, shaded his eyes against the bursts of light, and tried to see through the rain. Hard rain. Almost as hard as hail when a gust splattered it against the glass.

He watched the storm, reached out to press a palm against the window, and within seconds it had calmed him, drove his doubts into the corners, and left him knowing exactly what he had to do. He could not stand to be laughed at, which is what they would all do when Ollie told practically everyone who mattered. It was as simple as not being able to stick around anymore. As simple as that. Ollie had betrayed him, had made all those promises, and then had gotten herself pregnant. To trap him. To pin him down. To force him to share her with someone—no, some*thing* else.

And he wouldn't have it.

As he watched the lightning burn through the sky, watched the rain gouge trenches in the yard, he would not have it.

When it was over, when the fury outside was done and gone, he went upstairs, went to the phone, and vacillated only a moment before calling Eban Parrish.

"This man of yours, Mr. Parrish," he said without preamble. "Is he still interested in the Antique Bazaar?"

The line crackled with waves of static.

"Mr. Yardley, this is a surprise. And am I to assume that you would actually sell now?"

An implied question: *do you know what you are doing?*

"I would, and I am, Mr. Parrish," he said as firmly as he could. "I absolutely am."

"I see. Well. This is a rather late development, Mr. Yardley."

"The offer was a good one," Bud said. "If your man still wants to make it, we'll accept. I just wanted you to know."

"I see."

"Is there going to be a problem?"

"Not for me," Parrish said. "But Mr. Yardley, may I suggest that we talk about it further? Perhaps tomorrow, at the affair? You are going, aren't you?

He hadn't been. He was going to stay home, among his own children. "Yes," he said. "Yes, sir, I'll be there."

"Excellent. That's excellent, Mr. Yardley. And may I recommend you think it over very carefully, so there are no more last minute changes of mind."

"Mr. Parrish—"

"Until tomorrow, then, Mr. Yardley."

A vicious explosion of static made him pull the

handset away from his ear. He turned, walked to the living room window, and watched the street. He didn't know what he expected to see, but all there was was the rain puddles, the twilight, and the odd red glow that made him think of dying.

3

Piper decided he was going crazy. Or worse—he was getting senile. For years he had been going along just fine, keeping his health, nursing a steady business with the hounds, staying out of Nell's and Wilbur's way; now, without warning, his mind was slipping. He was standing outside the Depot, and he recalled . . . no, he seemed to recall speaking with Eban Parrish earlier that afternoon. But that couldn't be. They had barely exchanged two words in twenty years outside what he was being paid to do. No call to. He wasn't buying houses, and the mummy sure wasn't buying hounds. Yet there was this odd sensation that they had actually had a conversation. Today. But he couldn't remember what was said, and he couldn't remember where it was said. He just suspected it, and the suspicion turned his stomach.

It was twilight. Shadows were breadking from behind the trees, slipping out from under the porches, a few sifting into the air like black mist. The streetlamps were on, partially smothered by the foliage, and doing little more than illuminating tiny round stages along the sidewalks.

A hiccough made him cover his mouth. Shame made him walk away from the bar and head for the highway.

He had been drinking. For the first time in years he had taken more than a token drink, and he was disgusted. It was Dumpling's fault. That dumb hound running off, not saying a word, taking her litter to get killed in the woods. He sniffed back a tear. Stupid bitch.

Wilbur, as usual, was no help. He hated the dogs, a hatred fostered by that big-titted wife of his. Nell. What the hell kind of a name was that, anyway? It was something you called a horse. And she wasn't any help either. She had practically run him out of the Shade Tree when he came in for his supper, said he stunk of dogshit, why the hell couldn't he at least take a shower after he handled those animals. Those animals. She called them that, not once that he knew ever giving them a chance to prove they were special, loving, ready to lie down and die for you if you were to ask them not even nicely.

Wilbur—the spineless little creep, how could he be his son for god's sake—Wilbur just stood by like a wimp and nodded. He was always on her side, always against his very own father.

Shit and damnation.

At the amber light, reflected in dying suns trapped in roadside puddles, he turned right and headed for home. Sitter was folding up his chair. Piper waved; Sitter waved back.

Another bad feeling.

Didn't he see McMahon before, sometime this afternoon? Wasn't the dope heading down for Winterrest with a big canvas sack in his hand?

That couldn't be. The demons would've got him. Sitter thought there were witches there, but Piper knew it was the demons. Waiting behind the windows to grab the souls of travelers too stupid to stay away. Demons. Shadows tangled around his legs and made him trip over his own feet. Cars swooped past him, radios loud, voices loud, lights so damned bright they hurt his eyes. He tugged on his cap and tried to ignore the dark of the hill looming on his right.

Like he tried to ignore the Hollow where Douglas Muir lived. He didn't like it there. There was no one around, you couldn't hear the traffic, and that dumb horse was always trying to take off his hand. But then,

192

Muir and his horse were just as crazy as Sitter, only he was seeing cars instead of witches on broomsticks.

Crazy, all of us, he thought. Crazy. It must be the heat.

He turned into the lane, sniffed back another tear, and began calling for Dumpling.

He missed her. And since Nell and the wimp would be at the restaurant until after eleven, he was going to crank up Carmel Quinn, stand on the porch, and listen to the voice that made him wish he were all Irish. And he was going to bawl his damned eyes out because everyone was going crazy and his favorite pup in all the world was missing.

4

On any other Saturday night Bernie Hallman would have flatly refused any emergency calls that came into the gas station; he was closed at six and that was that and the hell with stranded motorists who didn't have the brains to take care of their cars. Tonight, however, Wanda got a damned bee in her bonnet and started nagging at him about modernizing the place, about doing his duty as a husband, about fixing the plumbing, about every damn thing that came into her mind. So when the call came from Parrish, he was glad of it. Shit, there was still an easy hundred bucks to be made, and Parrish was very upset that his rich friend hadn't been where he said he was. Very upset. Hell, Bernie thought the guy was gonna cry right there on the phone, for Christ's sake.

Well, Parrish was gonna cry even more, because Bernie was tired of running around like he was some kind of servant, waiting in the damned dark and there was still wasn't anyone here he could do business with.

When he had arrived at the estate, the gate was

193

open. He'd finished his beer, tossed the can onto the floor, and drove in slowly, making sure he didn't scrape his truck on the wall. Then he'd headed for the house, peering and swearing because while the sky was still streaked with light, it was almost midnight down here. The moon was already up, a few stars were making attempts to break through, and then he had been stuck in the cab during the downpour.

He didn't think about the absence of clouds, just counted the bucks he was going to get if that guy would just get his ass in gear and come on out. He had to be in there; there was a light in one of the first-floor windows. Faint, but steady, like a candle or a lantern. And when it seemed that no one was going to answer the sound of his horn, he climbed stiffly to the ground, walked to the door, and slammed a fist against it. Once. Just to let them know they weren't dealing with some half-brained Triple-A driver who had more forms than an insurance agent to fill out before they would even say hello.

Nosir, this here was Bernie Hallman, the best mechanic in the county, and he was glad to be out of the house, glad for the money. And he'd be a damnsight gladder once he plopped his aching butt down on one of Judy's stools and polished off a bottle of Jim Beam while watching the waitresses strut their stuff in their beautiful tight jeans.

With the headlights behind him, casting his shadow on the door, he looked around and shrugged as if to someone in the truck. Then he knocked again, tried the knob, knocked a third time, and stepped back.

"Hey!" he shouted. "Hey in there, it's the tow truck!"

The pickup creaking a cooling behind him.

"He ain't gonna like it, Mr. Parrish ain't, me havin t'come out twice like this!"

The truck creaked again, a weight settling on it.

"Well, fuck ya," he said. "You and the horse you rode in on." He gave one last slam on the door, winced at the pain that shot up his arm, and managed two steps back before he stopped.

The truck was creaking louder, swaying side to side, winch and chains in the back groaning and clanking. The driver's door slammed shut, swung open, slammed shut.

Puzzled and annoyed, Bernie took another step forward before he looked down, and saw that the tires were disappearing into the gravel that filled the drive.

It had to be a trick, because the damned truck was sinking.

"Jee*zus!* Hey! Hey!"

The metal began to shriek like nails drawn across slate, the chains clanged tonelessly, and all he could do was leap off the drive and onto the grass and dance around helplessly, shouting, once running back to the door to pound furiously on it for help before turning around to run back. He couldn't leave his truck; it was the only one he had. And he couldn't stop it from sinking. Couldn't stop the gravel from skittering around the vehicle, slamming against it, denting it, spilling into the back, and forcing it lower.

To the door.

To the window.

The glass exploded outward, and he threw himself on the ground and covered his head. Something landed on his back and he yelled, rolled over and picked up a small rock. He threw it as far away as he could, and widened his eyes when it landed back at his feet.

A piece of fine-edged gravel struck his cheek; he gasped at the burning and swiped at it—his palm came away bloody. Still another bounced off his boot and gouged the oil-smeared leather.

The cab roof and the angle of the winch were the only things above the drive now, and he could still hear it groaning, screaming, while some of the gravel shifted direction and headed straight for him.

He pushed himself to his knees, and groaned when they were sliced open by stones hidden in the grass.

Stumbling up and backward, he heard *skittering, slith-ering,* and saw in the last of the light stones tumbling toward him. They swarmed over his feet. He kicked out, and they clung like razored burrs, spinning, drill-ing through the leather, drilling through his feet.

He screamed.

Gravel swarmed up his legs, shredding his trousers, knifing his calves, his thighs, throwing him back again when he tried to flail at them. He leaned down once and saw for the first time what was left of his legs.

He screamed.

Drilling without a sound, save for the tearing of skin, the faint splash of blood, the protest of hard bone.

A handful reached his groin, and he bellowed, began running, not caring that his legs were barely carrying his weight, not caring that he was on his hands and knees, his back covered, his spine exposed and glint-ing pinkly in the moonlight, his hair turning red, his arms no more than skeletons holding him up.

He screamed hoarsely.

The gravel avoided his throat, and he screamed more like a whisper and was driven face down into the grass by the weight on his back.

Drilling.

He shuddered once, and prayed Wanda to forgive him for not getting the hundred bucks.

He shuddered again when the gravel finally drilled through his lips and into his throat.

And he didn't move at all when the gravel turned him to bloody sand.

FOUR

1

It was eight-thirty. The food was in the kitchen, still in its bags; the beer was in the refrigerator, cooling; the liquor was in the living room, opened.

"This," Doug muttered, "is ridiculous."

No one denied the assessment—no one heard him. At his feet Heather, Keith, and the Mohawk Gang were crowded eagerly around one of the speakers, listening to an episode of *Straight Arrow*, giggling at the commercials, yet paying strict attention to the lurid sound effects that created the images and sparked their imaginations. He repeated his disgust, and Keith looked up, alarmed.

"Are we too loud?" the boy asked over the hushing of the others.

He shook his head, indicating with a gesture he was only talking to himself.

Ollie was on the couch, Liz and Clark flanking her, speaking soothingly and ignoring him completely.

He and Heather had ridden over on Maggie; Keith had applied a bit of wheedling directed more at him than at his mother to have the Gang included since they were going to listen to the radio shows, and when permission had been granted they had been driven over by Ian's mother; Liz had taken the battered BMW; Clark and Ollie had arrived less than twenty minutes later, laden with brown bags of groceries and liquor. There was no word about Bud.

The false excitement they had brewed over Winterrest was enough to provide momentum for the next hour, until the sky finally turned black. The lights had been low, and Clark was at the window, a glass in his hand. He had shaken his head and whistled.

"Christ," he said loudly, "We're at the end of the goddammed world out here. You can't even see the stars."

A harmless statement, but the memory of the freak storm palled them. They sank into their chairs and only half-listened to the squabbling among the kids hunting for tapes to play, until finally, inevitably, Ollie began weeping.

"Ridiculous," Doug said a third time and walked into the study. He switched on the overhead light and stared blindly at the bookshelves. Who the hell's idea was this anyway, he wondered; not that he wasn't taking any of the blame. The party had been the perfect excuse to turn their minds from the storm, the odd week, the abrupt spate of personal problems that had, he thought, turned them all into temporary emotional cripples.

It wasn't working.

He knelt in front of the overloaded shelves near the floor. One by one he pulled out back issues of his architectural magazines and flipped through them until he found the pseudonymous articles he had written. Aside from the tapes, these had been great therapy for him, and calmed him now, though his confusion was still there. Something caught his eye then, a reminder of the puzzle he had been mulling over earlier in the week. He held up the glossy page and studied the photograph he had seen.

"Goddamn," he said. "I was right."

"About what?"

His head jerked around, and the magazine slipped from his hand. Liz was behind him. An impatient hand raked through her hair, and when he pointed at the floor she knelt beside him.

"How's Ollie?" he said as she picked up the magazine and flipped the pages over, one finger marking his place.

"Better. Clark's convinced her that Bud is pulling a Casey—hiding out and trying to decide if he's man enough to face the future."

"Jesus, Liz," he groaned. "Did he really say that?"

She chuckled. "With a perfectly straight face."

"And Ollie bought it?"

"I don't know, but she claims to feel better. What are you doing in here? You're supposed to be the host, y'know."

An elbow in her ribs made her gasp, and laugh. "This was not my idea," he said. "But I was just going through these when"—he took the magazine, opened it to the photograph, and handed it over—"I rememebered this."

It was in black and white, one of eight on a page that featured architectural styles popular during the forties. The house he indicated was obviously fieldstone, alone on a featureless plot of land, and by the front door stood a tiny man in a dark suit, squinting at the camera as though taken by surprise.

"God," she said, "that looks like—"

"Right, I saw it earlier, but I had other things on my mind. I just remembered it."

"But it can't be," she said, tilting the page, holding it away, holding it near. "That's silly. Parrish would be . . . hell, by the looks of him he hasn't changed a bit."

Spurred now, the puzzle gathering more pieces, they rummaged through the rest, and were soon joined by Clark and Ollie who were shown the photograph. They were given time for amazement, then handed more copies to glean and discard.

After a few comments on some of the *outré* styles, on some of the houses they coveted, they were silent. Only the radio, only *Inner Sanctum*.

An hour later there was a stack of eight magazines on the floor. In each, a picture of Eban Parrish, the dates of the taking ranging from 1914 to 1955. He was in the same dark suit, the same hair style, in front of the same house, though each of them by their captions were in eight different states.

They hadn't been able to find a single one that identified any of the structures as Winterrest, despite the fact that each of the houses looked exactly like it.

Clark, sitting cross-legged, scratched at a temple. "So? This is supposed to mean something, but it beats me what."

"It means," Ollie said blithely, sitting back against the shelves, "the man has discovered the fountain of youth, that's what it means." She grabbed an issue from the pile and flourished it after reading the caption. "This says 1935, right? Okay, well, that's almost fifty years ago. Now it's possible he was born old, or something like that, you know what I mean, but a man has got to show his age sooner or later. I figured he was only about sixty. He would have to be ten or twenty back in thirty-five. And I'll bet my savings he doesn't get any more exercise than pushing away from his desk."

"A relative?" Liz suggested. "His father or something."

Doug slapped a hand lightly on the pile. "Eight pages, Clark, and five different magazines. Who's going to notice? The oldest magazine here is 1973."

They were bewildered, sensing they had found something and not knowing what it was. Finally, Doug pushed himself to his feet. "I think we shouldn't wait for Judy. I'm going to get her and," he said with a wink to Ollie, "drag Bud back as well."

"And what are we supposed to do?" Liz asked, more sharply than she had intended.

"Your mission, should you decide to accept it, counselor, is to come up with some explanations. Then we'll tell each other why Parrish has another mansion to peddle—which I bet he isn't peddling at all, don't ask me why. We will also know why he wants to buy our homes, use Clark as his attorney instead of Liz, and make us all suspiciously rich."

"Suspiciously?" Clark said tolerantly.

"What would you call it?" he said. "Manna from heaven?"

His tone was light, but he did not look at Liz and left before she could speak. He was out the front door without anyone stopping him.

The night was humid, warm, and before he was clear of the woods his shirt was clinging damply to his back. A dog's bark curled into a howl; bats flitted over the hood and swung away blackly. Lights from the Cleary house crept onto the road, strings of headlamps emphasized the black that hovered above the trees, and the blinking amber light swayed slightly, making him think of a conductor on the tracks, trying to slow down a hurtling train.

Judy was at the register when he walked in, and she didn't argue when he took her to one side. The Depot was crowded, and he could see she would have been much later had he not come. She protested when he insisted she leave with him, a formal demurral that vanished the moment he feigned giving in. Her apron was off, a shouted order to Gil, and she pulled him from the tavern. Once out, she headed for her house, explaining that the clothes she had on smelled of grease and beer and she wasn't about to face the others without at least changing.

He agreed and followed, watching her slight form dart through the shadows of the porch. Casey, she explained without his having to ask, had not been seen all day, and she claimed in a huff that she didn't give a damn.

The moment the inner door was closed she fell against him, wrapped her arms around his waist, and kissed him. Surprisingly hard. Surprisingly hungry. His eyes were still open, and he made a move to ease her away. She clung to him, and he responded before he knew what he was doing.

Then, just as abruptly, she broke away without releasing him, and said so solemnly he almost burst out laughing, "Douglas Muir, I want you to marry me."

His mouth opened to say *what?*—but nothing came out but a hissing.

"Well?"

Her voice was soft, a spider web quivering.

"Uh, Judy, look . . . I mean, this is awfully, uh, out of the blue, you know what I mean? I mean—"

She kissed him again, hips pressed hard against him, shifting back and forth, not quite grinding, not quite demanding.

This time she only tilted her head back, her eyes bright with moisture. "Marry me."

"Judy," he said breathlessly, shaking his head to find some calm. "God almightly, I—"

"Please!" she insisted, and in the shadows of the foyer he saw what he could have sworn was something akin to rage. "Marry me, please? I'm tired of waiting for you to ask." Her eyes softened. "I'm tired of being alone. And we can protect each other."

"From what?" he said kindly. "Neither one of us is exactly terrified of the wolf charging through the door."

"From old age." She twisted out of his arms into the living room, where she stood in a shimmering patch of moonlight and took off her shirt. "I have to change." Half her face was ivory, half in a deep shadow that sank her eyes into her skull, turned her lips a dead flat black. Her jeans slid off easily. "I can't go on like this." She lay on the rug, only shoulders to knees caught in the light, dismembered by the moon. Her voice was disembodied—spider web, waiting: "Doug. Please. Let me protect you."

He hesitated, thinking of Liz; Judy whispered, and Liz vanished; he felt himself responding, felt his legs lower him to the carpet, felt his hands skim over her, lightly, not recoiling at the mooncold dry flesh though his fingers began to jump. He nearly stopped when he thought, *she feels like stone,* then felt his chest constrict as she tugged at him to straddle her, plucked at his buttons, his belt, his zipper.

He could not see her face—the moonlight shaft had cut off her head.

"Marry me," she whispered, beer on her breath, perfume in her hair, while his shadow became her blanket, her chest his pillow.

When he glanced up, the room was black; when he looked down, her one eye was staring. Blindly. Like a corpse.

"Forget about Liz," she whispered. "I want to protect you. I want to feel alive."

Her tongue played at his ear, her hips rising to meet him; and she gasped when he entered her, grunted when he thrust.

The moonlight was cold on his back and soles, the carpet abrasive on his knees, but he felt nothing at all, not even her rhythm, an act and nothing more in the dark living room of her darkened house, while she demanded an answer and drained the breath from him.

When it was done, when she was done, she caressed his back with her nails (spiderlegs walking), clutched at his buttocks (spiderlegs digging), pulled teasingly at his hair. "Well?"

He swallowed an immediate *no*, thinking of a way to tell her about Liz, and in the hesitation felt her hands stiffen, felt a nail penetrate his skin like the dull edge of a razor. Then she rubbed the spot quickly, apologizing, finally shifting and rolling her eyes.

"I'm crazy, right? Jesus." Softer: "Jesus, Doug, you have no idea how long I've been waiting for this. You have no idea at all." Lightly: "Of course, you realize I had rather hoped for a bed."

"It wasn't my idea," he mock-scolded. "I think I'm crippled for life."

She pecked his neck, his chest, hugged him so tightly he thought he would suffocate before she released him, led him by the hand to the bathroom upstairs and left him to dress.

From down the hallway he could hear her singing to herself, giggling once, laughing once and cutting herself off.

He looked in the mirror, expecting to see his soul's accusation of his betrayal of Liz. But there was no guilt. There couldn't be. His hair was unmussed, and there was no blush on his cheeks—it was as if it hadn't happened. Except for the cold, and the ache in his groin, it was as if nothing had happened at all.

Judy hummed as she dressed; it was all going to be fine. The poor helpless man never knew what hit him.

She put on cotton slacks, a light blouse and light sweater, wore loafers and white socks, then allowed him to drag her over to the Bazaar—to find Bud, he said, and bring him back to the party. Ollie needed him, and they wanted him to feel as if they weren't taking sides.

The VW was still in the driveway, but the lights were all out and no one answered their ringing, or Doug's increasingly angry pounding on the door. She tried to make it a game, hide-and-seek and they were It, and shrugged to herself when Doug refused to be anything but solemn, anything but quiet. It was to be expected. She had ambushed him, and it was only natural that he retreat—to figure out what was going on.

She knew.

No matter what he thought about Liz or anyone else, she had him, he was hers, and unless the unforeseen tripped her up, he would still be hers long after tomorrow. This time there was no mistake. This time she had chosen wisely, and the best of it was, this time she really cared. This time the buoyancy that floated her over the yard and into the Jeep when Bud went unfound, was unquestionably genuine. He was hers. He belonged to her now. Nothing Liz could do tonight could alter that fact. Hers. All hers.

The next fifty years would not be spent alone.

* * *

They checked the restaurant, returned to the Depot to leave word with Gil, and drove on to the Hollow. He filled her in as they went, trying to be as rational as he could and realizing that by the time they reached the lane she was much too silent.

"Sounds dumb, doesn't it," he admitted sourly.

"It doesn't sound like anything at all, actually," she said. "I just don't know what the big deal is."

"Neither do I," he said. "That is, the Winterrest sale thing is a big deal, to be sure. Deerford as far as anyone has told me has no history of planned growth except for Meadow View, and with all the people who will be coming in here, there'll be too much strain on what little services we already have. It really doesn't make sense when you think about it. And the more I do think about it, the more I wonder if Parrish isn't just out to make a fast buck or two and the hell with what anyone else around here says."

They passed Piper Cleary's; all the lights were out.

Judy squeezed his arm. "Well, you're wrong about Parrish. He's not like that at all. Besides, the big deal I was talking about was those pictures you found. I don't get the excitement."

"It's not excitement, exactly. It's a feeling. A very strange feeling I don't like at all."

"Ah," she said. Her chin tucked in, her voice deepened. "We have a premonition, do we? A little touch of the old ESP, eh? You think maybe Eban Parrish is a demon or something?"

For some reason he couldn't laugh. "No, I don't think he's a demon or something. That kind of crap I leave to Sitter and Piper. Be serious, Judy, okay? The others—"

"Are crazy too if they're getting chills just because you found some pictures of an old man who sells real estate."

He gripped the wheel harder, not understanding why she should be so negative when she hadn't even seen what they had. He concentrated then on weaving with the road through the woods, flickering in and out of the waning grey moonlight until his vision began to blur and he was forced to slow down. When she squeezed his arm again, he gave her a one-sided smile.

"I didn't come on too strong, did I?" she said.

They pulled into the garage. The engine faltered and died, and it was too dark for comfort.

"I was . . . not really prepared."

mooncold, like stone

"Who would be?" she said, and pressed close to his side as they walked to the house. "Just don't forget what I said."

"How could I?"

She said nothing more, only smiled and patted his arm as he opened the door.

The kids were at the kitchen table, thick sandwiches piled on a platter in front of them, soda cans open, their voices raised in earnest argument about the name of Straight Arrow's horse. The others were in the living room, TV trays laden with cold cuts. Doug noted that the study light was off, and the magazines were now piled on the coffee table.

There were questions then: about the weather, about Bud, about what Judy thought they should do about the sale. She stood at the hearth and told them she hadn't the faintest idea. Yes, it was a lousy prospect, and yes, she agreed with Doug that Deerford was not the place for such abrupt growth, and yes, the more she thought about it the more pissed she grew.

Doug sat on the windowsill and listened, and was reminded of men he had known in prison, men who spent hours in the library teaching themselves the law, the same hours again every night preaching passionately to each other about the injustices of it all and what they were going to do about it the next time their lawyers visited.

It was preaching to the converted.

An hour later they realized it as well, and decided they would confront Parrish at the party tomorrow and pump him for all the information they could. They quieted then, and waited until he had spread the magazines in front of Judy and asked for her opinion.

None of them were prepared for her response.

The first photograph made her grow pale; the second had her left hand shaking; the third and the fourth made her drop the magazines and push herself to her feet.

"Lord," Clark said with a grunted laugh, "he's not all that ugly, you know."

"Judy," Liz said, "what's the matter?"

She waved away the question, waved away Doug when he took a step toward her. "I'm all right. I . . . it must be the food. I ate too fast." She hurried to the staircase, to the bathroom, and slammed the door.

Doug stood with one hand on the newel post and looked up. "Clark," he said quietly, "I think you'd better take her home, if you don't mind. Ollie, too, We've done enough for one night."

"No, hey," Ollie protested angrily. "All you guys are forgetting about me, aren't you? I mean, what the hell are you going to do about me?"

Liz wrapped an arm around her shoulder to hold her down, to comfort her while she struggled not to cry again, struggled not to lose control. "Ollie, the doctor—"

"Shit on the doctor!" she snapped, and stood up. "Clark, please. I want to go home." She strode to the front door, one hand absently on her stomach, and waited while the attorney's face shifted from petulance at being elected chauffeur again to a firm decision that someone ought to be the man around here since Doug was clearly not offering himself.

Then Judy burst out of the bathroom, ran down the steps no more composed than before, and nodded brusquely when Ollie told her Clark was their cabbie. She did not look at Doug. She ignored Liz's good night. And Doug stood in the doorway until they were gone.

Liz joined him, a hand at his back. "I'll take the kids."

He didn't look around. "Yesterday, I want to Winterrest. Just to look at it. I like to, it's an impressive piece of work. Liz, I leaned on the wall, and it moved."

She said nothing immediately. Then: "Your imagination. Walls don't move."

"And New Jersey doesn't have earthquakes. And women don't get pregnant overnight."

Her hand slipped away from his waist. "That isn't the same, Doug, and you know it. There are explanations for earthquakes, and there are denials of unwanted pregnancies. But walls just do not move."

"Yeah," he said softly. "Yeah, I know."

She backed away and called the children. They protested, saw that Doug was no longer on their side, and grumbled out to the car. Liz turned on the stoop.

"Doug, what are you going to do? I mean, about the tea party tomorrow?"

He stared at the dark. "I don't know, Liz. I don't know."

"Well, I can tell you now I'm not going. I don't give a damn if he builds those condos from here to Pennsylvania, I'm not going to set a foot on that place tomorrow."

He nodded and watched them leave, watched the moon make corpses of the trees straight ahead.

Five minutes later he closed and locked the door, locked all the windows, and stood in the dark—listening, not thinking, to the terrified race of his heart.

PART FOUR

THE MENU

ONE

1

Doug rolled over too quickly in the bed, clamped his hands gingerly to his temples, and cursed, damning himself for even thinking of moving. What had awakened him was a none-too-subtle ache in his head—it settled there, digging in with dull claws, stirring only when he shifted to sit on the edge of the mattress and massage his brow, the back of his neck.

Through a vertical gap in the draperies he could see sunlight as if diffused through grey glass, and a strip of black cloud scarred white around the edges. *Rain*, he thought; *good god, it's going to rain.*

But the only chill he felt was the one that coasted along his skin, tightening it, making him shudder to send it away.

He forced a groan for the sake of his conscience, jammed his knuckles into his eyes and rubbed, pulled, then lowered his hands and blinked until he could see without a laving of tears. His head still complained, but he managed to feel a bit more alive, and could remember what had gotten him here in the first place.

After the others had left and he had gotten control of the fear that had gripped him, he had wandered into the kitchen, had seen an unopened bottle and poured himself a dram of scotch. Back in the living room he had sifted through the magazines again, sipping, puzzling, refilling his glass and sipping.

He had no idea when the thought *herded* first surfaced. He only knew that he had abruptly given up the pretext of genteel drinking and had taken a long numbing swallow straight from the bottle. Later, with the window dark and the air leaden around his shoulders, he had made his way to the bed; sometime after that he managed to pass out.

Now he stumbled into the bathroom, gritted his teeth, and let the shower run hot; thirty minutes later he was shaved and dressed, out in the stable providing fresh water and hay for an impatient Maggie. As he spoke with her, apologizing, he stepped back from the scene and took a close look at the week.

He was right—they were being set up.

It was like the first few days after he had arrived in prison—the stripping away of his civilian clothes, his civilian dreams and attitudes, the brusque and terrifying orientation not only by the authorities but by the inmates as well, and the gradual, horrifying acceptance that for the next several years manipulation and intimidation would be the rules of the game.

But if they were being set up, what was the purpose?

If they were being set up, who was pulling the strings?

Maggie followed him to the paddock, nudging his back in her hurry to have him open the gate. And as he watched her break into a playful, high-stepping canter across the grass, he wondered what part Parrish had in all this.

Breakfast was quick, his movements more urgent as he strode into the study, stood at the drafting table, and stared at the measured lines that would, in time, give birth to a new home. He wanted to work, but the Scotch-muddled thoughts of the previous night returned, maddeningly out of order. He grabbed the magazines from the living room and swept the Branchville design to the floor. With an Exactoblade he sliced out Parrish's photographs and spread them across the slanted board. Then he sat on the stool and stared at them, one after another, rearranging their dated sequences as if playing the shell game.

Nothing changed.

The houses were the same, and Eban Parrish was the same, even as far back as seventy years ago.

Setting aside the impossibility of the man not changing, not aging a day in almost a century, he concentrated first on the duplication of the mansion's basic design.

It had nothing to do with Clark's suggestion of an ambitious realtor—no matter what else he was, Parrish wasn't the type. And it definitely had nothing to do with randomness. Just as there was nothing random about the way he pieced a house together line by line, there was nothing random in the way Parrish was spreading carbon copies of Winterrest across the country.

Purpose here, too; there had to be a purpose. And he was positive it wasn't just because the old man liked the design.

He saw it ten minutes later—the only caption that gave him the name of a town. Flat River, Nebraska.

Spinning around, he grabbed for the telephone book and opened it to the front pages where the area codes were listed by state. There were two for Nebraska, and he stared out the window.

Who would he call?

He knew no one there, and contacting the police to find out if there was a Winterrest estate in or near the town seemed prankish. They would probably hang up on him, after chewing him out for wasting their time.

Who would he call?

He slipped an invisible coin and dialed 308 Information, asked for a listing for Flat River, and when the operator found it his heart paused, started again when she told him no one or no business called Winterrest was located in her territory; when he dialed 402, in case there were two towns with the same name, he was not surprised when he learned there wasn't.

He paced into the living room and back, telling himself there was nothing to worry about, that what Parrish did with his time was his own affair. Yet there was still that growing conviction he was being manipulated, being prepared for something he would not like.

A look to Maggie, then, and he dialed 308 Information again and asked for the local Flat River newspaper, no he didn't know the name, but it was very important and he'd appreciate the help. The operator, friendly enough to joke about his memory, found it after only a few minutes' searching. And before he lost his nerve he dialed, listened for eleven rings, and had decided the office was closed for the day when his silent prayer was answered.

It was a secretary, her turn to cover the phones on Sunday, and she was suitably impressed, and considerably mystified, that he was calling all the way from the East Coast.

"Miss," he said, "I'm trying to locate the owner of a piece of property out there. I'm an architect, you see, and my secretary took a message from the owner on Monday, while I was away."

"You oughta try Information," she said, and suddenly sounded as if she had decided to gargle. "Sorry." She laughed. "Got a Coke here, lots of ice at the bottom of the glass. Straw."

He laughed with her, and tapped the photograph she could not see. "I would," he said regretfully, "but there's a problem. I can't read the woman's handwriting. All I know is, he lives in a place called Winterrest."

Silence; more gargling.

"Miss?"

"Winterrest? Sure, I know it."

He gripped the edge of the table tightly. "You do?"

"Sure, who don't?" She giggled. "Well, I guess you don't, do you, but we sure do. Biggest place around here, 'cepting some of the bigshot farms. There's a party or something out there today, in fact." Her voice soured. "Very exclusive, so I'm told."

Doug sat heavily on the stool. "So you're told?"

"Well, I didn't get an invitation. 'Course, I never had anything to do with them out there, so I don't suppose I should have. Still, it'd be nice, y'know? Keep on good terms with the press and all."

"Yes." The word was forced out; there was no breath left in his lungs. "Miss," he said, "forgive me for sounding stupid, but how big is Flat River?"

"Oh, I don't know. Last count I heard was eight, nine thousand. Not counting the cows." She laughed merrily, an old joke on a new customer. Then he heard a buzzer in the background. "Hey, Mister," she said, "I gotta go. Got someone waiting on me out front."

"But Winterrest—"

"I can't help you there," she said. "Far as I know, Mr. Parrish never put in a phone all the time he's been there."

"And how long has that been," he said mechanically.

"Mister, I wouldn't know. He was here before I was born."

I do not believe in immortality, he thought; I do not believe a man can be in two places at the same time.

And I definitely do not believe in magic.

The telephone rang. He answered with a brusque "Yeah?" and instantly knew Parrish was on the other end.

"Mr. Muir?"

He cleared his throat, and stared at the pictures, one by one. "Yes, Mr. Parrish, what can I do for you?"

who are you?

"I am truly sorry to bother you on such a lovely Sunday, but the offer I mentioned—"

"No," he said heatedly. "No, I'm still not interested."

"I see. Well, that's very good."

More coolly: "Sorry if I've disappointed you."

"Not at all, Mr. Muir. If I were able to accommodate all my clients all the time, I'd be immorally wealthy."

"I know what you mean. Believe me, I know what you mean."

Parrish chuckled politely. "In that case, I shan't bother you any longer. Will I see you later this afternoon?"

Without thinking, he shook his head.

"Mr. Muir?"

He stared at the pictures, at Maggie, at the room. "No," he said. "I have . . . work, a lot of work. I'm afraid I'll have to pass."

"I see." A slow inhalation; bubbling. "I'm sorry to hear that." A pause filled with static. "Forgive me for asking, Mr. Muir, but you're not feeling under the weather, I trust."

who the hell are *you?*

"Fighting off a cold, I think. Nothing serious. But it's not easy to work with it, and I can't spare the time."

"Ah. Well, do take care, Mr. Muir. Things like that have a habit of cropping up and turning nasty."

"I will," he said. "Thanks." Then he pushed at one of the pictures with his finger. "Magic," he said softly.

"I beg your pardon. Magic, Mr. Muir?"

He jerked his head away from the earpiece, not aware he had spoken aloud, thinking the man had already hung up.

"Did you say magic, Mr. Muir?"

"Uh, yes. Yes, I did."

"And why did you say magic, Mr. Muir?"

This is ridiculous, he thought. "Just thinking out loud, Mr. Parrish, that's all. My mind was already somewhere else."

"Ah. Well, if you want my advice, you will put no credence in so-called magic, or in so-called miracles for that matter. It's difficult enough for some people to believe in the living. And perhaps, after all, I will see you later."

"But—"

The dial tone hummed.

He lowered the telephone to the floor, straightened, and chastised himself for lacking the courage to ask the man directly about Flat River. Not that he would have received an answer; Parrish would have denied knowing a thing.

Lying, he thought, right through his teeth.

He inhaled slowly, deeply, and checked his watch—it was after eleven. The instant decision not to go to Winterrest did not, as he'd hoped, lift any burden from his shoulders. If anything, he felt worse, more nervous, and more determined to find out if Liz was right and it was only imagination that was keeping his mind off balance.

Right about now, though, he thought it might be worthwhile to talk to someone like Piper Cleary.

"Funny, but you don't strike me as bein the kinda guy that thinks about things like that. No offense."

Doug sat uneasily on the top step of the Cleary back porch, his hat pulled low as much to keep the cloud-diffused sun from his eyes as to prevent Piper from reading his expression. Cleary himself sat on the browning grass, his three remaining hounds frisking around him, every so often smacking him with their wire-whip tails when he grabbed for their heads to wrestle them to the ground.

"No offense taken, Pipe. I'm just curious."

"Are you, now."

Doug nodded.

Cleary adjusted his deerstalker and squinted at the house. They had passed the pleasantries already, Doug complaining about a mild hangover, Piper commiserating and explaining how Wilbur and Nell had chewed him out for his drinking last night from the moment the sun came up until they had left for the restaurant. They were worried, he said acidly, about his being decent this afternoon; like they were some kind of gentry instead of folks who made their living slinging hash and breaking eggs.

When they were settled, however, a can of beer passing for the hair of the dog in their hands (Piper obviously having begun treatment long before Doug arrived), he waved his free arm at the estate hidden by the trees behind him.

"I've been sayin it for years, y'know, but people don't like to hear it. Y'know, like hearin a son or a husband or somebody's died, they say it can't be, they only saw him last week. If they can't touch it, smell it, taste it, they don't know it.

"Me, now, I got the woods. I got my hounds, and we tramp all over the damned place, we see things back in there you'd never think in your whole life'd be true."

"Like Sitter's witches," he suggested, anxious to have the man stay on the subject. And not at all sure he wasn't a little crazy himself for listening to all this.

Piper drank deeply, belched with a glassy-eyed grin and shook his head. "Nah, not like that at all. Sitter's a good man, don't get me wrong, but his head's not exactly screwed on right. Take me, f'instance. Would you believe I used to be a hell of a big guy?" He lifted one arm, palm parallel to the ground. "Not big that way." He spread his arm wide. "That way. Two-hundred-and-fifteen pounds of solid flesh. Then a doc says I gotta lose or I'm dead before I'm sixty. So I lose. Now I got all this skin and nothin to put in it.

"You believe that, Doug?"

He sipped at the beer, trying not to grimace. "It is hard to believe, Pipe, you have to admit it."

"Sure it is, but it's true. What you see ain't the real me. The real me is as fat as a pig." He emptied his can, and opened another. "Now, do you believe in God?"

He leaned away from the odd question. "God?"

"Yeah," he said, pointing at the sky. "You know. God."

"Well . . . I suppose so."

"You believe in the Devil?"

"No." A quick answer, no thinking required.

"Wrong," Piper answered sternly. "It's like the woods, Mr. Muir. Everything's got a reason for bein there, and everything that's there has a shadow. You got sparrows and hawks, you got mice and bobcats, you got all that stuff. You also got God and the Devil. It don't make sense to believe in one without the other. You got your good, and you got your bad, it's as simple as that."

No argument was offered; he only pulled at the beer and nodded for the man to go on.

"Now that house back there. I been around a long time, Mr. Muir, and I notice things. I have to, it's my business, bein a hunter and all. And I really can't prove it—that is, I ain't got somethin I can pull outta my pocket, so you'll have to take my word for it— Winterrest is a demon place, sure as I sit here."

He squinted to see if Doug was laughing; he wasn't—he was listening.

"See, it goes back to the beginning," he continued, shifting until he was sitting Indian fashion. "You read that report thing from that fella down in Princeton?"

Doug nodded; he had.

"Well, it goes back to then, I think. The way I see it, that professor that found out all those things about Deerford and the house, he wasn't really listenin to what he was hearin. Talked to a lot of the old folks, the ones that keep the stories, and he picked what he wanted to and ignored the rest. Me, now, I hear it all, I hear the details, so to speak. That man that built that place, after all that terrible stuff happened to his family, he knew the land was cursed. Don't laugh! Cursed is what I said, and cursed is what I meant. There are places like that. You travel enough, you can see them all over. Places so damned ugly they look like God shat on them he was so pissed. Places, too, that look so beautiful and *no one's there*. Now the first ones, it makes sense you don't do anything there. I mean, who wants to live on a garbage heap, so to speak?

"But the second sort of makes you wonder. Such a lovely spot, peaceful, maybe a stream, some trees, but it could be a desert for all you find there. You can't even find a robin huntin worms.

"Yep, it really makes you wonder."

Doug emptied his can and leaned back on his elbows.

Piper pushed off a hound with a good-natured oath and slapped his deerstalker against his leg before yanking it on again.

"Now, when this long-ago guy got here, there wasn't anyone on the land. Lots of folk around with their farms and things, but no one here. Great property, worth a fortune. Right on the coach road, looks to be good farmin, but not one of the others took it. Now this new one, he doesn't notice, he just wants a place to live 'cause he's been travelin a long way, so he builds.

"It has to do, you see, with the living and the dead."

Doug sat up: *it's difficult enough for some people to believe in the living.*

Piper emptied a third can, opened a fourth, and took half before taking a breath. Doug didn't want to guess how many the man had had before he'd arrived, and he was puzzled by the sudden indulgence.

"A man that lives out here away from everything, he knows about living. The crops, the trees, the animals, all that stuff. Now the fella that built Winterrest, he's from the city so to speak in those days, and he don't notice that no one else had farmed the land, not even the Indians that was still around. Then all those terrible things started to happen, and it just stands to reason, don't it, that he wasn't gonna let any of it stop him."

He paused, eyes glazed, mind drifting. Belching, he shook his head.

"Now in those days, the best way to fight was to have yourself a fort. A wood fort was okay, but a stone fort was a damn sight better. Which he went ahead and did 'cause he knew how. What he didn't know, though, was that the demons that had cursed this place were gonna make him and everybody else crazy. He probably figured he could beat that curse with plain old hard work and a lotta sweat.

"But there were bad winters that time, and the way I see it, he just went crazy. Cabin fever. Killed his family, saw what he'd done and killed himself he was so miserable. And the demons that made him do it just never bothered to leave."

A sharp nod; the point finally made.

"Mr. Muir, on the other side of that wall there be demons, and there have been since who knows when. It's just cursed, like I said. And because that sap built his house there, it got itself cursed too."

He hiccoughed, belched, lay on his back, and stared at the sky while his hounds sniffed around his side.

"Demons, Doug ol' boy, and we're gonna have tea with 'em this very afternoon."

He didn't comment, but rose with a sheepish grin and asked about the bathroom. Piper waved him grandly toward the house. He pulled open the rusted screen door and stepped into a kitchen of cracked linoleum on the floor and white metal cabinets on the walls. The bathroom was to his immediate right, and he hurried in, shut the door, and leaned heavily on the sink while he ran cold water.

He splashed his face and shook his head at his reflection. Douglas, ol' boy—

And he couldn't finish; he couldn't tell himself it was all a madman's crock.

Instead, he gaped at a yellowing snapshot tacked to the wall by his shoulder. It was of Piper is his deerstalker cap, looking as wasted as he did now, not a day older or a pound thinner. He was standing at the gate that led to Winterrest, and right beside him was Eban Parrish. Remembering a habit his mother had, he pried up the bottom corner with one finger and looked for a date.

He found it just above center, in ink almost faded to gold.

It was June, and the year was 1935.

221

2

The suitcase lay open on the bed. The drawers of the maple dresser were pulled out, the closet door was open, and two pairs of boots and a pair of shoes lay on the mattress. Doug strode in from the bathroom and dumped a double handful of toiletries into the suitcase, then turned to the dresser and began to grab for socks and underwear, tossing them behind him, not checking to see if they landed in the case.

His movements were smooth, almost practiced, but the muscles in his wrist and neck were strained to cords, and there was a mask of perspiration forming over his face.

A folded shirt dropped to the floor, and he paused, stared, then kicked it under the bed.

1935

He stuffed as much as he could into the case, belted and snapped it closed, and left the room to stand by the gallery rail. Below, the speakers hissed, nothing on the turntable, nothing on the tapedeck. He looked at the beams, the walls, remembering with choking clarity the mess he and Piper had made getting everything into place without it falling on their heads.

Flat River

The debate was over. Manipulation had somehow been shaded into threat, and the merely unusual had taken on hues of the preternatural. He didn't know if such a thing existed. But after he had seen the photograph, his mind rejected hoaxes and the normal.

What was left, though he had no name for it, frightened him too much for him to remain.

He took the stairs down as fast as he could, dropped the suitcase by the door, and hurried out to the paddock. Maggie trotted over to the fence and nuzzled his hand while he stroked her neck.

"I'll be back for you in a while," he said. "If I don't, someone will be over to take care of you until I do."

The buckskin tossed her head, snorted, and raced off with tail high, and Doug couldn't watch. He spun around and ran back inside, swerved into his study, and began gathering his designs into a large briefcase.

The telephone rang.

He ignored it until he had all he wanted, then snatched it up, listening for the bubbling husky breathing that would tell him it was Eban Parrish.

"Doug?"

He almost collapsed on the floor in relief. "Liz, hi!"

"Doug, I thought you were going to call me."

Confusion dropped him onto the couch. "Hey, I'm sorry. I don't remember, though—"

"You didn't promise," she said. "I just thought . . . I just thought you'd call, that's all. You were kind of spooked last night."

"Pot calling the kettle black, Liz."

"Yes," she admitted. "And I'm still not going. Have you made up your mind yet?"

He tugged at an earlobe, felt the weight of the luggage behind him. "In a way, yes. Look, I'd like to come over for a minute if I can. Do you mind?"

"No, of course not. What's—"

"Be there in five."

He rang off before she could ask him anything, and was out and into the Jeep before he could ask questions of himself. At the end of the Lane he waited impatiently for a line of cars to pass, noting as he did the thickening overcast that sagged here and there to touch the tops of the hills and create a fog that blurred the foliage. The breeze was not yet a wind, but it was ambitious enough to turn the leaves over and prophesy rain, turn the cattle's backs, and send the crows into sporadic flight, wheeling like buzzards before settling on fences to watch the traffic darkly.

He took advantage of the first break and spun east, tempted to stop and have a word with Sitter, to see what excuses he would make for Winterrest; but as he approached the lawn chair and the waving left hand, he changed his mind. Piper was drunk and Sitter was probably crazy and the only thing that would come of it would be further confusion.

For the first time in years he forgot to wave as he passed.

And it wasn't until he had turned into Meadow View that his breathing eased and his hands calmed. The Mohawk Gang was playing touch football in the front yard, and they waved as he hurried up the walk. Keith yelled to him over the shouts of the others, but he didn't hear it; he pushed the bell and turned to follow the game, such as it was with two kids to a side.

Normal, he thought; god, it's all so normal.

Liz opened the door and stood alongside him. She was smiling, though the smile did not extend quite as far as her eyes.

"What's up?" she asked.

"Liz, this morning I had a talk with Piper, and I got to thinking about . . ." He paused and shook his head. "I started packing. I was going to run away and knew I couldn't, at least not without seeing you first."

"Really?"

"God, Liz, c'mon."

She took his hand, then, and led him around the side of the house, stopped near the back, and told him, "I'm scared, Doug."

He shifted his hands until they were in his hip pockets, one hip cocked, one foot slightly ahead of the other. The game in front was loudly reaching its climax.

"You frightened me last night," she continued, "and you're frightening me even more. Here," and she pressed a fist to her temple, "I know you're nuts. I know I am for giving credence to anything we've said about Parrish and the rest. There are always adequate, if not always perfect, explanations for just about every phenomenon around here, including Eban and his infernal love for a single house. And that's good. I know that if I sat down and thought about it hard enough, I could come up with an answer that would satisfy all the criteria. I could go in front of a jury and acquit Parrish in an afternoon, for whatever stupid crime we're determined to accuse him of."

When he lowered his head, the shadow of the hat brim buried his eyes.

She faced him, and she was angry.

"But I *haven't* been able to sit down, Doug. I can't sit down! Not for more than five minutes at a time." She jerked her gaze to the sky. "I haven't been able to *think,* Doug. I can't *think* straight anymore, and I don't like it! And now you're going to take off, just like that. Just like," and she snapped her fingers hard, like a gunshot.

He almost lost his own temper when, quite unexpectedly, she stepped close to him, took his elbows and pulled him into an embrace. Tenderly. Fearfully. Until the Gang appeared at the corner of the house and he released her quickly, moving back until she looked over her shoulder and saw them.

"Go away," she ordered, too loudly. "Go!"

The Gang exchanged puzzled looks, and vanished in an excited whispering.

"Liz," he said when they were alone, "you didn't let me finish."

"Upstairs." And they climbed to the redwood deck. He sat at the round plank table while she fetched Dr Pepper from the refrigerator. The sky lowered; the breeze died; the air felt as cool as the can of soda in his hand.

"Finish," she told him, her eyes glinting with a hint of tears.

The words came, but slowly, as he told her about Piper's demons and the photograph he had seen in the Cleary house.

"We are," he said, looking over the lawn, "two perfectly normal people in a perfectly normal town. At least I thought so until the other day. Now, I'm not so sure. I was packed to leave an hour ago. Until you called." His smile was sardonic. "There are times, you know, when I have to be hit rather smartly with a two-by-four to straighten me out. I couldn't leave and not see you. In fact, if you stayed, I couldn't leave at all."

"Doug—"

He waved her silent and fussed in his jacket pocket for a cigarette. He lit it, and watched the smoke hang in the air, dissipate so slowly he still saw it until he blinked. Then he leaned over the table, his forearms a triangle with the push of his stomach.

"Look," he said, and wasn't sure precisely what he would say, "I've decided to go to the party this afternoon." He avoided her startled look, took a drink of soda, a puff of the cigarette. "I have to, I think. I've done a lot of traveling, as you know," he said wryly, "and I guess what I'm saying is, that it's about time I stopped. Something's going on around here. What, I don't know, but it affects us, and only us, and since there's no guarantee it'll stop if I, or we, leave, the only way I'm going to find out is by going there and talking to Parrish."

"Why him?"

"He . . ." He stopped. "He knows, Liz. I don't know why, but I know he knows."

"What about Piper's demons?"

"Piper was drunk."

He isn't always drunk."

He swirled the soda in its can, blew smoke, blew air, and pointed at her. "I do not believe in demons, Liz. I do not believe in demonic possession or spectral domination or centuries' old curses on houses."

"You didn't believe in earthquakes in New Jersey, either. Or gale-force winds that don't hit anyone but you. Or women who get five months pregnant in a week, if that's what really happened."

"Touché," he muttered.

"Touché what?" she cried in frightened frustration. "I don't even know what the hell I'm talking about."

"In that case," he said calmly, "the way I see it, there's only one way to find out if we've suddenly gone crazy, which I doubt very seriously—we go to that damned party and see if there's someone here who's trying to pull our strings."

She shook her head and looked away, one hand drumming on the table. "Do you want to?"

"Do I have a choice?"

"Yes!" she said. "Of course you have—you just don't go. You—"

"What, Liz, ignore it? Pretend it's all the product of my poor, overworked imagination, that none of it is happening? Or should we just move away and try to forget it all?" He stared at the house and cursed the losing of his temper. Then he directed his gaze back to her, and lowered his voice. "Liz, Parrish called you this morning to be sure you weren't selling."

She said nothing.

He leaned closer. "That is no coincidence, I know that now. For some reason, he's made sure that neither you nor I nor Bud and Ollie is ready to give up our homes, even for more money than we've ever seen in our lives. He has made absolutely sure that none of us want to leave town despite the enticement. That means something to him so much so that I can't just walk away without finding out why."

"But he hasn't threatened us or anything," she protested.

"No," he said. And didn't have to say *not yet*.

3

Maggie wandered around the paddock, grazing, testing the air, shaking her head and snorting at the presentiment of the storm. She tried running a few paces, and drew herself up; she tried scratching her back on the grass and found it unpleasant. She stood at the gate and stared at the house.

She ran again, and reared to thrash at the air; ran again, and stopped.

Her tail twitched, her mane trembled, but nothing she did brought the squirrels out to play.

She returned to her grazing, snorting angrily whenever she heard the rumbling underground.

4

Sitter McMahon sat alone in the dark.

The television was off, the blinds were all drawn, and the door was as locked as he could possibly make it. He told himself it was a poor day for making people happy, that they wouldn't appreciate his waving at them in all that gloom, and when Douglas Muir didn't wave back he knew it was true.

But he didn't scan the channels for signs of the witches' coming.

Today was the day.

He was safer inside.

5

"Deeeeeeemonnnnnnsssss!" Piper cried from his place on the ground. "C'mon, you goddamned deeeeemonnnnnsssss, this is the Cleary you're temptin, ya goddamned bastards!"

When he felt the ground rumbling, Piper Cleary began to cry.

6

The air was shadowed, but there were no shadows on the ground.

Liz didn't want him to go. *Before you do anything foolish, let's at least check it out.*

The air was chilled, and damp, and the temperature stayed high.

We can't take anything at face value anymore. Let's go to town and see, okay!

Agreement came slowly, and he was ashamed of himself for giving in only when she said she would go with him.

Don't worry. The whole town can't be in on it.

He parked in front of the Depot, and they walked slowly across the street, hands brushing but not clasping. They had considered recruiting Olivia and Bud, but changed their minds when Liz suggested they were probably too involved with sorting out their problems.

The real estate office was closed, its blinds down, the door locked. Doug knocked so hard the glass threatened to break. They walked around to the back, one on either side, and failed to find an open or unlocked window, or a venetian blind open enough to see in. No one they asked in the crowded restaurant had seen Parrish all day, though it was suggested that he was probably at the estate, getting ready for the party. Few seemed to care that it was up for sale; those who did promised support when he mentioned that he might confront the agent with the distress of the community.

"Now what?" Liz said when they were back outside.

"Ollie," he said. "We can't avoid it now."

The Bazaar was closed, and they exchanged worried glances before he knocked, as loudly as he dared. Liz shielded her eyes with a hand and peered inside, and after a long minute saw Ollie weaving her way through the furniture toward them.

"She seems all right," she said, and stepped back as the door opened.

Ollie was dressed in white, all white, from the satin ribbon wound through her single braid to the leather sandals on her feet. Her eyes weren't puffed or red, nor was there despair in her expression. She greeted them lovingly and asked them inside.

"Can't Ollie," Doug said before Liz could accept. "We're on a hunting expedition." A jerk of this thumb over his shoulder. "Have you see Parrish today?"

"Nope. Guess he's making the salad, huh?" She laughed.

"I take it, then, you're going?"

"Oh sure! Why not?"

Liz looked pointedly around her and into the shop. "Is Bud coming too?"

"I don't know," she said stiffly. "He's locked himself in that stupidass Retirement Room and won't come out. I tried half the night, but he doesn't even answer me. Charles Yardley, for all I care, can eat shit for dinner."

Doug kept silent; he was suspicious of her bright eyes and her too-perfect smile.

But he couldn't deny that she was stunningly beautiful, her cheeks shining, her lips moist, her arms when revealed alabaster and unblemished.

Her white muslin top was voluminous, with wide sleeves beautifully embroidered in floral reds and golds; around her neck was a fine gold chain, which dangled hanging between her breasts a small brass sunburst medallion. She fingered it absently, and gave them both another smile.

"I want you to know I've decided you're right, Liz. What's happened to me isn't normal, but it isn't all that unusual, either. It took me a while, but I've pretty much put my head on where it belongs, and I'm not going to baby Bud. Either he believes me or he doesn't. And if he chooses not to, I'll put his ass in the

230

street." The smile broadened. "See you this afternoon, okay?"

And she shut the door in their faces, gently but firmly.

"Well," said Liz as they walked back to the Jeep. "Well, feature that, will you."

"What do you think?"

"You're kidding!" She examined his face closely. "No, you're not kidding. Jesus, she's miserable, can't you see that? She's probably depleted half their stash. If her eyes were any bigger, they'd pop out of her head."

He looked over his shoulder. "No kidding."

She groaned and shoved him into the driver's seat. Then she reached out and held his arm. "Doug, you'll be careful?" She took a deep breath. "Take care, please. You . . . well, hell, you mean a lot to me."

He didn't think about it. He kissed her hard, long, and held her close while he took her back to the house. Then he kissed her again and watched as she walked inside without looking back.

He drove past Hollow Lane and stopped on the shoulder, at the Winterrest gate.

There were no cars in the drive, no tables on the lawn, no sign at all there was a party that afternoon.

He slid out and walked through the grass to the wall, looked down, and punched the stone. He kicked it. He shoved it. He leaned his full weight on it.

Nothing happened.

Then he looked at the house and whispered, "Who *are* you?"

TWO

1

4:00

There was no blue left to color the sky.

The sun was gone, interred as it westered without leaving a shadow.

The overcast had become less of a haze, more of a cloud that was shading to pale grey, spotted with black, smooth and lowering and defining a new horizon. The hills were smoked with drifting fog, the air was autumnal, and the grass almost brittle.

There was only a light breeze, infrequent and tepid.

The crows that had perched on the sagging telephone lines lifted one by one, silently circling, forming an ebony flock that wheeled south over the highway. They made no calls; there was only the muffled flutter of their large black wings.

2

A gold and green canvas canopy was centered directly in front of Winterrest's back door, and beneath the second-story window. It was easily twenty feet on a side, its corners held eight feet above the ground by smooth, arm-thick posts wrapped in gold and green streamers; its edges were scalloped and fringed in pale yellow, its center hoisted to a circus tent peak. At the tops of the poles, and hanging from single linked chains from the inside supports, were brass and teak carriage lamps already lighted, kerosene flames filtered through the amber glass. Beneath the vaulted center were three fifteen-foot buffet tables covered in white linen—two were laden with china plates of hot and cold meats, breads of all descriptions, cheeses, candied and glazed vegetables, and four huge crystal bowls filled with salad greens. The third table held coffee urns, punch bowls, teapots, the plates, glasses, and silverware needed by the guests.

Beyond the tent, arranged haphazardly, were white wrought iron tables open to the sky. The chairs were white as well, filigree and standing slightly unevenly on the uneven ground.

The guests had treated their invitations in an almost formal manner; the women were all in airy summer dresses, many in white gloves and hats, not a single one wearing a pants suit or anything provocative or remotely revealing; the men, though none wore a hat, wore their Sunday best suits of pale colors to white, sharkskin to polyester; more than a few surreptitiously polished their shoes on the backs of their trouser legs.

Their milling and strolling covered the lawn, but the mansion itself seemed oddly deserted, almost aloof from the activities building in its backyard. Its six upper-story windows were blinded by drawn curtains of undetermined color, the four lower ones reflected fragments of the assembly, and the colors of the open-sided tent in darkly muted shades.

Doug stood off to one side, dressed in a green courduroy jacket and sharp-creased tan slacks, glass in hand, eyes narrowed in a thoughtful squint.

He had been among the last to arrive, though he had arrived on time; the gate had been wired open, the front lawn dotted with automobiles, bicycles, and a few newly washed pickups. A delicately hand-lettered sign on the locked front door directed him to the back. Once there, he took several moments to reluctantly admire the studied courtliness of the arrangements and the lavishness of the food. Filling his glass, then, with what tasted like rum punch, he drifted off to the left, away from the hundred or so others who were eating, drinking, and trying to find something else to do.

He was angry.

From the moment he had seen to Maggie and had left the house, he had felt the manipulation, the intimidation, but by the time he had emptied his glass and refilled it halfway, he knew that most of it was directed at himself.

He had wanted Liz with him, to support him, and she wasn't here. Her fearful unease had made her protective of her family, and his own doubts had prevented him from seeing it.

Now he was alone, ashamed he had not been more sensitive, simmering because he was unsure what he should do next. As for his nerves, the house itself was doing a perfect job of setting them on edge.

From the front, Winterrest seemed perfectly innocuous. It was a large stone house, nothing more and nothing less. But here, in back with the others, he felt something else, an undercurrent that linked the guests in a way he did not understand, in a way that let him out.

And even as he watched, that link grew stronger.

The party, though somewhat subdued at the start, seemed now to be a success. Stage-whispered gossip flowed, greetings were pleasant and enthusiastic, and suddenly he was caught up in passing conversations that courtesy dragged him into, and polite smiles pulled him out of. Wilbur and Nell Cleary, who had evidently catered the affair, spent most of their time bustling in and out of the house to replenish the plates and urns; Gil Clay, in a pink polo shirt and blinding white slacks, hovered around the last table, sipping at the punch and smacking his lips for all the world like a baffled wine taster; Wanda Hallman, unashamedly obese and bleached a platinum bouffant blond, stalked around the fringes, cornering everyone she could to

234

ask if they had seen or had word of her ne'er-do-well husband. Farmers' families tended to stick together; those who lived in town split up almost as soon as they arrived.

Only Piper Cleary and Sitter McMahon were conspicuous by their absence.

Go home, Doug, he thought then; go straight back to the wall, climb over, and go home.

It was a thought so tempting his hand began to tremble, but it was also one he could not obey. He had knowingly opened the door behind which *something* lurked, not because he was stupid (though he might be, at that), but because if he didn't, he would have to start running. And once started, there was, as he'd told Liz, no guarantee he would ever be able to stop.

Or that he would ever be able to get away.

He heard a familiar voice then, high-pitched and laughing. For a moment he couldn't place it and turned sharply to his right, to the lawn that spread westward. Punch slopped over his hand, and a chill that had nothing to do with the clouds overhead stalked his spine, touched the edges of his lungs.

It was Keith, and the Mohawk Gang, and Heather was with them.

The glass almost fell from his hand. He looked back to the crowd, blinking his confusion, not seeing Liz until she was almost upon him.

She wore a plain, pastel green blouse opened two buttons down, and snug designer jeans that flattered her hips, and were unceremoniously tucked into the tops of new, pointed tan boots. Her hair was ribbon-tied in a loose ponytail, accentuating the high forehead, and the eyes that were at once enraged and dark with fear.

She stopped at his side and stared across the grass at the children. Her lower lip was pulled between her teeth, and her chin thrust out when she tried to swallow. When he touched her wrist, the skin was cold.

"What happened?" he said quietly.

235

The children swerved and swirled like a school of bright fish, and others swept quickly around to join them, yelling, laughing, arms high and swinging. Goaded by the Mohawk Gang and anxious to escape the stringent bounds of party etiquette, they started a ragtag game of touch football, their shouts and groans, cheers and escaped curses considerably louder than the adults' conversation.

"I could ask you the same thing," she said.

"Nothing yet."

"And you," she said bitterly, "are still going to play Gary Cooper, right?"

"I thought you understood."

"I do," she replied with a sad shake of her head. "God, I do now. When I got inside, I didn't see the damned note."

Doug frowned.

"On the kitchen counter," she told him as if he should have known. "They're supposed to put their messages on the fridge with the ladybug. It was on the counter and I didn't see it until fifteen minutes ago." From her jeans pocket she pulled out a wrinkled sheet of yellow, lined notepaper. He took it and, after a glance to the children, read it.

Mom, I really like parties. Heather does too. Summer is very boring. We're going to have fun. Please come.

It almost sounded like a command.

After he'd read it a second time, she took it back and jammed it into her pocket. She started forward, her mouth open to call Keith and Heather. He took her arm gently. She hesitated, started to pull away, then walked with him reluctantly, her head turned to watch her son who, when he caught her eye, waved and grinned and punched his sister's side.

"I'll strangle him," she said.

"Is it that bad?"

Her expression began as disgust, then wavered into the unease he had seen earlier, on the porch. "He's not the same."

He almost stopped. "Huh? What are you talking about, Liz?"

She looked back again. "He's . . . I don't know. Not literally different, I don't mean that. But he's like Ollie. That wasn't really her we saw this morning, you know that, don't you. She wasn't the overgrown flower child who's supposed to marry Bud Yardley. That was an Ollie I've never seen in my life. Keith, he's . . . he's never done anything like this before. He's never deliberately disobeyed me, and then flaunted it. Never. Ever since the other night I don't know him anymore."

Her hand became a fist, and he took hold of the wrist until the fingers relaxed. "Liz—"

"I want to get them out of here, Doug. I want to get them home. And you," she added without pause. "You can't stay here either. I'll bet you don't even have a gun or anything."

He could feel the tension in her arm, could see her eyes widen and dart from side to side, like Maggie when she saw lightning and didn't understand, knowing only the fear.

He lit a cigarette and smiled politely at those who saw them and waved, nodding at those who nodded to him. A stout man in a charcoal grey three-piece suit was orating by the house's far corner, his audience mostly men who jeered and slapped their thighs. Gil was still puzzled by the punch. An impromptu barbershop quartet began singing east of the tent and drew most of the crowd there. The others sat, or wandered, but no one entered the house.

"Douglas, help me."

He was about to turn, to agree, when Olivia came around the corner from the front, spotted them, and waved gaily as she headed without pause for the tent and the buffet. She was still dressed in white, the breeze filling her blouse now, catching the sleeves and pulling them back along her arms. Her hair was unbraided, tangling itself, weaving, flowing like a sable banner that made half the men stop to stare.

237

"It isn't polite to drool in public," Liz said dryly.

He grinned and poked her side, relieved she seemed not about to lose control, at least not yet. She poked him back and shook her head. "Douglas, for god's sake, don't you feel it?"

He did, and was relieved it wasn't his imagination. Now if he only knew exactly what it was, he might be able to do something about it.

"Doug, let's go home."

His answer was delayed when Judith appeared in the doorway.

She wore a loose-fitting peasant blouse that exposed a generous portion of her lightly freckled chest, and a dark blue skirt stiffly pleated and girdled by a wide-ribbon gold sash. A dark green ribbon wound through her black curls like a laurel wreath; her feet were bare.

He waited; she didn't look.

"Doug," Liz said, "let's go home, please? Let's forget all this and get the kids and go home."

"Let's take a walk," he said instead, extending a hand. "Don't worry about the kids. They'll be all right for the moment. Come on."

She took the hand without arguing, and they strolled away from the party, away from the house toward the back of the estate. The flat of the lawn ended fifty yards along, where it began lifting into low swells separated by troughs running with twilight, swells that eventually merged with the slope of the hill behind and the hollow where Douglas lived and Maggie waited. They stopped at the first rise, and he pulled her down gently to sit beside him. He raised his knees and wrapped his arms around them; Liz stretched her legs out and leaned back on her palms.

"View from the top," he said, though they weren't that much higher than the lawn they faced.

She didn't smile. She only said, "Well?"

When he didn't respond immediately, she reached into his jacket pocket and pulled out the pack of cigarettes; when she had one, he lit it without moving his gaze from Judy in the doorway. She appeared to have recovered from the night before, he thought; yet she still made no attempt to establish eye contact with him even when she looked in his direction. She appeared not to be in the slightest bit of trouble. It wasn't an act. She was perfectly normal, just looking for someone else, and all others had been blocked out until she located who she wanted.

The Mohawk Gang, led by Keith and a red-faced Heather, sprinted toward the open-sided tent, only pausing long enough to wave at them and pantomime a starving man eating before running on again.

"I swear to God I'll kill the little bugger," Liz said, almost rising. "If his father were alive—" She cut herself off, and lowered her head.

He ran a gentle hand along the plane of her back, and decided that she was right and he was wrong. Whatever was here, whatever had brought them here, wasn't worth the pain; it certainly wasn't worth the pain he heard in her voice. And startled by the value he had suddenly given her feelings, he almost laughed with delight. He was about to grab her shoulders, turn her around and tell her, "I love you," when she said, sharply and without warming, "Look!" and pointed down at the party.

When he did he saw nothing out of place. The singing was still in full flourish though not always on key, the buffet was still under attack, and the white lawn tables were filled now with animated conversation. Staring, he searched for a face, saw neither Clark nor Bud—but Ollie was in the midst of a group of young men, laughing and tossing her hair as she let out all the flirting stops.

"Try harder," she said.

"I don't get it."

"Try!"

"But Liz, I don't even know what—" And he saw it. It was in the movement of the guests.

Before, they had been stilted, almost timid, their voices low and respectful in the shadow of the all too familiar house; now they were shifting about in abrupt, oddly static stop-and-go patterns, rarely remaining at ease in one place for more than a few seconds at a time. Conversations were interrupted or broken off in mid-sentence, plates and glasses were returned to the tables half-empty, hardly touched. The voices carrying in the still, warm air were tinnier, louder, the laughter more explosive, more raucous, and once in a while couples and singles would hurry through the back door, and return a minute later with strained smiles on their faces and their eyes averted. A word or two, and they headed for their cars.

Restive; high-strung thoroughbreds being led to the starting gate.

"It seems," he said with an enforced calm, "as if the big moment is arriving."

He looked over, and Liz's face was strained. The skin was drawn taut over her cheekbones; her lower lip was pulled between her teeth, her eyes were narrowed as if she were trying to see through a dense fog.

"Liz?"

She pointed.

The party had come to a complete halt.

Judith had left to join the others, and now Eban Parrish was standing in the doorway.

3

5:00

The overcast had thickened perceptibly and laced itself with black, the air was darker grey and still, and the lanterns dangling motionlessly from their chains under and around the tent were crystalline bright as if a mist were trapped inside them. The door was closed. All the windows were black now, reflecting nothing.

"Doug, we can still go."

"No," he said. "No, not now."

And the anger returned, apprehension replaced by a silent promise to end once and for all the manipulation of his life.

He rose awkwardly and pulled Liz to her feet. They took the slope slowly, watching as Parrish, smiling and nodding, walked toward the tent. The others closed around him expectantly, nervously, the barbershop quartet cut off in mid-verse by a matron's imperious scowl. The kids had already grabbed their food and drink and were streaking back to the site of their game; no one raised a voice to stop them.

Parrish stood in faint shadow just beneath the canopy's fringed overhang, his back to the mansion, his hands folded loosely in front of him—a respectful and humble speaker waiting patiently to be recognized. He smiled blandly as the townspeople who remained filled in the gaps between the buffet tables, waiting until the shifting for position was completed, the accidental elbow knocking a cup or a platter placed under control. Someone coughed; someone blew his nose; someone hastily crushed a cigarette under his heel.

Doug and Liz stopped at the back of the crowd, and she gripped his hand, hard.

"Winterrest welcomes you," the realtor said. He seemed to speak in a normal tone, but there was no one who had to crane to hear his words. "May I assume that Mr. and Mrs. Cleary have done their usual fine job?" He paused for a smattering of self-conscious applause to fade with the breeze. "And of course, our equal thanks to the Depot and the lovely proprietress, Miss Lockhart, for the, shall we say, slightly spicey punch?" Again the applause, this time laced through with polite laughter.

Doug couldn't see Judith; he imagined she was grinning.

Parrish cleared his throat.

The overcast lowered.

"I will make a third assumption, if you will permit me." He glanced around the crowd blindly, not caring

241

about eye contact, enveloping them all with a single sweep of his head. "I imagine you have heard by now that certain highly interested and well-financed parties from outside our little community here have made certain inquiries into the availability of Winterrest—for purchase, that is, not for rent." An uneasy stirring; less people knew than Doug had suspected. "I assure you the respectable concern engaged in these preliminary exploratory inquiries has in mind turning this wonderful old estate into a—how shall I put it?—into a—"

"Development," Doug said loudly, ignoring the sudden yank on his left arm, ignoring the alarm he felt by blurting out the word before he had time to think.

Parrish stretched without taking heel or toe off the ground. Heads turned; there was whispering.

"What was that?" he asked, a slight frown on his brow.

"The word you're looking for," Doug said, shaking off Liz's hand. "It's development. As in Meadow View."

"Perhaps, but hardly a common one, Mr. Muir," Parrish said without a single change in intonation. He paused, and blinked once. "The generous people who will eventually live here should this matter be concluded in the way they wish, will be used to a standard of living quite naturally above what the rest of us are accustomed to.

"As for Winterrest itself," he continued, now addressing the guests generally, "it will be something like but definitely not your usual hotel. A clubhouse, so to speak, with accommodations for overnight guests. These magnificent lawns will be completely preserved, except for those sections utilized as a golf course and a relatively small number of tastefully contemporary townhouses and condominiums. I expect, my friends, that as time passes quite a lot of business will be done with the town proper."

"Rich or middle class," Doug said just as loudly,

"it's still a development. High-toned, ticky-tack, no matter how you slice it."

Heads swiveled again, the whispering more intense and the looks frankly quizzical.

Liz yanked his arm a second time, cautioning him with a frown to watch what he said. He didn't mind the attention, however; Parrish had forced him into speaking out before they could get him alone and make known their objections; and though he saw little support among those facing him, he also did not sense any outright condemnation. They were annoyed with his behavior, not with what he said.

"The interested parties," Parrish said, with a nod to note the architect's objections, "have made this little gathering today possible, in the hopes that you will not dismiss their plans out of hand. They wish you to understand they are neither hostile nor indifferent to your feelings, nor are they desirous of creating any ill will among you."

"Where are they, Mr. Parrish," a man's deferential voice asked from the crowd. "Do we get to meet them today or what?"

"In time," Parrish answered warmly. "In time, sir, in time you will see."

"What are their names?" another wanted to know. "Are they from around here?"

"In time," Parrish repeated. "For now, let me say only that the duly chosen representatives in this matter are myself," and he ducked his head modestly, "and the legal firm chaired by Mr. Clark Davermain, of Newton."

Liz gasped softly; Doug's puzzlement grew.

"Mr. Parrish," said Nell Cleary, "what's this all gonna do to our taxes?"

Wanda Hallman wanted to know if traffic was going to choke up the town, and did anyone know where the hell Bernie was?

A woman Doug recognized as Archie Mancuso's mother worried aloud that an influx of new citizens might mean they would have to start building schools, which would raise their taxes and force the creation of a school board which none of them, at the moment, were qualified to man.

Doug was pleased. If the agitation in the air was as real as it sounded, he may have at least solved one problem today; and if not solved, he had at least driven it out into the open where it could be properly examined. Parrish, however, seemed unaffected by the barrage of questions and comments that grew steadily in volume.

The canvas above began snapping sharply at their heads; the breeze had returned.

Liz hissed when he cleared his throat. "Mr. Parrish," he said, shouting over the heads of the people in front, paying little heed to a woman who wanted her chance to put in a word, "would you mind telling us who owns this place? Who hired you and Clark Davermain to deal with this so-called concern?"

"Excuse me, Mr. Parrish?" Judith's unexpected voice was clear, and unforced, and turned Parrish's gaze away from Doug's eyes. "Mr. Parrish, excuse me, but isn't this a matter for a town meeting? You really should have asked for one, you know. This honestly isn't the time or the place to spring something like this on us. It smacks . . . well, it kind of smacks of coercion, or bribery, you know."

Jesus, what the hell is she doing? Doug thought, craning to find her; what's she trying to prove? Though it appeared as if she were merely consolidating the objections, what she had done was to rob the infant fire of its fuel.

Parrish, meanwhile, accepted the remarks, and their respectful echoes in the murmurs filling the tent, with evident good grace. A brief lowering of his head in acknowledged guilt for a misstep in procedure, raising it again with the first smile Doug had ever seen on his face.

"Our Miss Lockhart, as usual, gets straight to the

point. I will attend to it straight away. Meanwhile, may I suggest we do not insult our host by ignoring all this fine food and drink? You may stay as long as you like, and of course the house is open for your inspection and delight. And please," he added, a palm raised in caution as the gathering began to fray at the edges, "do please be careful once you are inside. I must ask that you neither bring cigarettes in nor light a match once through the door. Winterrest is expressly preserved as it was in the beginning; we certainly don't want it to think we are clumsy bulls in a china shop."

There was laughter and applause, and Doug stood with Liz as the others milled around them, averting their faces now, not bothering to stop to either decry or declare. He had expected one or the other and was braced for it; he was not prepared to feel the complete absence of caring. It was as if they had been told there was rain in the forecast—any fool can see that, all he had to do was look up.

Within moments they were alone. The buffet was deserted except for a few stragglers, the rest heading for the tables and chairs, to watch the renewed ball game, or to the queue up at the doorway for their Parrish-guided tour.

"Son of a bitch," he said helplessly. "Can you beat that?"

"Doug," said Liz, "have you seen Ollie?"

5:30

It's marvelous, Ollie thought in headspinning delirium, her cheeks aching pleasantly as if they were about to split open; it's absolutely and totally fabulous! I'm making a fool of myself.

But she didn't stop grinning, didn't stop giggling, couldn't get over the way the men rushed to fetch her food, rushed to fetch her drinks, ate her up and drank her down with their eyes while she stood there in the middle of it all and could feel them, just feel them straining and panting against their little-town morals. Any of them, would have gladly emptied his wallet just to get her alone in the house; any of them would have cut off his right arm just to be able to touch the swell of her breasts.

Oh god, it was beautiful!

And that damned sonofabitch ought to be here now, ought to be taking notes on the way his imaginary rivals suddenly weren't very imaginary anymore. He ought to *be* here, damnit, to see the way they treated her, to see the way she played peekaboo with her hair, squared her shoulders to position her breasts, stretched the thin muslin over them so they could see, if they looked closely, the lace roses on her bra and the dark shadows of her nipples.

Oh Christ, the bastard ought to be here!

If he needed a father for the kid so damned badly, he could take his pick of half the town.

She drank, then, and ate, and let her constantly changing escorts do most of the talking; she felt her cheeks flush, her neck grow warm, and decided as Parrish came out of the house that she really should go stand with Doug and Liz in case they thought she was pissed at them, too. They had tried their best to make things easier for her, tried to show her how wrong she was to get so hysterical over . . . well, maybe not exactly nothing, but not the end of the world, either.

It definitely wasn't the end of the world.

God, it had taken her hours last night to find the right screws for her head, the right way to reset it so she was thinking straight for a change and not having bastard Bud do it all for her. Hours and hours, and now, though she wasn't drunk, she was feeling no pain and feeling the best she had since . . . since God only knew when.

She covered her mouth with a palm to stifle a guilty laugh. If Bud had thought the goods were tainted before—him and his damned paranoia flushing it down the damned toilet—he should see the colors her secret stash was giving her now: all those greens sometimes so bright they made her eyes water, all those golds shimmering and swimming on the circus tent, all those incredible blacks up there in the sky, like holes opening onto the soul of the universe, showing how it really was and whispering to her that she knew more than she thought.

All the colors, all the sounds, and the beautiful feeling that her stomach had grown, that she was much like a woman only days from her term.

For a moment, when Doug first interrupted Parrish's speech, she felt a twinge in her abdomen and shook it off as too much rum and set her glass down—it was too soon for the kid to do anything but swim around in there and have himself a good time before the world crashed into sight.

By the time the speech was over (it was too bad she hadn't heard any of it), there was this nice man who looked a lot like Judy's bartender in the godawfulest pink shirt and silly white pants who seemed determined to hand-measure the circumference of her waist and the diameters of her breasts; he breathed something she couldn't understand into her ear that made her lungs fill with fire, made her head giddy, and she was about to turn around and introduce herself when the twinge came again.

She winced, swallowed a moan, and ran a soothing hand over the swelling.

It was bigger. God, it *was* bigger.

The twinge became a streak of pain across her gut.

She gasped and grabbed hastily for the edge of the nearest table, shaking her head when Gil Clay asked if she needed any help. It would be all right; all she had to do was find a chair and stop her damned drinking. Christ, she'd have to remember she had a kid to watch out for now, and all this slurping the sauce wasn't going to do her a bit of good.

There wasn't a chair nearby, and the pain arrowed up her spine and into her brain. She whimpered, and whispered Bud's name, looked around to find Doug, to find Liz, and found herself staring into Eban Parrish's eyes.

"My dear Miss West, aren't you feeling well?"

Her brave smile was replaced by a squeak of pain. She shook her head.

"Oh my poor dear," he said solicitously, his eyes abruptly filled with concern. "Well, we certainly can't have you giving birth right here in the middle of the party, can we? Good heavens, I shouldn't think so. It's much too soon, am I correct?"

"Yes," she said, and almost added "mummy,' but he was being so kind she swallowed the word instead.

"As I thought," he said, and put an arm around her waist (funny how strong these little guys can be) and took hold of one hand (funny how cold those fingers can be). Smiling, and murmuring unintelligible words of comfort, he guided her across the lawn and into the house.

The central hallway ran the width of the mansion, and before she could protest, he had brought her closer to the front, the wall on the right plastered and divided with thin pale beams above black walnut wainscoting, the wall on the left painted white and faintly marked with fingerstreaks of dust. The light was dim but not uncomfortably so, glowing from glass-globed gaslamps now harboring light bulbs in the shape of quivering candle flames.

"Mr. Parrish," she managed at last, "I'm all right now, really."

He shook his head at her display of courage. "You young women these days certainly do have your stamina. But," he continued with a raised finger, "may I be presumptuous enough to suggest a short rest before you attempt the walk home? After all, you must think for two now, isn't that correct?"

"Well . . ." She supposed he was right, after all. A little too much attention, perhaps too much of that punch. She guessed it wouldn't do any harm at all to lie down for a while. A nap. Until the dizziness went away and she could stand alone again.

"Fine, that's fine." His voice was eager, two hands scrubbing each other.

They climbed the narrow staircase to a landing which branched left and right to a hallway above. The stairwell was encircled by a low oaken balustrade, and she leaned on it at his direction while they made their way to the front corridor and turned right, where he opened the front door.

"Oh . . . my," she said, blinking away the light from the single high window. "This is . . . weird."

The room was small, its ceiling low, the bed Parrish indicated stretching out from the lefthand wall barely her size. A wood canopy extended over the frame, a red and black quilt covered a thick mattress. A mahogany wardrobe took up most of the space beside the door, a straight-backed chair next to the window the only other piece of furniture in the room.

There were no pictures on the walls, but cracks in the plaster formed faces and creatures and rivers of shadow.

"They were, as you can see, much smaller in those days than we are now," he explained as he assisted her onto the bed, fluffed the pillows and waited until she lay prone. Her ankles rested just on the footboard. "Even I, who am certainly not very tall by today's standards, feel obliged to duck each time I enter one of these little rooms."

She looked to the window—the sill-length white curtains had been tied back, and she could see the wall, the highway, and the trees on the other side. The sky was considerably darker, gloom spilling through the panes until Parrish turned on the light switch. It wasn't much better, there was only one wall lamp beside the door, but it helped. She smiled her thanks.

"I shall leave the door open for you, of course," he said solemnly. "And I will have Mrs. Cleary—I think you kow Nell, don't you?—look in on you in half an hour. I would hope that by that time you will be feeling much better."

"Yes," she said. "Yes, thanks."

Her eyelids felt uncommonly weighted, sand scraped at the corners, and she astonished herself by yawning the moment the old man left her.

"Too much," she said quietly. "This is really too much."

She yawned a second time, and tears filled her eyes.

Damn you, Bud, she thought, punching the top pillow with her fist; damn you, you should be here taking care of me instead of that funny little man. Damn you, Charles, you bastard. Jesus, Bud. Jesus.

She was almost asleep when she heard the walls groan.

5:30

"Cluck," said Ian Backster delightedly. "Cluck, cluck, cluck, cluck."

"Shut up, creep," Keith grumbled. "Shut your face before I smash your glasses."

"Keith!" Heather scolded.

He shrugged; he didn't care. They were all being stupid, and it was all Archie's fault. The football game had just broken up, and they were sitting in a tight circle on the lawn, plucking at the grass and muttering dark oaths at the other kids who had been called away by their parents—either to go home, or to take the stupid tour through the stupid house. There didn't seem much point in playing anymore with just the four of them—Heather really didn't count because all she wanted to do was be the referee so she could stand on the sidelines and look for Archie's big brother, Barry—so they had dropped where they stood, listening to the wind gathering itself for a big blow off the hill behind them. Then Archie had decided it was time they took a tour of their own. They could go in the front way, he said as he scrambled to his fat knees, his stomach almost lying on his fat thighs. Everybody else was hanging around the back and who would notice, right? It was a big place, right? They could hide in closets and stuff and scare the shit out of the old folks.

Dirk was eager, as was Ian, who couldn't stop bouncing. Heather kept looking over her shoulder for Barry, so it was up to Keith to talk them out of it.

"Cluckie, cluckie," Archie sneered.

Ian giggled.

"Hey,' Keith said, "who's the chief around here anyway, huh? Who's the—"

"Oh, dry up," Dirk said in disgust. "Boy, as soon as someone else comes up with the neat idea, all you can do is play the big man, like you know everything that's going on. Well, I think it's neat, and I think we oughta do it."

"Yeah," Ian said, eyes wide behind his glasses. "We could moan and groan and do all kinds of things like that."

"In broad daylight?" Keith said. "Are you kiddin? They're gonna know it's us. It ain't gonna work."

Archie puffed his cheeks, shook his head, and shrugged at the others. "He's a chicken, what can I say?"

"I am not a chicken," Keith said, keeping his voice low. "But if we get caught in there by Parrish the creep, he gonna ream our asses good."

"Keith!" Heather snapped. "Watch your mouth."

"Oh pardon me," said Archie, eyes wide and rolling. "We gotta lady present, Keith. We gotta watch our terrible language."

"You kids make me sick," she said, pushing herself up and brushing off her jeans. "I'm going back." She took a step away, and looked back. "Maybe Maggie is hungry. Maybe I'll just go over and feed her."

That was for Keith, who thought of the buckskin and nearly changed his mind to join his sister. But he hesitated too long, and Heather tossed her head and walked on.

"Be sure to say hello to Barry honey," Dirk sang, one hand on his hip. "Give him a big one for Archie."

She paused only long enough to brandish a fist at them before stalking over the lawn toward the house. It was enough, however, to drop the Gang into hysterical laughter. They rolled, they kicked at the air, they called Heather's name and asked her what she and Barry did when they were out in the field after dark and thought no one knew they were being watched. She ignored them. Eventually they quieted. The sound of starting engines drifted toward them from the front yard.

"Shit, man, everybody's leavin," Archie complained, sitting back on his heels. "A bummer, y'know?"

"Don't matter," Dirk said, pulling at the grass. "The food stunk."

"Gee, I kinda liked it," Ian said. Dirk scowled at him and he sighed. "Well, I guess it wasn't all that great," the boy admitted quickly. "I mean, it wasn't all that great, right?"

They sprawled. They stared at each other. They rose as one and looked around listlessly.

The sky darkened, clouds lowered, and Keith noticed the field of stars trapped around the tent, noticed as well that every light in Winterrest had been turned on. Most of the adults were gone from the lawn.

whispering

a darksoft voice, whispering

"Got an idea," he said, keeping his voice calm.

"Great," Archie said grumpily. "What do you want to do, go wash old man Parrish's car or something? I still wanna go in the house and scare some old farts."

"I think we oughta go see what's back there, in the trees," he said.

"What trees?" said Ian, peering myopically around.

"I ain't climbin no wall," Dirk said. "Besides, we've been on the hill before. Unless," he said, suddenly brightening, "you mean we sneak around to Muir's place and get his horse or somethin."

"Hey," Archie said brightly. "Hey, okay!"

"Gee, I don't know," Ian said, sniffing and pushing at his glasses. "I don't know. My mother wouldn't like that. She'd kill me, you know? If I was caught in the Hollow, she'd kill me. She says Mr. Muir's a—"

"No," Keith said. "We're not going there, and we're not climbing any walls."

"Then what the hell trees are you talkin about, idiot?" Archie said.

"Those trees over there, stupid," he said, and pointed to the heavy stand of hickory and birch, oak and willow that dotted the rise behind the spot they had made into their playing field earlier that afternoon.

Dirk looked, and scratched his head. "Where the hell did they come from?"

"UPS came by. They were just delivered," Keith said. "Boy, what a stupid question."

"But I don't remember—"

Suddenly, Archie grabbed Dirk's arm and pointed. "There!" he said breathlessly, leaning forward, squinting. "Over there. Did you see it?"

"What?"

Ian stood close to Keith, frowning but saying nothing.

"A lady," Archie said, already starting forward. "I saw a lady back there. Maybe," and he grinned, "we'll see somethin good."

Before he could be stopped he was trotting away toward the trees, Dirk hesitating, then following. Keith made to join them, and was stopped by Ian's hand.

"What's the matter?" he asked kindly. "They're only trees, Ian. They won't hurt ya."

"But they weren't there before," he said, wincing as if expecting to be hit. "They weren't there, Keith."

"Sure they were," he said, slapping the boy's arm lightly. "We were playing, you just didn't notice them, that's all."

"My mother—"

"—won't even know you're gone. She's looking at

old stuff in the house, right? Old chairs, old forks, old fogies." He laughed at Ian's grin. "See? We'll find out what Archie spotted, then come right back, okay?"

Ian was still doubtful.

"The chief says it's okay." He glowered, and pursed his lips. "Unless you want a torture, kid."

Ian relaxed. "Okay, chief." They had covered less than ten feet, however, before he stopped Keith again. "What did Archie mean, about seein that lady doin stuff?"

"I don't know. He's got a dirty mind. She's just probably pickin flowers."

Another twenty feet.

"Keith, there aren't any flowers there. Like there wasn't any trees."

Keith looked down; the darksoft *whispering* made him smile.

5:30

In the VW, Bud waited patiently on the bare shoulder while a handful of cars, two pickups, and a station wagon loaded with kids pressed through the gate and headed back for Deerford. Two of the drivers waved to him, one calling out with a harsh laugh that he had probably missed all the best goodies, but he only waved back and smiled inanely and raced the sputtering engine until he was able to pass through. He parked beside Douglas's Jeep, had his hand on the door latch and one leg lifted before he froze. He was too anxious to get out; he would create the wrong impression if he plowed straight into the mob, hunting for Ollie. He had to calm. He had to get hold of himself and be absolutely calm.

He had left the Retirement Room only when he heard Ollie slam the front door, and he couldn't believe it when he saw her walking boldly up the street toward the highway, all dressed in white like she was some kind of bride, her hair loose and licking at the air, her hips swinging back and forth like she was advertising herself to the first man who'd look.

And they'd look; damn, he knew they would look.

He had shouted at her wordlessly, impotently, then walked around the counter by the door and pulled up the loose floorboard to expose the safe they had had embedded in a steel-lined concrete sheath. The combination came without him thinking about it, and he didn't pause until he had the canvas bank sack out, the lock opened, and the money from the week's sales in his hand. She had been at him for days to deposit it before they had a robbery; he had procrastinated. Why should he go when he only had to drive back just to get the household money? That wasn't the way you did things, she had said. But he hadn't gone, and now he was glad. This money, even without counting it, was going to take him a long way from Deerford, and the woman who had betrayed him.

He had taken his time dressing.

Then, while he was wandering through the apartment, saying goodbye to a bench that he discovered meant nothing to him, he thought about taking the bankbook too, and decided that was being too cruel— Ollie being the expert would know all about that—and drove the VW out to the county road.

He didn't notice Sitter wasn't in his usual place.

He saw a blinding white Mercedes pull into the drive and recognized it as the one belonging to Clark the lawyer. He made no attempt to call when the big man slid out, straightened his tie, and walked around the side of the house. He didn't care. Clark the lawyer was someone who was less than a ghost in his life.

Time, he thought. No more stalling.

He opened the door and got out, closed it quietly, and looked with frank amazement at all the lights burning in the house. It made him think of Casey, and made him wonder if Lockhart had had enough of this place, too, and had taken off for better parts. He smiled. Casey, he thought, was more than likely still out on a drunk, or hung over in a cave somewhere.

The first thing he had to do was find Parrish. He had decided that Ollie probably wouldn't sell the Bazaar on a bet, and he would have to disappoint the old man, apologize but explain nothing.

Then he would find Ollie and tell her goodbye.

He faltered.

That was going to be harder than he thought. Six good years down the old tubes. Maybe he should be more charitable. Maybe he should give her a second chance.

But she's pregnant. She's been pregnant for five months, maybe more, and she didn't tell him a thing.

Fuck her, he thought, and giggled—somebody sure as hell did.

A minute's thought, and he decided to forget her. She didn't need a goodbye, or a smile, or even a wave as he drove out of her life. She obviously didn't need anything about him.

Hesitantly, then, he began to search for Parrish and get it over with so he could get the hell away. But when he walked into the yard and saw the few remaining people—where did they all go, for crying out loud?—he could not shake the feeling they were all staring at him, pointing at him and sniggering. Muffling a cry behind a sweat-slicked hand, he ran back to the car, slumped over the roof, and clenched his fists against his head. Stupid; he was being stupid. Jesus, did he really want to leave Ollie, Deerford, the shop? Deep down, did he really want to go? Maybe it would be better if he just went home. He could leave the keys on the dash so she wouldn't have to walk, and he could walk back himself.

He needed time to think again; he needed time to decide.

You'd be lousy in a corporation, Yardley, he thought as he started up the drive; you can't even decide when it's time to take a shit.

At the gate he reached down for the latch, and his hand cracked against stone. Blinking, he stepped away and looked down.

"Damn," he muttered, and looked left and right before he knew he wasn't dreaming.

The wall was there, but it was unbroken, and shoulder high.

4

6:00

Ollie was nowhere to be seen, and Liz finally grabbed for Doug's hand. "Well, that was just wonderful," she said flatly, pulling him steadily away from the tent. "That was really great." She refused to release him when he tried to yank away, and stopped only when they were clear of the few people still hanging around the depleted buffet. "Do you have any other great ideas up your sleeve?"

He knew full well he had erred in trying to antagonize Parrish. At a town meeting the discussion would be, in the long run, much more profitable. But at least, he said, more people are aware now than before of what was going on; that in itself can't be all that bad.

"Oh no," she agreed, but barely. "But you saw the way that man handled them, didn't you? By the time he gets through with them at the meeting—if it ever happens, which frankly I doubt—he'll have no trouble convincing them it's the best thing that ever happened to Deerford, if not the world."

He glared at the ground, kicking himself for losing control, and waited for Liz's complaining to fade. When it did, they stood side by side and searched again through the remaining faces for signs of Ollie. He was puzzled now; she should have joined them by this time.

A breeze shoved his hair down over his eyes. He snapped his head back and fumbled for a cigarette.

257

The breeze was too steady; the flame wouldn't stay lit long enough for him to catch the tobacco.

"Hey, take it easy," she said in weary apology, stroking his arm with one finger. "I'm just getting frustrated, that's all." A disturbed glance at Winterrest, at the windows blinking as shadows passed behind them.

"Yeah," he said. "It's the day and—"

"It's strange," she said quietly, as if she hadn't heard him, "but I get the terrible feeling someone's watching us."

He understood, covered her hand, and squeezed it. "I think it's time. We'd better find the kids and leave."

Her head moved; it might have been a nod.

He looked then for the ballgame, and it was gone. There was no one on the grass, no one near the trees. When Liz saw where he was looking, and saw the empty lawn, she scowled, and put her hands to her face as if to keep the muscles there from jumping too hard.

"Inside," he suggested when she began turning in a slow circle, searching for her children. "I'll bet, knowing the Gang, they went inside for a little mischief-making. You go check there, okay? I'll look around out here. If you find them, tie them up and stick by the back door until I get back."

She didn't smile. She hesitated, then whispered angrily, "I'll kill him," and hurried off, slipping neatly through the short line at the door with an apologetic smile and soft words he could not hear. He watched for a second the space where she had stood, on the verge of deciding to go with her on the off chance she might be in trouble; then he shook it off and walked slowly around the tent toward the lefthand corner of the house. It was still bothering him, and while he would indeed keep an eye out for Ollie and the children, he decided to check the house once more. Just once. To see if it was only a trick of the light.

On the south side he was alone. He wiped his hands against his trousers before brushing them lightly over the weathered grey stone, feeling, testing, until he had covered nearly fifteen feet of its length. The window-sills were just at eye level, but he did not look in. He was waiting for the oddity to make itself clear, and just as he reached the corner he had it.

He shook his head, and rubbed at a temple; not only was it unlikely he had missed it all the times he had been here before, it was impossible.

A voice called his name urgently.

He leaned closer, his nose less than an inch from the stone, and he poked, pushed, traced a thumb along the wall.

'Hey, Doug!'

He looked to his left, annoyed, and saw Bud running toward him.

"Doug, hey!"

Backing away from the house, he waited, looking sideways at the sprinting younger man. Here too was something out of kilter, something about the way he charged and the way his hands punched at the air. He closed his eyes, opened them, and realized the per-spective was all wrong. Bud seemed too far away, yet it was only seconds before he was holding onto the edge of the house, hair matted over his brow, chest swelling for air.

"Doug," he gasped, swallowed and shook his head. "Doug, something's wrong around here."

Doug took his shoulder and gripped it, shook it gently. "Take it easy, Bud, take it easy."

Bud grimaced; it was supposed to be a smile.

"Okay, what are you talking about? What's wrong?"

Bud pointed vaguely behind him. "The wall." He tried to stand, then fell back against the house, his hands pressed hard against his sides. "Look at the wall."

"All right, take it easy," he said again, smiling nervously. "God, you're a hell of a mess."

Bud shook off the hand and pointed. "Goddamnit, Doug, will you look at the wall!"

He looked, looked away and back, and saw what Bud meant—the wall was six feet high now, and the gate was gone as if the stone had grown together and sealed them in. He took another step back and scanned its length as far as he could see through the grey gloom of the lowering clouds. Mist freckled his cheeks, and he brushed at it impatiently. The breeze ruffled his hair damply.

"No," he said automatically.

"I tried," Bud said, breathing easier now. "It's no trick, Doug. That wall . . . it's changed!"

Doug waved weakly. "It couldn't. Not in just a couple of hours. My god, do you have any idea how long something like that takes to build? Do you have—"

"Jesus!" Bud grabbed him roughly and shoved him forward. "Then go look for yourself, damnit! The friggin wall has grown!"

He stopped himself after a dozen running steps. From here the stone looked black and shining, as if muddy water were trickling off its jagged top. Then he felt a rumbling beneath his feet and blinked his astonishment as the wall stretched even higher.

It was no illusion; the wall was growing.

"Jesus," Bud whispered beside him. "Jesus."

He put a fist lightly to his mouth while he tried to think, dropping the hand to rub at his chest thoughtfully while he returned to the house and leaned against it.

"What is it?" Bud asked, unable to look away from the wall.

Trapped, Doug thought; we're being caged in.

"I don't know," he admitted. "But take a look at this while you're at it."

Bud stared at the place where Doug's hand rested, frowned, and shook his head. "I don't see anything."

"Look again," he insisted. "Look down this side, especially at the blocks, and where they join the windows."

Bud balked. "Hey, Doug, what's going on? We got a

260

. . . a thing out there, some kind of wall that's growing like a plant, and you want me to . . ." He stopped when he saw Doug's expression, shrugged resignedly, and stopped to examine the greystone blocks, the juncture at the sills, and window frames as high as he could see. His hands quivered the entire time, and with every step he glanced over his shoulder at the glistening black now rising high enough to block all but the tops of the trees on the other side of the road.

"There are no seams," Doug said flatly.

"What?"

"Seams," he repeated fiercely. "There are no seams there, goddamnit!"

Bud jumped, and quickly reexamined the stone—where mortar should have joined two large blocks just under the center window there was only seamless stone. He looked at Doug, looked back and checked again, this time bending to peer under the sill's overhang. His hand rested against the frame to balance him, and it was several seconds later that he looked up in amazement.

"Doug."

"Yeah."

"Doug, that's not wood, that's stone."

"Yeah, I know."

"But that's impossible, right? I mean, even for the old days, that's not right."

Doug nodded shortly, then turned on his heel and started for the wall. He broke into a sudden run and didn't stop until he had to fling out his hands to prevent himself from crashing headlong into it.

It *moved*.

He leapt backward, spun around, and ran a few steps toward the house, then spun again and charged the wall. He jumped, and just managed to get a grip on the tooth-like projections that had sprouted along the top.

It *rippled*, it *moved*, and it tossed him to the ground.

No, he thought; no.

Bud knelt beside him, helping him to sit up. "It's a trick, I guess," he said, his calm desperate. "Right,

Doug? Some kind of trick. Hydraulics underground, that kind of thing. A shaft the wall comes up when someone inside presses a button." Doug lurched to his feet. "What I can't figure, though, is what they did to the gate. Unless the wall's hollowed out over there, see, and the gate just slides in." He brushed manically at Doug's shirt. "A trick. Hell of a neat one, too. Scared the shit outta me."

Doug heard the man's voice, but he didn't hear the words. Instead, he began walking stiffly toward the back lawn, Bud babbling at his side, almost skipping once to keep up as Doug moved more quickly.

Once on top of the first rise, he took a minute to gaze at the far corner beyond which lay his home, then he turned and faced Winterrest.

"Hey," Bud said, puffing up to join him, "I think I oughta go get Ollie, y'know? I mean, this is really somethin she oughta see, don't you think? She likes stuff like this. She really does. She really oughta see . . . Doug, what the hell are you looking at?"

"There," he said with a jerk of his head.

Above them, the overcast had begun to strip away from itself, streams of languid dead white drifting out of the black, specters of fog dancing alone with the wind. The lanterns on the tent swayed, the lights in the windows turned amber and brightened.

"There," he whispered to himself. "There."

Knowing now what his examination had showed him, the building altered itself to accommodate his new persepective: rather than seeing an extraordinarily skilled stonemason's perfect cut and fit, he saw Winterrest as a single block, one massive stone out of which had been carved windows and doors; a sculptor's masterpiece.

Or one of Piper's demons.

Sitter's witches.

His first thought was the most terrifying, and it tore at his throat like a burr: *it's alive*.

"Now that's crazy, man," Bud said as he started back down the slope. "You've got to be kidding. It's hydraulics, I told you. Man, you must've gotten some of Ollie's stuff, right? Or you got some of your own."

Doug realized he had spoken aloud, knew it was crazy, and knew that if Winterrest wasn't alive, then there was something in there that was.

"Hey," Bud called, "why the hell did somebody leave this out, huh? It's gonna get ruined, for god's sake."

Doug rubbed his face hard with both hands, feeling relief as the blood rushed to his skin. A startled look around at Bud's yell, and he saw Yardley trotting over to a dark form far to the left, where the rise sank and met the flat of the lawn. He took a step forward, and saw a tall chair sitting on the grass, ornate and massive as a throne, with lion's paw feet and armrests that scrolled under toward thin carved panels. Bud was running now, shaking his head at the stupidity of people who didn't know what they were doing, and Doug watched numbly.

That chair hadn't been there before.

He would have seen it; Liz would have seen it.

And it hadn't been there when he and Bud had climbed up here to look at the house.

Bud reached it, walked around it, threw his hands in the air and kicked at the ground. "Can you believe it, Doug?" he shouted. "I mean, can you just believe it? Jesus, this thing here is worth a fortune!"

Doug looked at the house.

"My god!" Bud exclaimed incredulously.

He looked at the chair.

"Jesus!"

"Bud, no!" he yelled.

Bud ran a loving hand over the chair's outline, purring to it, grinning at it, finally turning with a flourish and dropping onto the seat. He continued to caress the armrests until he paused, looked at his hand and looked more closely at the chair.

"Hey, Doug," he said, clearly puzzled. "You know something? This thing's made of stone."

"Bud, *no!*" he screamed.

He broke into a frantic shambling run, angling toward Yardley and waving his arms frantically. Bud only looked up, however, waved back, and was about to stand when his face suddenly flushed, and contorted with pain. The chair's armrests were unscrolling, winding upward, inward, snaring his hands in a loop that pushed them toward his chest. He shrieked as his wrists snapped like dry twigs. Doug yelled helplessly, and the chair's high, triptych top curved outward, downward, the center steeple aiming for the middle of Bud's head.

He was thrashing now, and screaming, pleading shrilly for help, for God or Doug to save him; but Doug was slipping on the damp grass, going down on one knee, propelling himself forward, going down again while the chair began to rock, and to sink into the ground.

The steeple reached the top of Bud's skull, and pierced it; the flanking peaks pressed against each cheek, and crushed them; his arms were folded over his ribs, and shattered them.

Doug heard the screams gurgling and sputtering into silence, saw the thin trace of blood that split from the bridge of the man's nose. Then he fell a third time, less than five feet from the chair.

He couldn't get up. His legs would not hold him, his eyes would not look away as the chair quivered and rumbled and Bud stared at him, eyes red and bleeding, stared at him as the chair sank below the surface.

Staring at him.

Begging.

Until a banner of fog floated out of the black and covered the hole.

Doug threw up.

There was no stopping the violent contractions, the pockets of warm acid that boiled into his throat. He crawled away from the spot where Bud had vanished, coughed, and lost all he had drunk since arriving at the party. Tears welled and slipped over and drenched his cheeks; he crawled again, shaking his head like an animal in pain, rolling onto his back at last and staring at the sky too dark for the hour. He could feel his mind scrambling for cover, for protection against the insanity he had just witnessed, could feel his heels thumping the ground as if snapping out the last vestiges of an epileptic fit, or a violent dying. Strips of fog continued to separate from the overcast; mist tickled at his face. His mouth opened to swallow the moisture, and swallow the air that had been punched from his lungs.

Not true, he thought; not true, not true.

An hallucinogen in the drinks, or in the food. Of course it was. It had to be.

But years ago it seemed he had touched the front wall and it had *moved,* and he had just tried to climb over it and it had *moved,* and Bud had been seduced by a wood-stone chair and had been crushed to death and dragged into the ground. That had not been his imagination; he *knew* it, just as he knew now that Winterrest was not populated by vengeful demons or used as a witches' haven; there were no ghosts that haunted or spirits that possessed; he didn't know how yet, and didn't know why, but Piper had been closer than he knew when he'd said the place was cursed.

He dried his face with a jacket sleeve and pushed himself to his hands and knees. A sobbing gulp of air cleared his head, and he looked out over the lawn into the windows of the house.

Parrish would know.

Parrish knew it all, knew everything, and had known it from the beginning.

And Doug suspected that the beginning was at least three hundred years ago.

Swaying to his feet, he staggered across the grass, not looking back, not wanting to see where Bud had died.

Winterrest welcomes you: my god, a literal invitation?

we don't want it to think we're clumsy bulls in a china shop: not a slip of the tongue, and not a reference to the men supposedly interested in buying the place.

It.

The house.

Winterrest.

He reached the tent and fell against one of the poles, the lantern above banging softly against the wood. Staring at the doorway, seeing the townsfolk crossing from one room to another, he wondered if some of them knew, and if so, how could they stay so goddamned calm?

His breath came slowly, came loudly, a wondering for a moment why Bud had to die? Then his eyes opened wide: Casey? Bernie Hallman? Jesus, Piper's Dumpling?

He couldn't think.

Jesus, he couldn't think!

None of this was logical, none of it rational; and he could not resist the ghastly feeling that it all made perfect sense, or would as soon as Parrish told him what the hell was going on.

He slipped a hand wearily over his eyes, dragging moisture from his brow, and looked at the house again. A dark figure stood in the doorway, backlighted in flickering gold. Using the pole for balance, he straightened, and gnawed briefly at his upper lip when Eban Parrish stepped outside and began walking toward him.

A faint rumbling like thunder, and Doug looked up and around the tent's fringe.

It was like peering into a caldron filled with black smoke: the clouds rolled, wove, dove into themselves, every so often casting forked tongues of dull white into the wind that curled them around the chimney pots on the roof, danced them around the corners of the house.

A faint rumbling like thunder, or an animal's growl lodged in its throat.

He pulled his gaze away to avoid a sweep of vertigo, and watched as Parrish approached. The man walked past him calmly until he was standing under the tent, a long table between them.

"Who are you?" Doug asked, his voice rasping.

Parrish, in his three-piece suit, his hair darkly plastered down on his skull, smiled and opened his hands. "I am who you see."

He shook his head. "Bud," he said. "Bud Yardley."

Parrish—voice bubbling, inhaling like a man taking a breath before a dive—allowed him a smile at the corner of his mouth.

"I see."

"Well, I don't, damnit."

Parrish inhaled, hissing. A shadow in spite of the lanterns above them.

"Shall I begin at the beginning?"

Doug clung to the pole to keep his legs from collapsing.

"But you know the beginning, don't you, Mr. Muir. At least, you know some of it."

He nodded. "The stonemason—"

"Ah yes," Parrish said, drawing out the word and nodding to himself. "Yes. He was a bright man in many ways. Not so bright, however, when he refused to listen to his neighbors. They warned him, you know. They told him to stay away from this place, to move on, it made no difference in which direction. But he had already been driven from one home, and he was not about to be driven from yet another. Poor man, he did not believe in curses, he did not believe that life is not something restricted to flesh and bone."

"You talk," Doug sneered weakly, "as if you had been there."

"Patience, Mr. Muir. Patience."

The canvas slapped the air; the tent fringe writhed. He sagged against the pole again, and shook his head violently to clear it of Bud's image, Bud's pleading staring eyes.

"He believed," Parrish said softly, "in the *rightness*

of his life. He truly believed that nothing would ever harm him again if only he believed hard enough, and worked hard enough. A splendid man he was, no matter how misguided. He took the stone for his house from this very field. He loved it, the stone; for a while he was so frantic to give his family shelter that he *loved* the stone. It was his savior, Mr. Muir. It soon became his god."

Doug felt the demand rise: who the hell *are* you?; and he knew the answer: *patience, patience.*

Parrish glanced idly toward the house, then clasped his hands behind his back. Rocked once on his heels.

The tent billowed and groaned softly.

"It came a time, Mr. Muir, when the stonemason would not permit anyone but himself to work on the house, or even to quarry the stone and block it. He was obsessed. He was fighting, you see, for his life on many different levels, and each night before he retired he would walk around the house and give each block he had carved his personal blessing. For him it was not blasphemous, because he did not believe in God."

A sad shake of his head.

"He should have, you know. He really should have. For, a belief in God would have taught him, at the very least, that there are other forces in this world besides the forces of good. Any god would have done the job, and had he believed, he would have believed in places like this.

"He would have believed, you see, that there is life that blossoms, and life that is static; it is the way of things. He would have realized, in time, that his care had . . . shall we say altered the material he worked with?

"He would have seen the development of life, Mr. Muir. He would have felt the changes in the stone. He would have felt, and he would have believed."

"Clap if you believe in fairies," Doug said bitterly.

"If you like, Mr. Muir, if you like."

Doug's left hand wiped at the foul taste that had

settled on his lips. An urge to spit became a swallow instead. "The stone . . . is alive," he said.

Parrish lifted an eyebrow: *if you like*.

"And this place is cursed."

"Cursed, damned, an oversight of Creation—call it what you will, Mr. Muir, but it exists. You know it exists. Life in places like this is static, and patient, waiting for the right person to feed it, and to let it grow."

"Who are you, damnit!"

Parrish winked. "The man's name was Parrish. Eban Parrish."

Doug had seen too much; it was impossible not to believe.

"You?"

Parrish surprised him again. "No, Mr. Muir. The name I have is only a convenience, nothing more. I am—"

He raised a hand, an old hand, over his head, curled it into a fist and smiled again. Then the hand descended sharply, smashing against the table and splintering the wood. The table collapsed, plates and cups and silverware clattering and shattering onto the grass.

When he held the hand up again, there was not even a bruise.

"I am Winterrest, Mr. Muir."

If it grows, Doug thought, it demands to survive. And to survive it needs contact with the creatures around it. In this case, people.

Parrish nodded: *very good, Mr. Muir, very good*.

And . . . oh my god my god . . . if it grows, it needs nourishment and strength and therefore food. Food. Jesus, it needs to eat. All the time? No. It doesn't move, it doesn't travel. So, only sometimes. Every three or four decades enough to sustain it, and to let it live until the next time.

Like everything else, it just wants to live.

Parrish stepped through the rubble, and Doug shied away, keeping the pole between them.

"What else?" he said, curiously less frightened now that he knew what he was facing (though a part of him still screamed that he had finally lost his mind).

Why me? he asked silently, with his eyes.

"You love it here," Parrish said simply. "You would not give up your house, and you would not accept a most handsome profit. You love this place as much as Eban Parrish did." Inhale. Hissing. "You are not obsessed, naturally, but you are willing to fight to preserve. In that way, you are little different than I, don't you think?"

"I don't destroy innocent people!" he said, nearly yelling.

"You killed a man, Mr. Muir."

"It was an accident, damn you!"

"Besides, Mr. Muir," Parrish said as he walked a circle around him, his eyes focused on Doug's, his head swiveling to keep the contact strong, "Besides, how many people do you think would live in Deerford if every so often half the population disappeared?" His lips quivered, and his sudden smile was knowing. "How many, Mr. Muir? How many would stay?"

"Wait a minute," Doug said, staggering to the next pole. He looked at the house, and back to the old man. "Are you saying that those people willingly went in there to die?"

"They cannot die, Mr. Muir, if they are already dead."

The pole turned to ice in his hands, and his breath to acid in his lungs.

"They are not aware of it, of course, and some do not return. A few have an inkling of . . . strangeness now and again, and I do have a few friends who are fully aware and do not mind it at all. Not, you see, when they consider the permanent alternative. No, they do not mind when they realize what they have."

"Judy," he whispered.

And Parrish only smiled as he stood again in the doorway, and turned his head slowly.

"Wait!" He reached out a hand almost pleading. "What about Piper and those rocks? What about the earthquake, the gale—"

Parrish raised a silencing palm as the light behind him dimmed, and grew stronger.

"Mr. Muir, when you wake up each morning to a bright new day, you stretch and groan, you rub the sleep from your eyes, you test your muscles before you leave your bed. You flex, Mr. Muir, to be sure all is in order."

Doug swallowed, thinking of Maggie in her paddock, striking out against the wind.

"And when you have awakened, Mr. Muir, and are ready to engage your schedule for the day, you need a bit of breakfast, don't you? A spot of lunch, nothing heavy. Just a little something to tide you over until dinner."

The bile rose again, and Doug grabbed for the last pole, slick from the mist that fell from the writhing clouds.

Parrish sighed; he was growing bored with it all. "As for Piper's brief travels—and Sitter, too, I might add, though neither really remembers, it's much more convenient that way—well, Mr. Muir, is not one of the prime rules of survival the necessity of procreation?"

Doug gaped.

"Goodbye, Mr. Muir. I do hate to leave you, but I'm afraid it's time for dinner."

Doug pushed away from the tent, reason gone, murder stretching out his hands—and the door slammed in his face. He pounded against the frame, against the door, bellowing at Parrish to let him in, to answer the rest of his questions.

How could he fight, he thought desperately, standing away from the house to stare up at the windows, to stare back at the door; how could he save himself if he didn't have all the answers?

Dead? They're—

Liz!

"Liz!"

And as he grabbed hold of the doorknob, the screaming began.

5

6:00

"Shhhhh!" Archie hissed in exasperation, waving a hand frantically behind him. "For Pete's sake, you wanna get caught, you dopes? You wanna get caught?"

The others crowded expectantly around him and made him squirm, Ian and Dirk at his back, Keith beside him and peering through the staggered rows of trees toward the ghostly white figure that walked hurriedly away from them. They could not make out a face, but its outline when it had passed them was clearly that of a woman. A young woman, and she checked behind her constantly to see if anyone was following.

"Know her?" Dirk whispered.

"Heather," Archie said, and Keith punched him smartly in the middle of his back. "No, of course I don't, stupid," he admitted, "but did you see the size of them melons? Did ya see them? Jeez." Said quietly, almost worshipfully.

"What are melons?" Ian asked. "Hey, Keith, what does he mean about the melons?"

Archie rolled his eyes and nudged Dirk into giggling, and they edged forward again, darting from tree to tree, lining up behind each trunk until the way was clear again. Keith tried to stay by Ian, to reassure him if only by his presence that nothing could go wrong, that they wouldn't get into trouble. The kid had not joined the Gang's other spying missions, and probably

272

wouldn't have understood what they had seen if he had. Keith barely did himself, though he knew most of the language involved; it seemed to him somehow inhuman, more like what animals did in a barnyard than what men and women did on a bed of leaves, or grass, or on a blanket they carried to places they thought no one knew but them.

Archie, of course, claimed to have already lost his virginity (whatever that was), and had unarguably preempted the chief's slot as resident expert in matters like this (whatever this was).

What bothered him most, however, what really made his skin crawl this time were the trees they were sneaking through. He had been trying like crazy since they entered the grove to figure out what had made him direct their attention here. He hadn't spotted the woman yet, nor by twisting his face in a painful attitude of thought could he remember ever seeing this place before.

It was strange.

It was creepy.

Ian stumbled over an exposed root. Keith grabbed for the kid's arm, smiled an *it's okay,* and they ran on tiptoe to catch up with the others.

It was much darker now, the foliage above them dimmed almost to extinction in the deep grey light that softened the rough edges off all the bark, blotted out their shadows, and made the lower branches seem to glitter with dewdrops. The breeze scratched through the leaves; an occasional belt of fog wound out of the sky and hung a few inches over the grass until either the breeze or their feet tore it to shreds.

They could hear nothing, and when Keith looked over his shoulder, he could see no sign of Winterrest or the grownups.

He licked at his lips, but said nothing. This wasn't the time for Archie to see how nervous he was.

"There!" Archie said suddenly, dropping on all fours behind a fat-boled hickory.

They gathered around him, crouching, breathing

273

heavily through their mouths, and finally realizing they couldn't all use the same tree for cover. With emphatic hand signals and a few mouthed curses, they agreed to separate—Keith crawling to an oak only a few feet away, Dirk dropping back to the left to a cage of white birch, Ian staying with Archie not because he wanted to but because there was no way he was going to be left alone in this spooky place.

Less than twenty feet ahead the trees stopped, forming the arc of a half-circle whose diameter was described by the low Winterrest wall. The woman stood in the clearing, looking around as if searching for someone she was supposed to meet here; at her feet were clustered a profusion of waist-high wildflowers whose colors seemed unnaturally dark against the stark white of her dress. She cupped her hands around her mouth then and whispered a name. None of them could hear it. She whispered it again, stepped away from the flowerbed, and hurried to the wall. With her hands braced on top, she leaned over and called into the woods behind.

Archie rubbed his hands on his trousers and grinned, poked Ian's arm, and gave him a broad wink.

Dirk watched solemnly.

Keith couldn't be sure he hadn't seen her before, and wished she would turn around so he could get a good look at her face.

Then she backed away, hands gone in front of her. Again she stopped among the wildflowers, and shuddered when mist was shaken loose by a gust rattling the leaves. Her hair, Keith saw now, was short and black and curly, and she wasn't very tall. A dark green ribbon dangled midway down her narrow back, and it flopped from side to side suddenly, like a garter snake with its head caught in a trap.

Keith blinked, and heard Archie gasp.

The woman was taking off her dress, exposing first the gentle, speckled round of her shoulders, then wriggling side to side to inch the soft white material slowly down the undulating length of her spine. Her back was veiled by diamond droplets of mist, her shoulder blades working, the skin flexing and stretching and rippling and moist.

At the same time, she began lowering herself to the ground, as slowly as she slipped the garment from her body, kneeling in the high flowers, her arms folded demurely over her chest, her fingertips peeking over the lush curve of her shoulders.

Keith swallowed dryly, and looked over at Archie, who was gaping and blinking rapidly, forgetting all about Ian who was trying to ask him silently what was going on. He couldn't see Dirk, but he was sure that he was just as puzzled as the rest of them.

The woman dropped forward now, her gleaming white buttocks rising briefly through the stems before she sank, and the blossoms rocked gently to and fro from her passing, from the wind.

They watched breathlessly.

A white hand rose languidly out of the floral sea, spread its fingers wide, and made a loose beckoning fist before lowering again.

Ian finally gave up trying to get an answer from Archie and scurried over to Keith, pressed his cheek against his shoulder and whispered a question in his ear.

"I don't know," he answered truthfully from the side of his mouth. "I don't have any idea."

"She must be crazy, right? She's *naked*, Keith."

"Yeah, she's crazy."

"I think so, too. She's really crazy."

Ian scrunched closer, standing in a crouch with his left hand against the tree. Keith could feel his breath on the top of his head, and he shook it, pushing an elbow back so the kid would move away. Ian pouted, but twisted until he was looking around the trunk's other side.

"Now what?" he asked. "Can we go back now?"

"Not yet, dope. We gotta—"

Archie hushed them with an angry snarl, brandished a fist and jabbed it at the flowerbed. Keep your eyes peeled, Mohawks, the best is yet to come.

The trouble was, Keith didn't want to see the rest. It was getting wet out here, and chilly, and if that crazy woman was just gonna roll around in a bunch of stupid flowers, he'd rather be back at the tent waiting for dessert. Ice cream, maybe, or chocolate cake. He leaned back as far as he could to see around Archie and catch Dirk's eye. He jerked a commanding thumb back toward the house, tilted his head toward the flowers and made a face of exaggerated disgust. Dirk frowned, then shrugged his agreement though he made no move to retreat.

Archie was on his hands and toes now, knees and elbows bent as he scuttled away from his position. Keith couldn't believe it; he couldn't believe the fat jerk was actually heading for the woman. He wanted to call out, but that would only alert her and get Archie into trouble.

Ian gasped, and stood up in full view of the clearing. "Hey," he said. "Hey, lookit him."

Keith lunged to drag him back out of sight, but Ian jumped away, pointing, making strangling noises as if he wanted to yell and dared not. Keith lunged a second time, and cracked a shoulder against the bark, grabbing at the trunk while he shut his eyes tightly and waited for the pain to pass.

Grabbed it, and yanked his hand away.

"Ian," he said.

Ian shook his head; Archie was almost halfway there.

"Ian," he insisted, and the kid scrambled to his side.

"I'm sorry," Ian said. "I'm sorry.

"Shut up," Keith ordered, took his hand and pressed it to the tree.

Ian struggled, tears filling his eyes because he knew he'd angered his friend and didn't know what to do next.

276

"Feel it!" Keith snapped, and dragged the boy's palm over the bark. "Feel it!"

Ian fought him for half a minute before looking away to stare at the tree, before standing and using both hands to read it like Braille. "I don't get it," he said. "Keith, is it some kind of new tree?"

"Don't be a dope," Keith told him angrily. "The thing's made of stone!"

Dirk couldn't make up his mind whether to stand up, sit down, use a crouch, climb the tree, or get down on his hands and knees and go after Archie. There were three slender trunks to the caged birch, two of them in his hands, one foot propped for support against the back one. He saw the hand rise and fall again, and was positive that this time he had seen part of her bare knee and a white sliver of thigh.

God god god, he thought; Archie, you creep, you're gonna ruin it all.

One hand slipped then and and he fell forward. The side of his head slammed against the white bark, and he bit down on his lower lip to keep the pain and the bright lights inside.

Damned thing's like glass, he thought, and kicked back as hard as he could to teach the tree a lesson.

Archie couldn't believe his luck, and wished Barry were here to see what real luck is. Right out here was this woman taking off all her clothes. She knew he was watching; he could tell. He really could tell. He knew she was doing it just for him, and when that hand came up like that a second time and it waved at him like that, he almost dropped his pants he was so surprised. Now his fingers were hurting from holding up all that weight, but he didn't dare drop to his knees or they'd get all cut up, and he didn't dare stand because then she would see him before he got any closer.

He didn't want to take the chance that he was wrong, and he didn't want any of the stupid guys to come out and get him. That'd be just like them, to screw things up just when he got lucky. Too bad the four-eyed shrimp was along; he didn't know diddly about women, he was too little, and all those stupid questions . . .

The flower bed rose like a wall ahead, and he forced himself to slow down. The light was dim, but he could still see through the stems a jigsaw piece of her skin, white and soft and shivering a little. He licked his lips, tried to suck in his stomach, and after a moment's hesitation decided to try to get even closer.

There was just enough room between the outer stems for him to slip through without much trouble. But he moved slowly, so carefully it seemed as if he wasn't moving at all.

She was there, right there now. He could see more of one leg, and holy Jesus that was her breast he was looking at! There it was, as big as the women he had seen in the magazines his father kept in the bottom drawer of his dresser, under the sweaters. Big. Humongous! Shaking a little, the nipple brown and covered with little brown dots.

He had no idea what he was going to do when he finally got there, but he was sure glad Keith wasn't with him. If he had come, he would have to tell him that he'd been lying about all the virgin stuff, and Keith wouldn't ever let him forget it.

The stems were closer together toward the middle, and he began to lose sight of her as his shoulders pushed them aside, and they snapped back like whips. He swiveled his head to look up at the blossoms, and looked back just as the stems started to sway again.

He hadn't touched them.

They were moving, and he hadn't touched them.

Something slammed suddenly and sharply across his hips. He barely restrained a yelp, and cursed as he swung his head around to see who had gotten close enough to throw the damned stone.

The flower swayed.

278

There was no wind.

He looked ahead again, upper lips curled as he searched for the woman, and again he was struck, this time on the left shoulder. When he looked, something hit him on the right, and immediately on the rump. He couldn't help crying out then, more in rage than in pain, but when he tried to stand up to defend himself he was cracked on the head.

"Hey, damn you, Keith, Dirk, cut it out!"

There were pretty whirling stars—he thought that was only in the cartoons—and there was a pain that brought unashamed tears to his eyes.

He stared, hoping the naked woman in the flowers hadn't heard him, but he groaned when he realized it was no use, she was gone; there was nothing ahead but the damned rattling flowers, and strands of stray mist that slipped between the stems to coil on the ground.

"Aw . . . shit!" He spat, rolled over until he was sitting, and glared back in the direction he'd just taken. "Aw, damn!"

He flung out a hand, and his knuckles struck one of the stems. He opened his mouth to yell, but nothing came out. His fingers closed around the green, and he stared at it, puzzled.

Jeez, he thought, that thing feels like—

A flower slammed into his temple, and he jerked away, cupping the stinging wound with a palm; a flower cracked across the back of his skull, cracked over his right knee, cracked against his arm and he fell back, sobbing, looking and realizing it wasn't Keith or Dirk or even the kid.

A beautiful white blossom raked across his ankle, and he felt the blood flowing.

A soft yellow blossom nearly gouged out his eye, and opened his cheek.

Finally, as he rolled helplessly side to side, finally Archie screamed.

The stone flowers swayed, back and snapping forward.

The stone blossoms beat fiercely and rapidly against his limbs, against his chest, against the forearms that were thrown protectively over his eyes.

He heard Dirk screaming.

And the stone petals sliced easily through his shirt, swiftly through his trousers, exposing the black-and-purple welts that swelled on his skin until they burst into red flowers that ran down his side.

Swaying.

Clacking.

Twisting, and bending, and beating Archie to death.

Dirk saw Archie vanish into the flower bed, and decided that the game was over. Any second now that crazy women was going to jump up screaming and hollering and wanting their blood, and before they knew it their folks would be in here with whips a hundred feet long to take off their hides.

The dumb shit.

He wrinkled his nose in disgust, looked over at Keith and Ian and lifted his hands: *what can I say? The sucker blew it*.

But Ian and Keith were staring wide-eyed at the flower bed. Dirk peered between the trunks, waving a hand in front of him as if hoping to disperse some of the gloom so he could get a better look.

The flowers were moving.

It must have been Archie plowing his stupid way through, but the flowers were moving, swaying back and forth, drawing wider and wider arcs in the air, finally whipping so fast that their colors began to blur, blur and hurt his eyes.

Archie yelled.

Dirk saw a red blossom rise and fall, and heard a spongy thud, another, saw a yellow blossom lash forward and come back up, dripping red.

Archie was screaming, begging for help.

The flowers, Dirk thought in numb astonishment, holy shit, they're killing him!

He lunged forward, pushing hard with his foot off the trunk behind him, and grunted in surprise when he discovered that he couldn't slip out between the boles of the cage the way he had slipped in. There was no time for figuring it out, though. Archie's screams were filling his ears and making his head hurt, and tears were in his eyes as he spun around and tried to get out another way.

Above him, the leaves clattered together; around him the trunks moved slowly inward.

He put his back to one and grabbed another in both hands. And pushed. Red-faced, sweating, spittle bubbling out of his mouth. He pushed again, harder, and his elbows bent inward. Archie screamed. Dirk closed his eyes, lowered his head, and pushed. *Pushed.* Felt his upper arms sliding back along his ribs, felt his legs straighten as the trunks pressed against his knees.

The leaves clattered and fell around him, bouncing off his head and stunning him not with their weight but with their number, leaves of stone cutting his hair, his scalp, rasping the skin from his nose and cleaving his chin.

"Keith!" he shrieked. "Keith! Help, Keith!"

Archie screamed.

The tops of the three birches merged and spilled their leaves, and the trunks began to wind around each other from the crown, turning slowly, grinding, while Dirk shrieked and wept and the ground beneath him rumbled, while the slick stone bark rubbed the skin from his muscle, rubbed the muscle from his bone, and finally closed tightly, leaving only an arm dangling from the center, only a leg kicking at the ground, two inches above it.

A leaf landed on Dirk's shoe, and bounced off, and shattered.

Ian began screaming the moment Dirk did. He jumped around and waved his arms because he didn't know which direction he should take. Archie was out there dying, and Dirk was over there dying, and he couldn't think of anything to do but shout and shake his hands and wonder why Keith was just standing there, staring at him like that.

"Keith," he sobbed. "Keith, we gotta—"

"Shut the hell up," Keith said with a snarl, picking a stone off the ground and shaking it in his face. "Shut up, shrimp, before I bash your head in."

But he couldn't shut up, he had to keep talking, had to keep yelling or else he would hear Dirk and Archie and the way they were crying and the way they were begging and this wasn't the way the Mohawks were supposed to be, this wasn't the way Keith said it would be at all.

Keith threw the stone anyway, and it bounced off his chest, making him stagger back and clutch his shirt. His glasses flew off when the next one came too close to his head and he had to jerk away.

"Keith! Keith, stop it!"

Keith told him to shut up, and though he could barely see, Ian knew it didn't sound very much like his friend. It was a different voice, and he even looked sort of different, and when he picked up another stone, Ian started to run.

There was no trail to follow, but he was always proud of the way he would never get lost because he had what his mother said was a great sense of direction. So he ran, dodging around the trees, listening to Keith shouting at him to come back, come back, it was all right, he wouldn't get hurt if he would only come back.

He ran anyway, shouting until he was hoarse, crying until his eyes dried up and there were only knife-blade sobs that made his chest hurt and made his stomach hurt and made him stumble into the trees that were made of stone.

The ground began to shake then.

He faltered—there's no such thing as an earthquake here, move, move, move!—and ran on, scrubbing the backs of his hands over his eyes so he could see better, not looking back because he knew Keith was chasing him, looking for big stones he could throw that would hurt him. He ran around what was supposed to be a birch tree, and as he passed heard it *craaaack* in half and thunder to the ground just after he left it.

Another one, big and dark, falling right beside him, a branch sandpapering down the length of his back, ripping his shirt into gleaming pink tatters, into flapping bloodied ribbons, making him fall onto the grass because the pain was so bad and he could feel the running wet spreading over his back.

He leapt to his feet when he heard Keith yelling.

He spun around, but he was awake, it wasn't a nightmare and he wasn't home in his bed.

He ran, swerving blindly—I can't see, I can't see! Ma, I can't see!—when yet another stone tree split and splintered at its base and thundered down to crush him. It missed him by less than the breadth of a shadow. Fragments of stone chipped into the air and rained over his head, cutting him, hurting him, making him shriek, and Keith was getting closer and closer and calling his name, it's all right, Ian, it's all right, if you stop they won't hurt you, stop running, they won't hurt you.

The thunder again, the ground shook and rumbled, and Keith suddenly sounded just as afraid as he was—and he couldn't help it, he had to look back because that was the old Keith, the one who was his friend, not the one who wanted to hurt him.

He stopped to look back.

And he blinked.

At the weeping willow behind him, growing and growing and growing and growing and all he could say was "oh" before it slammed him to the ground.

6

Doug thought the screaming came from inside, then heard it again and leapt back from the stoop. He whirled to his right and saw Keith racing toward him through the odd grey light. The boy was waving frantically, his strides awkward as though exhaustion were about to drive him into the ground. He stumbled twice. The first time, Doug started for him at a hurried walk, calling out and waving a hand to show him he was there; after the second, he was spurred into running himself, seeing the boy's fear-widened eyes and the horrid contorted features.

They met in a collision, fifty feet from the house.

Keith in his panic tried to swerve away, but Doug lunged to his left to snare the boy's chest. They fell in a writhing tangle, the boy calling for help until, amid the rolling and kicking, they butted foreheads. The sharp pain dazed them both slightly, but it gave him the chance to gather Keith into an embrace and rock him until he finally quieted down.

"What?" he said then, gently. "What happened, chief?"

"The trees," the boy said, sobbing again.

Doug looked to the estate's far corner, saw nothing but the grass and a hard-to-pierce shadow-wall where the hill behind ended its slope. There were no trees, no shrubs.

"Keith," he said, stroking the boy's hair. "Keith, where's the Gang, huh? Where's Heather? They leave you out there all alone?"

"Heather . . ." He fell silent for a moment, struggling to remember, then lifted his head. "Heather said

284

she was going to feed Maggie. She said she was hungry and ought to be fed."

Thank god, he thought as the boy wiped his eyes and nose with a sleeve.

"And the Gang? Where's the Gang, chief?"

"They . . ." Keith struggled and pushed himself away until he was kneeling in front of him. On his face were blotches of dirt, grass, a straggle of hair that put a crease on his brow. His white shirt was torn at the right shoulder.

"It's all right, chief, it's all right, take it easy." Doug smiled and brushed at the blades clinging like leeches to the shirt. "It's okay, you hear? Just take it easy, take a deep breath and take it easy."

Keith swallowed, but the deep breath turned into another bout of sobbing, though now without tears. "The trees," the boy insisted, peering over his shoulder. "They . . . Archie, Ian, Dirk . . . the trees, the flowers. It wasn't me, it was the trees!"

"All right," he said, and put an arm around his shoulder, climbed to his feet and started walking him back. "It's okay, chief, it's gonna be okay, you just take it easy." A broken record, he thought; a damned broken record.

It's time for dinner

They hobbled across the lawn while Keith muttered to himself and shook his head as if trying to drive something out. The house closed in on them, its amber light in rotoscopic flickering, dropping swatches of gold onto the lawn, reflecting off the underbelly of the clouds still roiling, still peeling off strips of white to test the strength of the wind.

The kids, he thought as they staggered into the backyard, and he lowered the boy into one of the white chairs; Jesus, even the kids. The party feeds the guests, and the guests feed the house. Oh god, those poor kids!

It wasn't a matter of fighting now. He had to find Ollie and Liz and get them all out of here before it was too late. Later, when they were safely beyond the thing's influence, they'd figure out a way to get rid of it if they could. Later, when the nightmare was at arm's length.

He started for the house, and Keith leapt from his chair, jumped around in front of him, and held out his arms.

"Where are you going?"

"Sit," he ordered.

"But where are you going?"

"To get your mother," he explained. "And Olivia. When I do, we'll get out of here and go home, okay? Now stay here, Keith, please."

"No," the boy said, shaking his head and backing away. "I'm not going to stay here all by myself."

"Then you can come—"

"No!" Keith screamed. "No!" He spun once in a direction-seeking circle, then sprinted for the corner, disappearing around it before Doug could take a step to follow. He called out Keith's name, called again and slapped his hands to his head. Which way now? The boy? Liz?

The canvas tent snapped in the wind, the only sound in the yard.

The clouds began to smooth over.

He groaned with indecision, then raced off to the side of the house. Keith was already gone, and he realized the boy could be anywhere by now; they could end up chasing each other around the place like riding a carousel. He punched a fist against his leg, went back to the door, and shoved it again.

The house was silent.

The lights on the walls danced frozen in their bulbs; the corridor stretched ahead of him for what seemed like miles to the front entrance.

There was no trace of the people he had seen step inside, no voices, no footsteps overhead. The bare flooring was unscuffed and held no signs of damp shoes or boots tracking mud or grass over it. They were gone, yet he knew that the wall outside would prevent any of them from leaving the grounds.

"Liz! Ollie!"

No answer but the lights mocking him peacefully on the walls.

All right, he told himself; one step at a time.

He could see at a glance how much smaller the place was than it appeared from the yard, consistent with the probable height of the seventeenth-century man who had built it. Yet he could not help but admire the structure of the rooms, the way the walls and floors, though somewhat irregularly canted, gave it the bulk, the size, the sense of proportion one would need if—

He groaned, and clenched a fist until his nails almost punctured his skin.

Winterrest was disarming him, smothering his sense of danger with a show for his love of houses and his architect's greedy eye.

Fuck you, he thought, and froze momentarily, as if expecting it would read his mind and kill him.

Two paneled doors flanked him; he jerked open the right-hand one and looked into a large kitchen empty save for aluminum foil-covered trays on a wall counter, a large trash can filled to brimming, and piles of dirty glasses.

The floor was made of tile-shaped stone.

"Nell? Wilbur?"

He crossed the room quickly—ignoring the sound of his heels snapping like dry twigs—to a closed door in the far wall. He hesitated only fractionally before flinging it open to face a long narrow pantry.

"Hey, Clearys!"

Running back to the corridor, he wondered what had happened to Piper. He hadn't seen the old man at all since they'd talked earlier that afternoon, but there was no time to worry about it. He opened the opposite door and stepped into a square room against whose walls were tall ladder-back chairs and four walnut tables. A larger table took up most of the floor's center, and the wall and ceiling beams were dark with age and rough-hewn.

He didn't need to touch them to know they were only stone simulating wood.

"Hey, anybody! Hey!"

The next door opened onto what was probably a study. A polished roll-top desk, spartan chair, secretary, dusty shelves on the wall. A lantern. A braided oval rug. The walls not quite true, the dusty white ceiling sloping slightly toward the center of the house.

"Hey, is anybody here?"

He closed his eyes as he turned to walk back and took a deep breath. The air was unmoving, nothing to it but age and the faint clammy stench of ancient moist rock. He had smelled it before, during searches of old houses for designing ideas, when he walked into a just-finished home to check to be sure that his plans had been followed—it was emptiness, a void. No one lived here, no one spent time here, nothing in the air but the materials used to build it.

He had seen at least thirty people walk through that back door, and now it was as if they didn't exist at all.

Walking the central hallway was like walking down the center of a deserted road—he heard nothing but his own footsteps, and had no desire to call out to see if anyone was there. Yet he knew someone was. He could feel it in the way his skin stretched tight across his shoulders, could feel it in the way the hair on his nape tingled as though brushed by static electricity.

At the foyer he found himself panting as if he'd just run a hard, fast mile. The double doors on the left had been opened, and he could see though a sparsely furnished sitting room to another room that stretched to the far corner. Low ceilings, white plastered walls, a fireplace in each room large enough to walk into, deep enough to place a narrow bench in when the winters grew too vicious.

But that was all.

No people.

On the right it was the same, though the setting was more formal: a dining room dominated by a refectory table surrounded by tall chairs with throne backs and scrolled arms; beyond it a smaller room, used only by the family on ordinary occasions, for dining, for evening reading, for the men to talk about the day's work while the women worked on their knitting, their weaving, their planning for the future.

And still, as he stood in the foyer and peered up the shadowed, narrow stairwell to the balustrade that rimmed it on the second floor, he felt the watching again.

It was the house.

Winterrest was watching.

And soft footsteps were approaching him from the room on his right.

He spun with fists ready, and saw a woman coming toward him. He recognized her at once and almost ran to take her in his arms before he remembered.

"Judy," he said dully.

She smiled. "You've been talking with him, I hear."

A tremor raced the length of his spine, and he grit his teeth against it. He reached into his pocket and pulled out a cigarette. Then a match, which he struck several times before it ignited.

"Put it out!" she commanded sharply. "Put it out!"

He was so startled he shook the flame out immediately and shoved the match into his pocket. But he couldn't move fast enough to prevent her from reaching up and grabbing a handful of his hair, yanking it until he yelped, until she pulled his head down close.

"Are you going to marry me?" she demanded, her breath ice on his lips.

"Judy—"

She took her free hand and ran it gently across his stomach. "Now is the time to decide, Douglas." She leaned into him, and he could smell the must from her living room, could feel her moving beneath him on the rough, hard carpet. "You promise to marry me and I'll

289

protect you." She kissed him, grinding her mouth against his until his teeth threatened to cut through his lips. A moment later she pulled away, chest rising, falling, perspiration on her brow. "And if you don't, there's nothing I can do to prevent him from making sure you don't come back. You'll be dead, Douglas. You'll be dead, and buried."

It was ludicrous, and terrifying, and he couldn't help it—he started to laugh.

"Damnit, I want to protect you!" she cried. "I do, and you won't let me!" Then, abruptly, her expression faded to dull resignation. The muscles around her eyes and mouth went slack, and for a moment there was nothing on her face at all.

"Liz Egan."

He had stalled long enough. Whatever it was he was facing, whatever it was that called itself Judith Lockhart, was of less concern now than finding Liz and getting her out. He started for the stairs, was halfway to the landing when she screamed, "I love you, you goddamned son of a bitch!"

The vehemence and language stopped him like a slap, and turned him to look. She was at the foot of the stairs, a large brass candlestick in her hand. She glared, and in a single whipping motion threw it at his head. He ducked as she raced after it, felt it graze his shoulder before crashing behind him. He snatched it up and spun just as she reached him, and there was nothing he could do but bring it down on her head. On her forehead. Splitting skin, cracking bone, reeling her backward until she fell.

The candlestick dropped from his hand.

The house trembled. A vague distant rumbling more sensed than felt turned him cold as he pulled himself up by the railing.

Judy sat up.

Oh god, he thought; dear god.

She rose easily to her feet, paying no attention to the gap in her skull that exposed the white bone, the grey brain behind.

"Oh Christ, Douglas," she said sadly. "I wanted to show you I could protect you."

Then she took a step up, and he could see she was not bleeding.

Dead, Parrish had told him. They were dead, and they were alive through Winterrest's grace.

And he had made love to the woman, to the *thing* coming after him up the stairs.

There was no time to try to understand. As soon as she took the first step he launched himself to the landing and grabbed a post, flinging himself into the hallway to race toward the front. He shouted for Liz, for Ollie, and yanked open the first door he found. He had turned to run away from the empty room when he stopped, looked back, and saw clothes stretched out on the floor, piled on an armchair, spread out on a mattress sagging in a thin wooden frame. Six or seven, he was unable to count, though he recognized Wanda Hallman's flame pink dress.

Jesus, he thought, staggering back and stumbling to the next door; Jesus.

The second room was the same.

And the third.

He ran back to the junction at the stairwell and saw Judy halfway up and looking at him pityingly.

He sprinted for the north corridor this time, and wasn't surprised when he opened a bedroom door and saw Clark Davermain standing against the far wall. The lawyer looked astonished, then somewhat fearful, then terrified as the wall curved inward, reached outward, and embraced him until only his face was showing. Doug almost stepped in, until the wall took Clark completely, leaving only his clothes to slither down to the floor.

He slammed the door and raced on, shutting off thought, refusing to feel.

The middle room was the same as the others.

The door nearest the stairs was locked.

"Liz!" he shouted, pounding on the door, kicking at

291

it, pushing and yanking on the doorknob. "Liz, it's Doug!"

He heard nothing, and whirled just as Judy rounded the corner.

"Doug," she said, smiling encouragingly. "Douglas, please, you don't understand."

"The hell I don't," he countered, backing away fearfully. "This place is . . . taking these people, right? Taking them, damnit!"

"Not all of us. I thought Eban spoke to you." She was still advancing, still smiling.

"He did." Still backing away.

She stretched out her hands. "Doug, love me again. Please? Love me and we'll never have to say till death do us part." Her forehead was clear. "We're not dead, not really. We gave a little, the house gives a little back. That's all. That's all it is." Her skull was unmarred. "What's a little hurt for fifty years of barely aging? She pulled the neckline of her blouse down with one finger. "You could have me, Doug. You could have me for almost ever."

He felt bile rising in his throat, and he wanted to gag.

"Doug, love me."

He pressed himself against the wall and, just as she reached him, punched her square on the chin. Without waiting to see her fall, he ran to the stairwell, to the back corridor and checked the single room on the left. The door opened, the room was empty, and he was beginning to sob now as he heard Judy struggling to her feet. The door on the right gave as he punched and kicked it, and he had begun to spin around and leave when he spotted a foot poking out from under a low bed in the corner.

He dove for it, grabbed the ankle and pulled Liz slowly toward him. Whispering her name. Pleading with her. Turning her over and placing a hand over her heart, sobbing when he felt it beating. He slapped her cheeks gently and closed his eyes briefly when her eyelids began to flutter. Whispering her name and pulling her to her feet, he saw in her expression no need to explain. Either Parrish had already spoken to her, or she had already figured out as much as she wanted.

He guided her silently to the doorway, looked out and saw Judy standing in the hall.

Smiling sadly.

"Don't bother to look for Ollie," she said. "She's already having her baby." She lay a finger on her chin. "He'll look just like Eban."

Doug slammed the door and locked it.

Liz, her clothes disheveled, her face showing sign of bruising on the cheeks, swayed before turning to look for another exit. There was only the window, and the door to the hall.

"I passed out," she told him with a shrug and an apologetic smile. "Clark said it wouldn't hurt me. He said a lot of things and gave me some water." She put a hand to her throat and made a face. "A mild drug, I guess. To keep me calm, huh?" A weak smile now, and she bit down on her lower lip. "He said it wouldn't hurt and he said that the whole family would be together forever. He said—oh god, Doug, where are Keith and Heather?"

She ran for the door, and he grabbed her, dragged her away while she kicked at him, shouting her children's names and begging them to come to her. They struggled for several seconds while he tried to tell her Keith was outside and all right, that he hadn't seen Heather, but they couldn't do anything until they got out of the house.

The doorknob turned, and they froze.

A voice called their names, sweetly, with venom.

Doug ran to the window and looked down on the yard, on the canopy tent, then jumped when a booming crash against the door made the whole room shudder.

Liz staggered to his side and looked out, looked at him and said, "Why doesn't it take us?"

He didn't know. They were trapped, as trapped as all the others, yet the house had not made a single move to absorb them.

The booming continued, and a jagged crack appeared down the door's center panel.

Liz grabbed his arm, and he watched as the door began to splinter, began to flake, began to grind and squeal and tear at its hinges. He thought of shoving the bed up against it, but a single glance told him the frame was bolted to the wall. The only loose pieces of furniture were the wardrobe (too heavy), the chest (not tall enough), and the chair.

The top hinge cracked in half, and the door sagged in front of the ceiling. Judy's arm snaked around, probing like a serpent testing the air.

"Douglas," she said calmly. "Douglas, love me and I'll protect you."

Liz grabbed up the chair and drove it into the arm; Judy shrieked and pulled back, and the booming began again.

"We can't get out," she said, startled at herself. "We—"

"Well, sooner shot for a sheep as a lamb," he said suddenly, took the chair from her, and whirled around in a single fluid motion; the chair left his hands at the wide sweep of the arc and crashed through the window.

The house trembled.

It did nothing.

Doug stripped off his jacket, wrapped it around his arm, and dashed it around the window frame to clear it of glass shards and what was left of the panes' inner frames. Then he put the jacket back on and reached for Liz's hand.

"You wanna fly?"

The door scraped inward.

Liz looked out, and down at the tent snapping in the wind. "You're crazy."

"I'm still alive."

"It won't hold us."

The bottom hinge snapped.

Doug stepped back from the window to the middle of the room, looked to Liz *(will you follow?)* and ran, reached the sill and dove headfirst through the empty frame, kicking at the outer edge to give himself one more inch of distance.

The wind soughed, the canvas bulged and drew away, and hitting it was like landing on hard-packed sand; he gasped and rolled, stretched out his arms to try to stem the slide down to the edge, felt his feet kick empty air when Liz landed not far from him. The canvas surged and flipped him over, the posts groaned, and one of the center four buckled and let the tent sag further.

He didn't stop.

Though the tent was collasping slowly inward, it wasn't giving enough to prevent him from going over the edge. He hit the ground with a grunt, a yell, and rolled out of the way to make room for Liz. He wanted to stand and catch her like they did in the movies, but his legs and ankles stung, his lungs were empty, and all he could do was watch when she toppled off and landed perfectly, feet and hands, a sideways tumble, and up now and running to him.

In the window Judy watched and shook her head.

"Where?" Liz said, panting as they scrambled away from the house.

His right leg ached, his palms burned, and he hissed in a deep breath when something lanced up his spine.

Liz shook her head. "Clark . . . good god . . . Clark showed me all the rooms, all those people just . . . just sitting there. They wouldn't help me, they just sat there. They were just sitting and smiling. What were they doing?"

He told her as quickly as he could—about Judy, the candlestick, what he saw happen to Davermain, and what Parrish had told him. All of it so breathlessly he felt himself gasping, and he wondered if he were making any sense, if she understood at last what they were up against. Then she turned away and held her stomach tightly, twisting her neck as if fighting a cramp until at last she looked back.

"Doug, we can't just stand here. I can't . . . I've got to find Keith and Heather."

He tried to stand upright, tried to cast the pain someplace deep in his mind. Judy was still watching them, hands on her hips, a mother waiting for her children to do something against the rules. The back door was open. He swayed while his body fought the urge to collapse, then snapped his fingers when he remembered what Keith had said.

"Maggie," he told her. "Keith said Heather was worried I hadn't given her enough to eat and went to feed her. If she came back, we would have seen her."

"Then Keith," she said.

And Keith came around the corner.

7

7:45

Ollie dreamed of castles on cliffs overlooking an emerald green ocean, of castles in valleys surrounded by emerald green hills, of courtiers and knights serving no one but her, of armies and champions fighting only for her; she dreamed of darkness that comforted, of light that bathed, of men in processions bringing gifts for her child, of women in silks who would tend her at birth.

An ache centered in her belly, an ache that had settled in for at least a century or more; it was part of her, but it hurt her, and finally it expanded and began to spin and sharpen its edges, expand and whirl in waves of red lava, filling her stomach, filling her chest, filling her mouth until she opened it to scream.

She opened her eyes and saw Eban Parrish.

He stood at the foot of the canopied bed, and it must

have been the pain because he was turning to stone—light flesh to dark rock in blotches and streaks while he leaned over the footboard and pushed her skirt to her knees, pried apart her legs and rubbed his hands together.

She couldn't speak.

She could only watch.

While lava crested inside her, and Parrish appeared to shrivel as he gloated, shrink as he smiled, vanish as he fell forward between her legs.

And she couldn't move at all as she felt the baby coming.

8

7:45

Piper sat up suddenly. "Huh?" he said, looking around for the person he thought called his name. "Wha? Who's there?"

But the backyard was empty, the hounds dozing on the porch, and the sky overhead couldn't tell him the time. Nausea made him shudder as he dusted off his trousers, slapped his deerstalker against his thigh, and stumbled over the burnt grass to the porch, into the kitchen. He peered at the clock; it was blurry; he rubbed his eyes.

"Jesus, Mary, and Joseph," he muttered when he saw how late it was. "Good god, I fell asleep."

He started for the door, then sighed and shook his head. There was no sense going to the party now; it would be just about over, and all he would get would be a scolding from Nellie and some harsh words from Wilbur, and he certainly didn't want to see Mr. Parrish at all.

So he took two cans of beer from the refrigerator and walked into the living room, found all his Carmel

Quinn records and stacked them on the turntable. After several adjustment for volume, for bass and balance, he slumped onto the couch and started to sing at the top of his voice.

Later, he decided, he would go over to Sitter's and explain what had happened.

Not now, though, not now; he could feel them demons walking.

9

7:45

Liz ran to Keith and engulfed him with a cry, looked at Doug and grinned though tears filled her eyes. *He's all right,* she mouthed gratefully while the boy squirmed in her grasp; then he broke away and stood shivering while the clouds lifted, and grew black. "Keith?" She started for him again, fearful now, glancing at the house with every step, at Judy still watching. "Keith, come on, we have to get out of here."

He matched her step for step, holding the same distance and keeping an eye on Doug. "I want Heather. I can't leave her."

"She's at my place, chief," Doug said. "C'mon, we haven't got time to fool around."

Keith shook his head, and Liz made a grab for him, shouting angrily when he ducked under her arm and raced for the house. At the door he stopped and looked back, then leaned against the frame and his arm *merged* with the stone.

Liz blinked, it was a trick of the light, until he pulled the arm out, and did it again. Then she screamed.

"I want Heather," he demanded. "I want her now!"

She would have run to him, grabbed him, but Doug took her shoulders, shaking his head, matching her cries with shouts of his own, telling her it was too late, that Winterrest had him. As if to confirm it, Judy began to laugh, and the ground began to rumble, swaying the grass, toppling the chairs. The lights in the house winked out one by one until there was only the hall that framed Keith in gold, and the light in the window where Judy remained, laughing.

Liz denied it with a shake of her head, sobbed when the boy stomped a foot on the ground. A gap appeared in the grass and the mangled body of a young dog rose to his feet. He kicked at it, and splattered his shoes with droplets of blood.

"Keith!" she shrieked.

The boy laughed, and hugged the doorframe as if it were her waist.

Doug was startled when Liz suddenly ran to one side and searched through the party's ruins for a weapon. Cursing loudly, he screamed at Judy while Liz screamed for her child.

Madness, he thought, tossing aside plates and puny knives and jagged shattered cups; madness, I can't think, Jesus God, let me think!

Then Liz broke away, and he heard Judy and Keith shouting. He lunged toward the house where he thought she'd be heading, spun around when she wasn't there and saw her racing for the first rise. He frowned until he heard the sound of a horse running.

Oh god, no! he yelled silently, and wanted to weep when Heather and Maggie rode over the crest. She slowed abruptly; Maggie reared and stopped when the girl saw the destruction, the darkness, and her mother racing at her from one direction while Keith ran from another. And Judy called lightly to her, inviting her in.

Maggie reared halfway, backed off a step and tossed her head.

Doug started for them with a cry, and tripped, falling on his hands and knees. He punched out at the object that had tangled under his feet, but stopped and grabbed it instead.

No! Judy had commanded when he'd tried to light his cigarette.

neither bring a cigarette in or light a match once inside, Parrish had warned.

Doug looked down at the Sterno can that had kept the food warm on the table.

The stone is alive, he had said; *if you like,* Parrish had answered.

If it's alive, it's not stone . . . at least not stone as we know it.

Keith was trying to pull Heather from the saddle, his lips drawn back, his voice deep as he filled the air with obscenities. Maggie was turning away, confused by Heather's frantic sawing of the reins as she tried to decide what was wrong with her brother, what was wrong with her shouting mother who kept flailing at Keith as though he were a stranger.

Doug scrambled through the party's wreckage, burrowing under the canvas for other cans. Then he ran to the pole nearest the door and pulled at it, saw it bend in the center and pulled again until, with a ripping screech it came free of its eyelet in the corner. The canvas flapped feebly to the ground. He kicked and pulled at the rest unti the tent collapsed completely.

He looked up at Judy and showed what he held in his hand.

She lifted her palms and begged him with a shake of her head, a wild look over her shoulder and a terrified call for Parrish. Doug dropped the cans on the grass and pulled at the canopy. It was heavy, too heavy, and he shouted for Liz.

She heard him only after the fourth call, and turned just as Keith raced by her and sliced a foot into her leg. She bellowed and went down on one knee, watching helplessly as the boy tried to get at his sister again. Maggie, however, had made up her mind and was rearing despite the orders given by Heather; she reared and lashed out, and Doug saw her that first day, lashing at the air, only now Keith was there and trying to escape the hooves and the bared teeth.

Maggie knew.

The ground rumbled; to the left of the house the

earth began to fall back, and dark stone forms began to rise from the grass.

Liz swayed and stumbled her way back to the tent, saw where Doug was pointing and took hold of one edge. They pulled, and the slick grass enabled them to slide the canopy toward the house. A chair crashed on the ground near her shoulder; a lamp shattered across his shoulder, and he ignored the cuts he felt sliced into his scalp and back.

The back door slammed shut.

The ground shook violently, knocking them off their feet, so they crawled and dragged the canvas behind them, feeling the house trying to shift on its foundation, feeling the grass slowly turn to blades of rock.

He stood, arms out for balance, and grabbed as much of the tent as he could; but even with Liz's help the huge canvas was too heavy, weighted by itself and the light rain. He cursed, he railed, and suddenly he grinned when Liz lashed out with a foot, lifted a piece of the tent and uncovered a lantern.

He grinned, and laughed, and within moments they had found a pair more.

The window began closing.

Judith appeared in the room just as he tossed two of the lanterns inside and heard their faceplates shattering on the floor, on the wall.

He pulled out his lighter, snapped the wheel and touched the flame to the lantern wick Liz held out. It caught despite the wind, a faint blue flame that twisted away as Liz cursed the house for taking her child and threw the lantern through the window.

Nothing happened.

A shed appeared in the middle of the yard.

Maggie called out, turning on her hind legs and catching Keith on his shoulder. He fell, and Maggie snorted, pawing at the ground while Heather screamed and held the reins to keep from tumbling from the saddle.

Doug relit the lighter and tossed it over the sill, hoping to catch some of the fuel spilled on the floor.

Maggie reared, and crushed Keith's skull, reared again and began to trample him.

Doug didn't wait. Liz had already started to run away as best she could over the rolling ground, and he followed, trying not to hear Judy screaming for help, trying not to imagine he heard the house join her.

They ran toward the mare, averting their eyes from what had once been Liz's son, and he boosted her into the saddle, took the reins and began to run.

The clouds boiled and parted, and a drenching rain fell, a gale wind blew and nearly knocked him off his feet.

Maggie stumbled once, Liz grabbed her daughter's waist and reached forward for the reins. But the buckskin seemed to find a rhythm in the earth's turbulence and ran with it, calling, dragging Doug along behind her.

Then the wind stopped, and the rain and quaking—a sudden vacuum that made him look over his shoulder.

The stillness continued.

And ended with a roar that made his ears pop, made him stagger as air rushed toward the mansion, fed the fire, and exploded. Within seconds, the entire house was covered in flame, bellowing at the clouds now shifting away, reaching higher and drowning the lawn in snapping red light.

He saw it then.

Behind the flames, an anguished face that writhed and breathed fire, that glared and charred and peeled away burning flesh that fell to the burning ground like gobbets of molten hail.

The face of Eban Parrish.

A tower of fire erupted and billowed out of the low hill opposite them, and they swerved away; patches of fire lifted from the grass, disks of fire spun into the air and chased after them, fell short and rolled on their rims until they sagged into the ground. Like a beam pulled in half, a gap opened screaming in the trough between two mounds and filled itself with fire, forcing them back in the other direction; a tree sprang from a hollow, a torch that crashed and shed sparks picked up by the wind.

Doug ran, dodging flame, ducking spirals, calling to Maggie to keep her calm. Finally, he tore off his jacket and handed it to Liz, gesturing as best he could with one hand. She nodded and leaned over Heather to drape it over the buckskin's eyes. The horse bucked, and he talked to her; she trampled around in a panicked circle, and he pleaded with her, scolded her, took the reins and pulled until she followed him again.

The house burned; and beyond it, the wall.

Toward the north, the wall in flames.

Toward Cleary's, the wall and some of the trees.

They raced for the corner, and stopped. The wall here was burning as well, though it was far enough away for the trees not to be touched, and low enough still not to endanger them yet.

Firelight streaked across the grass, flickering, sapping, and Doug inched toward the low barrier, shaking his head.

Behind them a boulder rose, a boulder of writhing flame that began to roll toward them.

When Doug saw it, he grabbed Heather's shoulder and pulled her roughly to him, told her what she had to do in spite of the fire, and though she was wide-eyed with terror, her tongue licking away tears, she nodded. Snatching the reins away, she gave a wild shout when Doug slapped Maggie's flank.

The horse bolted forward.

Doug stumbled after.

Liz clung to Heather's back, looking back once to where her son had been lying, then looked away when Maggie gathered herself at Heather's command and lifted . . . sailed . . . Doug weeping and praying until the horse was over and galloping through the trees.

The boulder closed hard on him, and he swerved, leapt away from the crackling it left in its wake, and stared as it crashed into the wall. It hesitated, and began rolling the other way. Flames spit sideways, skyward, bored into the ground as it thundered back toward him.

Almost the entire estate was afire, and he had only one way to run.

He charged the wall where the boulder had struck it, wrapped his hands around his face and leapt through the flames. Burning scored his lungs, searing scorched his hair and the backs of his hands, and he felt the boulder reach the boundary only a few steps behind him, and shatter. A violent explosion that showered flaming rock on his shoulders, on the trees, and made him scream until he broke into the open and saw his house just ahead.

He fell, and rolled in case his clothes had caught fire, rolled and listened to the fire, listened to his whimpers, felt the oddly cool grass beneath his back and legs.

Then he stopped, and stared at the suddenly cloudless dark sky.

And gasped when a dark figure stood over him, and snorted.

Liz laughed almost hysterically when Maggie peered down at her master. When the shock was over and he joined her, she pushed the animal to one side wearily and, weeping now, dropped down beside him. Heather was quiet, arms crossed over her chest while she held her own shoulders.

Maggie nudged him, and snorted again.

"You," Doug said, "are a pain in the ass."

PART FIVE

DESSERT

The elaborately long camper, and the horse trailer behind it, was parked on the side of the road. Liz in a faded red tube-top and cut-off jeans sat in the driver's seat, her exasperation clear as she waited for Doug to puzzle over the map. Finally, with a loud sigh, Heather reached over his shoulder and took it from him, snapped it fully open and, after a moment's concentration, stabbed a finger at a thin blue line.

"Here," she said. "This is where we are."

Liz shook her head and looked at him, an eyebrow raised, a faint smile at her lips. "I thought you were supposed to be able to read things like that."

He shrugged. "Blueprints, yes. Maps, on the other hand, belong to a far-flung alien race devoted solely and single-mindedly to the utter confusion and eventual complete lostness of the human race."

"There's no such word as lostness," Heather declared as she handed the map back, another jab of her finger to show them the direction they should take.

He laughed, looked at Liz and was pleased to see that she was laughing too. Such delicate moments were few and far between, and he treasured them, tried to store them accurately in his memory—between the slots his mind stubbornly reserved for lingering fragments of the nightmare.

It was October, and they were in New Mexico, trying to beat the crowds to Albuquerque in time to

307

find a place to stay for the annual hot air balloon festival. They had left Deerford the day after the . . .

No, he thought; *just . . . the day after.* There was no other word. They had left before dawn, not bothering to check on the town; they had taken what clothes they could grab and left as fast as they could in the Jeep.

Neither mentioned the green grass where the mansion had been, or the grass that had taken the place of the wall.

It was all gone, and they kept on moving, and did their best to explain to Heather what had happened, and why.

And as they talked—in stretches of five, ten, fifteen minutes before turning away, the road slipping beneath them, the sky unchanging above—he found most of the pieces to fill in the gaps.

Deerford had been seeded with a score or more people who belonged only to Winterrest. They were alive—perhaps—and every time the mansion needed nourishment again, they offered themselves to it in order to stay alive longer. If they aged, he didn't know it; if they eventually died, he suspected it was because whatever the house found it needed in them they didn't have anymore in the quantities it required. They were little more than willing fodder in exchange for not dying.

And when they were lost to it, it found others.

It searched for them in the changing, real people who lived there, people who loved the town and would not surrender their lives and their homes there for any inducement—himself, Liz, Bud, and Ollie.

As for Eban Parrish—Doug told them he was Winterrest itself.

"An extension of it," he said, scarcely believing it himself, and wouldn't have at all had he not seen the photographs and heard the man himself. "It needed a contact, and it created one. Parrish was never human. He was—"

"A demon," Heather suggested.

"Yes," he said, thinking of poor Piper, hoping someone had taken his hounds. "Sure, that's close enough."

He never said a word about Judith; but Liz knew. Judith worked with Parrish because she held onto life longer than most. When she had been born, they didn't know; when she died, it was when Winterrest did. But when she was . . . alive, she wanted Doug because she didn't want to spend her eternity alone. She wanted company she loved; she picked Doug; he turned her down.

They bought the camper in Sparta and drove west with the idea of never returning to the East Coast again.

In Ohio, Heather wanted to know how little kids could never grow old and not have anyone see it.

"Oh, they must have grown," Doug said, knowing he was only guessing. "But they did it slowly. Kids can do that, you know, not grow for a while, and people figure they'll do it all in one spurt. So when it comes time, the Winterrest people move on."

"Where?"

"Flat River, Nebraska," Liz answered for him. "Places like that."

Heather said nothing; in her wallet she kept a picture of Keith she cried over at night.

They avoided the Midwest, sweeping down into Texas and finally west into New Mexico. They listened to the CB, the portable radio, once in a while watched a portable television when a signal was strong enough not to distort the picture. They read. They went to movies. They cooked inside, they ate in restaurants when they were too tired to stand.

The dreams were still there, they held each other at night, but they slept longer, felt better, and told themselves each morning they might never forget, but they might soon begin to live.

When they arrived at last in Albuquerque, they took

two rooms at the Winrock Inn—one for Liz and Heather, one for him. Then they spent the rest of the day trying to find a place to board Maggie, locating one in a suburb near the Rio Grande. That night they decided to celebrate with dinner.

No one spoke of the other places, the other Winterrests. Instead, they exclaimed over the balloons seen floating over the city, of the volcanos on the horizon, of perhaps riding the tramway to the top of the mountains on the city's east side.

They were happy, and Doug finally knew Heather wouldn't ask about Ollie, and was glad. He thought this was sometimes the worst of the memory—that Parrish, being old, needed special renewing. That Ollie had been chosen to give birth to him again. He had no doubt, as Judy had said, that the child would look just like Eban. The only thing he didn't know was if it would be born full-grown.

Dessert came, and they made pigs of themselves, later walked through the cool desert air and watched a spectacular sunset over the mesa. It was fine. It was almost normal.

But he suspected that before the year was over they would separate. Liz and her daughter would go . . . somewhere, and try to find the pieces that would bring them back to living; and he would try to remember the places in the pictures. Try, locate, and burn every one of them down.

Liz understood. And before they slept that night, she asked if he would follow them when it was over, if he would come back to them and be with them. He told her yes, without hesitation, and she smiled and kissed him lightly.

He would, he thought. He had too much to lose now to abandon them forever.

But first there was the other thing—Winterrest was dead, and still alive somewhere.

But to find it, all of it, he would have to return to Deerford and hope his house was still in the Hollow.

He would have to search Piper's home, to see if the old man had left records of his travels. When they'd stopped on their way out, the man and his truck were gone. Beer cans littered the lawn, and Carmel Quinn was singing endlessly on an endlessly spinning machine.

He would have to ask Sitter, too, and kill another dream.

Assuming, that is, that Sitter hadn't found his witches the way Piper had his demons.

They slept alone that night.

The next morning they hired a car in order to tour the city and the Sandia Mountains that rose above it; they decided that the next day they would ride north and explore a pueblo, see the Rio Grande, maybe take a look at Sante Fe and the desert between.

Heather was excited, and Liz smiled and held Doug's hand as they crossed the lobby for the front doors.

Someone called his name.

He turned, and the desk clerk beckoned.

"Mail for you, sir."

Doug froze, then walked over to the counter slowly, not liking the way his feet sounded on the tiles.

Too much like midnight.

Too much like stone.

"Are you sure?" Liz asked, peering at the postcard the woman held in her hand.

"Mr. Douglas Muir, right?"

He nodded, took the card, and looked at the picture.

Liz pulled away with a soft cry, grabbed Heather and ran out.

It was a greystone building in a large city, flanked by two others, its stoop filled with grinning people, every one of them facing the camera, laughing, and waving.

Standing in the doorway, a broad smile on his face, was Eban Parrish.

"Sir? Sir, are you all right?"

He turned the card over, read the message, and grabbed the counter.

Douglas,

> I want to protect you.
> I will protect you.
> See you soon.

> Love,
> Judith